THE
SECRET
GENERATIONS

THE
SECRET
GENERATIONS
John Gardner

G. P. PUTNAM'S SONS
New York

G. P. Putnam's Sons
Publishers Since 1838
200 Madison Avenue
New York, NY 10016

Library of Congress Cataloging in Publication Data

Gardner, John E.
    The Secret generations.

    I. Title.
PR6057.A63S4   1985   823'.914   85-6520
ISBN 0-399-13037-3

Printed in the United States of America
1   2   3   4   5   6   7   8   9   10

AUTHOR'S NOTE

While this is a work of fiction, set against reality, many of the characters actually existed—some being the very stuff of history. I trust I have not offended in my portrayal of them, though in at least one case, for the sake of the narrative, a most extreme theory has been used which places a very great figure of recent times in an uncertain light.

Many of the sideshow events are based on fact, though the obviously fictional "Cromer" episode has its genesis in a remark made in a letter from Clementine Churchill to her husband, Winston.

It should also be said that a slight readjustment to history has been made regarding ships sunk by possible sabotage, though in the main the details are accurate.

On the fictional side, as far as I am aware no family called Railton has ever been closely connected with the Secret Intelligence or Security Services of Great Britain. The Railtons are purely a figment of imagination and should not be confused with any other family.

Many people deserve thanks for help in preparing this book. Some must be nameless, others are well enough known through their own works of reference. As far as publishers are concerned, I owe a debt of gratitude to Peter Israel, Joan Sanger, Tim Manderson, Sue Macintyre, Ros Edwards, David Godwin and Brian Perman for their constant enthusiasm and assistance.

John Gardner
Oxfordshire 1985

For Margaret
Who Has Put Up With My Secret Generations

Contents

THE RAILTON FAMILY

General Sir William Arthur (1834–1910) = m. Nellie Maude (1840–188
        Railton   Catchpole

John Arthur (1860) = m1} Beatrice Emily (1867–1893)
      Railton   Dance
                  2} Sara Elizabeth (1885–)
                    Champney-Owen

James Arthur (1893–)
     Railton

Charles Arthur (1874–) = m. Mildred Elizabeth (1876
        Railton   Edwards

Mary Anne (1894–)
     Railton

les Arthur (1849–) = Josephine Marie (1855–1890)
    Railton   Simon

ndrew William (1875–) = Charlotte Hester (1875–)
    Railton   Michael

Caspar Arthur (1893–)
Railton

Rupert William (1895–)
Railton

Ramillies Giles (1895–)
Railton

Marie Simone (1876–) = Marcel (1870–)
    Railton   Grenot

Paul (1895–)
Grenot

Denise (1898–)
Grenot

Malcolm William (1877–) = Bridget (1880–)
    Railton   Kinread

For God shall bring every work into judgement,
With every secret thing,
Whether it be good, or whether it be evil.

Ecclesiastes XII. 14

The rapid, blind
And fleeting generations of mankind.

The Witch of Atlas: Shelley

Prologue

All the nurse could see was the fine old head against the white pillow. Her intuition and experience told her the man was very close to death. Had she been blessed with some odd form of second sight, enabling her to read the thoughts and see the images in the dimming brain, she would probably not have understood them. . . .

He felt a terrible weight on his chest, and pains down the left leg, but could not at first tell where he was. Then the roaring noise bore down on him—the dust choking his throat. Hoofbeats receding, and the sound of cannon. Now he knew.

He had been hit. Badly. Try to get breath. Gently. There. All would be well; they would take him back to the neat rows of white tents and hutments at Balaclava Harbor. For a second he could see the rocky inlet, cliffs rising around the deep water: a natural harbor for the myriad ships which had brought the soldiers to this place.

But something had gone very wrong after they trotted out, as ordered, then turned—at the sound of the "Gallop"—making straight for the Russian guns. Madness. Had he called out? Madness; particularly as, only the day before, he had been sent with a corporal and three troopers, to reconnoiter. The maps he had made, and brought back, showed the exact position of the Russian guns and the way in which they were digging in the Turkish cannon, so that the main Russian batteries were protected on both flanks.

Had nobody heeded his maps? Certainly that seemed to be the case; why else would they have gone straight into the trap once the charge was sounded? Why else would he be lying here in dust and blood?

The weight on him? Of course, it was his poor horse; his beautiful gray. For the life of him, Cornet Railton could not remember his horse's name.

The nurse, looking at the silent, sleeping old man, could never know that his mind had wandered back, vividly, over half a century, in this, his last, coma.

The old man stirred, then opened his eyes. The nurse knew he could not see her, but his voice was clear as he said, "Patience."

So he died. General Sir William Arthur Railton VC KCB DSO, of Redhill Manor, Haversage, in the county of Berkshire, with nobody to know that he had slipped away imagining his near death, so long before, on the battlefield of Balaclava, the day after he had spied out the land for Lord George Paget.

It was the early evening of January 1st, 1910, and the whole family gathered within two days of the death.

Giles Railton, "The General"'s younger brother, widowed but surrounded by his own kin—his sons, Andrew and Malcolm, with their wives; his daughter, Marie, and her French husband; and some of his grandchildren.

The General's own sons came to the Manor House—John, the MP, and his young second wife, Sara, together with James, the son of his first marriage. Then Charles, wastrel of the family, with his wife and daughter.

Later, Giles was to consider that of all those present for the funeral, his deepest love was for his daughter, Marie, and his young nephew James; while his contempt remained reserved for Charles. He wondered, now that the General had gone, what lay in store for the Railtons, and what he could do personally to shape their future. It preyed on his mind, causing anxiety, then a sense of resolution, with the iron entering his soul.

By rights, Giles, the eldest member of his great old family, should now take the place of his dead and revered brother. But, by natural lineage, it was John, the politician, who took over the bequeathed lands, Manor and most of the money. This was yet another worry for Giles: having spent a lifetime among plots and counterplots, intrigue and secrets, he saw the family as a microcosm of his own country. His concern for the family was even greater than that for England, and, while all at present appeared set fair, stable and calm, he knew of the political and military storms which could appear so suddenly on a sunny horizon.

He hoped for a future blessed as an era of tranquillity, but knew the truth in the adage, "In time of peace prepare for war." His own duties to his country were thus slanted, so he considered he must look to his family and take precautions now.

Like a Grand Master at the game of chess, Giles planned his moves—to protect the honor and possessions of his clan; to see that those he loved remained safe; to use the weak to save the strong.

With the death of the old General, the Railton family was entering a new and vital stage in its long history. Giles would play a crucial part in the navigation of the family through the next decade, which is but part of a wider, more complex tale, the fuse of which had already been unknowingly lit almost a year before, in a bar near the German Naval Dockyard at Kiel.

PART I

To Learn a Trade
(May 1909–August 1914)

Chapter One

1

When he walked into the place and found it was the roughest, sleaziest, most whore-ridden, drunk-filled and dangerous bar on the Kiel waterfront, Gustav Steinhauer thought he had possibly made a mistake; when the big Petty Officer started the fight he knew it.

Steinhauer believed his vocational world to be full of idiots and amateurs, so he held to the axiom that the professional, such as himself, must take heed and never stand out like an extra bridegroom on a honeymoon. Now he had broken this solemn rule.

The Petty Officer, named Hans-Helmut Ulhurt, was possibly his last hope, and he had traveled from Berlin to see him. Steinhauer, carrying a pigskin document case, was dressed like any other civil servant. The officer of the watch told him that Ulhurt was ashore. Herr Steinhauer would probably find him in the Büffel, his favorite drinking place.

Steinhauer should have known better; should have gone away and returned in the morning, but, to be fair, he was getting desperate and the Kaiser expected results. So off he went to the Büffel, where he tried to look inconspicuous, sitting in a corner and peering through the gloom and smoke, trying to size up the Petty Officer, whom he immediately recognized from the photographs, and descriptions already obtained.

From time to time, a whore would come along and offer herself. Steinhauer tried to turn them away with tact, but that made matters worse. The whores were loud and abusive when rejected, and several rather effeminate sailors looked hopefully in the direction of this oddity who had come among them, in his gray coat, gloves, high fur collar and neat cravat. You did not often see a dandy like this in the Büffel, but, thank God, Ulhurt was holding court—telling raucous stories and hurling the cheap fiery schnapps down his throat as though he would never get another drink after tonight—which, as it happened, was almost the case.

The Petty Officer was a big man, but well-proportioned, with shoulders and arms that looked as if a sculptor had fashioned them out of granite. He could well be the man who was needed. Certainly he had the background, intelligence and talent.

Then the doors opened and the three English sailors arrived, a little drunk and very naive. They were also petty officers—off *HMS Cornwall*, Steinhauer guessed, for the Royal Navy had this cadet-training ship in port on a courtesy visit, though they would have to search hard to discover any courtesy among the German naval personnel at Kiel. For everyone knew, in that May of 1909, that the Kaiser was making a bid for ultimate seapower, so that the High Seas

Fleet could claim that they, and not the British Navy, dominated the world's oceans. The Kaiser was very touchy over the constant English claim that Britannia ruled the waves, and for the past few years a flurry of activity, building and counterbuilding had been going on in the great dockyards of Germany and England. The Royal Navy was not really welcomed in German ports, and members of that Service were certainly not considered to be good news in a den like the Büffel.

A silence fell across the drink- and smoke-filled air as soon as the three Royal Navy men came in. It had the same feel to it as the atmosphere which precedes a tropical storm.

The foreigners appeared quite unperturbed by the sense of aggression in the bar, walking straight in and ordering schnapps in a mixture of sign language and a few words of badly learned German.

Steinhauer noticed in a flitting second that everyone had looked to the big, fair-haired Ulhurt, and he remembered the man's reputation for violence.

Even the proprietor turned, as though seeking the Petty Officer's permission to serve the foreign sailors.

Steinhauer was to recall that moment many times in the years to come. The brown-stained walls and ceiling; the rough wooden benches and tables; the bar with its bottles and barrels; the men with sailors' faces, beaten by wind and spray; and the girls whose eyes moved like those of snakes. Most of all, he remembered Ulhurt, whose look became bland and open, half-amused but laced with something deadly.

"So the Royal Navy has taken to murdering the German language now." Ulhurt spoke a perfect English—which surprised and pleased Steinhauer—with no trace of the guttural accent which so often prevents the German from mastering other tongues. Though Steinhauer had seen men like this on many occasions, the Petty Officer looked relaxed. He was poised, ready and willing to beat the living daylights out of the three Englanders.

"What you talking about, kraut?" The tallest, most muscular of the English sailors took a pace forward.

"Kraut?" Ulhurt still appeared amused. "What is kraut, Englishman?"

"Cabbage face," one of the other naval men said loudly.

"You know what?" Ulhurt began. "The Royal Navy is shit." And with the final word, he launched himself at the biggest Englishman, butting him in the stomach, his great arms delivering axlike blows into the man's solar plexus.

There was a brief lull before the whole bar erupted, and it was during the pause that one of the other Englishmen hit Ulhurt with a chair. Steinhauer saw quite clearly that these three men were but an advance guard, for suddenly the whole bar was full of English sailors, swinging fists, and even—to his horror—knives.

Steinhauer, making a dive toward the exit, was thrown to one side like a discarded doll, and viewed most of what followed through a haze.

He saw one of the girls sail across the room as though possessed by the power of levitation; an English sailor bury a knife to the hilt in the ribs of a young German; a German seaman deliver two hammer-blows, left and right, which connected with the jaws of two British seamen; he heard the crack of bone quite clearly, and was fascinated by the odd angle at which the mouths hung just after being hit.

He was aware of the terrible noise; the screams of agony; the screeching from the women; the grunts of pain and exertion from men of both sides as they fought with no holds barred; and he saw the small concerted rush of six English ratings—able seamen—smashing their way through to the bar, vaulting it and grabbing at the bottles, which immediately became weapons.

Most of all, Steinhauer watched Petty Officer Ulhurt. For a big man, Ulhurt was exceptionally nimble, and very strong— a streetfighter, an experienced bar-brawler, who appeared to deal almost perfunctorily with his enemy. He fought with hands, heads, elbows, knees and boots, rarely leaving himself open to attack, always ready for the enemy coming at him from behind.

But Ulhurt was gradually driven back, to make a stand, not against the wall but the bar, which was his undoing.

By this time they were breaking the bottles and using the sharded, jagged ends as weapons, and there was blood everywhere. Ulhurt, back against the corner of the bar, had done this, and now jabbed a shattered bottle at any Englishman who came near. He did not think, or expect, the two young sailors behind the bar to have the muscle it took to lift a full cask of beer.

But not only did they lift it—a great cask containing something like a hundred liters—but, as though engaged in tossing a bag of potato peelings into the sea, they hurled it toward Ulhurt, who had no exit, no escape.

He saw it coming, too late, and leaped to one side, but the full weight of the cask caught him on the right thigh and he fell, badly, trapped against the wall, his right leg outstretched, taking the force of the cask. Steinhauer watched as the man's mouth opened in a noiseless scream of agony. Later, he maintained that he actually heard the terrible crunch of bone as the leg was crushed— broken in twenty-eight places, the surgeon later said.

Oh shit! thought Steinhauer. His last hope. Ulhurt, who knew the sea, was familiar with dockyards, violence, wireless telegraphy, and spoke five languages well, had been the ideal. Now Steinhauer's search had shattered with Ulhurt's leg.

Then the dockyard police and the British naval shore patrol arrived. Some men were arrested and taken away, others were loaded into wagons and moved to the nearby naval hospital.

Outside on the pavement, Steinhauer showed his credentials to a German naval police officer, who then treated him with great respect and left him alone, wrapped in a misery he could share with nobody.

"You want to have a good time?" a whore asked him.

In his anguish, Steinhauer looked at her and saw she was young and attractive. Probably not in the business very long. What the hell, he thought, and went back to her room, which was none too clean.

In the night, between the bouts of purchased sex, Gustav Steinhauer thought again, and wondered. Was it just possible? Could Ulhurt's accident be a blessing in disguise?

In the morning he went to the hospital to discover that the Petty Officer's leg had been amputated at the thigh. It was touch and go, but the surgeon considered it was probably go, because the man had the constitution of an ox.

Gustav Steinhauer returned to Berlin. Two weeks later the now one-legged Petty Officer Hans-Helmut Ulhurt was moved, much to his consternation, to a private clinic in the Berlin suburb of Neuweissensee. He did not know it then, but his secret war was about to begin.

Chapter Two

1

The market town of Haversage, nestling in an almost private strategic hollow at the foot of the Berkshire Downs, had known many moments of triumph and sadness in its long history. Here Alfred the Great came to recruit men to fight his bloody battles against the Danes; the Doomsday Book shows taxes collected from both bondmen and free—whose main occupation was with the land and cattle—all living in the vicinity of Halfting, which eventually became Haversage.

In the tenth century, Benedictines arrived at what was by then a thriving settlement, its people living off the good growing and grazing ground of the area. Work began on the Abbey—little of which remains, though the major part of the Parish Church of SS Peter & Paul dates from those early builders, with additions constructed in the 1780s.

The church itself is a monument, not only to the glory of God, but also to the men who went out from Haversage to do battle throughout the world, and at home in England. There are the tombs of four crusaders within its walls, and at least three other noted soldiers lie under the main aisle.

The Benedictines were, naturally, ousted by Henry VIII's commissioners, and, like so many other monasteries, the Abbey was sacked and burned when the King reformed the Church, splitting from the Papal authority of Rome. In place of the peace-loving monks, a new landowner arrived—Richard de Railton, descendant of that Norman knight, Pierre de Royalton, who had distinguished himself at Hastings with Duke William in 1066.

Within eighty years the family had dropped the "de," to become plain Railton, having built the great Manor House at the top of Red Hill—a vantage point which probably derived its name from bitter skirmishes and the shedding of blood centuries before. They then set a pattern for other landowners by organizing their farming and extending a building program.

Over the years the Railtons evolved into the true backbone of Haversage. There was usually a Railton living at the Manor, running the Estate and acting as squire to the local community. At the same time, other members of the family spread abroad, serving Monarch and Country in the Army, Navy, or some branch of the Diplomatic Service; and the best of them, the natural patriarchs, returned to Redhill Manor to see out their last years.

So it was with General Sir William Arthur Railton VC KCB DSO—known to all within the family simply as The General.

The entire family had spent the Christmas of 1910 at Redhill, as was the custom. The General's younger brother, Giles, had been there with his naval officer son, Andrew, who brought his wife, Charlotte, and their three sons— Caspar, and the twins, Rupert and Ramillies. Giles' second son, Malcolm, had traveled from Ireland with his recent wife, Bridget; while Marie—Giles' only daughter—had come with her French husband, Marcel Grenot, from Paris, together with their two children, Paul and Denise.

The General's own two sons were present—Charles, the younger, with his oddly dowdy wife, Mildred, and their daughter, Mary Anne; and John, the Member of Parliament, proud with his young second wife, Sara, and the son of his first, tragic, marriage—James.

It was the happiest of holidays, for this was a special time at Redhill, and the General was in excellent spirits.

On the Tuesday after Christmas they had gone their separate ways, leaving the General to celebrate the New Year at the Manor with his staff—Porter, his old servant; Cook; her daughter, Vera the head maid; the two undermaids; Natter the groom; Billy Crook the odd-job boy and the others.

Giles was to see-in the New Year with Andrew, Charlotte and his grand-children, and was just preparing to leave his Eccleston Square house, during the early afternoon of New Year's Eve, when the telephone message came from an almost incoherent Porter to say his master had been taken ill with a seizure.

Giles immediately warned Andrew, but did not stress the seriousness of the situation; then set out for Haversage, arriving at the station to be met by Ted Natter with the dogcart.

Even on this bleak evening the golden-red brickwork of the Manor appeared as inviting as ever—a sight which remained constant in Giles' memory. For here was his childhood: the holidays from school, the first riding lessons, Christmas, his own father and mother, an age of autumns and a wealth of winters, a cycle of springs and summers.

The dogcart stopped within the square-U of the Manor frontage, and Giles looked up, a sudden weak last flicker of winter sunlight glancing off one of the big leaded windows of the second floor, as though God were vainly trying to flash a heliograph message of hope.

The doctor was there, with a nurse; and the house, usually so lively, had taken on that quiet hushed quality of places where death has come, suddenly uninvited.

William lay unconscious, as though asleep, upstairs.

Once the doctor had told him it was only a matter of time, Giles sent for young Billy Crook to run down the hill and warn the Vicar. He asked the nurse to let him know as soon as there was any change, then, with professional speed, went to the General's Study.

The room faced south, to the back of the house, and in summer you could step through the tall windows, into the sheltered rose garden, from the top of which almost the entire Estate, together with the Home Farm, could be seen.

Giles went quickly through the papers, knowing what should be destroyed and what kept. So it was that he became the first to read the will and perceive the immediate problems.

Only when he had completed the careful sorting of documents, did the General's only brother set about informing the family that the old soldier's end was near. He died at ten o'clock that night, and the nurse reported he had clearly spoken the word "Patience" at the end. It puzzled the nurse, though Giles merely nodded.

Soon, from the town below, the Passing Bell began to toll; the tenor, "Big Robin," the ringers called it: great melancholy booms of resonance, vibrating the frost already forming on the trees; the sound creeping like a warning into every household.

In the Market Square, the butcher, Jack Calmer, blew his nose, looked at his wife, and their daughter, Rachel, pausing in his eating. "We should make a prayer for him, I reckon. A good brave man. A gentleman."

They heard the bell in the Royal Oak, the Blue Boar, the Swan, the Leg of Mutton, and the Railton Arms. Men who had known the General, and even fought under him, put down their beer mugs and stood in respect, for they knew it meant inevitable change.

The bell notes were heard for miles, clear above the town. They heard it in the almshouses halfway up Red Hill, and old Miss Ducket shed a tear, for she had known the General as a young man. To many people, the steady bell-notes brought home the fact that the winter of their own lives was upon them, and the clock ticking on the mantel ticked for all. The Redhill Manor Farm Manager, young Bob Berry, heard it, and felt fear for other reasons, as indeed did the Estate Manager, Jack Hunter.

John, Charles and their families arrived before luncheon on the next morning; Andrew and his family were there by the afternoon. Marie and her husband, Marcel Grenot, were again making the journey from Paris, having only just returned following the Christmas festivities; while Malcolm and Bridget— spending the New Year with Bridget's parents in County Wicklow—would get to the Manor by the next evening and stay until after the funeral.

So it had been Giles who made certain the family secrets remained safe, and

Giles who broke the news of the General's will to the old man's two sons; Giles who anticipated the trouble and did his best to counteract it.

The difficulties presented by the will were threefold, resting wholly within the areas of property and finance, together with the individual characters, and ambitions, of the General's sons, John and Charles. With John, the problem was multiplied by his young wife, Sara, considered by some of the family to be immature, spoiled and headstrong.

John had been unlucky in marriage, his first wife, Beatrice, having died giving birth to their only son, James, now in his seventeenth year. The boy had been brought up by a series of nannies and then went through his baptism of fire, first at a preparatory school and finally within the disciplined life of Wellington College—the family school.

John's life was politics, and from the year after Beatrice's death he had been Member of Parliament for Central Berkshire, unusually hardworking for a politician, devoted to his country, with a vain ambition to attain Cabinet rank or more.

Unlike his brother, Charles, John had never been thought of as much of a ladies' man. It was therefore with almost a sense of shock that the family heard, just under three years before, that John William Arthur Railton MP had announced his engagement to Miss Sara Champney-Owen—a girl twenty-five years his junior. Within a year they were married, and since then John had seen more of London society life than ever before.

Whatever was thought privately of Sara, she appeared to care deeply for John, and made such a hit with the true powers within the government that her husband's career stood every chance of distinct advancement.

But now, with the General dead, the prospect of John Railton being able to continue in politics at all hung in the balance—and that was a matter of property and duty.

Apart from several small financial bequests, and an important £2000 a year to Charles, the basis of the General's last will and testament lay in the whole question of family property.

Because of their position, the Railton family had, over the years, amassed both wealth and lands. By 1910, as well as Redhill Manor, with its estates, Home Farm, and a large income from rents in the town of Haversage itself, the family owned four further properties in London—the excellent house in Cheyne Walk, in which John lived with his bride; the house just off South Audley Street, comfortable enough for Charles, Mildred and Mary Anne; and a tall, terraced home in King Street, where Andrew lived with his family during the periods of his service in the Royal Navy when he was in England.

The Eccleston Square house—the finest of all—had been designated as a family property until Giles', and the General's, father had bequeathed it for all time to Giles with the proviso that it should not be sold or passed out of the family.

Now, the General had obviously considered it was time to leave the various

London properties to individual members of the family. The King Street house was to go to John's son, James, when he came of age or was married; South Audley Street was left to Andrew; Charles was to have Cheyne Walk, while John Railton became the principal beneficiary, receiving Redhill Manor, the Farm and Estate, together with all existing moneys and revenues, which meant a considerable income from the people of Haversage and the surrounding district.

Nobody had to be over-astute to see the dilemma presented by what to most people would be an incredible boon.

Redhill Manor was a full-time occupation, its owner being required to remain in residence for at least six months of the year. John was a professional politician—at this very moment engaged in fighting the General Election, called by Prime Minister Asquith just before Christmas. Could he in all conscience now continue in politics and run the Manor? It would all depend on Sara.

2

During the late afternoon on the day following the death of the General, Giles Railton spent an hour in the General's Study explaining the will to the dead man's sons, John and Charles.

Charles was gleeful, for the bequest gave him a freedom he had long sought. But John Railton MP climbed the great staircase, which curved to the round gallery overlooking the main hall, with his mind in torment.

The fact of his inheritance came as no surprise. Yet he was confused, being a busy and dedicated man engrossed in two things only—his vocation and Sara. Now his mind centered on how best to soften what would undoubtedly be twin blows to his young wife.

They were sleeping in the room situated almost directly above the General's Study, with windows looking down onto the rose garden, and he gave their secret knock, opening the door immediately. The heavy crimson curtains were drawn, a fire burned in the grate, sending a pack of shadows dancing across the bed, on which Sara lay, only partially clad. The firelight flickered red over her face, and she looked as though she had been crying. Sara had adored the General, so appeared more upset by his death than either of his sons. She asked John to lock the door, holding out her arms, making it plain that she wanted him—either to give or take some solace.

He crossed to the bed, not locking the door, sitting beside her, taking one hand in both of his. Then, as gently as he was able, told her that he might well have to give up politics, while they would definitely have to hand over the Cheyne Walk house to Charles and come to live at the Manor.

Her long blond hair was let down, spreading fanned across the pillow, and as he spoke, so her large eyes opened wider, her face taking on a shocked look, as though someone had unexpectedly set out to hurt her.

Slowly her manner turned to disbelieving anger. "You can't give up politics! How can you give up in the middle of a General Election?"

He said he would probably go on for the time being, "Just to make sure the seat's secure. . . ."

"And *our* house!"

"It's never been *our* house, Sara. It's family property and I have new responsibilities. I doubt if I can combine running this place   the Farm, the Estate, and all else with my life in politics."

"You mean we'll be buried down here?"

She liked Redhill Manor for visits, but often said it would be difficult to live there.

"But, Johnny, we'll be so far from—"

"From London, yes."

Be firm, Giles had said. So John calmly told her the facts. *His* grandfather had given up a career in government service to run the Manor. "It's part of one's duty," John said.

"Then why not Charles?" Her voice became querulous.

"Because he's my younger brother. The General left the estate to me. It's like a family business, Sara."

"Oh, don't. You make it sound like trade." She bit a lip. "Very well. We have to live here. But don't be a fool and throw away your political career. After all, didn't Asquith suggest a Cabinet post after the election?" As she said it, Sara's hand went to her face, palm to cheek, an act of guilt, though she knew exactly what she was doing.

"When?" This was the first John knew of a Cabinet post.

"I'm sorry." Sara did not look him in the eyes. "I'm truly sorry. I wasn't supposed to say anything. Please don't tell Mr. Asquith that I let it slip. Please." Her concern sounded genuine enough, as well it might. There was certainly truth in the story, but Sara had reasons for keeping her husband from speaking to the Prime Minister.

"He's serious?" John asked, and she nodded, saying that Asquith had talked about it for almost half an hour at a ball they had attended just before Christmas.

The news put a new complexion on matters. Could he possibly combine the two things—run Redhill and stay on in politics?

"It makes a difference, doesn't it?" she asked softly.

He barely nodded, moving to the window, pulling back the curtains. Yes, it made a difference, but still meant that she would be mistress of the Manor. She would have to compromise.

Viewing the whole cartography of the events from the high ground of hindsight, this was probably one of the most significant moments in Sara's life.

3

Giles Railton looked around the dinner table, only half-listening to the muted prattle of John's young wife, Sara, seated to his left.

He had little time for the chattering Sara, for she appeared to think only of herself. That was his deduction, anyway. Odd, John marrying such a woman. Now, if it had been Charles. . . . Well, Charles was always too much of a good thing in that way. Women, and the drink.

He caught sight of young James, at the far end of the table. James had the Railton bone structure and nose, but his face was closed, with a muted look. Poor young tyke, Giles reflected. First losing his mother at birth; then trying to adjust to a stepmother only a few years older than himself; now the death of his dearly loved grandpapa. William often remarked that young James was the one to come to him most often with his problems.

Giles' son Andrew was in discreet conversation with Charles, across the table, while his wife—the delicate, porcelain-like Charlotte—talked quietly to John. Charles, Giles could see, was already in his cups, the eyes becoming glazed and hooded.

Andrew's and Charlotte's children—Giles' grandchildren—sat in silence, knowing, though not believing, that their great-uncle, the family patriarch, was dead. Young Caspar, a month or so James' senior, appeared to be lost in a world of his own, while the twins—Rupert and Ramillies—were having a fit of nervous giggles. Giles wished he could recall how it felt to be fifteen again. His other son, Malcolm, whose one obsession in life was farming, would be with them soon; as would Marie and her husband.

Suddenly, as these things happen, there was a silence: a stopping of conversation as though by mutual consent. Faces slowly turned toward Giles, as if expecting him to say something important.

For once in his life Giles Railton was lost for words. "His . . . the General's . . ." he began, realizing the twist of emotion within him, "his . . . his last word was 'Patience.'" He paused, pulling himself together. "'Patience,' name of his horse. Name of the horse shot from under him at the Battle of Balaclava. *Patience.*"

It was all he could think of to say.

4

The Railtons had provided moments of great pleasure, as well as sadness, to the people of Haversage. Countless Railtons were married and buried in the Parish Church, but none with the pomp, solemnity and spectacle attending the obsequies of General Sir William Railton, where even King Edward VII was officially represented by the Lord Lieutenant; and six staff officers—from regiments with which the General had served—walked beside the pallbearers.

The band of the 2nd Battalion Oxfordshire Light Infantry played the Dead March from *Saul,* as a color party and guard of honor escorted the cortège down the long, winding hill, through the town, to the church.

Hardly a house stood without some visible mark of respect—from flags lowered at half-mast, to black rosettes pinned onto doors. The shops were closed for the entire day, and the locals braved a bitter wind, standing silent and bareheaded, as the procession went by.

The family met at Redhill Manor after the committal, and though its contents were already known to them, listened while old Mr. King, senior partner of King, Jackson & King, of Gray's Inn, read the will.

Giles Railton did not return to London until the next day, though Andrew left with Charles and their respective families by the late train from Haversage Halt on the night of the funeral.

Giles particularly wanted to stay. He had business to discuss, at some length, with his daughter-in-law, Malcolm's wife, Bridget, who would be returning to Ireland the next day. He also spoke with his daughter, Marie, and her husband. They too would begin the return journey to France early in the morning. Both conversations were secret and full of intrigue. The General would have smiled.

5

Dublin was shrouded in freezing fog, and Padraig O'Connell turned up the high collar of his greatcoat. There had been snow in the Wicklow Hills, so after two days of failure he had gone up to see a Fenian comrade near Blessington. Then the Dublin–Blessington Steam Tram had been three hours late into Dublin. Cursing to himself, he hurried into Sackville Street—or O'Connell Street, as most people now called it. A tram clattered by like some noisy wraith in the thick mist.

He strode on, past the Gresham Hotel, the Crown, and the Granville, turning left into the small bar, smoky and clamorous on this night.

Fintan McDermott—a little terrier of a man—sat in his usual place by the fire, a chair drawn up, empty, beside him.

Before joining his friend, Padraig bought himself a glass of porter at the bar.

"Yer late, then, Paddy." Fintan did not even raise his head as O'Connell took his place in the vacant chair. The two men did not need to look at each other, for theirs was a life-long bond, strengthened by the same ideals. Both were intelligent men welded to seeing the long-delayed Home Rule Bill go through Parliament: helping it, if need be, with the bullet and grenade, yet alive to the dangers a new Republican Ireland would face from the Protestant communities, most active in the Northern counties. A United Republican Ireland would be hard to establish.

"So, I'm late," O'Connell agreed.

"Now you can tell me then."

"Tell you?"

"What the great secret's been. What took you out of Dublin all yesterday, and then today."

O'Connell shook his head slowly. "Just an idea."

"Ideas. So what was this idea?"

"Well, Fintan"—for all their closeness, O'Connell was reluctant, like a schoolboy with a secret which needed to mature before it was told—"I went to have a word with Bridget Kinread, so."

"That's a fair notion, Padraig, but I thought she was wed."

"Isn't that why I went to see her? Isn't she married to an Englishman— *Mister* Railton? And isn't there talk that she's coming back for good, and that her husband is to farm in Wicklow?"

"And you didn't see her?"

O'Connell shook his head. "Yesterday I just thought she was away for the day, but she's been gone this last week—the day after New Year, on the Kingstown boat."

"Across the water, so."

"A death in her husband's family."

Fintan bowed his head. "And what's so special about Bridget Kinread, or Mrs. Railton as she now is?"

For the first time that day, Padraig O'Connell smiled. "Because she is now a Railton, and that's the kind of English family we need an ear to."

Fintan McDermott nodded slowly. "And she'll be back? With her husband?"

"They'll be back. And I'll be there to tell her where her duty lies. Bridget Kinread needs reminding of her country. She'll be no bother. You'll take another drink?"

6

On January 17th, 1910, at about eleven o'clock in the morning, Charles Railton made the short journey from the Foreign Office to a small room in the War Office. For Charles the appointment was unexpected, but those few people with a detailed historical knowledge of Britain's Intelligence and Security Services will tell you that the visit was an important milestone.

Although there are plenty of recorded events containing the name Railton— for the family appears to be synonymous with Intelligence and Security—there is not any existing record of Charles Railton's visit to the cubbyhole which served Captain Vernon Kell, the first Chief of MO5: later to become what it is now, MI5.

Charles, himself, was a typical Railton: tall, over six feet, with thick light hair, a strong jawline, high forehead, a long patrician nose flaring slightly at the nostrils (the Railton nose, as it is still called in certain circles), and clear blue eyes which when necessary could lie as easily as his tongue—and it had often been necessary as far as ladies were concerned. Yet, untypical of the Railtons, until that morning Charles considered himself a failure.

Adventurous by nature, Charles had been shunted into the Diplomatic Service against both his inclinations and wishes. His brother John, his senior, had gone into politics via the Army, so Charles was sent in the direction of diplomacy, for which he had little flair. In fact, during the last few years his disenchantment had become complete. His present posting, as a ministerial liaison officer between the Foreign Office and the Admiralty—a situation which he shared with five other young men—was a backwater into which he had been towed merely out of respect for his father. But now the General was dead, and on that morning of January 17th, Charles had gone back to his duties at the Foreign Office with a letter of resignation in his pocket.

His wife, Mildred, the quiet, dark-haired, clergyman's daughter, had that day watched him leave their small house, just off South Audley Street, with many misgivings. Since the General's sudden death and the news of Charles' legacy, she deeply feared that without the disciplines made by the normal demands of the Foreign Service, Charles would lapse into the ways in which he had been accustomed to live before their marriage, and even after. During that time she knew there had been other women, and she had wept bitterly over it, along with concern for his drinking habits. Then, with the birth of their only child, Mary Anne, nearly sixteen years before, Charles had changed. Also, on the previous evening, Mildred had plucked up courage to tell him she was again—after so long—pregnant: a fact which she did not exactly relish. She knew of her husband's feelings for the dull drudgery of his work, had listened to the string of wild schemes which had been his constant song for the last two weeks, and so feared for him as well as herself, their daughter and the unborn child.

But neither she nor Charles had taken into account the General's brother, Uncle Giles. Giles had seen the problem, found an answer and set matters in motion. Hence the message that Charles was required to visit Captain Vernon Kell at the War Office, an instruction so sudden that Charles did not have time or opportunity to deliver the letter of resignation.

7

The door carried the legend MO5. CAPT. V. KELL. Charles had never heard of MO5. He knocked, and a pleasant voice called for him to enter.

Vernon Kell sat behind a small desk in an unprepossessing room. Besides the desk, there were a small table, a couple of chairs and a wooden filing cabinet. Maps hung on the walls, and a pile of pamphlets lay on the desk in front of Kell—very much a military man, with mustache to match; square-faced but blessed with friendly, open, features. As he rose, Charles noticed that

Kell momentarily allowed his shoulders to droop, then straightened them, as if with effort. The same effort went into the labored intake of breath.

"Railton, I presume." The Captain sounded as though he were in difficulty. "Sorry about this." He tapped his chest. "Be over in a minute. Asthma. Confounded thing's crept up on me again. Had it as a child. Be a good fellow and give me a minute, eh?"

Charles nodded, took one of the spare chairs, and waited for Kell to regain his breath. He seemed in poor health for a man of—Charles calculated—about the same age as himself: mid- to late-thirties.

"Lord, I'm sorry," Kell said eventually, color coming back into his cheeks. "Should've stayed away today. Had an attack over the weekend. Martyr as a child. Thought it'd gone by the time I went to Sandhurst, but back it came." He smiled, giving Charles a casual glance. Charles, however, had the distinct impression that Kell had almost looked into his soul, examined the secret places of his mind and summed him up in one quick look.

"Well, what've you been working on of late? Nobody'll have told you what this is all about, I suppose?" Kell's manner was easy, relaxed, with no trace of what the General would have called "side." The General hated side.

"Sort of errand boy between the FO and the Admiralty for a time, and the answer to your question is no." He held Kell's eyes and quietly told him about his proposed resignation.

Kell grunted. "Diplomatic's not for you, eh? Suppose you should've followed your father. Sorry about him, Charles—if I may call you Charles?"

"Of course."

"Good. My name's Vernon. Should still be with the South Staffs. Would be if it weren't for the dysentery and asthma. Pegged me to a desk here. Then threw me into this job. Been clamoring for help ever since we began. Mind you, there's Sprogitt—the clerk." He inclined his head toward a door in the corner. "Sprogitt lives in what should be a broom cupboard. Apart from him, there's only me, though I've got my eye on another fellow. Typical, isn't it? They appoint me head of MO5 and then give me no staff."

There was a tiny pause before Charles asked what the MO5 stood for.

"Military Operations 5. Look, I'm a new boy at this, like yourself. How much do you really know about Intelligence—well, Security anyway? What d'you know about what the yarnspinners call the Secret Service?"

Charles admitted he knew very little.

"Well, I suppose I'd better give you the state of play."

During the next hour Kell demonstrated one of the reasons he had been asked to form his new department: a clear, lucid picture of the current situation regarding clandestine matters—as far as Great Britain was concerned. Toward the end of the last century there had been a two-headed, ineffectual monster— Military Intelligence and Naval Intelligence, each with its appropriate DMI and DID (Admiralty). Now only the Director of Intelligence Division at the

Admiralty remained, and the Committee of Imperial Defence, concerned over the lack of any well-organized machinery during the Boer War, had for some time been attempting to unravel the various strands of the complex business.

"There's a Foreign Section running around the Empire, and Europe. A handful of agents. Some are rogues; others dedicated men and women." Kell threw up his hands, going on to explain that the Foreign Office had been more than unhappy with the way in which Intelligence was being handled by the Military. "A lot of people were, rightly, furious when the War House, here, disbanded the Field Intelligence Department. It was better than nothing—in fact it was the best thing we had. As it is, the Army's left with precious little, and the General Staff don't trust the Foreign Office. The Navy have an organization that's moderately good. But some of those within the Committee of Imperial Defence have decided to reorganize."

So now the Foreign Office was determined to see a proper Service established. "They've been working on the Foreign Section for some time," he confided, "though it still comes under the War Office, even with a naval man in charge. Smith-Cumming. Able fellow."

"And this section? MO5?"

"Early days, Charles. Couple of years ago, the CID claimed me"—he spoke of the Committee of Imperial Defence—"and finally winkled me into this little spot. Me, the furniture and Sprogitt." He waved toward the clerk's door.

"To do what, exactly?"

"MO5's brief is to study the possible vulnerability of the country to foreign espionage, tell them what we should do about it and then get on and do it. The term espionage, incidentally, covers our own particular brand of subversives."

"You mean extremists? The Irish Fenians and the like?"

Kell nodded. "Yes. Revolutionaries, Fenians, anarchists, agitators—all of 'em."

"And where do I come in?" As he said it, Charles knew he wanted only one answer.

"I hope you'll come and help. What is it King Lear says?

> Take upon's the mystery of things
> As if we were God's spies.

Come and be one of God's spies with me, Charles."

"But I know little of—" Charles began.

"Nor do I," Kell said grittily. "But the job's interesting, a challenge, particularly because nobody's really done it before. If I could recruit my own staff, arrange my own methods and training, we might eventually become a formidable force. So, are you with me, Charles?"

With a tiny hint of reservation, Charles nodded, and Kell crisply said he was pleased, if only because *he* needed help. In fact, the first Director of MO5 did not particularly like Charles Railton, detecting in his manner, face and eyes, something a little below standard for a man of his upbringing. But Kell was a believer in conversion, and if anyone could make Railton into a reasonably efficient officer in this new department, it was himself. Now he quickly told Charles that he had already begun to learn the job mainly through his most important contact, Superintendent Patrick Quinn—Paddy Quinn—head of the Metropolitan Police's Special Branch.

Quinn had been in charge of what was once known as the Irish Branch—formed to combat the Irish extremists—for over six years, and, according to Kell, the man was not merely an able policeman but an expert in many things that would be very useful to them: "Interrogation techniques, knowledge of the way subversives work, surveillance, underhand methods. Quinn's also a Royal bodyguard. So we have a good helping hand there."

"So, when do *I* begin?"

"No time like the present. Don't worry about a posting from the FO. That'll all be taken care of."

There were several pages of notes, and memoranda, for Charles to read then and there in the office; and within the next few hours he discovered some of the things that would be expected of him.

Kell believed that time waited for no man. Charles would have to follow in his new chief's footsteps: do a course on wireless telegraphy, and another—at the Admiralty—on codes and ciphers.

On that first day at MO5, Vernon Kell and Charles Railton worked until well after five in the afternoon, not even pausing for luncheon. By the time military and civilian personnel were beginning to leave the War Office building, the two men already had a framework of the organization, which in later years would become known as "The Firm."

The evening was cold, with a slight frost rising around the gas lamps of Whitehall. But Charles did not take a cab home. Nor did he, as was his usual habit, head for The Travellers Club, which was, and is, known as the Foreign Office Canteen.

Instead, he walked home, enjoying the crispness of the chill air.

There was a sense of starting anew in the South Audley Street house. After dinner Charles talked with Mildred. He told her there had been a change, that he had been reappointed, though he said nothing of the true nature of his duties.

Before sleep took him that night, Charles pondered on one aspect of the day which intrigued him. He had casually asked Vernon Kell who had recommended him for work at MO5.

"Why, your uncle—Giles Railton—of course." Kell sounded as though this should have been obvious.

But why, Charles wondered now, should something like that be obvious? Indeed, why had *he* been chosen? Certainly Uncle Giles was a senior member of the Foreign Service, but what on earth would a rather dull old bird like Giles know of Intelligence matters?

Chapter Three

1

Earlier, almost at the same moment as Charles arrived home, an important bell was clanging in another part of the capital—in the Caledonian Road, a mile or so from the Great Northern Railway's King's Cross Station, and hard by Pentonville Prison.

Among the many abroad in that part of the city, midst the clanking trams and bustling people, one in particular made his way, with purpose, down the Caledonian Road, stopping finally at the familiar striped pole which signified a barber's shop, pushing open the door of number 402A and causing the automatic bell to clamor.

Inside, the gas jets were turned high, the two barber's chairs vacant, and the sweet scent of cheap bay rum mingled with that particular smell of London, wafting in from the street—an amalgamation of grime, horse and the prevailing odor of soot.

For a moment the man stood inside the door, his head cocked, listening as the spring bell slowly stopped its harsh warning. He was dressed more fashionably than those who normally frequented this seedy neighborhood, wearing a long, dark greatcoat with a fur collar, the design of which was certainly foreign.

As the bell ceased, a young man in a not over-clean apron appeared in the doorway at the far end of the shop.

"Good evening..." he began, his accent thick, guttural. He stopped suddenly when he saw the stranger's face, turning to call urgently up the stairs. "Karl!" he shouted. Then, in German, more loudly: "Karl, come! The gentleman is back."

The visitor took one step inside the shop, paused, then walked forward with confidence, his well-waxed mustaches quivering, like an animal picking up an interesting scent. The young barber waited in the rear doorway, nervously glancing upward at the sound of heavy footsteps now descending the stairs.

The second barber, entering from the staircase, was obviously the owner of the shop. He moved with a familiar authority, his appearance neater and cleaner than that of the young assistant—hair cut short, to the scalp, above slightly bovine features. "Ach!" The grunt contained some relief as he set eyes on the newcomer. Then, to the younger man: "Wilhelm, the door if you please."

The blind was quickly pulled down, the key snapped home in the lock. Only when this was done did the owner speak again. "It is good to see you ... Herr ... Weiss?"

"Names do not matter. We can talk in private, yes?"

The barber motioned his visitor to the stairs, giving Wilhelm a nod, telling the lad to stay where he was.

Once upstairs, the visitor asked, "You have come to a decision? Made up your mind?" He dusted off the seat of a stand chair with his gloves and sat down, small eyes never moving from the barber, who now spoke slowly, as though choosing his words with great care.

"Yes, I shall do my duty for the Fatherland. But it is necessary for me to have help. I cannot do it alone. Young Wilhelm is reliable. He'll keep his mouth closed. I shall do it if he is also paid a small amount."

"There should be no difficulty with the money. But *you* have the responsibility." He drew out a large piece of heavy-grade folded paper. "Before I leave, you must memorize the names and addresses I have here. I do not care how long it takes, but I shall not leave until I am satisfied that you are word perfect. *Verstanden?*"

The barber took the paper with immense care, as though it were some kind of explosive device—which, in a way, it was.

2

The man the barber had called Weiss boarded the midnight ferryboat to Ostend.

He stood by the rail, gazing at the lights of England disappearing into the cold night, but his thoughts did not even touch on the barber or the work going on in London. Gustav Steinhauer had larger matters on his mind: things which gave him a particular power, an almost unique position within the diplomatic and military regimes of Prussia.

He was also anxious to get back to Berlin. These little forays abroad were important, but it was his special work, for the Kaiser himself, which took pride of place in his life. At the heart of it all was Hans-Helmut Ulhurt, who had taken several months to regain his health. Now, still in the private clinic, he had learned to walk again, with the aid of a wooden leg, and was doing well.

Only one thing appeared to puzzle Ulhurt. He was surprised the Imperial Navy had dropped any charges against him concerning the affray at the Büffel. Steinhauer told him not to worry about it; as far as the Navy was concerned, he had disappeared from the face of the earth. There was work for him to do, and it could well include the kind of fighting he seemed to enjoy so much.

"You are to concentrate on getting fit again, learning to walk and move with a wooden leg as well as you did with two real ones," Steinhauer counseled.

"In time you will learn all things. Some of your friends have paid a high penalty for that night in Kiel." He cocked his head to one side. "Some have been executed. Do as *I* tell you. Keep silent. Obey only me and you will not suffer the same fate."

3

At one point during his return to Berlin, Steinhauer found himself again becoming anxious. It was now two years since the Kaiser had sent for him privately—not only an honor, but the moment he had fought, schemed and planned for over the years.

Gustav Steinhauer's background could in no way be described as aristocratic in the Prussian sense. However, he had relations at court. The Steinhauer family were what the English would call well-to-do, though not quite top drawer.

Gustav was exceptionally bright—a quick learner and a very hard worker. By his early twenties he spoke four languages fluently, had made friends in influential areas and secured a place for himself in the Foreign Ministry on the Wilhelmstrasse.

It was during his first years at the Wilhelmstrasse that Gustav Steinhauer discovered his taste for intrigue and duplicity. Within two years he found himself in a position to travel regularly between the Wilhelmstrasse and the court, taking with him drops of gossip and tittle-tattle which might prove useful to the Kaiser and his many advisers.

In the forefront of his mind Steinhauer remembered that the long-deposed Bismarck had relied on one man for intelligence, and a complex system of spies—the hated but very powerful Eduard Stieber. As the years passed, Steinhauer's one ambition had been to become the Kaiser's Stieber, and the opening appeared quite suddenly just before Christmas in 1908. What happened then finally led him to Petty Officer Ulhurt in Kiel.

In England, nobody connected with MI1(c)—the Secret Service—or the tiny MO5 could possibly know what a part Steinhauer and his one-legged protégé would play in the future. Certainly none of the Railton family, even if they had known of the men's existence, could have foreseen the havoc and the harvest that would be reaped.

The meeting with the Kaiser had happened so unexpectedly that Steinhauer did not have time to reflect or become nervous. He had been visiting his uncle, and on reaching his office, found the man in a state of excitement.

"His Majesty wishes to see you!" Uncle Brandt paced up and down. He was in full uniform, being on duty that day.

"Me?" Steinhauer swallowed. "When?"

"Now. The court leaves for Austria in two days. His Majesty sent for me yesterday. He asked for you: when you would next be coming. . . . He is waiting now."

Within minutes Gustav Steinhauer found himself being marched through the marbled corridors, and before he knew it there was the Kaiser himself, looking serious and rather terrifying, with the waxed mustaches and the strange aura of power and dignity which seemed to surround him.

For a full minute the Kaiser looked him up and down as though appraising him. Steinhauer thought of undertakers. Then the Kaiser spoke:

"You are Gustav Steinhauer from the Foreign Ministry?"

"Majesty."

"Good. I commend you. You have brought some useful items of information to the court. I am in your debt."

"No, Majesty. No! I simply wish to serve Your Majesty and the Fatherland. I am dedicated—"

The Kaiser took no notice. "I commend you," he repeated, as if to say, "Stay quiet, man. If I say I commend you, then that is all."

"Thank you, Majesty."

"I have work for you, Steinhauer. Work of a special nature. Dangerous but rewarding. Will you undertake this work for me?"

"Anything, Majesty. Say the word. For you and the Fatherland, anything."

The Kaiser gave a brisk nod. "Good. You know that I am basically a man of the sea?"

"I've seen Your Majesty's beautiful painting of the torpedo boats attacking the ironclad warships . . . in the Berlin Academy of Art. Inspiring. It is—"

"Thank you." The Kaiser began to talk quickly, rapping out the sentences like orders, not giving Steinhauer a chance to interrupt. "I am also versed in military matters, naturally, but above all I love the sea and the Imperial Navy. It is imperative that the world should see the Fatherland, and not England, as master of the great oceans." He took a quick breath before rattling on. "When you start this duty for me, you must remember this."

Then the Kaiser began to get down to the details.

Gustav Steinhauer became elated, almost heady with the power that was being placed in his hands.

4

Giles Railton carefully replaced the telephone earpiece, cradling it into the U-shaped arm projecting from the instrument's column. He had answered Vernon Kell's call in his usual manner—a series of monosyllables—for Giles disliked the telephone. Well, the news was good, even though Kell did not sound very enthusiastic about Charles. At least it brought his nephew into that world which Giles had inhabited for so long.

Giles sat in his study, on the second floor of the elegant Eccleston Square house, a few doors from where Winston and Clemmie Churchill were basking—between a hectic political life—in the joys of parenthood with their first child, the five-months-old Diana.

When his French wife, Josephine, was still alive, Giles' Study was known to the children as "Father's Hide." Indeed, the children were never allowed into the room, and he recalled Andrew's sense of injustice at the age of ten: "Why cannot we play soldiers with Papa?"

Josephine had found it difficult to explain to the small boy. Five years later she was not there to explain: coming into the hall, on a Friday evening, bright and happy after a shopping expedition, and dropping dead of a brain hemorrhage at the foot of the stairs.

Giles rarely dwelt on that terrible day. In fact, he seldom thought of his own past except when it was necessary to draw on personal experience. The events of the last weeks, however, had forced his mind from the safety of its private battlements. The death of his elder brother had brought more than mere memories, it had also produced an avalanche of pressing problems. One of these had, for the time being, been settled by Vernon Kell's telephone call.

Unlike most of the Railton males, Giles had never grown to a full tall stature. The General, even at the age of seventy-six—when he died—had maintained a full six feet two inches. But Giles, though far from stunted, had reached five-seven at the age of fourteen and stopped there. He did retain other Railton features—the nose, eyes and a full head of hair, just beginning to gray as he entered his sixty-first year.

It was strange, he considered, how often in the family history there was a great gulf fixed between the arrival of children. There were over a dozen years between the General's sons, John and Charles, the same hiatus which had existed between himself and the General. Indeed, Giles knew of yet another child sired by his brother, never spoken of, yet born only twelve or so years ago. The General had certainly been active with more than one woman since his wife's— Nellie's—death in a riding accident during the autumn of '84.

As far as his colleagues were concerned, Giles Railton was merely another senior civil servant—a timeserver waiting for the inevitable autumn of his days. Nothing could have been further from the truth, for Giles Railton was only just reaching the apogee of his career.

The memos and documents called him a Senior Adviser: Foreign Policy. Yet his official dossier contained more fiction than fact, going back many decades. It did not mention such things as the part he had played in the purchase of shares, for the government, in the Suez Canal; the visits to India and the two years in Egypt. The copperplate handwriting gave little away about the many, and various, visits and journeys around Europe, nor their purpose. Among other matters, the clandestine meetings in Russia remained uncharted, for, while other diplomats met the Czar and his advisers, it was Giles who, in secret, spoke with men like Lenin, Trotsky and other dedicated revolutionaries, trying to understand and analyze their dangerous political ideology.

Some imagined he would have been happier at a university, possibly a chair in History, failing to see that his passion was confined to military history, the study of strategy and tactics—hence his private preoccupation with playing soldiers in the Hide, surrounded by maps, books and hundreds of lead replicas. This obsession came from a childhood competition with his elder brother. To Giles, even in the last years, brother William had been godlike and, possibly, the only other living being from whom he had no secrets.

If the truth were known, Giles had found himself becoming involved in political ideas that disturbed him considerably. He worried about Asquith's government and their plans of reform—particularly concerning the Irish question and Home Rule. The true vocation of his life was the way in which his country could be provided with essential information for trade, foreign diplomacy and the Military. Yet the largest portion of guilt concerned the family. Paradoxically, he held the family and its history in highest esteem; yet he also found himself querying the whole matter of privilege and the injustice of rank.

Knowing what they did, his sons, Andrew and Malcolm, and his daughter, Marie, tended to make allowances for their father's somewhat odd way of life.

Andrew could not escape contact with his father's arcane calling, for he had spent the past two years at the Admiralty as Flag Officer to the Director of the Naval Intelligence Division—the DID.

Marie, and her French diplomat husband, were more deeply involved, and there had been much private discussion over Christmas at Redhill Manor and again after the funeral.

Malcolm, however, refused to be drawn, though his recently taken Irish wife, Bridget, was becoming more pliable. Giles wanted to use her as a most particular investment in secrecy.

Now, after talking to Vernon Kell about Charles' recruitment to MO5, Giles had things to do which might assist Marie and the work in which she was most privately involved in Paris.

Putting on his greatcoat, he stood in the hall for a moment as his one manservant, Robertson, hovered in the background.

"I don't know what time I'll be back," he told the man. "Tell Cook to leave something cold for me. You can all go to bed. I'll let myself in," and he went out into the freezing night, not even looking back.

First, he took a cab to Trafalgar Square and walked through to the Strand. Out of habit he paused for a moment or two after turning corners, and constantly crossed and recrossed the road, looking for any familiar shape or figure who might be following.

Only when he was certain that he was alone did he double back toward Charing Cross, making for a narrow alleyway which housed, among other things, a small newspaper and tobacconist's shop. Here, Giles Railton was known as Mr. Harding—a gentleman, the owner considered, who liked a little fling now and again: for he paid handsomely for one room above the shop, reached via a street door, the keys of which were in Mr. Harding's keeping.

Inside the street door, stairs mounted to a minute landing and to another door which led to a tidy room containing two stuffed chairs, a bed and a table.

No pictures, books or papers, for Giles wanted nothing to distract those who met him in this place.

He drew the heavy curtains before lighting the gas mantles and the small fire, for the room was almost as cold as the street outside. Only the most astute observer in the street would note the small gap left between the curtains.

The girl had been given her instructions, sent directly by hand—from Redhill Manor to an address in Putney, then forwarded by two separate carriers. The time limit was between seven and ten in the evening. If Mr. Harding's light was not on, she was to come back at fifteen-minute intervals until ten. After that she would try again on the following night.

In her late twenties, the girl dressed fashionably though inexpensively. If anyone was interested, she looked like a lady's maid on her day off, or traveling, for she carried a small Argyle cowhide bag as well as her handbag in which lay a French identity card and the equivalent of £200 in French francs, as well as a little extra English money. She was known as Monique.

She knocked on the street door—a quick tattoo of three—and once in the room, Giles helped remove her coat, then waited as she made herself comfortable in one of the stuffed chairs.

"It's really quite simple this time," he began. "I should warn you that the people concerned are related to me. However, you must put that to one side, do a thorough job and always give me the truth, however unpalatable." He then proceeded to give Monique the address of Marcel and Marie Grenot—his own daughter and son-in-law.

"I'm only to observe?" She had no trace of an accent: not surprising as she originally came from Warwick. Hers was an old Army family, and she spoke French fluently.

He nodded. "Observe, and report to me. You will also protect. You're clear about communications?"

She said it had all worked well enough during her last duty in Paris. This time she would try to get very close.

Giles looked pleased. It was important, he told her. "All the same, I need to know everything. The French authorities can become difficult, even with their friends, when it comes to spies."

There was still more to say, but finally Giles handed her a ticket: the night boat to Calais and a third class to Paris. Both tickets were one-way.

5

Returning to Eccleston Square by a different route, Giles thought of the last time he had spoken to Marie about the work she was doing. It had been Christmas afternoon, in the General's Study, with the frost white over the rose garden, and the light fading. Her husband, Marcel, sat in a leather chair and berated the apathy of his own country.

"They say, 'Why should Germany bother us? They will not fight again, and they certainly will never draw the English. After all, the royal families are related.'" He had an almost theatrical French accent. "The senior politicians of my country are like deaf-mutes. In fact they have little comprehension." He shrugged. "Mind you, our generals are also ill-equipped for any modern war."

Giles said war was probably remote, but thought one should be aware of possible enemies. "It's the same here." His voice betrayed fatigue. "Politicians, like the people of this country, are more occupied with preserving the status quo. Neither learn from history."

After a short silence, Marcel gave his wife a sidelong glance. "Marie is doing all she can. As you have instructed."

Giles smiled, as wintry as the weather outside, asking if his daughter was still keeping up the pretence of a liaison with the German Military Attaché.

There was no humor when Marcel growled that there were doubts about the *pretence* of the liaison.

"Hypocrites!" Marie became angry. "I love my husband and nobody else. France is my adopted country, and I'm also still British." Suddenly she grinned. "Anyway, he's not the Military Attaché; he's the Attaché's assistant."

"Klaus von Hirsch"—Marcel spoke without enthusiasm—"has an unfortunate reputation with the ladies."

"Which, as my father has pointed out, makes him all the more vulnerable." She said the Attaché's assistant in Paris talked a great deal once you had his confidence.

"And you have that confidence?" Giles made no exceptions, treating his daughter as he would any other agent.

"Enough to be within months of getting details of the German battle plan—should they ever need to use it."

"Which plan?"

"Oh, you know some of it—the Graf von Schlieffen's famous plan. I'll have the whole thing for you in time."

Giles suggested that von Schlieffen's plan was almost certainly out of date, the Kaiser's Chief of General Staff having retired some three years ago, plagued by ill health. His successor—the able General Moltke—would doubtless have his own new battle order and plan.

"I would not be too certain." Marie could be as stubborn as her father. "Von Schlieffen is still held in great awe and the plan certainly concerns France and Belgium. So, I continue? Yes?"

Giles nodded. "You go on as before. Get as much of the battle plan and order as you can. *Any* way you can."

As he thought back on these things now, while returning home from briefing Monique, Giles Railton realized he had no compunction about allowing his daughter to form what could be an immoral alliance with the German officer.

He was not a squeamish man. Some years ago, in the late '80s, he had garroted one of his oldest friends on discovering that he had passed information to Irish agitators. He did not think twice about it, and lost no sleep after the act. Later he had a recurring dream in which he was carefully pulling the wings off exotic butterflies. He still had the dream occasionally, but never associated it with the act he had performed, of his own volition, for his country.

It was well past ten o'clock when he got back to Eccelston Square, and the house was in darkness. He ate and returned to the Hide, selecting a large-scale map of the field of Crécy from the case which housed his comprehensive collection. He had drawn the map himself—as with all the others—now he pulled out several trays of finely detailed lead soldiers: the troops of Edward III and the Black Prince; archers, foot soldiers, cavalry, baggage wagons and accoutrements, together with the larger forces of Genoese archers, the men of Bohemia and Alençon, Blois and Lorraine, with the armies of Philip VI.

Setting the English Army back behind Abbeville, Giles started to study the moves which had occurred in the late August of 1346. He was a firm believer in the theory that one learns from the follies and wisdoms of the past, but, as he moved the blocks and fighting men around the map, part of his mind dwelt on his daughter-in-law, Bridget, who, with Malcolm, would now be well on her way back to Ireland. He hoped that, in spite of Malcolm's lack of interest, Bridget—now a Railton in Giles' eyes—would see where her duty lay.

6

As his train finally pulled into the Lehrte Railway Station, Gustav Steinhauer recalled the Kaiser's particular orders to him, on that day just before Christmas 1908.

The Kaiser had discovered the officers of the Army High Command were anxious to take over all matters concerned with intelligence, including the handling of agents already placed by the Foreign Ministry into other European countries. They were planning to effect this takeover within the next two to three years.

The Kaiser had confided to Steinhauer that his great worry was the way in which this would affect matters of intelligence—particularly over the question of seapower.

"I realize that you are in a position to contact our spies already buried on foreign soil, Steinhauer," he said, "but these men and women will come under military control when the High Command gets its way. What I need is my own man, and I see *you* as my man. Am I correct?"

"Of course, Majesty."

"Good. Then you will report certain matters to me—and to me alone. When the Military establish themselves as the Fatherland's spymasters, you will co-operate with them. But you will not betray this one confidence to them. You will place your own agent—a man who is well trained, knows about naval matters, is familiar with sabotage and the other skills of spies—in England. You will control him. You will not betray him to those who will be your new masters."

"Yes, Majesty."

"You would be able to do this, and mislead your military spymasters?" The Kaiser frowned, looking directly into Steinhauer's eyes.

"Of course, Majesty. They'll never be able to find, or identify, him."

"Good." The Kaiser gave a short nod. "Very good indeed. Now, to this man. You will select him, train him, and send him out and report the full facts to me alone. You understand?"

Steinhauer nodded.

He interviewed eleven possibilities, all of whom turned out to be flawed. Then the Petty Officer, Hans-Helmut Ulhurt, came to his notice. A man with all the right credentials, but a man who would have to be not only trained but also tamed. A man who required discipline.

As he boarded the Stadtbahn train for Neuweissensee, Steinhauer hoped the crushing of Ulhurt's leg had almost performed the taming for him. Soon, the training phase would end, and his tame spy could be tested in the field. Ireland, perhaps, would be a good starting point. He was pleased with that idea.

Chapter Four

1

Giles Railton had trained himself to manage on only four hours of sleep each night. Between three in the morning and dawn he was often at his constructive best.

On a Wednesday night, a few weeks after the General's funeral, he walked the streets of London. He knew every road and alley blindfolded and in fact could always find his way, even in pitch darkness or thickest fog. It was not a knack, but a self-taught art, for he could do the same in most of the great capitals of the world.

On this morning the journey was simple. Eccleston Square to his son's house in King Street. The task was one which a messenger could easily have carried out, but the intriguer in Giles' nature made it a pleasure for him to do the job alone.

Nobody either heard or saw him enter King Street, slip quietly to the house door and deposit a letter through the box.

In the morning, Lieutenant-Commander Andrew Railton RN rose early, out of habit. While shaving he peered hard into the mirror. The General had seemed indestructible. Now he was gone—like a man dying in battle. Many Railton men had looked hard at themselves over the past days, as though searching for the seed of destruction which lies in all men.

Examining his reflection, Andrew found it hard to credit the fact that he had passed his mid-thirties, let alone reached the rank of lieutenant-commander. He also marveled at his happiness and good fortune. Though, like all sailors, he preferred to be on a ship, he was content with his profession; one of his sons, Caspar, was nearing the moment of decision regarding his future; while the twins, Rupert and Ramillies, now approached the first hurdle which would shape their futures. Andrew was inordinately proud of his sons.

There was also the intense happiness of his private domestic life. In all respects, even after the seventeen years of their marriage, Charlotte was an unbelievably ideal wife and mother. She had a good, interesting mind, always anxious to learn, so that the couple could talk about most subjects under the sun. She also ran his home with an almost naval precision, even if she occasionally took a little more drink than was good for her.

After all this time, she appeared to enjoy their lovemaking with the kind of abandon Andrew associated with a completely different sort of woman.

Dressed, he went through to Charlotte's room. In spite of the early hour, she was awake. He said he would be home at the usual time that evening and merely wished to see her before breakfasting and leaving for the Admiralty.

She gave a sleepy smile. "Oh, my dear, what do you find to do with yourself all day at the Admiralty?" Then, suddenly becoming wide awake: "Andrew— you never talk about it nowadays. What *do* you find to occupy yourself? You used to say so much..."

Andrew had been reluctant to tell his wife about the nature of his work with the Director Intelligence Division (Admiralty). "It's just that the Admiralty isn't quite as exciting as in the old days." He hoped the question had been turned.

Her face fell. "Oh well, I suppose you're working with this new Naval War Staff."

"Something like that." He bent over to kiss her. "I shall see you tonight, my darling."

"And I shall look forward to it." She grinned, sinking back onto the pillows.

Tonight, he thought. One of these tonights he would have to speak to her about the very sensitive nature of his work. Wives needed to know these things in order to avoid gaffes in public, particularly at naval functions.

He went down for breakfast, which was ready in various dishes on the sideboard of the dining room. An envelope lay by his plate, and he immediately recognized his father's hand. Inside, a single sheet of paper was neatly covered with a series of numbers. Urgent it might be, but he would eat first. Helping himself to bacon, eggs and an excellent sausage, Andrew applied himself to *The Times*. When he finished, he took a second cup of coffee and went into his study, on the far side of the hall.

Having locked the door, he spread his father's message out on his desk and took a book from the case which stood against the right-hand wall.

Andrew was barely fourteen when he became interested in secret writings and codes. As a quiet, secret pastime, his father devised the simplest form of cipher, an ordinary book code with messages passed by giving blocks of figures equivalent to page, line and number of the word. It was hardly professional, though most serviceable, for the numbers were useless to anyone else unless they knew what book was being used. Initially they used the works of William Shakespeare, for all the Railtons were dedicated to the Bard—some said they used the plays more than the Bible, and certainly regarded them with greater reverence. Then, Giles made the cipher more obscure by discovering two copies of a three-volume history with the pompous title, *A View of Universal History, from the Creation to the Present Time.*

It had been published in 1795; by G Kearsley, No. 46, Fleet Street, London; and written by The Revd. J Adams, AM., and they had often used the cipher to communicate with one another during the intervening years.

The current message, left by Giles in the small hours, was ciphered to Volume One, and Andrew took less than three minutes to unravel it. The book, being old, was written in a flowery language which made literal messages sometimes difficult.

When deciphered, this one read: THE AUTHOR SUGGESTS YOU BE NOT WITH YOUR CAPTAIN AT THE MILITARY TRIBUNAL THIS DAY.

So—Andrew allowed himself a cynical smile—was this a case of father not wishing to be distracted by son? Or was it merely a question of too many Railtons spoiling the broth of intrigue? The military tribunal was the first full meeting of the CID's sub-committee for the reorganization of the Secret and Security Services. Under normal circumstances, Andrew would have accompanied his superior, the DID.

On the way to the Admiralty he thought of Charlotte's remarks concerning the unfair treatment of Admiral Fisher, recently resigned from his duties as First Sea Lord.

It was so damned unjust, for "Jacky" Fisher had changed the whole shape and capability of the Royal Navy more than any one man since Henry VIII.

After arriving at his office, Andrew went straight to give his excuses to the DID and make sure he was not at the meeting that afternoon. Then he got on with the important, most secret, work entrusted to him.

2

After that very first meeting with the Kaiser, during which he was left in no doubt as to his orders, and duty, Gustav Steinhauer contrived to take care of his own situation lest anything should go badly wrong.

He managed two more private conversations with the Kaiser and overcame the vain man by the use of his own silver tongue, extracting from him two things. First a general-purpose letter, so phrased that the reader would be left in no doubt that Steinhauer was acting on the Kaiser's personal orders. Second, he pleaded for money. The cost of recruiting and training the kind of man required by the Kaiser was, Steinhauer explained, prohibitive. The Kaiser appeared to understand this, just as he saw that Steinhauer would be unable to get funds directly from the Foreign Ministry—and certainly never from the Military, once they took over.

In this way Steinhauer had gained a special private kind of power and was in a position to make certain Hans-Helmut Ulhurt was properly cared for at the clinic in Neuweissensee. He simply bought the place out and introduced his own staff.

When he was in Berlin, Steinhauer tried to visit the clinic every other day. He found the big sailor had started to respond. The aim was to make Ulhurt dependent on him alone.

Soon, he discovered two things—Ulhurt could be gentle, kind and talk with great knowledge about a hundred different subjects; he was also full of pent-up anger and could be as dangerous as a snake. He would be trained, as one taught an intelligent dog, to flush out quarry, to bring home messages, to maim and to kill. Altogether a most suitable subject.

Steinhauer told him there was special training ahead. He already knew a good deal about wireless telegraphy, but he would also have to learn violent skills, including the use of explosives, as well as some kind of a course in ciphers.

"As soon as you're really moving well, and are fit," Steinhauer told him, "I will want you to go to sea once more."

"To get my sea legs back?" The sailor flashed a rare smile.

"Something like that. There are people to meet and countries just over the horizon. Call it experience."

"Call it what you like." Ulhurt pulled himself from the bed and walked, unaided, to the door and back again.

"Soon we will have some new instructors here." Steinhauer was only just starting to formulate the course he wished Ulhurt to follow. "There will be people to teach you many skills—and some gymnastic experts."

"I smashed up the teeth of a gym instructor one time." Ulhurt looked at his hand. "Tried to practice some physical exercises on me—know the kind I mean?"

"I think so."

"Look." He held up a hand the size of a small bunch of bananas. "Look— you can still see the scars where his teeth went."

"You have a good, interesting future." Steinhauer tried a smile, for the big sailor appeared to have become sullen.

"Even without a leg?"

"Especially without a leg."

"Shithouse English dogs!" Ulhurt slapped his wooden thigh. "A life and career ruined."

"I've already told you, your career is not ruined. Far from it. The reason you are here is to prepare you for future work for the Fatherland."

"Fuck the Fatherland!"

"Ulhurt, my friend, do I have to remind you of your luck? Others have—"

"Died? I know, died. Damned bastard English sailors are the ones I want to see rot."

"And you may well have that chance. Listen for a moment. The sooner you can get used to this wooden leg, the sooner you can get your own back on English sailors. Already you have achieved miracles. I know it is hard, but I will let you into one small secret. And kindly remember it is a *secret*. Something between us alone."

The big head gave a surly nod.

"The work I am to prepare you for concerns English sailors. It will bring you into close contact with them. If the opportunity arises, you will be able to exact revenge. Work hard. Learn what we are about to teach you and there is a good life ahead." Steinhauer smiled, one hand patting the large man on the shoulder. He felt the hard flesh under his palm and thought, not for the first time, that this man had enough power in his body to kill with consummate ease.

In a moment of near affection for the wounded giant he asked if there was anything he needed.

"A woman." Ulhurt sounded surprised that Steinhauer even needed to ask. "A good woman. Preferably black. Black is the fashionable color at the moment—I mourn for my leg."

That evening a henchman brought a tall, fine-looking mulatto girl to the clinic. She came from the Alexanderplatz area, in a closed car, with the blinds down, and was returned there—in the early hours of the morning—with enough money to take a couple of days off. The male nurses reported to Steinhauer that their patient performed well, and that he made an extra effort the following day.

Within thirty-six hours, Steinhauer returned to the clinic and sought out Ulhurt in his room. The huge sailor lay on his bed, and Steinhauer—his head reeling with devious decisions—pulled a chair close to Ulhurt.

"You are to start," he announced quietly, as though someone might be listening.

"English sailors?" Ulhurt grinned with crooked pleasure.

"I fear not. Not yet. Something has happened. Serious—and you are the only man I can trust to do the job."

Ulhurt stared at him, eyes dull.

"Together," Steinhauer continued, "we live in a land of shadows, my friend.

Secrets are sometimes not kept. We have an agent who works here in Berlin—no need for names." He glanced nervously at the door. "This agent has acted in a treacherous way—working for us while giving the appearance of working for another country. We arranged this, so that the country concerned should be given false information—"

"What country?" It sounded very important to Ulhurt.

"England."

The sailor smiled and Steinhauer continued. "It has been discovered this agent has, in fact, been passing useful—correct—intelligence to the British."

"So."

Steinhauer glanced around again. He seemed particularly agitated. "You see, it is *my* fault. If the agent is questioned, my head will be on the block. Is there need to explain more?"

"You're in the shit, unless—" Ulhurt smiled happily.

"It's a way of putting it, yes." Steinhauer nodded. "Unless this person is silenced. Unfortunately my superiors are already suspicious. The agent lives in a small, cheap apartment over the Pschorrbräu—the beer hall off Friedrichstrasse, on the corner of Behrenstrasse. Number 165. Apartment 4, on the second floor. You get to it through the beer hall or the private door around the corner in Behrenstrasse. You know the area?"

"Well enough." Ulhurt's eyes had lost their dullness. "You want me—"

"You'll be rewarded well. A quick, professional job. Quiet. Just go to the apartment at seven o'clock tonight—the agent is expecting one of my men. Just kill."

"Leave it to me."

Steinhauer fiddled with his hands, still looking nervous. "There is one small problem." He hesitated. "The place is being watched. You must get in and out without being spotted. Heaven knows, we've taught you—"

"Don't worry. Seven o'clock."

"I'll be waiting here for you. For your return."

At half past six that night, Ulhurt limped his way into the busy beer hall on the Friedrichstrasse. The tables were full, and pretty girls performed intricate choreography around the customers, holding four, sometimes five, foaming steins.

Ulhurt found a place, called for a stein of the Kulmbach beer for which the place was famous, and began to drink. He spent nearly twenty-five minutes taking in the scene and in particular watching the archway that he discovered led to the stairs, and so to the apartments.

At five minutes to seven he paid for his beer, rose and headed for the stairs. In the few remaining minutes left, he discovered the way down to the other exit—an ill-lit passage, and stairs down to the street door, which opened onto the Behrenstrasse.

There were only four apartments above the beer hall—two to each floor—their large doors grimy and in need of paint. Certainly, Ulhurt thought, these would be cheap places. Outside the door marked Number 4, he slid a hand into his pocket, pulled on a pair of thick gloves and removed the piano wire from inside his coat. Winding the two ends around his wrists, he reached for the knocker, tapped three times softly and then dropped his hands, holding them together.

For a second, he was surprised when he saw the agent who opened the door for him. It was the mulatto girl they had brought to the clinic. She wore only a thin, silky robe through which her dark enticement clearly showed.

"Well! Come in." She seemed pleased to see him. After all, Ulhurt was exceptionally satisfying, even to a whore. She opened the door, and, without any hesitation, Ulhurt kicked it closed behind him, turned her around, slipped the wire over her head and killed her without a sound. It was done in seconds, and the mulatto did not cry out.

He lowered her body to the carpet, left the piano wire embedded around her lovely neck and let himself out onto the landing.

There were not many people about in the Behrenstrasse, and Ulhurt did not pause to see if he could spot a police watcher. He moved with speed, limping along in the direction of the nearest Stadtbahn station.

He had gone five paces when he detected movement—men closing in from behind and to the side. As far as he could see, there were four of them, coming at him fast.

Ulhurt ducked down the first alley to his right—narrow, dark, and with a light at the far end, bracketed high to the wall. With his training, he could take all four if they were foolish enough to follow.

They were stupid, two of them coming at a rush, one of them shouting for him to stop.

Ulhurt turned, braced himself against the wall, tripped the first man and heeled him between the legs with his one good foot. The other, a small pudgy fellow, walked straight into the sailor's rocklike fist and went down with a dreadful silence.

The other two were calling, but they had only just reached the alley. Smiling, Ulhurt decided he had time to get clear. He found he could walk very fast when it was necessary and had almost reached the far end of the alley when a figure stepped into the pool of light thrown by the lamp attached to the wall.

The first thing Ulhurt saw was a pistol held in the man's hand. He calculated that he could not reach the pistol in time. They would shoot him down. Well, he would go fighting. He gave a terrifying roar and had started to launch himself forward when Steinhauer's voice cut through the night: "You just passed the test. I would have been almost too frightened to use this thing." He returned the pistol to his pocket. Ulhurt stood, staring at him, not knowing whether to be furious or to laugh.

"I had to know how you would behave," Steinhauer told him later. "If you would kill to order, no matter who it was."

"I very nearly had you as well." The sailor gave an unpleasant smile. "Pity about the girl. She was good."

"Plenty more where she came from."

On the following evening another car arrived at the clinic, delivering a further reward for Ulhurt—another mulatto girl: tall, with long, splendid legs which gripped the sailor like those of a wrestler. She was sent to him each week. Usually on a Thursday. He was never asked to kill this girl.

3

Now that their patriarch, the General, was gone, the Railtons began to adjust to their various new roles as the next few weeks went by.

The weather did not improve. If anything it became colder.

As had been predicted, Asquith won the election—though the Liberal majority was greatly, even alarmingly, reduced. For John, who attained a handsome majority, no immediate call came to join the Cabinet.

Charles darted around the country, his movements and occupation cloaked in discreet and cloudy silence.

Mildred began to feel more miserable as her pregnancy advanced. She did not confide in Charles, though she had the most terrible premonition about this baby, and this labor.

The younger people returned to school, and Giles went about his own private war—sometimes in secrecy, more often in committee, where he soon discovered that his battle was with the stone-faced men of the Treasury, and the even more granitelike Military. It was obvious that the Generals, and those who controlled military thinking, foresaw any future war as mere skirmishing with tribesmen around the Empire. The Navy had a greater understanding of what the collection and use of intelligence would mean should a modern war erupt. But the Generals could not even envisage the possible strategy or tactics of a future conflict.

He clashed, on a number of occasions, with Sir Douglas Haig, who, on hearing that part of the operations mooted for a Secret Intelligence Service would be the recruitment of foreign nationals, exploded, "I've rarely heard of anything more infamous! A member of His Majesty's Civil Service suborning foreigners into betraying their own countries—and paying them to do so."

On another occasion Haig maintained that "The gathering of military intelligence has always been, and will always be, the role of the cavalry. If I want intelligence, I get it in the field, by fair and square methods; and if it's obtained by an officer in disguise, then he is aware that if discovered, he will be shot like a gentleman."

Giles Railton suffered many moments of anguish, for his own logic told him that Europe was fast becoming a powder keg, and, sadly, he guessed the first explosions could easily detonate very near to home—in Ireland.

Chapter Five

1

No born Railton had ever been blessed with the jet-black hair and eyes that Bridget Kinread brought to the family when she married Malcolm. Both the General and Giles had approved her looks, clear skin and sparkling personality. Neither of them had ever seen her in a mood which matched the hair, for Bridget's black moods came upon her like a violent summer storm—all crash and lightning.

The blackness was upon her now, as she sat at her old bedroom window, watching the mist gather closer, sweeping in over the valley. She prayed that even at this late date Malcolm might change his mind.

But Malcolm had done it. One hundred and fifty acres and a Georgian house, bought and paid for. Glen Devil Farm. They were to move in within the month—and everybody knew it.

It was always the same in the country of her birth. She often felt that Ireland was more of a village than a country, for all its national pride. Within a day, the "interested" people would know that the Englishman, Malcolm Railton—himself who wed Bridget Kinread of Ballycullen House—had paid a fair sum for Glen Devil Farm.

If only Malcolm could have bought in England. For all his education, the Army, his upbringing, the man had no idea of what it would really be like: nor what strain it could eventually place on her. She had tried to tell him; but, like so many of his compatriots, he just failed to understand. No Englishman alive— or dead for that matter—had ever truly understood. If they could, then the bitter river of enmity which ran skin deep under so many Irish lives would have dried up long ago.

Many times, in her childhood, Bridget had sat in this very window, wondering at her own melancholy. It was wrong, she knew, very wrong, to think of her own people and her own country as she did. But it had been the same from the time she could first remember; and the feeling had grown with the events which shaped her life, for she had left Ballycullen House at eleven years of age, to be educated in England, living with her aunt near Virginia Water.

Until she returned to Ireland as Malcolm's bride, Bridget had visited the country of her birth only for short holidays. Now she was back, a changed woman with new horizons, married late, at thirty, into one of the great English families.

In the event, her husband was infected by the wizardry of people and country. This was where he would farm. The blackness descended from the moment she realized what would happen.

Ballycullen House was empty but for Michael Bergin, the stablehand, for both her mother and father had gone with Malcolm into Wicklow Town. "We'll live in better style than any of the Railtons in England," Malcolm said as he kissed her before leaving. "Bridget, my dear, here in your Ireland we can afford to farm and live like lords. What's more, there's greater respect."

For the first time she detected the innate snobbery of the family into which she had married. It was not so obvious in people like her father-in-law, Giles, with whom she had pleaded after the General's funeral.

"He's set on farming, Papa Giles. Is there no way he could farm here, at Redhill? He'd be an asset."

Giles looked at her with cold eyes, shaking his head. "Bridget, my dear, there is no legal way, and, if it's what he wants, I cannot stop him. However, you are a Railton now, and there are things you can do for your new family. Things of great importance."

She waited, puzzled, not realizing what he meant until he began to ask questions about her past, and the people she knew in Dublin and elsewhere.

"I live by old honors," Giles said. "Love of Country, King, Empire and God. Those things grow thin with age, of course, but I trust you will live in the same way. The family, your new family, lives by these things, and we are all dedicated to service. You would wish to be of service?"

She said yes, and he then began to talk, telling her what she must do.

And now, Bridget Railton was alone in her parents' home. Any one of *them* who wished to talk with her would know, and come. As she thought this, so Bridget caught sight of the horseman coming across the fields at a gallop. And even through the drizzle, which had now reached the house, she could see it was Padraig O'Connell, whom she had known since they were both barely five years of age.

She slid from the window seat and peeped into the mirror, smoothing her hair and adjusting the lace collar on her simple brown woolen gown. From the top of the stairs she could already hear Michael Bergin admitting Padraig into her father's house, through the kitchen door at the back.

"I can hear you, Padraig O'Connell," she called, surprised at the calmness of her own voice. "And shame on you visiting when a respectable married woman's alone in the house."

His laugh was gruff and carried little humor. The laugh of a dead man, her father had once called it after they had been up until dawn, drinking and arguing politics.

He stood in the hallway, at the foot of the stairs, his clothes damp from the soft rain he had tried to outride; dark eyes looking up at her, his hair long and tangled, and the mouth smiling—like his laugh, the smile of a dead man, not reaching the eyes.

"If you wanted Father, he's in town with my husband." She stood at the last stair, the blackness of her own eyes almost outfreezing his.

"Sure and I know that. Would I have come here if your husband was at home?" Then his voice fell by one note, like a scale on the pianoforte. "Or your father either, Bridget. No, we must speak. Where?"

She motioned toward the parlor and he went on ahead of her as though he owned the house and not her family.

"You know why I'm here?" He turned toward her as she closed the door behind them.

"You tell me and I'll know—though I'd rather not, Padraig, I'd best be truthful."

"Tut! And is that the way to be talking to someone who was your friend from childhood? Almost kin to you."

"*A little more than kin, and less than kind.*" She muttered the quotation from Hamlet.

"You're talkin' in riddles, so. Is that how they speak in your polite London society?"

"I mean I do not want you here. You or your kind. You know well enough what I mean."

He nodded, and she thought there was an almost tangible calmness within this man. The inner peace of certainty: a mark of his cause. "Aye, so, I know what you mean, but there's no escaping kin and country, Bridget. In the next few years things may go peacefully, though I doubt it; and it's my duty to call on you." He laid one thin hand on her wrist. Everything about him was lean, she thought, from the dead laugh to the body, even the way he breathed: shallow, lean breaths as though all his energy went into it. She tried to shake off the hand, but his grip was deceptively strong. "Your English husband's bought Glen Devil Farm, so that can only mean you're back to stay."

"There's talk of putting a manager in," she lied.

"There's no such talk. There'll be no absent landlord at Glen Devil. Now you listen to me, because it's of your country, and your people, that I'm talking. You know what's going on?"

"I can guess."

"The next few years'll see it happen, Bridget. For good or ill, this is the crucial time. If they force through this Home Rule Bill, the Protestants—the Unionists and Orangemen—will not have it. It's already been said in Belfast, and in Dublin, that if the Bill goes through, the Unionists will form a Protestant government in Belfast. We've heard it all before. Didn't the present British Home Secretary's pox-ridden father, Lord Randolph Churchill, say long ago that if the Bill passed, then Ulster would fight, and Ulster would be right?"

"I'm not one for studying the politics of it."

"No, well, he did say it, and they would fight. Only they would *not* be right. We deserve a united Ireland, ruled by ourselves, governed by ourselves." The dead laugh again as he spoke in Gaelic: "*Sinn Fein—Ourselves Alone.*"

"Ourselves alone," Bridget laughed back in his face. "And what do you expect ourselves alone to do? Massacre all the Protestants here and in the nine counties? Kill the English? Butcher the soldiers, and be butchered?"

He tightened the pressure on her arm. "Look now; whichever way it goes, the thing must be finished soon—within the next few years. Maybe sooner. Now you listen. If that Bill is passed, then we'll get what we've always wanted, though there'll be trouble. Fighting, yes; and killing as well. For if the Bill doesn't pass this time, then the Republicans will rise up and pass it of their own accord. The feelings are high, and they'll run even stronger...."

"You and your kind will see to that, I've no doubt."

"Then have no doubt. There's hatred flowing again. Arms are already being brought in. If the Bill passes there'll be fighting; and if it doesn't pass there'll be revolution in this green country. Either way, the storm'll break. Sooner rather than later."

"So what has it to do with me? I shall be here, at Glen Devil, and probably see my husband slaughtered...."

"There's no need for that. Many English will hold to our cause, because it's right. There are two things, though, Bridget Kinread...."

"Railton!" she corrected sharply.

"To me it's Kinread until your husband's proved otherwise. You see to it that your Englishman knows which side to butter his bread."

She gave a shrug that could have meant anything. O'Connell continued: "And there's more to it than persuading Malcolm Railton to keep the butter right side up, and not put the country's plight on the long finger. I know of his family. I know what they are, who they are and what they do."

"So?"

"So they're full of power: diplomats, military men, and politicians. Doubtless you'll be visiting them or they'll be coming to Glen Devil. This is the second thing, Bridget—you'll hear talk from them, and you will *be* hearing things. You understand me?"

"I understand you're asking me to spy for you; report to you."

He shook his head. "I'm not asking. That is what you *will* do. Anything of value; any crumb of information you pick up from the tables of your grand new English relatives; anything of importance to the cause of Ireland, you will pass on to us. You follow?"

She shrugged, giving a half nod, knowing it was a sign of commitment, yet not wanting to know.

"Good." This time the smile almost reached his eyes. "You only have to tell young Michael Bergin, out in your father's stableyard, and I shall arrange to see you privately. When you've moved to Glen Devil, there'll be someone else there, employed by your husband, who'll offer the same service. Nobody else need know."

She stepped away, telling him to go.

"Nobody, Bridget," his hand on the door, "will ever guess where the information comes from; but you can be our lifeline...otherwise..."

"You'll kill me just as you'll kill my English husband."

"Only if you make that necessary." He pulled the door open and did not look back. She heard his boots heavy on the polished boards of the passage running toward the kitchen.

A few moments later Bridget caught the sound of his horse thumping out of the yard. She went from the parlor into the hall. Michael Bergin leaned against the kitchen door. He gave her a knowing nod, then turned his back and walked away. If it came to it, Michael would be the one to cut her throat.

Bridget went upstairs, took paper and envelopes from her father's table and began to write. Her letter was addressed to a Mr. Harding at a Poste Restante— a newsagent and tobacconists' in London—near Charing Cross.

Giles Railton had taught her how to do it. The letter was a simple inquiry about a subscription to a lady's periodical, unobtainable out of London. But there were key words in the short note. When Giles Railton read it, he would know that the Fenians had made contact.

"I shall give you things to pass to them, my dear," he had told her on the afternoon of the General's funeral as the bitter dusk gathered in around Redhill Manor. "They will be things for them to know, and believe. In return you will let me know everything—names, times, plans: all you can glean. You'll do it?"

She had said yes, just as she had nodded affirmation to Padraig O'Connell, not knowing what she would really do, until she saw the evil in Michael Bergin's eyes. Now, Bridget Kinread was a Railton. If Malcolm would have nothing to do with his father's intrigues for sovereign, country and God, then she would.

2

The middle of March found Sara alone at Redhill Manor. John was tied down to parliamentary business and insisted that she stay in Haversage. It was a good opportunity, he said, for her to establish her position as mistress of the Manor.

She had hoped her stepson, James, would also be at Redhill, as Wellington College was on holiday for ten days. But at the last minute he had written to say he was going to stay with a friend in Farnborough—the son of a local doctor, by name, Savory.

Since the changes that had come with the General's death, Sara spent the bulk of her time at the Manor, and though she was loath to admit it now acknowledged that the new peace and tranquillity of Haversage had advantages.

It would have been wrong to suggest she did not miss London: after all, until now London was everything she knew.

But in the relatively quiet, different atmosphere of Redhill Manor and Haversage, Sara began to question the whole tenor of her life. She could never, of course, forsake London entirely, but the Manor had already begun to cast its spell.

She spent a great deal of her time wandering through the house, captivated by the sense of history which seemed to ooze from the walls. She loved the huge hall, the great staircase and gallery, the reception rooms with their high ceilings, the oak panels in the long dining room and, especially, in the General's Study. The views from nearly all the windows also entranced her—in particular those from the upper rooms at the rear of the house, from where you could see the whole rise of the Downs.

From her own bedroom, which she shared with John when he was there, the skyline curved, treeless, for several miles; yet, right in the center stood a small clump of bushes which from the distance of the house looked like an oasis. The household—servants and family alike—called this view "Egypt," for the bushes look exactly like a group of palm trees standing alone in a seemingly endless series of dunes.

The house, while in good order, still retained the decorations—the wallpaper, paint, hangings and carpets—of the past forty years, and as Sara roamed its rooms and passages, her mind turned constantly on change and improvement.

There had been little snow that month, but the cold and frost was lingering, though this did not stop Sara from going down into Haversage whenever possible. John said she should make herself known locally and patronize individual tradesmen who would take it as a great compliment if she went to their shops personally.

So on several occasions she got Ted Natter to take her down the hill into Haversage, usually in the governess cart pulled by a good-natured quiet little gray pony.

On this particular day, muffled against the cold, they returned to the Manor, taking the now familiar way east, along Hill Street from the market square, and up Red Hill itself, to the Manor gates on the left. The wheels crunched on heavy gravel, the great elms, bare against the cold clear sky, flanked the drive for a quarter of a mile to the house, standing with the pale glory of winter sunlight on its soft brick.

Redhill Manor was all the more imposing because of its size. The oldest part—"the core of the house," as the General used to call it—lay, almost an exact square, in the center. It stood now, just as it had been built, in the early sixteenth century, with its unusually large leaded windows and the main iron-bound oak door, set into a stone drop archway with carved and decorated hoodmolds and spandrels.

The additional building consisted of two large wings, erected to left and right, making the whole place, if it could be seen from above, into the shape of a giant H: a square U at both back and front. These wings had been added so skillfully that it was difficult to detect change in style or stone.

The family maintained this was due to the patience and determination of Walter Railton—known in his day as "Buck" Railton—who had commissioned the building's enlargement in 1718, using a grant presented to him by a grateful Duke of Marlborough, with whom Buck had served with courage and distinction at Blenheim and Ramillies.

To Sara, and many of the Railton women, Buck appeared as a romantic figure; but they judged him by the portrait, which hung with the other Railton likenesses in the library, access to which could be gained only through the General's Study. Buck looked a swashbuckler, and the painting, which showed the smoke and skirmishing of the initial attack on Blenheim village in the background, gave the impression that his eyes still mocked or invited, depending on your sex, as if sending strong signals forward across the centuries.

John could have had the same look, she liked to think, had he not gone into politics.

For all his brilliance and devotion to duty as a politician, John lacked something present in all the other Railton men Sara had met—and certainly visible in the painting of Walter Railton. It was indefinable, but not, Sara concluded, the sexual thing—though she intuitively knew from the start that her husband was not the most driving of lovers.

She pondered on this after her return, having gone to the library with the great fire crackling behind its metal mesh guard. The room had no need of a fire for warmth, being already full of life from the hundreds of books and the long row of Railton ancestors preserved in oils.

She glanced up at Buck's portrait, half-formed questions flitting through her mind. There was surely a special kinship between her and Buck Railton, for family legend held that he was a deceiver, loaded with lust. Like herself, she thought, and the guilt of it gnawed at her conscience, while she worried that John would say something openly to Asquith.

Certainly, there had been promise of a Cabinet post for John: but never from Asquith. The Chancellor of the Exchequer, David Lloyd George no less, had promised. "What's your payment, then? What do you ask?" His hand cupped about her breast as he spoke, mouth close to hers. As his other hand reached, starting to lift her dress, willpower had drained away and her juices began to flow as never before. The magic of the man—his eyes, the mystery of his lilting accent and body. When she replied, her own voice held a rasp of dryness in the throat. "A Cabinet post for my husband," she had said.

The Welsh Wizard laughed. "Is that all? It's done, my dear. You have my word. John Railton's a lucky man. There . . . there . . . and there."

So he worked his enchantment, and she understood why his reputation stood as it did. After her wedding, her mother had told her, "Promise me, Sara, if you are to mix in the world of politics, never allow yourself—not for a minute— to be left alone with Mr. Lloyd George." She had promised. Another promise broken. Her marriage vows broken: not just once, but on four occasions, and Sara knew it was not for the sake of a Cabinet post. It was for her own body, a need for the little Welshman, with his winning ways and the peace he brought after the passion.

Feeling a deep moment of depression, here in the library, Sara went over to the windows which, like those in the Study, looked out onto the rose garden. The chill sun still shone, and she gazed out, dead-eyed, at the line of cypresses following the path, at the far end, to the bower, and what they liked to call the maze. To the right lay the walled kitchen garden, and far off on the left the Great Lawn. Beyond, to the west and south, the lands of the Estate reached for miles, up to the Berkshire Downs where once the Roman legions had passed by. You could just glimpse "Egypt" from here.

The depression was coupled with a moment of self-hate, partly because of her folly—particularly in lying to John, telling him Asquith had promised the post—yet also for her own dissatisfaction. The gloominess turned to anger, so that during the lonely luncheon, served by Vera, she felt the old fire rekindle in her loins, the flames licking at her imagination.

Immediately on completion of her meal, Sara retired to rid herself of the obsession. Then, in a sudden need for cleansing, she sought out a pair of her old riding boots, and by three in the afternoon—knowing there was less than two hours' daylight left—she hobbled, now in her riding habit, to the stables.

Billy Crook had been sent over to warn Ted Natter, who prepared Fancy, a docile roan mare, for Mrs. Railton.

"Her be sweet-tempered, M'm," Natter told Sara when she appeared in the yard.

But Sara's mood was not for sweet tempers. "When I want a docile animal I'll tell you, Ted. I need something with spirit."

In the harness room, while their mistress paced up and down the yard, Natter grumpily told Billy Crook, "Her wants somethin' spirited, then 'er can 'ave Turk, an' to 'ell wi' 'er."

Though he grumbled, Natter was no fool. Turk was the General's gray, a fine animal, spirited but easy to manage. Natter had loved his master, and knew better than to let a man of well past seventy out on a difficult mount. So he had no qualms about seeing Lady Sara—as they incorrectly thought of her—trot from the yard, having turned away all offers to be accompanied by either Natter or Billy Crook.

She rode hard and with concentration, the sting of cold on her face, the excitement of managing a large animal. As she rode, so the fantasies disappeared, and with them the fire. She knew that men talked of taking cold baths. They would be better taking a horse out, alone and at a wild gallop. She was now herself again, mind and body centered into staying on Turk's back; maintaining command.

So Sara became conscious only of the noise: the wind, her own breath, the great drumming of Turk's hooves, while, around her the rolling fields went by. She skirted two small copses, then began to gallop, intending to make a long curve that would eventually take her back toward the house.

She was aware of a particularly high hedge ahead, but urged Turk to take it. He seemed to slow slightly, hesitating, but she shouted at him, excitedly, for this was the first time Sara had jumped such an obstacle at full speed or on such a big animal.

Then she was in the air, with her stomach left behind; hands, feet and knees all working madly to stay in place. For a second the world seemed to stop.

Turk appeared to remain suspended in space above the hedge, and it was in that split of time that she saw the true danger.

Below, and in front of her, on the far side of the hedge, as she leaned back in the saddle hauling on the reins, Sara caught a glimpse of figures—a knot of men working in the ditch directly below her.

She heard the cries, saw at least one startled expression, and was aware of men scattering. After that there was simply the sensation of hanging in midair; sky where earth should be. Then turning upside down; earth; a pain reaching out slowly, swallowing her into darkness.

The next thing was a sense of warmth. Sara knew she was on her back. Voices drifted from the air a long way off, making little sense. As her eyes opened, a weathered young face swam above her as though detached from its body.

"Is he safe?" she asked. "Is Turk safe?"

The young man was kneeling beside her. "Spadger went after him, Ma'am. He was still galloping, but I doubt if he's come to any harm. It's you I'm worried about."

"And the men? There were men."

"No damage done there." He smiled, his voice holding the traces of a Berkshire accent, yet not broad like that of Ted Natter's or the girls at the house. "I've sent to the house for the doctor, Ma'am."

She pulled herself up, testing each limb carefully. "Doctor? What doctor?"

"You had a very heavy fall, Mrs. Railton."

"Just had the wind knocked out of me, that's all. Tell them not to bother with a doctor."

He nodded, gave a quick order and one of the farm workers—she recognized them now—hurried off, shouting, "Willum Plum . . . Yer, Willum . . . Come baack Willum . . . No cause for the doctor . . ."

"I'm so sorry." Sara felt sick and shaken, but was certain there was no serious damage done.

"As long as you're not hurt, Mrs. Railton."

She smiled. "Who are you?"

"Berry, Ma'am. Bob Berry. Farm Manager for the Estate."

She shook her head, suddenly realizing that she was hanging on to his arm. One of the men was leading Turk back. The animal appeared to be docile, only occasionally tossing his head.

"You sure you're all right?" Berry asked.

"Few nasty bruises, that's all." She tested her legs and balance, conscious of the aches in her shoulders and, embarrassingly, all over her buttocks. "I've been lucky, Mr. Berry. It could have been very nasty."

He reached up and took Turk's bridle. "It was very nasty the *last* time . . ." Berry stopped as though he should not have spoken.

"Last time?"

"You were not to know, Mrs. Railton. The hedge. They call it Lady Nellie's hedge. Long before my time, over twenty years ago now. The General's wife, Lady Nellie, fell at the hedge. They were hunting and..."

"Oh my God!" Sara felt dizzy. She knew all about the famous terrible accident. Lady Railton had been killed instantly. "I didn't realize it was *this* hedge! Oh Lord!"

"You think you can make it back to the Manor, Ma'am?"

She nodded, uncertain.

"Perhaps if I walked the horse?"

"Oh, would you, Mr. Berry? I'm not really hurt, but... well, finding out this is Lady Nellie's hedge, and everything..."

"If you can mount, Ma'am, I'll lead him."

So they set off at a walk, and, to regain her composure, Sara asked Bob Berry about his work. As he talked, she found herself becoming intrigued.

He spoke of the dairy herd; the grazing land, and of the way they rotated the crops of corn, potatoes and other vegetables. His voice had a quiet, soothing quality, as reassuring as the seasons. A man perfectly content, she told herself; someone who loved the land and the animals; someone who saw results each day of the year.

"You're lucky to be so happy, Mr. Berry."

"Happy indeed." He paused for two long strides. "Happy as long as I remain here."

"You're not leaving us, surely." She reined in the horse, looking down at him.

"Not of my own accord, no, Ma'am."

"Then...?"

"I shouldn't speak of it to you, Ma'am..."

His brow creased, and she saw concern in his eyes. "Tell me." Sara heard a new note of command in her voice.

It was a simple story. Berry was an Oxfordshire man, son of a farmer from North Hinksey, a few miles west of Oxford itself. He had courted the daughter of a neighboring village innkeeper for two years prior to applying for the Farm Manager's post at Redhill Manor, three years previously. He suspected the General had given him the appointment on the strength of his forthcoming marriage. Certainly he knew the General's son, Mr. John Railton, expected a married man as Farm Manager. It had always been so at Redhill.

But life is never smooth. On the very day the letter arrived from the General offering him the post, his intended bride broke the news that she could not marry him.

"The General was a good man. Told me it didn't matter, and in any case the right girl would come along soon enough."

The right girl had not come along, though, and Bob Berry was very much aware that his appointment would come up for review at Michaelmas.

Sara began to walk the horse again. "And you think my husband will replace you because you're not married?"

"He's every right to, Ma'am. Every right, but I ask you, please, don't mention this to him."

She reined in again, looking him straight in the eyes. "I'll only mention it to him if he threatens to get rid of you before the right woman comes along." She smiled. "That's the least I can do. I will *not* see you leave, Mr. Berry."

Natter met them in the stableyard, and Sara thanked Berry for all his kindness, reassuring him that her husband would not see him out of the Farm.

"No harm done, Ted, thank God," Berry told him.

"Don't know 'bout that, Mr. Berry. There be trouble at the 'ouse, I can tell 'ee that for sure."

Trouble there was.

Vera Bolton—Cook's daughter, who was Sara's maid at Redhill—lingered by the door, trying to catch her mistress before she got in. "Oh, M'm, thank 'eaven you're back and safe. Mr. John's 'ere from London—waitin' for you. Worried out on 'is life he is; and when he heard you'd fallen at Lady Nellie's hedge—well! He's in such a state, about you and—"

"And what?"

"Best go in an' see 'im, M'm. In the General's Study. Then the . . . best go see 'im."

John was slumped in his father's chair, behind the big desk, his face gray, looking older than she had ever seen him. He was up and over to her the moment she appeared in the doorway. "Oh, my dear, thank God you're safe!"

"John, it's all right. I—"

"You *are* unhurt? When I heard it was Lady Nellie's hedge, I—"

"I simply need a bath, with something in it to ease the bruising. A nasty fall, that's all."

He made her promise never to go out again without either Natter or Billy Crook, but she could see from the creases on his face that his concern had not diminished.

"Are *you* all right?" Placing her arms on his shoulders. "John? What is it?"

"There's a telegram. From Dr. Savory, in Farnborough."

"James?"

He nodded, going to the desk and picking up the small slip of paper. "I said he should have come here to stay with you."

She took the paper and read: JAMES SLIGHTLY INJURED IN FLYING MACHINE ACCIDENT. FEEL IT BEST IF I BRING HIM HOME TO YOU TODAY. SAVORY.

Chapter Six

1

Throughout the rigorous years at Wellington College, those who came into contact with James Railton put him down as either a superior snob or a quiet, lonely boy.

At that time, Wellington—like most public schools—did not smack of luxury. The discipline was harsh, the training hard, the conditions and food worse than merely mediocre.

James appeared not to mind this and improved greatly when given some authority as a prefect—a natural progression, the Headmaster considered. After all, the boy was grandson to a general and destined to become a professional soldier himself.

When he took the Sandhurst entrance examination there were many prayers that he would pass—for even a general's grandson did not gain automatic entrance to Sandhurst.

The exams were difficult, but young Railton sailed through his "preliminary"—taken in the early part of 1909—and they expected him to pass the exceptionally hard "further," which lasted for six hours a day, covering eight days.

The "further" was in a real sense a detailed survey of the candidate's academic and physical condition. As James had remarked to his grandfather at Christmas, "What's the use? Soldiering's what I'm after, not writing essays."

The old man grunted and laughed. "You'll find out soon enough, boy. It all comes in handy. Think ahead. I've always tried to do that, which is more than can be said for some of the General Staff these days. Change in the wind, James; change in the wind."

"Like flying?" the young man had said rather slyly.

"Like flying, the internal combustion engine and the reorganization of the Navy. The Army'll come to it as well. Think ahead."

"It's what I'm trying to do, sir," James replied, then launched into the short speech that was to bring about the telegram from Farnborough.

James had discovered a true passion. He was desperate, and determined, to fly: like the Wright brothers, and Cody, who flew the first aeroplane in England.

With this new obsession, James harnessed an already well-developed military mind to the challenging possibilities of the future. He knew he was scheming when he brought up the future of flying with his grandfather, just as intrigue led him to cultivate boys like Martin Savory.

Savory had a "thing" about girls, which was yet to hit James, who had a thing about flying. More important, young Savory lived in Farnborough, where a lot of flying went on. It was as simple, and deceitful, as that. It should be added that he also told nobody about the £500 his grandfather had placed, with sworn secrecy, in Coutts Bank under James' name. Last, it was simple to get invited to stay at the Savory house during the break in the Easter term.

The days were clear and cold, with occasional mist in the evenings, and James came to an easy arrangement with Martin.

Each evening they planned a ramble in the area—for the next day—with Martin briefing James about the local terrain, sights and places of interest they would have seen.

The following morning the boys would leave together—Martin to "do a spot of mashing," as he put it, with a local girl, home from some ladies' school in Sussex and not averse to a bit of canoodling; James to go down to the large stretch of ground, dotted with wood and tin buildings, where, because of the clear weather, much flying was taking place.

Since Sam Cody had first flown from this field, still operating as the military balloon factory, many pilots, inventors and mechanics had made their way to Farnborough. Within a matter of days, James—who had devoured every available book about heavier-than-air flight—was able to make a few friends among the people working at the balloon factory. These conversations proved good supplementary experience to the books. Technically, James knew exactly how to fly.

On the day that would, in some ways, change his life, young Railton entered the aerodrome and set off in the direction of the large hangar where he knew Allicott Verdon Roe was working on his latest machine.

He had gone only a few steps when a new sound caught his attention. Already James prided himself on being able to recognize various engine notes, but the noise he now heard was unknown to him—a gentle, steady, beelike sound coming from the south. He turned, looking in the direction of this new engine note.

It was low over the trees, nose slightly raised, preparing to land—a beautiful, boxlike machine, superbly rigged, with a pusher propeller. Long triangular struts held an elevator well forward of the wings, while the open framework swept back to a pair of boxed rudders. Skids, like skis, hung below, each fitted with what appeared to be unusually small wheels, while another pair of even more minute wheels were visible forward of the box-kite rudder section.

"Farman!" James breathed aloud, recognizing the lines of the machine. A Farman biplane had carried off the distance prize at Reims last year. He watched, fascinated, as the aeroplane banked gracefully, losing height, its pilot plainly visible, exposed to wind, bitter cold and all weathers as the propeller whirred behind him.

The Gnome engine began to die as the aeroplane descended onto the grass, turned and came to a halt not a hundred yards from where James stood.

The pilot was bundled up in helmet, goggles and leather coat, so James could make out neither features nor age. When the man climbed down, it came as something of a surprise that he spoke with a distinct American accent— for the Farman was a French aeroplane.

"Where do I find the top man around here, son?"

James asked if he meant the Commanding Officer of the balloon factory or some other official.

"I guess the Commanding Officer. I'm supposed to be here on military business. You a flyer?"

"Yes," James lied. "Waiting to go to Sandhurst. Just filling in a bit of time here."

"Well, if you're not doing anything, could you keep an eye on the ship while I try to find out if I'm expected?"

James said he would certainly look after the Farman, and could he just climb up and take a peep at the controls?

"Don't see why not." The American thrust out a hand. "Name's Farthing. Richard—Dick to my friends."

"Railton. James Railton."

The American nodded, and James watched him walk away, a tall, muscular man—about ten years older than himself, he guessed. There had been a particularly attractive glint in the large brown eyes, as though the American viewed the world, and life in it, as some joke, not to be taken seriously by those who were the dramatis personae of history.

James climbed up onto the Farman—a Farman III, he thought—taking his place at the controls, checking which levers operated the ailerons, rudder and elevator. The mechanisms were all simple enough: strong bolted wood, wheels, and pinions, carrying wires to the various control surfaces.

He forgot cold and time; even the ground disappeared as James went into a daydream. He knew exactly what was required of a pilot in flight. What he needed was the opportunity; all the imagination in the world could not make up for the real thing: to look down on earth from a height of several hundred feet; feel the wind, see the horizon tilt; to be free, and touch the clouds with his hand.

Suddenly he was pulled from the reverie by the American voice calling, "James? James, you want to come down here a minute?"

Dick Farthing stood below the wings, grinning up at him.

"Just thinking how nice it would be. . . ." James began to climb down.

"Well, you could get your chance at that. For the time being, I guess it's me who needs help. I've got no place to stay. Know any good hotels?"

There was the Queen's Hotel, which James thought looked reasonable enough, but probably a shade expensive.

"The hell with the expense." Dick laughed again—he laughed a great deal. "Maurice Farman's paying. I'm just here to show off his wares to the British Army." He pronounced "Maurice" in an accentuated French manner—Mor-

reece. "Just help me get this ship across the field to the hangar over there."
He pointed at the hangar, which James already knew was empty, next to where
the Roe contingent worked.

"Hope they've given you some keys. The A. V. Roe people'll be swarming
all over this if you give them half a chance." James lifted his eyebrows.

Farthing dug into his pocket, producing a set of keys. "Courtesy of your
Army people. Strange, they *were* expecting me." He gave another laugh. "Mind
you, it's going to be a week before anyone'll come over to take a look."

James helped him start the engine. Swinging the propeller, he discovered
the Farman had its drawbacks, for you had to stand within the framework of
the two slim booms—which made up the wide, open fuselage—cocking your
ear for the pilot's commands. The engine started on his first downward pull of
the propeller: clattering into life, then soothed by Dick's experienced hand on
the throttle.

Ducking under the thin wood and canvas, James gave his new friend the
thumbs-up. The engine blipped gently and the Farman taxied across the field,
James running behind, head down, keeping out of the propeller wash.

The A. V. Roe people were friendly, though inquisitive about a new arrival,
but Dick managed to keep them at a distance by pleading that he had not
eaten for almost twenty-four hours. There was a professional briskness about
him, offset by a disarmingly easy manner. He seemed to keep up a flow of
conversation as James walked him to the main gate, and down to the Queen's
Hotel, where he registered, insisting that James should stay and lunch with
him.

However, it did not take James long to realize that, though Dick Farthing
appeared to talk a great deal, his chatter gave nothing away. On the contrary,
he interspersed his conversation with quick, telling questions, so that by the
time they reached the hotel, he had a good knowledge of James' background
and future prospects. "Your pa's a Member of Parliament?" he exclaimed with
what appeared to be some awe. "Now that could be a real help. Maurice figures
your military people may want some of his new designs. Getting to know an
MP would be a good start. Reckon I fell on my feet meeting you like this."

Over lunch, James began to learn something about the American. Their
family backgrounds were very similar—Army and Diplomatic Corps. "Yep,
my old man's one of the President's Foreign Advisers; and I have an uncle,
Bradley, in the Army; while the other one's a senator. I reckon I'm the black
sheep." When Farthing smiled, the right corner of his mouth twisted upward,
half-closing the right eye, as though the smile brought with it a conspiratorial
wink.

At twenty-seven, Richard was the eldest of five brothers. "Joseph's just
twenty; Michael's about a year older than you, James. Then we have young
Bradley, just turned fifteen, and Arnold, coming up twelve. We've a sister as
well—Maud. Guess my folks squeezed her in between Bradley and Arnold."

Dick had followed the military side of the family. A graduate of West Point, he was commissioned into the infantry. Then, like so many of his generation, he caught the flying bug. "Pa was scandalized, of course. Threatened to cut me off without a dime, but I used my natural charm." He grinned, to show the laugh was on him. "In time of war or national emergency, back I go into the Army—only I hope to hell they have some kind of Air Corps by then."

James said it was his hope also. "The General Staff drag their heels. Nobody sees the potential."

Dick shrugged, a gesture of agreement. "Well, your people do *seem* to be interested in Maurice's designs. They certainly want to see how the Farman III performs. You want to give me a hand or are you busy over the next few days?"

The invitation delighted James. "Hope you'll let me take her up."

"No problem. You got a certificate yet?"

"No." He could not lie about that.

"Well, if you have some experience, it's okay. She handles like a willing lady."

Dick's career in aviation had started with his hanging around flying fields in the United States. For some time he had worked for, and with, Glenn Curtiss, but eventually came to France. Now he was one of Farman's established pilots.

They arranged to meet on the following morning, and James could not wait to get back and give the news to Martin Savory.

The next day was like its predecessor—clear and bright, with a pinch of frost in the air.

They worked all morning, checking the rigging and tuning the engine. Dick Farthing had brought a hamper out from the Queen's Hotel, and said he would do a circuit after lunch—"Just to keep her in trim. Then I'll run through the procedures with you if you'd like to fly her."

There was really only one way to learn: get a thorough grounding by reading, listening and watching; then go up there and do it. James, with the supreme confidence of youth, knew he was ready.

They started up the engine, and the aeroplane trundled out onto the grass, with Dick at the controls. Fifteen minutes later it was back, nose turned in James' direction. Once the engine was switched off and the propeller stopped, he jumped down. "Okay, you want to take her around?"

Dick lent him his flying gear, and James climbed up into the hard little seat in front of the engine, while Dick went through the controls—the levers for elevators, rudder and ailerons; exactly how much throttle he would need; cautionary advice on not being heavy-handed with the elevator, and a word about judging his speed for landing.

His mouth was dry, and in spite of the cold he could feel the sweat moving from his pores. The palms of his hands were damp under the leather as he tested the control levers. There was a good forward view, allowing him to judge the angle of the elevator—directly in front of him—stretching out on the jutting triangular framework.

He heard Dick, behind him, calling to ask if he was ready; and they went through the familiar starting-up ritual.

James had not bargained for the vibration, or noise. You were aware of it from the ground, but once at the controls, everything took on new perspective. The Farman was translated from an inanimate object to a machine that had life and purpose.

He concentrated, feeling a sense of achievement at steering the aeroplane across the field, finally turning into the wind, holding back on the elevator lever to keep the boxed tail and rudders down on the ground.

He gave the throttle a touch, lowering the revolutions, but the rudder box wanted to rise—the rudders themselves needing hard handling to swing the front of the craft into position. Finally it came around, giving James a view of grass spread out in front of him, with the skyline and trees in the far distance, a couple of miles away.

He looked about him, as other pilots did, to ensure no other aeroplanes were nearby or overhead. Then, still holding the tail down, he pushed the throttle lever forward, calling up the power needed to launch himself into the air.

The racket behind him grew louder and more distracting as the machine began to move forward. At first the motion was hardly noticeable; then the whole aeroplane tried to slew violently to the left. Correcting quickly with the rudders, he had to push even harder on the elevator to keep the rear down as the Farman bumped over the grass, gathering speed at a frightening rate.

Everything appeared to blur as the speed rose, wind lashing at his face, trying to penetrate the leather of helmet and the glass in his goggles. Then the rear stopped swinging and he was moving in a straight line.

Now, he thought, letting the elevator lever loosen slightly. The curved control plane moved fractionally, ahead of him, and he allowed it to find its natural position before he tightened his grip, holding it as the rear of the Farman came up. The machine's angle altered as it tried to lift. Then, a slight bounce, and other noises: wind whining through the bracing wires; a rippling and creaking of fabric and wood; the clatter of the engine.

James was unaware that he was talking to the craft, just as he had talked to his first horse when learning to ride. Hold her there. Back, now! Back! The jutting front section holding the wide elevator seemed intent on dropping forward, and it took muscle to pull back on the elevator, bringing the whole flimsy triangular framework sharply up. For a second he thought the booms behind him would smash into the ground, but he held the position. Steady! Steady! The wheels and skids bumped and rocked on the rough grass.

Then came a new peace. No vibration from below; only the screech of wind over the wings and through the wires. There followed a sensation James was never to forget.

It took almost thirty seconds for him to realize that the machine had left the ground, finding its natural habitat.

The Farman must have reached almost a couple of hundred feet before he even had the wit to level off. He did not feel the cold, and the noise and the wind on his body went unnoticed. From where he sat, perched among the wires, with the great Gnome engine roaring away behind him, he felt as though he sat on the cusp of the world itself. Before him, the landscape of Hampshire spread to the horizon—clear and bright, the whole unrolling before his eyes like a live relief map. The sensation and heavy intoxication of the experience almost made him forget to reduce engine power.

As the revolutions gradually dropped, to his command on the throttle, the machine began to sink. He touched the aileron and rudder controls. Bank and turn to the left. Steady! The left wing dropped sickeningly, and for a moment he thought the whole aeroplane would slide out of the sky to bury him in the fields below. Opposite aileron. The wings remained dipped and the earth tilted. Now another touch on the elevator. "That's it, girl! Round we go. . . ."

Holding the Farman level again, James Railton marveled at the fact that *he* was really flying it—that it did what he told it to do, through the controls, just as others had said in books or conversation.

The gentle turn now brought him south of the field, on a reciprocal course to the one he had taken after lifting the aeroplane from the ground.

He was flying at about one hundred and fifty feet, he thought, and the sight of huts, people and the terrain beyond appeared unreal so that he began to shout, wildly elated, "I'm flying! Look, I'm flying!"

When he judged that he had traveled about a mile past the field, James gently tried his next turn—a wide, sweeping half-circle. This time he moved across the wind, then into it, so the machine required constant adjustment. Strange, he thought, on the ground there was hardly any wind; yet, up here above the earth, the breeze was strong enough to lift the aeroplane up and down, so that he had to make quick corrections with rudder, ailerons, elevator and throttle.

Everything now required concentration, but the magic of flight remained undiminished, enlarged by a sense of pride as he found himself in line with the field, throttling back, adjusting the elevator, bringing the machine into a glide, dropping fast toward the ground.

He must have come down to within fifty feet before realizing he was too low, dropping steadily. The hedgerow surrounding the flying field sped toward him at an unpleasantly fast rate.

For a second he did not realize what was happening, then came the swift kick of fear low in his stomach as he fought to bring the machine under control. The aeroplane appeared to have a will of its own, the front angling up steeply until it was almost standing on the enclosed, boxlike rudders.

The noise was terrific, and he was banged around in the hard little seat. Then, for a moment, he heard only the scream of the engine as the propeller

desperately tried to claw at the air. There came a terrible slapping sound, like
water running off the underside of the wings. The Farman refused to answer
the controls, tipping, starting to roll uncomfortably, until, with a grinding
sweep of air washing and eddying around it, the whole aeroplane dropped.

The rear hit the ground first, tearing the booms away, and James only just
had time to use his common sense, chopping back on the throttle and flicking
the gasoline cock closed. He was conscious of the wings being ripped off on
the starboard side and of a terrible buzzing and cracking as the propeller chewed
into the earth.

Then came the unbelievable splintering noise and blackness.

He came to lying on the hangar floor, with Dick Farthing leaning over and
calling his name.

He heard his own voice, disembodied, saying, "Sorry, Dick," then, slowly,
life returned. He was able to move each limb, gingerly, one at a time. Nothing
broken except the aeroplane. He could not stop saying "sorry," for his mind
was filled only with the pile of wood, metal and fabric which had been the
beautiful Farman—ruined, by him, beyond repair.

For the first time in years, James wanted to weep. He had not shed a tear
at his grandfather's death—for him, that grief manifested itself in other ways—
yet now he could sob for a machine.

A doctor had been sent for, and, by all the ill strokes of fate, he turned out
to be Martin Savory's father, who took James straight home.

He had suffered minor cuts, a lot of bruising, and shock; but this did not
stop the good doctor from quizzing him hard about the "rambles," and the
whereabouts of his own son. Dr. Savory was in no way unpleasant, but, James
reflected, he would not care to be in Martin's shoes.

To his surprise, James found his own father more irritated than angry. What
amazed him was that John Railton sounded very like the General and even
appeared to understand his desire to fly. "If you wanted to mess around with
aeroplanes before going to Sandhurst, why in the name of heaven didn't you
tell me?" Later, James heard about his stepmother's riding accident. It had, he
reasoned, upset his father and greatly affected him.

Sara insisted that James call her by her Christian name, and, in spite of the
shaking she had received at Lady Nellie's Hedge, tried to form a bond of trust
between James and herself. Since her marriage, Sara had attempted to foster a
special relationship with her stepson; now there was true opportunity, and she
even discussed the whole business of flying with him.

In the end, of course, everything had to come out, including the private
money the General had put away for James. John Railton was anxious to get
in touch with Farthing to see what expenses had been incurred by the accident.
James' inheritance, and the £500 in Coutts Bank would, he said, have to go
toward defraying the cost.

John also made it plain that until his son was fully commissioned, and out
of Sandhurst, all holidays, or leave, must be spent either at Redhill or at the

London house. James would be seeing much more of his stepmother. "If you must fly, do the thing properly, James."

James was quick to point out his beliefs. "It's the future, Father. It will eventually have great military bearing, and I want to be ahead—or at least out there with the leaders."

John Railton smiled to himself. He admired the young man's enthusiasm, but could not for the life of him see how these motorized kites could possibly be of military value.

2

Steinhauer was coming under increasing pressure. The Military were, as the Kaiser had predicted, taking over. They had even privately announced their nominee as Head of Intelligence and informed Steinhauer that he would be working directly under him.

An emissary spent several hours with Steinhauer, questioning him about the state of spies and agents in other European countries; police informers used by the Foreign Ministry's secret department; networks; communications and all the paraphernalia of espionage.

They were cleaning his cupboard bare, and, quite possibly, opening his correspondence in the bargain.

He started to take greater care, making his journeys out to Neuweissensee at irregular intervals, changing trains at odd stations, watching to see if he was being trailed.

Of one thing he was confident: if he could get Ulhurt trained, disciplined and into Britain, he would be able to keep him as a private agent, away from those who already existed. The way the Military was going about the business could, he concluded, lead only to disaster, with the current agents detected, arrested and thrown out of the countries in which they operated.

As the military takeover became more apparent, Steinhauer visited two old contacts. One was an expert in explosives and weapons who had long since retired from the Army to earn a more dubious living among the criminal classes. The other Steinhauer had used before—an ordinary-looking fellow with simple tastes, but in a trade which was expensive and used only occasionally by governments. The man was called Wachtel, and his vocation in life was that of an assassin. He had traveled the world and knew more ways of bringing silent, and instant, death upon the unsuspecting than any professional soldier. He was credited with over a hundred politically inspired killings, half of which had gone down as common murders. Never once had he been detected.

These two men would be well paid for training Ulhurt. They could also be trusted to remain silent.

Hans-Helmut Ulhurt progressed with speed. Where, at the start of it all, the bad surgery in Kiel had left him weak and somewhat diffident, the big sailor now seemed to have been given an almighty push forward.

When Steinhauer came to see him they always conversed in English, and Ulhurt's command of the language was even better than before. Also, the experts reported that he responded to their specialist training with skill and enthusiasm.

Now he knew exactly how much explosive was needed to do great damage to even the most sophisticated warship; he was able to assemble bombs; set simple timers and detonators; he could also kill, quickly and silently.

The assassin said it came naturally to the sailor: "Already he has a good knowledge of close fighting; he can handle the gun and knife with no problems, but what impresses me most is how the fellow handles himself when unarmed," he told Steinhauer. "He can kill with one blow—and do it quietly. I have to say that he's particularly good with the garotte, and the great thing is that he has a talent for improvisation."

Steinhauer worked with Ulhurt, going over maps and charts with him, making the man learn the geography of Great Britain and in particular the layout of the major naval dockyards. He also insisted that Ulhurt study drawings of all capital ships belonging to the Royal Navy, the procedures at harbors and drydocks, the way the Navy worked aboard ship, and the ritual traditions of that Service.

They also went through many everyday things such as traveling on English trains and buses, shopping, living in English hotels. Soon, Steinhauer knew, the time would come for his sailor to make some kind of familiarization visit to England. Ulhurt had of course been to most of the great ports of that country, but he had never had the opportunity to spend time there.

With this in mind, Steinhauer began to seek out ways and means of getting Ulhurt into England. He spent one evening with the captain of the merchant ship *Möwe,* and to his delight discovered that not only could the captain place Ulhurt in England for the best part of a month, a little later in the year, but also—on the same trip—give him a week in Ireland, a very useful proving ground for spies.

3

Giles Railton heard the story of James' escapade some ten days later while lunching with John at The Travellers Club.

"He's right, John," he chuckled, the usually cold eyes creased around the edges. For some reason which John could not fathom, Uncle Giles found the whole episode amusing. "He's absolutely right. Aeroplanes are going to be of great military importance, though I wish your boy could come over and din that into the heads of people like Douglas Haig. Anyway, you didn't ask me to lunch merely to tell me about young James, did you?" Giles already knew why John had sent the invitation, on House of Commons paper, and by the hand of a special messenger.

John looked about them as though he did not wish to be overheard. "No," he said softly. "No, there are other matters. Uncle Giles, I always knew you were involved in secret work, but I did not realize how deeply."

Giles shrugged. "What d'you mean, deeply?"

John then told him his own news. Two days before, he had been summoned to Downing Street to a private meeting with the Prime Minister.

Asquith did not beat about the bush. "Railton, though I announced my Cabinet immediately after the election, I wish to make an addition. I want you in the Cabinet." He held up his hand as John opened his mouth to offer a word of thanks. "I need you—*you* in particular—in the Cabinet for a special reason."

When John gave him a puzzled look, Asquith enigmatically said, "The Committee of Imperial Defence."

"Oh?"

"Oh, indeed," the Prime Minister nodded. "For some time your uncle, Giles Railton, has been actively concerned in one aspect of the committee's work. As either myself, or some member of the Cabinet, is required to sit on that committee, I want you to do it on a full-time basis. What is more important, I shall require you to be a member of the special subcommittee, chaired by your uncle. The General Staff have nominated Douglas Haig—bright enough fellow but a grievous thorn in Giles Railton's side. My desire is to outflank him—with Railtons if need be." The Prime Minister gave a dry laugh.

When he took the news to Sara, John had other things to tell her as well— that Charles' wife, Mildred, was pregnant, and Charles had, therefore, decided that they would not require the Cheyne Walk house for at least a year. "So you have no great upheaval there as yet." He put his arms around his young wife, watching the pleasure grow in her face. Secretly, she was delighted. The danger had passed. David Lloyd George had kept his promise.

Now John had sought out Giles, before the new post was made public, to reveal that they would be working together.

"This intelligence business—how important is it?" he asked his uncle.

Always economic with words, Giles attempted to imbue John with his own passion.

As he came to the end of his monologue he pensively said that he had dined with his neighbor, Winston Churchill, on the previous evening.

"And how was he?" John appeared preoccupied, as though Giles' talk of intelligence matters had taken his mind elsewhere.

"Winston? In a black mood. He fears for Europe—in fact for all mankind."

"Prophecies of doom? Winston has a tendency to look on the worst side at times."

"He believes we are on the brink of disaster."

"What nonsense."

Giles raised an eyebrow. "I wouldn't be so sure. He can be persuasive. Winston says that the King, the Kaiser, the Czar, not to mention the President

of France, and other heads of state and royal families—and their governments—
are fiddling while Europe is about to become a tinderbox."

"Too much brandy. Still worried about the Balkans, is he?"

"Not just the Balkans." Giles did not smile. "He is convincing about the
great gap between the aristocracy of Europe, the middle classes and the real
poor; the high rate at which countries are arming themselves; the instability
of currency; the smell of revolution. He believes we're heading for some great
and terrible conflagration."

"Oh, rubbish. There's plenty of wealth; trade is good. Oh, the Balkans have
their share of troublemakers—so has Russia. But the dockyards of Germany
and Great Britain haven't been as busy for years; plenty of work except for the
work-shy. Anyway, Uncle Giles, it won't be our concern if there's trouble."
John Railton smiled, a little patronizingly Giles thought.

"I wonder," said Giles, "how many of the good people of Rome were making
remarks like that just before the crumbling of their Empire?"

4

On the same day that John and Giles Railton met for lunch at The Travellers,
a visitor arrived unannounced at the Manor. Dick Farthing came mainly to
reassure James that Maurice Farman himself was defraying the cost of the crashed
Farman III. There were no hard feelings, but it was felt that James should
spend a little more time learning the rudiments of flying in a more simple
machine. "You really had me fooled, James." Dick's large brown eyes twinkled
with humor, one cocking into a wink as the corner of his mouth lifted in his
customary smile.

"Well"—James still bore some of the bruises and marks of the crash—"I'll
not fool you here. Stay at least for one night so we can talk. I also want you
to meet my wicked stepmother. She's a real corker."

5

After the lunch with his nephew, Giles went straight back to Eccleston
Square and up to the Hide. He had a great deal on his mind, and he set out
maps and lead soldiers, ready to fight the Battle of Blenheim, in which Winston
Churchill's ancestor had so well acquitted himself.

While he prepared the opposing forces, he pondered deeply on the new
involvement of John Railton in secret affairs. John was a sound man for the
usual hurly-burly of politics, but Giles considered he might be squeamish when
initiated into the darker arts of secret life.

As he moved the troops around the field, so he thought of the other Railtons
now involved. Most of all he pondered on his daughter, Marie Grenot, and the

news that was reaching him from his agent Monique. Marie could be the key to success in dealing with the stubborn British General Staff. He hoped this would prove to be so—and soon.

Chapter Seven

1

There was order and peace in England during that winter of 1910. Yet it was not so in other European countries. Churchill's comments to Giles Railton were far from unfounded. Below the placid, ordered, surface of life there was ferment, like the first sure signs of the onset of a giant earthquake.

During February of that year, the German Military Attaché in Paris, and his assistant—Klaus von Hirsch—had a visitor. The current arrival from the German capital was a military man—a captain by the name of Walter Nicolai, who was greeted with polite protocol, given a private audience with the Ambassador, Baron Wilhelm von Schoen, followed by an official luncheon. He was then left to the mercies of his military counterparts.

Early in the evening following his arrival in Paris, Nicolai found himself sitting over a bottle of schnapps with the Military Attaché and his assistant.

"You've landed yourself a nice pleasant duty, then, Walter." The Attaché lifted his glass. "Travel a little. A tour of our foreign embassies, so? Sounds like a holiday."

"It is not a holiday. It *is* a waste of time." Walter Nicolai tossed back his schnapps. "How do *you* like bowing and scraping with foreign diplomats? Would you not rather be getting on with soldier's work?"

"Ah, you soon get used to the bowing and scraping." Von Hirsch laughed. "I assure you there are many compensations. Here, whatever is at our disposal is yours, and there is plenty of fun in the City of Light. Wine, women and song. You will not find it such a free and easy life in London. You said London was your next call of duty, yes?"

Captain Nicolai gave an exaggerated sigh. "Yes, all those tilted noses and frigid women."

"And the greasy food." Von Hirsch wrinkled his nose.

The Military Attaché lifted an eyebrow, glancing toward Nicolai. "Klaus is enamored of a most attractive Englishwoman here in Paris."

"And unfortunately she is married to a Frenchman," von Hirsch reminded him.

The Military Attaché chuckled, then turned to Captain Nicolai. "But,

Walter, tell us—why this goodwill tour around the embassies? Rome last week; now Paris; then London."

"A fool's errand. Oh, work, work." The Captain held out his glass for more schnapps. "I'm a soldier, not a pen-pusher. However..." He hesitated. "Well, now that I'm here, I suppose it's best done with. Let's get the unpleasant talking over."

"You bring unpleasantness from Berlin?" The Military Attaché sat bolt upright.

Nicolai waved a hand. "Oh, not really. Not for you. Just the stupidity of generals—the High Command—who are of the opinion that if we must have an intelligence network, that organization will be solely military: run by the Army for the Army. *Military* Intelligence. No civilians."

"Except as agents, of course."

The Attaché intended the remark to be sarcastic, but Nicolai dismissed it as obvious. "It seems we have quite a number of agents already. England and France are well covered." He paused, as though the subject wearied him. "They are talking about making me Head of Military Intelligence—hence the Embassy visits. I am supposed to instruct you—"

"Instruct *us?*" The Military Attaché's voice was heavy with warning.

Nicolai made a gesture of apology. "I'm not yet appointed as Head of this new Military Intelligence. But I am supposed to instruct you—ask you—to relay possible names back to Berlin: to the High Command."

"Possible traitors? Agents?"

"So it would seem."

"That is neither a soldier's job nor the duty of a military attaché."

"I wonder?" Nicolai left the question mark hanging in the air. "Look, I've told you. There's an end."

"Why all this?" von Hirsch asked. "In time of war I could understand. But all is calm. Who would want intelligence at a time when peace is on everyone's lips?"

The Military Attaché grunted again. "It is when people begin to tell you war is impossible that you should look to your sword, Klaus."

"Yes." All lightness had disappeared from Captain Walter Nicolai's voice now. "Expansion, but not war, one hopes. However, there is still the question of that beloved old man in Austria..."

"Franz Joseph?"

"Old; frail; sick; never leaves his own four walls. Soon Franz Joseph will die, and who'll take his place?"

"Who indeed?" the Attaché agreed. "Franz Ferdinand, the Archduke?" He gave a nervous laugh. "Yes, the Arch-dupe. I've yet to meet a diplomat or politician who likes him. But these things are no cause for war."

Klaus von Hirsch, already slightly tipsy, raised his glass. "We shall have a century of peace."

"Let us hope so." Nicolai had become his benign self again.

They drank to peace, and the Military Attaché said that it was time to go out and sample the delights of Paris. As they left the room, Nicolai put a hand on von Hirsch's shoulder. "About this English lady of yours..." he began.

2

Monique had rented a small apartment almost directly across the street from where the Grenots lived, near the place de l'Opéra.

From her window, or even strolling nearby, she could log the comings and goings at the elegant building in which the Grenots occupied the stylish second two floors.

She posed as a young, middle-class widow who wished to live quietly ("And without a hint of scandal"—so the concierge), and was able to pass the days keeping an eye on the movements of the Grenots and their friends.

Monique certainly had suspicions regarding Madame Grenot's fidelity. Madame Grenot entertained. During the day; usually in the afternoon; and always at home. Her callers were men, and one in particular interested Monique—a fine-looking Prussian officer, tall, fit, and with the stride and confidence of an athlete, assistant to the German Military Attaché. He always arrived at three in the afternoon, each Tuesday, Thursday and Friday. Wickedly, Monique wondered what kind of athleticism went on inside the Grenots' apartment on those three weekday afternoons.

She was not to know that—until now—Marie Grenot had been keeping young Klaus von Hirsch very much under control.

"But why can't we, Marie?" The question had been asked many times. Now Klaus held her close, attempting to run a hand across her buttocks.

Marie Grenot twisted from him, walked to the sofa and sat down. She was surprisingly neat for a woman so long in the body, yet all her movements were sparse, economical. There was no sound to her footfall, no exaggeration when she poured tea. Her husband could verify that when she made love, his tall, striking wife became feather-light, as though by some strange magic she were able to melt into her partner's body. Now there was no mockery in her eyes as she said, "You stay over there, Klaus. Last week it went too far." Then, more kindly, "Give me time, my dear. You know what I'm like."

Klaus grunted—a schoolboy deprived of his favorite game.

"Oh, come on. Yes, Klaus, of course I wish to go to bed with you; but I know I would be plagued by remorse." She paused. "Do you think it possible for a woman to love two men at the same time?"

"A man can love two women, so I see no problem." Klaus knew this to be the right answer; just as he knew how much he desired her. He rose as if to cross to the sofa.

"No." Marie held up a warning hand. "No, Klaus. In a moment. I promise.

Truly. Let's talk. Maybe we can find somewhere on Thursday. Somewhere to be alone together..."

"I cannot see you on Thursday."

"Friday then. Why can't you see me on Thursday? You always come here on Thursdays."

Klaus said they had an important visitor at the Embassy. On Thursday he was detailed to accompany him to Calais. "He's going on to London."

"Lucky man. Imperial German Army, I suppose?"

Klaus nodded. "You must tell nobody, but this man is to be the new Chief of Military Intelligence."

"Intelligence? Spies?" She sounded thrilled by the glamour.

Klaus spread his fingers, pushing the palms downward, as if telling her to lower her voice. "It's not yet official, but there's little doubt. They wish to get rid of any civilian influence, so Captain Nicolai has the appointment."

"Goodness, how exciting! It must be important work."

"In wartime, yes. But in this peaceful world..."

She laughed—lightly, like a small glass bell. "In this peaceful world, Klaus, you have a war plan. You told me so yourself."

"All countries have war plans. The High Command has an old one. Old von Schlieffen's plan. But there will be no wars—it was decided last night." His head jerked back as he laughed, though Marie had the impression there was little humor in him.

"Who decided?"

"The Military Attaché—Captain Nicolai—and myself. We decided over much schnapps and champagne. So, my dear, there will be no war. Certainly not with England, because your King Edward's kinsmen rule most of Europe. Our countries are too close."

Marie Grenot felt her stomach turn over and the nape of her neck go cold.

"All's fair in war—and love." He stood, then crouched, teasing. "I shall make an encircling movement." He approached her so that she gave her glass-bell laugh, called him a fool and then surrendered to his kisses.

Before Klaus left, he extracted a promise from Marie. On Friday they would meet at a discreet hotel of convenience, where, he assured her, they would be safe from prying eyes.

Between Klaus' leaving and her husband's return, Marie wrote a private letter to her father. There was no reason to believe that any letters would be intercepted, so she wrote in plain language telling him, first, of Captain Nicolai's arrival in England and his proposed new duties for the Imperial Army; then of the long-suspected element within the Schlieffen war plan—the attack on France through neutral Belgium.

Across the street, in her little apartment, Monique logged Klaus' entrance and exit. An hour later she noted the exit of a maid carrying a letter. Later that evening she also sat down and wrote to Giles Railton. Her letter, however, was penned in careful cipher.

She did this twice weekly; and the weeks flew past. Soon it would be spring.

Two days later Giles received both letters and thought how best to use the information. He spent many hours hunched over his map board, moving small soldiers and contemplating Napoleon's strategy at Austerlitz as he allowed his mind to run free with the secrets it contained. His beloved daughter, Marie, and his agent, Monique, were not the only people from whom he had recently received word. At last his daughter-in-law, Bridget, seemed to have taken the bait and sent him a report from Ireland. Giles reveled in the intrigue, but his sixth sense told him of danger ahead. The games he played with maps and soldiers in the Hide were, in his other life, translated into real games which meddled with the politics of nations. Some sailed near to the wind of self-deception. And there were times, like now, when he smelled catastrophe in the air.

3

On instructions from his new military masters, Gustav Steinhauer left Berlin to visit the main agents already active in England. His duty was to indicate to them that they should be prepared to accept orders from another source as well as himself.

He went to Scotland, spending a few days along the south coast naval bases. Then he returned to London, to visit the barber in the Caledonian Road, whose shop was the hub of their work in England—the "post office" through which all instructions were routed.

Steinhauer was then able to lose a few days. His masters would never know it, for he had covered his tracks well, and the Embassy in London was kept in the dark about his real date of arrival and departure.

He arranged certain meetings, saw to the possibility of caching items which his man would need—things like explosives and detonators—then he crossed to Ireland, where he met a representative of the Fenians in a Dublin café.

The man was useful, a cut-out between the Fenian leadership and the rank and file followers, and therefore most pliable. Steinhauer fed him pleasant ideas, such as the definite possibility of arms being supplied through interested dealers in Germany. But, as always, there was a price to be paid—assistance to covert action.

Steinhauer spelled it out very carefully. "In the event of, er... unlikely problems between Prussia and Great Britain, we feel it only sensible to prepare ways to use Ireland to advantage—from a naval viewpoint, you understand...."

"Oh, I follow you." Padraig O'Connell nodded enthusiastically.

"I shall send a friend soon. You can talk to him freely. If there is anything you wish to tell him—about British military or naval operations here—we will reward you. This man will be prepared to do anything—shall we say, unpleasant?—for you. Understand?"

O'Connell grinned and said it was quite possible they could use such a man.

Then Steinhauer left, returning to Berlin to find Ulhurt straining at the leash.

"I want to do something useful!"

"In good time. Soon. Arrangements are at hand, but first I wish to talk to you about code names."

The giant gazed at him blankly.

"You will be known by two separate code names, but I'm going to call you 'The Fisherman' because you will be trawling the seas for souls . . . like St. Peter in the Bible."

Ulhurt gave a short, unconvinced laugh, so Steinhauer continued: "Your wireless cipher names will be 'Saint'—for St. Peter—and 'Angler.' You understand me?"

"You think I'm an idiot?"

"No."

"Well, then. Of course I understand you. Ciphers, code names—you seem to live in a world of ghosts and goblins, my friend." Ulhurt laughed again, this time rather unpleasantly.

Steinhauer's face froze into a stony look. "And you, *my friend,* do not know how close to the truth you are sailing."

4

The lights burned late in the Hide, on the second floor of Giles Railton's house in Eccleston Square.

Tonight there was no time for the maps or soldiers. Giles bent low over his table, strewn with papers, making notes for the next day's work. As he worked, part of his mind dwelt on the perils of the future. Everyone, he presumed, wanted to believe in a lasting, long summer of peaceful years; but wanting was not enough.

One name spelled out the dangers—Kaiser Wilhelm II.

Edward—the "Uncle of Europe"—was suspect to the Kaiser. The Encircler, the Plotter, was how the German Emperor saw him, and if the Kaiser had his way, his heel would be on his Uncle Edward's neck: while France would lie passively, her legs spread wide to accept his rape.

Nobody, Giles often argued, could doubt what the Kaiser really wanted: recognition of Imperial Germany as the one true power in Europe.

Tomorrow he had much to do. There was another meeting of his Sub-Committee for Review of Intelligence Structure, and only late that afternoon Giles had received permission to pass on the information he had already put before the CID Secretariat that day. He had doubts as to members of the Sub-Committee either believing or acting on his information.

His nephew John was to join his Sub-Committee as representative from the Cabinet the following afternoon, and Giles had been relieved to learn two days before that his son Andrew would not have to find more excuses to duck accompanying the DID. Lieutenant-Commander Andrew Railton had now been promoted to a more sensitive post within the Intelligence Division's structure.

He put his notes to one side and pulled another batch of papers into the glow from the green-shaded student lamp. First, the letter to Mr. Harding from Bridget Railton. That was moving well. Next, his daughter Marie Grenot's letters, together with the reports from Monique. They added up—Monique's reports and Marie's sources read like well-kept account books. Tomorrow he would act upon what had been given to him—indeed, he had already acted upon the business of Captain Walter Nicolai.

On the following morning Giles took a cab to the War Office, and within half an hour was sitting opposite Vernon Kell.

Kell was alone except for the clerk, Sprogitt. Charles was working. "Like a Trojan," Kell said. "You'll find him a much-changed man. Really hard at it. I'm running him around like a donkey engine. Crash courses in everything. Paddy Quinn's fixing up driving lessons with the Branch."

Giles wondered how long his nephew would remain so dedicated. Not many months, he thought. Briskly he turned the conversation to the object of his visit. "You'll guess what I've come to talk about?"

"Walter Nicolai?"

Giles nodded.

"You certainly have good sources of information, sir. Arrived exactly as you predicted."

"And how did the visit turn out?" Giles had left the whole business of Captain Nicolai's London visit in Kell's hands.

"Quinn's people took care of it. No personal details. Prussian Officer Corps. Military family. Young, more enthusiastic than most, rising junior staff officer." Kell gave him a mock-sly look. "It seems there's recently been a battle over intelligence matters between the Berlin Foreign Office and the Imperial Army. Apparently the Army's won the day. Captain Nicolai has an important patron. He's under the protection of Colonel Ludendorff—Head of Section 2 of the Great General Staff. They are to form their own Intelligence Department. From your information it would seem that Nicolai's got the top job."

Apparently Nicolai had remained in the Embassy during his entire visit to London, though he had received one interesting visitor—a civilian named Gustav Steinhauer. The Branch had taken a peep at the register of the hotel where Steinhauer was staying. He had given a false address in Berlin. The name of the street did not show on any map, so Kell took some expert advice from one of his many contacts—a Berliner.

The Branch had done some more checking. Steinhauer appeared to travel widely, claiming to be a paper manufacturer, yet he did not visit any firms connected with paper. Instead, Herr Steinhauer seemed to be interested in dockyards. He had also slipped across to Ireland for at least two days.

"By rights we should have arranged for Steinhauer to be followed," Kell grumbled, "but Paddy Quinn's men cannot do it all."

Giles reminded him of the Sub-Committee meeting that afternoon, and Kell wrinkled his nose. Too much time was spent in meetings. He wanted to get on with the job in hand.

"Come and have some luncheon." Giles allowed one of his warmer smiles. "Then we can go to the meeting together— 'cheek by jowl.'" Again the Railton love of Shakespeare, a habit quickly copied by their women. The thing Railtons rarely admitted, even to one another, was that they often "thought" in Shakespearean tags and derived much pleasure and comfort from the habit.

5

At half past two that afternoon, the Sub-Committee for Review of Intelligence Structure gathered in the somewhat gloomy room allotted to them at the top of the main War Office building.

Giles welcomed John as the new Cabinet representative, and then gave a bravura performance, illustrating what his family had known for years—his adroitness in handling committees.

Everyone was present: Sir Douglas Haig, with an entourage of two clean-cut young officers; the DID from the Admiralty; and a pair of faceless Treasury officials with eyes that showed as much charity as glass.

A Royal Marine captain called Maurice Hankey was there on behalf of the CID Secretariat; Kell, of course, attended in his own right; as did the Naval Officer, Commander Smith-Cumming, Kell's opposite number in the Foreign Intelligence Section.

Giles began with an assault on the Treasury, ramming home the fact that the new Secret and Security Services were going to mean a substantial allotment of both cash and men.

He quickly moved on to talk of the German reorganization and the intelligence concerning Captain Nicolai. Then he played his trump card, the Prussian Imperial High Command's work on the Schlieffen war plan. In dealing with this he made a clever plea for the impartiality of a purely civilian service.

"Military Intelligence in the field is one thing—you gain information and then immediately do something about it. Eh, Haig?"

Douglas Haig grunted a stubborn affirmative and Giles continued.

"An Intelligence Service, of the kind we are already organizing, is, however, something apart. Its job is to collect, collate and analyze information. Our kind of Intelligence Service is neither geared nor required to act upon that information. The duty of any Secret Service is to provide a facility for both the Diplomatic Corps and, more particularly, the armed forces. It would be military experts, like Sir Douglas here, who would make decisions on whatever information the secret departments provided for them. Yes, Haig?"

"I take the point." Haig was loath to accept any handling of intelligence outside the Army. He vaguely saw how Giles was outflanking him, so he turned the conversation back to the German war plan. "I must say, Railton, that this idea of the Germans tinkering with what you call the Schlieffen plan seems to make no sense. If my own diplomatic history serves me correctly, Prince von Bismarck himself laid down that Belgium would be inviolable. It's unthinkable."

"Really?" Giles raised his eyebrows. "Remember, Douglas, that Bismarck piloted Germany to unity. The present Kaiser threw him out."

"But you don't really believe that the German High Command, presuming they have designs on France, would risk clashing with us by walking into Belgium."

"It's exactly what I believe, and it's what our agents appear to have revealed. Remember Clausewitz—the genius of strategists—held that 'the heart of France lies between Brussels and Paris.' Von Schlieffen's plan is for the quick kill, going for the heart of France; and the only way to take France's heartland with speed is via Belgium. I have no reason to believe the current High Command thinking has changed."

"Cold-blooded," Haig murmured. "Unrealistic from a diplomatic viewpoint."

Giles pointed out that as a soldier Haig should know that strategy and diplomacy did not mix well.

"I suspect, from the information *my* people have provided, that the neutrality of Belgium is an unimportant obstacle; and that is how the present High Command sees it. I am passing on the kind of intelligence we believe our reorganized service can supply. I feel the General Staff should act on it."

By the end of the meeting, Giles felt that the information provided by his daughter regarding both Captain Nicolai and the adherence of the Prussian High command to the kernel of von Schlieffen's plan had been of great assistance in making his case for a Foreign Office–controlled Intelligence Service. But would the General Staff really take any notice? He doubted it as Haig departed with a curt nod and the one word "Interestin'." The attitude of the General Staff was fast becoming Giles' despair.

John Railton left, after giving brief, warm, greetings to Giles' family. As always, his uncle had impressed him, and he could report well to the Prime Minister.

As for Giles, he was oddly concerned about his nephew. There had been times when he detected John's concentration wandering, and it was so unlike the man that he made a mental note to ask a few questions in the right quarters.

6

Giles was correct. John was far from being himself that day. Overworked, he had started to miss Sara, who—to his surprise remained, uncomplaining, at Redhill Manor. His distraction this afternoon had been caused by a letter, received at the Athenaeum that very lunchtime. It came from his son James.

Dearest Papa,

I write to tell you that I have passed my 'Further' in grand style, so will be going up to Sandhurst on September 3rd of this year. I trust you will be pleased.

I have written to Uncle Andrew, giving him my news, for Caspar should also have his results by now.

The weather here at Redhill remains consistent. Spring cannot be far away, and this is ideal flying weather. I thank you so much for the payment to Dick Farthing who has arranged one of the new Farmans for my latest lessons, having agreed that, after all, this is the best machine available on which to learn. There is plenty of room on the Upper Down pasture, especially as it is clear of cattle at the moment.

Dick has flown up here three times in the past ten days to give me ground instruction. Yesterday, he allowed me to do a short hop, and appeared awfully pleased. I had no trouble controlling the machine.

Sara is most interested, and says *she* wishes to learn. She appears to have taken quite a shine to Farthing, who stayed on for the nights he was here, flying off at dawn.

One morning, Sara got up and went out to see him off. She really is a most splendid stepmother to have, and you will, I am sure, be pleased to learn of the great interest she is showing in both the Manor and Farm. She had old Froud up from the town, trotting around the house while she made suggestions about new curtains, and a carpet, for the General's Study.

Dear Papa, you must come and see us all soon. I know Sara needs you, but she is really more like a sister than a stepmother to me. She learns much about the Farm, and goes riding often, with Bob Berry. It appears he teaches her many things concerning the Farm, and how the land is managed.

I fear, though, she does not get on well with Jack Hunter. Yesterday, Hunter was giving instructions to the gamekeeper for the setting up of mantraps in the woods near the road. People have been getting in there, and Hunter said it should he discouraged once and for all. As it turned out, Sara arrived with Bob Berry just as the wretched things had been laid out in the stableyard. At first, Sara could not tell what they were, but when she learned I thought she would have a fit. She sent for Hunter and really gave him what for: told him he would have to wait for your return before any inhuman instruments of torture like that were set up on the Estate.

Hunter got quite angry, but she told him to mind his manners, and won the day. You would have been proud, I think.

Please come soon, Papa. I know Sara misses you. Our great American aviator arrives again on Tuesday. We are to fly on Wednesday morning, so he has agreed to come over a day early and dine with us. Sara has ordered a feast. She has been on at Cook, and had some capons brought up from the Farm. We are to have hare soup, soles à la crème, the capons and one of Mrs. Bolton's superb puddings. I wish you could be with us, as it is really to celebrate my 'Further.'

> Come soon,
> Your loving and affectionate son,
> JAMES.

John Railton, ever conscious of the age difference between himself and Sara, had wanted to bolt from his club, skip the Sub-Committee meeting and take the first train to Haversage — for it was now Tuesday. Never would he suspect Sara of any infidelity, but both Richard Farthing and Bob Berry were handsome, virile young men; and women of Sara's age were so easily tempted into flirtation.

There was much to worry him. People gossiped; Bob Berry was still unmarried, and only the Farm Manager. There could be a whiff of scandal, particularly if she had made an enemy of Hunter, who could be a vindictive man — especially when you considered his sexual proclivities, about which John had always been uneasy.

For the first time John wondered if he had made a terrible error in accepting his parliamentary seat, let alone the Cabinet appointment.

In the meantime all he could do was head for Downing Street, where he would wait for the Prime Minister. After making his report he could perhaps ask Asquith if he might take a week away from London to spend time at Redhill Manor. He could at a pinch get there tonight.

7

At the clinic in Neuweissensee, Steinhauer gave The Fisherman his first operational briefing. In a few weeks' time his agent would be setting off on his acclimatization mission — to take a look at England, and the English, at close quarters; to test himself and merge into the landscape. Then he was to spend time in Ireland, making contact with the Fenians.

He was ordered to engage himself in no espionage, but could offer *any* assistance to the Fenians. "If they should require you to use any of your particular skills, then you will do as they wish," Steinhauer told him. "However" — he wagged an admonishing finger — "take heed. No whoring, no drinking. You are on active service for the Fatherland."

"You think I'm going to drink my head off in London pubs and Dublin bars and screw all their women?"

"I think it quite likely, yes. And if you do, then you could become insecure.

My neck's on the block as well as your own. Just go—and bring back a good report to me."

The Fisherman merely nodded his big head. It was impossible to tell what he was thinking.

Chapter Eight

1

The Director of Intelligence Division, Admiralty, made a habit of calling into Andrew Railton's office when he returned from the Sub-Committee meetings chaired by Andrew's father. Being a courteous man, he liked to think this was a small sign of his confidence in Andrew.

Andrew's new job in the Division was to set up a special section dealing with all aspects of codes and ciphers, including their valid use, by the Royal Navy and its—possibly—paid agents; together with the way ciphers were being handled by the other great maritime nations of Europe.

"Well," the Admiral said on this evening, "looks as though this damned new Intelligence Service will eventually take over everything. Thank heaven we gave them the Head of their Foreign Section—at least we'll be able to keep an eye on him." He spoke of Commander Smith-Cumming, now in charge of the Secret Service, known as MI1(c). "Time to shore up, though. Weakest points, Andrew, weakest points?" The Admiral glared at him.

"The new chain of W/T stations along the coast, sir." Andrew had no doubts.

"You think we should press for that?"

The plans for a chain of stations along the British coastline had lain on the table for a long time. Too long. Both the Army and Navy had dragged their heels.

"Sooner the better, sir. I believe we should, as Shakespeare says, *put a girdle round about the earth.*"

"I'll have a word. Talk to their Lordships. Meantime get me a report on the other priorities."

So, when Andrew returned home, his head buzzed with the report upon which he would have to start working in the morning.

There was a letter from his nephew James lying on top of a small pile of correspondence on the silver postal tray in the hall. Andrew recognized it instantly from the way in which the boy added reckless flourishes to the otherwise beautiful handwriting.

Charlotte was in the Morning Room talking to Mildred, the detritus of tea not yet cleared away. As Andrew entered, the two women stopped talking, as though caught in some clandestine conversation.

In fact, they had discussed Mildred's pregnancy for most of their tea—Charles' wife, at thirty-four, being naturally anxious. Charlotte, with her experience as the traveled wife of a naval officer, appeared to have taken over the role of confidante within the family, and was able to cite chapter and verse on a number of her friends who had given birth to perfectly normal children relatively late in life. The subject exhausted, they began speaking of Sara.

Railton women, their menfolk often observed, had a knack of picking up family gossip, even at long range. Already Mildred knew of the American called Richard Farthing, and James' scrape at Farnborough. Charlotte knew more.

"Sara's a darling, and I love her dearly, but she is so very young." Andrew's wife had a quick, animated, manner of speaking. When she talked now, the tone became flat, as though sincerity were being strained.

"The American is visiting Redhill while John's away?" Mildred still had the somewhat churchy way of indicating that, while shocked, she could not wait to hear more.

Charlotte sighed. "It is not correct, even though James is there. Sara's left to her own devices in the country, and that must be difficult after the social whirl of London. Everyone expected her to be dashing up to London on the slightest excuse, but she stays at Haversage with little complaint."

"Surely you don't think . . ."

"A woman like Sara requires attention." Charlotte became emphatic. "Heavens, Millie, *you're* a long-married Railton now. You know what all our men are." Her lips formed a half-kiss, half-pout. "We can speak plainly, my dear. The women in the Railton clan also soon learn to enjoy that side of things. . . ."

"Charlotte!" Mildred sounded shocked.

"Millie, come along. We're experienced enough. The men have a reputation. You've been married what? Sixteen? Seventeen years? I'd be surprised if your desire isn't lit at least twice a week, even now. I'm not ashamed of it. Oh, I sometimes wonder if at our age we should be so wanton. I'll tell you, my dear, there are days when I long for Andrew to come home and plow me. I even lure him." She paused as though for a moment savoring a delicious thought. "So what of Sara? John's older, much older, and therefore an expert, I should imagine. I doubt if young Sara can do without it. He leaves her alone too often, and the Devil makes use of idle hands—though it's not the hands I'm concerned about."

"I don't believe she'd be so foolish," Mildred said primly. Her sexual experience with Charles had been somewhat different—a delicious, sudden and beautiful time in the first years, then nothing but guilt and unpleasantness.

Charlotte turned her lovely profile, catching sight of herself in the gilt-framed mirror above the mantelpiece. "In the country things are, well, different.

Look at the General. He managed, and not one member of the family, or the servants for that matter, ever acknowledged anything was wrong morally."

"I still can't believe that Sara . . ."

"No. I agree. But there is danger if she's left with young men. She's so very attractive," Charlotte added almost wistfully, "and young."

It was soon after this that Andrew returned. He kissed both women, and Charlotte took the opportunity to whisper that their eldest son, Caspar, was waiting anxiously in the study. "It's good news," she smiled, and Andrew, after a quick exchange with Mildred, made his excuses.

Thank God, he thought, that it was good news. Andrew had been the one Railton who since boyhood had longed for the sea and service in the Royal Navy. His most earnest hope had been that Caspar would inherit his obsession, but that was not to be. The boy had chosen the Army, surrounding himself with things military from around the age of ten.

When Andrew entered his study, Caspar got to his feet, and Andrew smiled, though his mind registered a slight shock, for the full realization struck him that Caspar was no longer a boy. He would be seventeen next week and looked it. His skin had changed to a rougher, more masculine, texture; while the boyish softness had gone from his eyes.

"Well." Andrew closed the door. "Your mama tells me you have news."

"Yes, sir." Caspar handed his father an envelope. It was addressed to Caspar Railton, Esq., and the coat of arms showed it was from the Royal Military College at Sandhurst.

Andrew gave a deep, satisfied grunt. "I don't really need to read it, do I? You've passed your 'further.' Right?"

"Yes, sir. I go in September."

Andrew offered congratulations, taking Caspar's hand, noting anew the firmness of the handshake. They talked for some minutes, then Andrew turned his attention to the letters he had brought from the hall, saying that he really must deal with the post before dressing for dinner.

There were two bills; the news from James (so both boys would be at Sandhurst together—no bad thing); a short, polite letter from Ramillies, still at Wellington; and another from Ramillies' twin, Rupert.

Rupert and Ramillies had been born six hours apart, and were not identical, which probably accounted for the marked difference in their characters.

Now, at the age of fifteen, the twins were well on their way along different paths. Ramillies was determined to enter the Diplomatic, for which he was obviously suited. Like most Railtons, he took easily to languages, and also had the ability to write in the terse, truncated manner of the Whitehall men.

Ramillies' letter was typical:

> Dearest Papa and Mama,
> Promotions announced today. I have taken over the House as House Prefect,

Also colours up on School Board. Awarded fencing Colours which I know will please you.

Nothing else appears to alter. The same old round and common task.

French and German well up to standard, according to M.R. and Herr B. English also, by word of Mr. H.

Must go and see House is well turned-out.

Deepest love to both. Please tell Rupert that he really should write to me.

> Fond affection
> Your obedient son,
> RAMILLIES.

Andrew read over the concise note twice, putting it to one side so that Charlotte could also read it.

The longer letter was from the son—though he would never admit or show it openly—whom he loved the most. Rupert, who, after his preparatory school, had broken tradition and gone to Osborne for the statutory two years of basic and academic study. Then to the Royal Navy College, Dartmouth, where he would leave, as a midshipman, to join his first ship at the end of this present year. Andrew was aware that his feelings for Rupert stemmed mainly from the boy's love of the Royal Navy and all things naval.

Dearest Pa and Ma,

Make do and mend, which includes the writing of letters to one's wives, sweethearts and loved ones, and as I have neither wife nor sweetheart (though I would not tell you if I had), I sit here scribbling to my loved ones. That includes my beastly brother, Ram, safe and tucked up in bed at Wellington; and my elder brother Caspar.

The word here is that those of us to become Middies at the end of the year are to go to *Dreadnought* or *Invincible, Indomitable* or *Inflexible.* Do not know the truth, but it would be tremendous. I think the story derives from the fact that we now have a full mock-up of a *Dreadnought* type 12 inch. turret, and learn the drill daily.

I find it difficult waiting to get out of here and into one of the Fleets now, and I do not honestly care which. To be in the Royal Navy, as an officer, even a lowly Snotty, is the greatest adventure for which a man can hope.

Everything else is shipshape and in good order. Discipline remains tight, with many scorched backsides; but that is the only way to run a

ship. Must finish now as Duty Watch has just been piped—and that's
me.

> My love to you both,
> Your affectionate and loving son,
> RUPERT.

Andrew was cheered, for the boys were doing well. His personal life was
good; and there was not a cloud on the horizon.

Andrew Railton rose, then went upstairs to dress and await the dinner gong.

2

James, having eaten all too well, pushed back his chair. The dizziness, he
reasoned, was due to alcohol.

"Don' know about you, Dick old man." He grinned at Dick Farthing, looking
positively stupid. "Don' know about you, but if I'm to soar like a bleedin'
eagle tomorrow, then I'd best be off to bed." He swallowed, shook his head
like a soaked dog, then pulled himself together and very carefully enunciated,
"We had best join the lady," collapsing into a giggling fit at the idea of there
being only one lady for them to join in the drawing room.

Sara, always precise in these matters, had left the two young men to their
port wine and cigars only fifteen minutes before. When they came into the
drawing room she was also laughing, holding a book.

She swallowed her mirth. "I can't believe this man Le Queux is serious. Just
listen to this." She was reading William Le Queux's *Secrets of the Foreign Office.*
Through giggles she now read aloud: "Before I could utter aught save a muffled
curse, I was flung head first into an empty piano case, the heavy lid of which
was instantly closed on me . . . I had been tricked!"

James clung to Dick, hardly able to breathe, while his American friend
merely smiled. At last James managed, "Whacked, Sara. Just tol' Dick I'm
whacked. For me—bed." He swept his arm in a dramatic circle. "I have been
tricked."

"By the wine, no doubt. You're as tipsy as a fiddler, James. Off with you."
Sara smiled at Dick Farthing.

James nodded gravely, backing unsteadily to the door. "Tricked," he repeated, now raising a hand in farewell. "'Night, Richard Farthing." Stumbling
forward, he bent clumsily to kiss Sara's cheek. "And 'night to you dear sister,
stepmother. Slayer of estate managers. Parting is such sweet sorrow—something like that."

"Bed, James," Sara laughed. Then, as the door closed, she turned to Richard.
"He will be all right to fly in the morning?"

Dick slumped into a chair. "The boy's not used to liquor." He snorted.

"Didn't have very much, if you noticed. Guess if he gets to sleep right away he'll be fine. It'll be clear and sharp up there in the morning. That'll blow the cobwebs from his brain in no time. The heart starts to pound when you're in charge of an aeroplane. It's like the man said, concentrates the mind wonderfully. Death always sits on the aviator's wing, my dear."

Sara was silent, staring into the fire. She had not seen, or looked for, faces in the fire since childhood. Now she saw several. Ugly, dancing, misshapen.

After a moment Dick said, "Sara, what are we going to do?" And she knew what he meant.

Still staring into the fire, feeling its warmth flush her cheeks, a whole army of images walked through her mind.

Though Dick Farthing had visited on only a few occasions, they had spent much time together, often talking late into the night. More and more, Sara had a terrible and disconcerting desire, wishing that she could become two people—one who continued to care for John and be a good wife; the other to love deeply and give herself completely to this huge, attractive American.

He moved across the room to sit beside her, repeating, "Sara, what are we going to do?"

Desperate, trying to evade the truth she asked, "Do? About what?"

His large hands were tender, the long fingers tracing down her hair. "You know very well, Sara." Then, after an unbearable pause, "Last week I tried to arrange for James to meet me somewhere other than here. I don't think I can come to Redhill anymore."

"Not come? You can't just—"

"No. No, maybe I can't," he almost whispered. "All I know is that I shouldn't come here. I'm more than fond of you, Sara. I want you. You understand?"

She could not drag her eyes from his: they were the color of rich earth, part of her realized, as though her thoughts tried to focus on something else. Rich, brown earth in the spring, tilled and ready for the first glint of green. Far away she heard her own voice say that of course she understood.

"I wonder if you really do."

"Oh, I do." Conscious of her folly, she placed a hand lightly on his thigh. The cloth of his suit felt rough, like putting her palm flat into a well-mown and rolled lawn.

His hand closed around her wrist. "No, Sara, I don't think you *do* understand. Yes, of course I want you in that way—what man wouldn't? But I want you in the impossible way. Completely. As a wife."

Her brow creased, real pain in her mind. "Please, Richard"—very level, not a whining, pleading voice. "Please, have me in the only way you can. Yes, I'd like you in all ways, but please, as that can't happen, would it be so wrong to be—"

"Lovers? Yes, I think it would be very wrong. That's why I shouldn't come back here. I don't know if I'm strong enough for it not to happen."

"Then don't talk of going away." She felt unnaturally controlled, and her voice remained calm. "We'll do no harm to John. Please take me, Richard. At least—"

Out in the hall, the telephone started to ring. For no reason she thought of the General, who had installed the instrument only a year before his death. Dick Farthing moved back to his chair. The ringing stopped, and, presently, Porter tapped at the door.

"I'm sorry to bother you, Madam." He said that Natter had been called out and the cart harnessed. The telephone call had been from John's club. He was arriving on the late train.

Sara thanked the old man, asking if there was food left, and ready, for her husband. "I was actually just going to bed, Porter. I've a slight headache."

"I'm sorry, Madam. Is there anything—"

"No, no," she said quickly. She would go up, and could Porter ask Mr. John to come and see her when he arrived.

The silence following Porter's departure was as violent as an assault by a thug. Dick Farthing rose and poured himself a brandy, while Sara slumped on the settee, still staring into the fire. Irrationally she felt her husband to be the intruder.

3

Sara did not appear at breakfast the following morning, and when John came down, James was startled to see that his father so suddenly looked tired and older. John greeted Dick warmly, thanking him for all he had done for James.

"Sara's not too well, I'm afraid," he told them.

"Lord, nothing frightful is it, Pa?" from James.

Dick, not able to look at John, remarked that she had seemed well enough over dinner. Then: "No, she had a bad head and went to bed soon after James."

"Bit of a cold coming on, I shouldn't wonder." John was not unduly concerned. "She isn't feverish, but sends apologies. Now, what about this flying?"

Asquith had given him a week. "You are on the telephone down there, after all. We can get hold of you if necessary." John was at Redhill determined to set all things right: to let Dick Farthing see that he did not neglect his wife; to give Berry some kind of warning; and to make peace between Sara and the Estate Manager, Hunter.

After breakfast, the men went up onto the downland, and John was impressed with his son's progress. James had now been given more freedom with the Farman, and did four trips that day—circling high over the Estate and town, making several low runs over the area they used for landing and taking off: demonstrating his confident ability and control.

Dick left at about three in the afternoon, while there was still sufficient light for him to get the aeroplane back to Farnborough safely. Father and son stood together, watching the great biplane dip its wings, setting course south-

east toward Hampshire. Then the pair turned and made their way slowly back
to the house.

Sara was waiting for them, composed and in brighter spirits. She did in fact
feel better, even though the terrible confusion still raged inside her. Her feelings
for Richard Farthing, she knew, would probably never change, but she would
remain a true and faithful wife to John, no matter what heartache she had to
hide.

Of one thing she had become convinced as she lay, red-eyed, on her bed
during the afternoon. If only she could have a child, a son preferably, then
perhaps the uneasy bond would be strengthened. She even said it aloud while
Vera Bolton was brushing her hair.

"Well, M'm, if all else fails, you should talk to Martha Crook—" Vera
suddenly blushed, thrusting a hand to her mouth as though to push back the
words. Martha Crook was Billy's mother, and worked as seamstress for the
Manor. Mother and son lived in the very pleasant Glebe Cottage, which stood
about half a mile from the main house and a mile or so from the Glebe House,
which was occupied by their surly Estate Manager.

Sara pressed Vera as to what she meant, but the girl was embarrassed. "I
shouldn't have said nothing, M'm."

"Well, you have, Vera. What do you mean about seeing Martha Crook?"

"Please, M'm. Please forget I said anything."

Presently, seeing she would get no further, Sara changed her tack. "At least
you can tell me one thing. Glebe Cottage is a nice little place, and Billy's a
help around the house and Estate. But isn't it unusual for the seamstress to
have her own cottage? What happened to Martha Crook's husband?"

Once more Vera colored and said she really should not have spoken of Martha
Crook. "I think you'd better ask Mr. John, M'm. Really I do."

After dinner, sitting in the drawing room, her mind still occasionally blurred
by the guilt of what might have occurred on the previous night, Sara asked
her husband outright about Martha and Billy Crook.

"I suppose I should have told you," John began slowly. "Damn it, everybody
else knows. Remiss of me."

So Sara quickly learned that Martha had been the last in a long line of the
General's mistresses. "He was a virile old man." John stared into the fire, his
voice odd, as though apologizing for something.

"Like *all* Railtons." Sara did not intend to sound coquettish; it was more a
word of reassurance.

James, who was with them, guffawed and received a sharp look from his
father.

It was a kind of family tradition, which began after John's mother had been
killed. Always the seamstress. "Always had one, and never a bad needlewoman
among them." John did not look at her as the story came out. "The tradition
was that the General chose the seamstress himself, just as he imposed the
conditions." Now he laughed. "I know of two who walked out pretty smartly

when they came to be interviewed. After that, the General went hunting on his own account."

Martha Crook had been the last. "We thought it'd be the usual. None stayed for much more than a year, but Martha was different. It seems she was once a midwife and nurse: so they say anyhow. Well, the rest follows. The General spawned a child of her. Billy's my half-brother, but he does not know, and there's a family pact. Martha still does the work of a seamstress, and she has Glebe Cottage, rent free, plus a handsome salary. In due course I shall see that Billy's looked after—should be thinking about that now, for he's a growing lad. Martha demands nothing, and remains silent."

Later, when James had left them, Sara told him that someone had suggested she should go to Martha Crook if she wanted a child. "Why should someone go to her, John?"

It was little more than Martha's merely having been some kind of nurse or midwife. "You seem to be learning fast about the country, so you must have discovered how they are here. The old ways are just under the surface; the old charms; magic, if you like. The country folk around here seldom go out on All Hallows Eve, for instance. Martha has a reputation and my guess is that she plays on it. I gather she still works as a midwife when it's necessary. But people *do* go to her, people who want children—and those who want to be rid of them, I shouldn't be surprised. She's become the local wise woman."

"In this day and age? John, it's 1910, not the Middle Ages." Sara had been rather shocked by the story of the General and Martha Crook. There was something unpleasant about the family just keeping her, having Billy put to a trade. She felt he deserved more.

"In the country, Sara dear, nothing's impossible. You *should* visit her sometime."

As they were on the subject, John decided it was time to bring up the question of the Estate Manager. "I hear you've had a run-in with Hunter about using mantraps," he began casually, not expecting the whirlwind he would unleash.

Sara's lips pursed, her eyes turning toward him. "Yes, John. I wanted to speak of Hunter. He's a vile beast of a man and must go."

"Go? But you'll never replace him. He was the General's confidant and—"

"And he's a pervert. A freak, who if it were not for your position would be arrested and locked up."

"Sara!" John Railton was taken aback by her vehemence. But also knew she was right. Many blind eyes had been turned to Hunter. "Someone's been—"

"Yes. It's like your Martha Crook and your half-brother, Billy. Something to be kept in the family. He's a criminal and you protect him because he was the General's man and a good manager. He's not only a pervert, but he's a law unto himself. Imagines he can play God."

"Sara, mantraps are regarded as part of life out here. We have to protect the game and—"

"It's not just the mantraps, it's the man. I'm the one who is here most of the time, and *I* don't want him working on the Estate."

John asked her what she knew, and how she had come by it.

"I felt a fool." She sat, straight-backed, her face set. John began to see that even in a few short weeks life at Redhill had changed her. "Hunter was blustering at old Natter the other day. Uncalled for, to upbraid another servant in front of me—unforgivable. But Hunter's a bully and insolent, as you know. Anyhow, when he rode off, old Natter muttered away, and I heard him say what Hunter was." She hesitated. "I didn't know what he meant, so I asked James. He told me, with some embarrassment. John, I don't think your son—and a lot of other people—really care for your employing a man who brings young boys and girls up to the Glebe House and commits such horrible, criminal acts. You protect him, and that's wrong."

She was correct, of course, John acknowledged to himself. The General had a strange outlook and did not regard Hunter's particular perversions as more than quirks. Yet it was against the law—God's law as well as the law of the land. Over the years, the men of the family had simply accepted Hunter and not dwelt on the implications.

"How would you suggest we replace him if I dismiss the man?" he asked.

"It's quite simple. Bob Berry's a first-rate farm manager; he could combine the jobs and do them both without difficulty."

"Ah." John smiled. "I also wanted to talk about Mr. Berry. It's a tradition here—in fact a necessity—that the Farm Manager should be married. The General made an exception with Berry. But I'm not going to allow it to continue. I've already decided—he'll have to go by the end of the year—well, at Michaelmas really; that's the usual time."

Sara slowly rose, standing in front of him, her back straight, eyes becoming as hard as any Railton soldier. "John." While her voice remained controlled, there was an edge to it that her husband had never heard before. "You are my husband, therefore my master—for I promised in church to love, honor and obey you. You are also master of Redhill Manor. But you need me here for the best part of the year. I did not like the idea, but I have come to terms with it. I even enjoy it. If you are to go on in politics, I must have a measure of power here. I would not threaten you, for you are my beloved husband; but if Bob Berry is sent from the Farm, then I shall pack my bags, return to London and never put my foot over this threshold again. The same applies to the decision about Hunter. He *must* go." The words, melodramatic though they were, carried conviction. Her tone softened. "John, dear. I've come to love this place. It has a sort of magic about it that ensnares a person. Other Railton wives have found the same, I know. You haven't the time to deal with every-thing. I have, and I mean what I say about Berry and Hunter."

John said nothing. He needed time to think. However, after two more conversations with Sara, he finally agreed. "I shall pension off Hunter and see Berry." Oddly, he felt that for a Railton he was being weak. Yet he wanted to dedicate the bulk of his time to the political work. Sara was happy at Redhill, and a few small changes would do no harm.

As for Bob Berry, the Farm Manager was already putting to rights the problem which had worried him from the moment of the General's death. He had formed a liaison with the sixteen-year-old daughter of Jack Calmer, the best butcher in Haversage. Young Rachel Calmer had first put in an appearance when she had been sent to the Farm on an errand.

The errand, a minor matter—a ten-minute chore—took her the best part of three hours, after which she began to walk out with Berry.

By late spring, young Rachel, who was a fine, slim girl, with dark, almost gypsy, looks, told her suitor that she was pregnant. She did not tell him that she had set out to become pregnant by him.

For Bob Berry, the future was prepared. The banns were read, and shortly afterward his new appointment as Farm and Estate Manager was confirmed.

Hunter left quietly, a fact which amazed many people. But John saw to it that he was provided with a regular annuity and a house far away on the other side of Oxford.

At Redhill Manor, things were changing.

4

Giles, in his own secret way, had been a one-man intelligence service for so many years now that he had long since ceased to be answerable to any of the official bodies. He shared his private knowledge—or most of it—and undeniably strode a delicate and dangerous path, with contacts which took him into strange areas, encompassing practically every country in Europe.

True, he had recently opened up a rich vein of information through his own kinfolk in Ireland, but long before his son Malcolm had even met Bridget Kinread, Giles had skillfully infiltrated his own agent within the now reblossoming Fenian movement.

In the past he had personally visited the man, interrogated him, and been the recipient of his private letters and messages, which provided a wide variety of intelligence concerning the Republican Brotherhood. The man's real name was Declan Fearon. They had coded him "Snake," which seemed apt, even amusing, to Giles.

Now, the elder Railton called on Vernon Kell to ask a favor. He learned that Charles was progressing well and suggested that his nephew could possibly receive further training by seeing the man known as Snake. For the first time Giles shared this secret source with Kell, who, suitably impressed, agreed that Charles might well benefit from a short clandestine operation.

So it was that Giles briefed Vernon Kell, who, in turn, gave Charles the details of what he was to do. The agent would be expecting him, on one of three consecutive nights, between seven and nine at his home in West Cork.

Passwords were arranged and Charles felt more than a small thrill being entrusted with bringing back detailed intelligence from Ireland. The dates set were in a matter of a fortnight's time.

5

Hans-Helmut Ulhurt—the Fisherman—sailed, ostensibly as Second Mate, on the merchant vessel *Möwe,* out of Hamburg, in early April.

They unloaded in Liverpool, leaving only machine parts in the cargo hold. These were to be delivered, during the return journey, in Dublin. The task in Liverpool should have taken four days at the outside. Unfortunately the ship developed trouble with her steering, causing her to wait for replacement parts to be brought from Hamburg.

In all, *Möwe* was in the Liverpool docks for almost two weeks, during which time the Fisherman traveled to Portsmouth, Southampton, Plymouth, London and thence to Scotland, via the industrial heart of the Midlands.

He was able to pass himself off quite easily as an Englishman, and had no trouble while traveling. On the contrary, he made some very pleasant friends, and, in all, had five liaisons with young women who were fascinated by his stories of the sea, his wooden leg, and other parts of his anatomy which provided hours of pleasure and homely fun.

He promised to visit these women again—in particular a Mrs. MacGregor, who kept a boardinghouse in Invergordon.

While he took pleasure with the ladies, the Fisherman behaved himself on other counts, getting drunk once only—and that in the privacy of his room at a small private hotel in London.

Finally they delivered the machine parts in Dublin, where the ship was to be berthed for six days.

On the first morning, Steinhauer's man visited Bewley's Café where he got into "casual" conversation with a man who gave him a number of messages for a mutual acquaintance in Germany.

"Our friend once told me that he had a man who could do almost anything for good comrades," the Irishman said quietly, after passing on certain intelligence which the Fisherman was sure would interest his chief.

"Yes." The Fisherman nodded. "Yes, that man is myself. Can I be of service?"

The Irishman looked at him with clear, hard, blue eyes which reminded Ulhurt of broken glass. "Some friends of mine have a great problem," he began. "You see, we've discovered a traitor in our midst, and there's really only one thing you can do with a traitor. . . ."

"How well I know it."

"You see, the fellow's well known and lives in a small community. If my friends did the job themselves, they'd be surely tracked down. They need an outsider; but someone who can come and go without leaving a ripple on the water, so."

The Fisherman nodded. "I'm your man. Just tell me where and who. It will be done in a matter of forty-eight hours."

"Well, now." Padraig leaned back in his chair. "Well, so. You'll be having to take the train. The fella you'll want lives in the village of Rosscarbery. That's in West Cork." He then started to give the German more precise instructions. "We'd like a real example made of him," he ended.

6

Charles had arrived in Rosslare in the steam ferry, complete with rod, fly box, and the usual impedimenta, looking every inch a visitor out for a week or so of pleasant fishing.

He took the train to Cork and then moved on, by omnibus, putting up for the night in an inn some five miles from Rosscarbery. In the bar he could not detect any suspicion. "There's a lot of people here for the fishing from across the water," they told him. So he arranged matters with the innkeeper, and spent the following day catching nothing in nearby fresh water.

At about four in the afternoon, Charles packed up his rods, returned to the inn and announced that he was off for a walk. Nobody seemed surprised—the English were mad anyway and there was no accounting for them. If the Englishman wanted to go walking at this time of day, who were they to comment?

Rosscarbery stands high on rocky ground, its one access being a steep rising road which takes you straight into its small square; the whole perched confusion of gray houses more than reminiscent of a Provençal village. The main road forks up the hill and is approached over a fine straight causeway.

It was a blustery March evening, with cloud lowering in from the west, and the last struggling rays of pale sun trying to cast slanting beams onto the sea lying to Charles' left. Ahead of him, the long causeway led to the road and the hill. He paused for a moment. Vernon Kell had told him not to arrive early. It was straightforward, he said, and merely a matter of timing. The man they called Snake lived in a small house on the far side of the town, on the western slope of the hill. Charles had studied a plan of the place. From the causeway it would take him about an hour to walk to their informant's door.

He rested, looking out at the sea, reflecting on its constant movement, aware of the noise as small breakers hit the rocks, but at the same time remaining alert, alive to the possibility of someone watching him.

At last, clutching his walking stick, Charles began to cross the causeway, walking steadily, timing himself; then, more slowly up the hill and into the square where lights were just starting to be lit. A woman, dressed in crow black, her head and shoulders covered by a shawl, hurried from the small general store, and three men lounged near a bar entrance. Nobody appeared to be interested in this tall stranger—though, later, his description was circulated to the police and military.

It was exactly five minutes to seven when he turned the corner of the narrow street where Snake lived—at the far end—in the three-room cottage known as Farnagh.

He could see it in the gathering gloom, and slowed as another figure approached on the far side of the road.

Charles did not look straight at the man, but took in the slightly limping gait, the fact of his size—tall and broad—and that he walked with his head lowered, the peak of his cap pulled down as though to avoid anyone seeing his features. The man walked steadily, unhurried, the halting clip of his boots on the broken pavement dying away as he headed back toward the square.

A few minutes later Charles was knocking on the door of Farnagh, three quick raps, ready to give the first password: "Can you tell me the way to O'Malley's Farm? I'm sorry to trouble you."

But nobody answered the door, even though a light burned, clearly, in the front room.

He rapped again, and as his stick struck the door, it swung open and he saw that the latch had been shattered. Charles felt the horror before he laid eyes on it.

Their informant had been a large man, heavy and fat. Now he looked like some grotesque deflated blimp that had been filled with blood and offal, then punctured unsuspectingly.

The little front room, once neatly ordered, had become an abattoir. Blood decorated walls and floor, soaked curtains and flung hideous patterns over pictures. The victim—the informer—lay hacked and split in the center of the room, his entrails spilling onto the carpet, his blood, still warm, dripping from the table. The instrument of this wild orgy of death, a large, sharp-bladed ax, had been tossed to one side, knocking over a small table so that the blade now lay half across a picture frame containing a bloodied sepia photograph of a young woman who had probably been the victim's daughter.

Charles retched once, then was violently sick.

It was not until he was halfway back along the street that three thoughts crossed his mind. First, as a stranger he would obviously be suspect; second, the frenzy of killing had not long taken place; third, the figure he had passed in the street was clad in a long coat, and he wondered what state that man's clothing would be in. If he were the killer, then whatever he wore under the coat must now be drenched with blood.

In fact, the body was not found for twenty-four hours, and by then Charles was well away on the return journey to England. Only later did Quinn tell him that two strangers had been reported in the area of Rosscarbery that evening: one was undoubtedly himself, the other matched the description of the man he had glimpsed near the informant's house. A week later the remains of burned clothing were found near the Rosscarbery hill. The killing remained unsolved, though one report, seen by Charles almost a year after, was of the opinion that, from half-charred buttons retrieved from the burned clothes, it was possible the murderer was German.

For several months Charles suffered nightmares, seeing again the mutilated corpse and hearing the dripping blood. Hardly a week passed but he recalled the figure with a slight limp and roll clumping toward him on the opposite side of the narrow street.

Chapter Nine

1

Winter slowly drifted away. By mid-April the blossom was showing, trees began to lose their bare, skeletal look, taking on a fine filigree of green, the true herald of spring.

Mildred Railton was only just showing her condition, but Charles already felt concern. The whole thought of Mildred carrying another child at her age nagged at the back of his mind.

By the end of April he was spending much more time in MO5's room, high and tucked away in the War Office itself. He was there on the afternoon of May 3rd, when Vernon Kell returned from a meeting at the Admiralty. He looked worried, and spoke even before closing the door. "Charles, the King's ill."

"Ill? Two much wine? He's only just got back from gallivanting around Biarritz."

"Don't joke!" Kell snapped. "It's serious." Before he could continue, the private telephone rang.

"Could you possibly get away, now, and come to Eccleston Square?" Giles asked quietly at the other end of the line.

Vernon Kell found Giles Railton in the Hide, a huge map spread out, with the opposing forces of Hannibal and Scipio arranged for him to study the tactics and dispositions of the battle of Zama.

"You've heard the news?" Giles did not look up from the model soldiers.

"The King?"

"Yes. It'll be public knowledge soon enough..."

"How bad is it really?" Kell asked.

"Very. It appears that he was not well while abroad. The Cabinet are on permanent standby. King Teddy's dying, and you must consider what this could mean in the long view of European politics. I cannot deny my own concern. Europe is in turmoil, and nobody seems to realize the underlying seriousness. Even the workers are restless—more than restless in other countries—and before we know it their grievances will spread to here."

The two men talked for almost three hours, and Kell left with a number of serious subjects for discussion with Charles and Quinn.

Giles had met his nephew, John, that morning, and they had certainly spoken of the gravity of the situation, though John was more interested in talking about Sara. "I find it incredible, Uncle Giles. When the General died, she hated the very idea of living in the country on any permanent basis. Yet it's taken her only a few weeks—weeks, mark you—to settle down."

Giles said that the speed with which Sara had adjusted was not unusual. "It was the same with your mother, John. That house has an odd effect on women."

Privately, he had his own thoughts about Sara. Redhill Manor, and the Estate, had become a new lover and husband for her. Time would see how things turned out—and time was sifting away from the King.

2

Two days later, in the evening, on May 5th, the whole country knew. King Edward VII was gravely ill.

At Buckingham Palace, the Queen sent for the King's faithful companion and mistress, Mrs. Keppel, but he continued to work, even on that last day, between fainting fits and having oxygen administered.

On the afternoon of May 6th, King Edward lost consciousness. Crowds began to gather, silently, in front of the Palace.

Just after midnight there came a great knocking at the door of the South Audley Street house.

Mildred awoke, agitated, asking what was wrong, and a maid appeared a few minutes later, saying there was a young gentleman for Mr. Railton.

Sprogitt stood, uncomfortably, in the hall. "Sir," he all but whispered, "His Majesty passed away about quarter of an hour ago. Captain Kell says would you please come to the office right away. He feels His Majesty's death is a matter for the country's internal security."

Charles nodded. The Uncle of Europe was gone, at the age of sixty-nine years. Charles did not realize this was truly the end of an era. His work was soon to begin in earnest.

3

The information brought back by the Fisherman was well presented but without much to interest Steinhauer, except for one name—Railton. He had heard it before, yet could not quite put his finger on it. The name had come in from the Fisherman via the Irish contact called O'Connell, who had boasted of a private informer—"name of Railton"—closely connected with the English Military in Ireland.

Steinhauer was still working out of the Wilhelmstrasse, and his new masters also had a few of their people in the Foreign Ministry, though the bulk of their operations were centered in a house on Courbierrestrasse, in the western part of the city, which they all referred to as Number 8. There was one old school-fellow of Steinhauer's—an Army captain, von Schurer, at the Wilhelmstrasse. He needed an unwitting go-between with the new regime, and could trust von Schurer, so it was to him that Gustav Steinhauer went on the day after the Fisherman's return.

He was greeted with a look of of surprise. "I did not expect to see you here, Gustav." Von Schurer was a tall, very handsome man, a shade of the dandy and thought of as a devil with the ladies. Only his intimates knew his particular sweet tooth for young boys. "Did you not get Major Nicolai's message?" Nicolai had been appointed overall Commander of Intelligence, with the rank of major, only a few weeks before.

Steinhauer had not even looked at his desk. "Nobody's said anything to me, old friend."

"Well, he wants you over at Number 8 immediately." Hermann von Schurer sounded as though he should have delivered the line with a stamp of the foot.

"Oh well . . . he'll have to wait. I'm tired."

"All that wine—and beautiful women spies." Von Schurer pouted archly.

"I don't think I've ever met a beautiful woman spy in my life."

"Well, Steinhauer, get over to Number 8—they've got a really lovely one there. Working hard with the gallant Major."

"Yes." Steinhauer feigned weariness. "I suppose I'd better go and see what they want."

At Number 8, Steinhauer was told that Major Nicolai had been asking for him all morning. "It's the bad communications," Steinhauer said blandly.

The officer who had spoken to him shrugged as if to say this was none of his business, and at that moment one of the doors opened. Nicolai himself came out escorting a dazzling, slim, fair-haired girl. "Ah, Steinhauer," he smiled, oddly jovial. "Meet one of the ladies we are training here." He mentioned no name, but the girl blushed when Steinhauer kissed her hand. Nicolai looked at him, smiled and said he would see her later. I'll wager you will, Steinhauer thought, bowing to the young woman as she left with another officer.

"And where did you find that little peach?" Steinhauer had never been intimidated by the Military.

Nicolai gave a frosty smile. "She fell off the tree and right into our laps. If there is ever trouble with England, she can be of great help."

"Trouble with England?" Steinhauer's heart missed a beat. For a second he thought they must be on to his own special agent. "God forbid trouble with England."

"Their King is dying," Nicolai said, as though that explained the whole thing.

"Ah."

"As for that girl, I might need your help there, but I asked you to come over to discuss reorganization."

"Since you people took over there's been nothing but reorganization. Walter, why can't you stick to pure Military Intelligence? It would make life so much easier."

Nicolai actually sighed. "That is what I want." He dropped into his chair. "I agree, but the High Command do not. I'm sorry, Gustav, but I've got unpleasant news for you."

"Go on."

"The various people you've carefully spread around England—watching the docks and so on . . ."

Steinhauer nodded.

"Well, I have been instructed to tell you that they are now to pass into naval control. You are required to see Captain Rebeur-Paschwitz and give him all the information—the way you communicate, the number of agents, codes and the like."

"Why the hell—"

"Because, in their wisdom, the High Command sees those agents as naval agents. Their targets are dockyards, the Royal Navy"—a shrug—"that kind of thing. So they are out of your hands. If you're short of work, I can give you some."

4

Thursday, May 19th, was the day on which, as all the newspapers bore witness, the earth was due to pass through the tail of Halley's Comet. Astrologers and prophets of doom saw the event as one of importance. Halley's Comet was the harbinger of disaster—though the only previous proven link was with the Norman Conquest, which was a blessing in disguise and never the tyranny represented by Anglo-Saxon propaganda.

It is unlikely that the thunderstorm during the night of May 18th and 19th had anything to do with the comet. It was restricted to the London area, and pouring rain followed throughout the morning of the 19th.

The body of King Edward VII lay in state within the Great Hall of Westminster, and the rain failed to affect the five-mile line of his former subjects paying last respects to their sovereign.

But Vernon Kell, Charles Railton, Patrick Quinn and some of his men— mostly invisible, mingling with the crowds—were nowhere near Westminster Hall that morning.

They had dodged the pouring rain, placing themselves, early, at Victoria Station. Quinn and his shadows had been actively on duty in that area almost since the night of the King's death, for it was at Victoria that the royalty of Europe and their entourages had begun to arrive for the funeral.

Plans were made, in MO5's room at the War Office, during the hours which followed Sprogitt's midnight call upon Charles. Quinn was already there, though

champing to get away, as he was required at the Palace itself. He had things
to say, though, and was going to say them now.

"We're going to see the largest gathering of foreign leaders, in London, in
living memory," he predicted. "It'll be bigger than that for her late Majesty's
funeral, you can count on it. My feeling, gentlemen, is that you should watch—
with my men's help if you so desire—for possible infiltration by intelligence
officers."

So, before most folk in the suburbs of London even knew that their monarch
was dead, the plans were already partially laid.

Now, Kell, Charles Railton and the Branch officers were at Victoria Station,
on the morning of May 19th, awaiting the arrival of the Kaiser Wilhelm and
his party.

The new King George V, formerly the Duke of York, paced the platform,
surrounded by his staff, seemingly anxious to meet his German cousin, the
Kaiser. The purple carpet had been rolled out, and a set of matching steps
stood nearby to give the German Emperor easy access from train to platform.

The Kaiser had already arrived in the Thames estuary aboard the German
royal yacht, the *Hohenzollern,* under escort of four Royal Navy destroyers. He
would make the journey into the center of the capital by train, just as the other
crowned, and uncrowned, heads of Europe—and the world—had been doing
all week.

From their vantage point, in one of the main station offices, high above the
spread of platforms, Quinn, Kell and Railton waited and watched, field glasses
at the ready, while an orderly, trained in shorthand, stood patiently by to take
down every comment made by the three officers.

The train appeared, gliding over the last few hundred feet of track, with
steam shut off to reduce the noise.

The figure, with the familiar curled and spiked mustaches, quietly descended
to be greeted by his cousin. They kissed on both cheeks, and the platform
suddenly came alive with the Kaiser's party.

The trio of officers barely glanced at the Kaiser. They were more interested
in the officers following in the wake of "the Bane of Europe," as his dead uncle
had once called him.

As various faces clicked into memory, either from previous knowledge or
well-studied photographs, one or the other of the three men spoke names. In
turn, the names were noted by the orderly: a litany of diplomats, advisers,
military and naval attachés, ADCs.

Quite suddenly, as the last carriages were due to leave and only lesser dig-
nitaries waited, Quinn let out a gasp. "Vernon! Look! To the right of the
German Military Attaché. See him?"

"What's that particular ferret doing with the royal party, I wonder?" Kell
also recognized the face and put a name to it.

5

"Captain Rebeur Paschwitz," he told Giles later that afternoon. The pair walked in Regent's Park. "Remember him? Rebeur-Paschwitz?"

Giles stumped along, lips tight. "Last time we saw him here was during Jacky Fisher's time at the Admiralty. He's most certainly Naval Intelligence What think you, Vernon?"

"Swine among pearls. He has no place at this particular event. Grand Admirals yes; but German Intelligence, no!"

A small child almost ran between their legs, chased by its nanny, scolding and apologizing to the two gentlemen.

They walked on in silence. "You're having him watched, I presume?" Giles could have been talking to himself.

Kell smiled. "Quinn says we'll have details of his every movement. Even his bowels. That's what he said."

Giles simply nodded.

6

Quinn was on duty, marching in the funeral as a bodyguard to the Royal Family. But Charles joined Kell and the orderly, occupying an empty room in a government office which afforded a view of the entrance to Westminster Hall.

Standing back from separate windows, they saw the entire moving procession of kings and emperors; princes and potentates; the military escorts; the regiments of the line; cavalry; bands; regiments of German, Russian and Austrian armies; and the whole heraldic panoply of England.

The bluejackets carried the coffin, wrapped in the Royal Ensign, from Westminster Hall, to place it on the gun carriage for the journey along Whitehall, the Mall, Piccadilly, and through the Park to Paddington—where the final lap was taken, to Windsor, by train for the committal.

Giles watched from a different vantage point, and as he looked at this incredible gathering, he had a strange premonition, based on his own particular sense of history. To see all this splendor and power on display was like watching the last act in an incredible opera. In his heart he knew it was never going to be the same again.

In their secret watchtower, Kell, with Charles, noted that Captain Rebeur-Paschwitz was present. Idly Kell again wondered why this particular intelligence officer was in England at all.

7

"Apparently he came over for a haircut," Quinn told them late on Monday afternoon, when they met at a house recently purchased as a "safe property" by the Branch for most private meetings or interrogations.

Quinn had put his two best men on the surveillance of Rebeur-Paschwitz—
"Detective Inspectors Drury and Seal. Drury telephoned me quite late last
night. The Captain went back to his hotel after the funeral. He changed out
of uniform, then ate a slap-up meal at the Café Royal."

The German had returned to his hotel, and the two surveillance men would
have lost him if they had not been so experienced. One took the front entrance
while the other watched the rear. Sure enough, fifteen minutes later, Rebeur-
Paschwitz came out—"Quite furtively"—from the back.

"Now, you'd expect a naval officer to go over to the Savoy or the Dorchester
to have his hair trimmed. Not so our man. Would you say it was normal for
a senior German naval officer to get his hair cut, late at night, in a barber's
shop in the Caledonian Road?"

They remained silent as Quinn told them that it was a seedy place, owned
and run by a man named Karl Gustav Ernst.

"Technically the fellow's British." Quinn's distaste showed, like a man who
has taken a mouthful of spoiled fish. "British born, but with strong German
links. I have men watching the place now. We've rented a little house across
the road."

Charles, naturally, wanted to barge straight in. "Kick the beggar hard."

Kell slowly shook his head. There could be large rewards if they played it
carefully. "I'd put money on the barber's shop being a 'post office'—and an
important one at that, if someone like Rebeur-Paschwitz takes the trouble to
visit."

Quinn agreed. "There are ways of finding out, Vernon. We have our own
methods, but I sense we should keep this strictly official. We'll need permission
to get all Ernst's post intercepted and opened. It should be done fast, I feel.
There's no point in putting this one on the long finger, as they say where I
come from."

"Charles"—Kell hardly turned toward him—"I think we should have a word
with your Uncle Giles." He actually winked at Quinn before turning to face
Charles. "Your Uncle Giles is a friend of the Home Secretary, is he not?"

"They live practically next door to one another, yes."

"If we have to get post intercepted, then we must see the Home Secretary.
Let's go and see Giles Railton and ask if he can put in a word for us. This
must be settled now."

The large operation that was now mounted by MO5 and the Branch against
the Caledonian Road shop became directly responsible for more staff and offices
being made available to Kell.

8

On a beautiful Sunday in August, at Redhill Manor, the full chapter of
events, springing from the German Captain Rebeur-Paschwitz's visits to the
barber's shop in the Caledonian Road, was discussed again.

The house party was Sara's idea. Giles had been one of the first to receive an invitation, and he telephoned to ask a favor. Could Sara ask Captain and Mrs. Vernon Kell? "Charles' boss," he said with no hint of intrigue.

This weekend at Redhill was a welcome break for everyone, though Sara had no inkling that Giles had managed to turn her invitation into a meeting for Kell, Charles, John Railton and himself to discuss clandestine affairs. He also wanted to view Charles at close quarters.

Charles almost turned down the visit, for Mildred was in the last weeks of her pregnancy—continually tired and warned by her doctors that she should rest even more than usual. But Mildred loved Redhill, and insisted that the change would do her good. To be safe, Charles had ensured that their daughter, Mary Anne, roughly James' age, should accompany them.

Mary Anne, a slender, vivacious girl with eyes, as Andrew once remarked, "the color of the North Sea in winter, though with more warmth," had become something of a problem.

Already they were talking of her "coming out"; but Mary Anne stubbornly refused to discuss any arrangements. Mildred, with time heavy on her hands, had even started to make lists to cover the ball they would give for her, following the usual ritual Presentation at Court and other social delights which surrounded girls of Mary Anne's age and station. But when it was mentioned, the girl showed no interest. At last, during one angry evening, Mary Anne claimed that she wanted none of the tradition, revealing her only aim in life.

"Please, Mama and Papa," she had spoken with cold reason, "I know you won't like it, but I think all the Season business is a waste of time and money. Besides, it isn't going to help me." It was then she told them that she wanted to become a nurse. "Eventually I shall be a doctor, and the way into that profession is through nursing."

Charles and Mildred were scandalized.

The skirmishes moved backward and forward, though Mary Anne's mind appeared to be unchanged. In time there would be an inevitable clash, but for the moment the real battle was carefully avoided.

Giles detected an uneasiness between the girl and her parents, but that was not unusual for headstrong young women of Mary Anne's age. In any case he had little time to concern himself with small family struggles. In truth, the maze of Giles Railton's mind was at this moment so full of twists and turns, so devious and confused, that even he wondered how he managed to keep all the threads together.

Giles had not seen John for nearly a month, and the sight of him at Redhill now gave cause for alarm. John Railton had lost weight, becoming almost gaunt. His hair had turned even more gray, and his color constantly changed from a sallow lack of pigment to sudden crimson flushes.

They met after dinner in the General's Study. John was slumped behind his father's old desk, looking listless and tired.

"Sara's worried, but I dare not tell her the truth," he answered when Giles asked after his health.

"And what *is* the truth?"

John gave a short, bitter, laugh. "That I'm the odd man out; a Railton who is not going to make old bones. . . ."

"But, my dear fellow——"

John held up a hand, shaking his head. "It's all right. There's nothing to be done. I've got what one doctor described as a dicky heart. The man I saw in Harley Street was more precise." He gave a resigned shrug.

"But surely you should rest. Stop, take a holiday. . . ."

"And gain an extra year? Maybe two? That's not my style: not the Railton style. The General could have died suddenly, in battle, from the age of sixteen onwards. I shall go in my early fifties. A year, two years with luck."

Giles nodded. He would have felt the same.

So, on Sunday afternoon, four of the men were seated on the rear terrace of the Manor—the women having taken themselves off; while the other male members of the party, including James Railton and Dick Farthing, were examining a new aeroplane—the prototype MF7 Longhorn—that Dick had flown down to Redhill.

Mildred rested; the sky remained clear, a deep blue, and the sun blazed hot on the stone terrace where the men sat, watching the butterflies among the lines of flowerbeds, conscious of the background drone of bees and other insects.

Giles began by saying he felt it was an ideal opportunity to review the situation— "Put the pieces together: particularly for John. He has only the barest of details, and, as a Cabinet minister with special responsibilities, he should know everything."

"We could have been badly hindered." Kell gazed at a stone urn as though the flowers cascading from it held some particular secret known only to him. "Could have been held up and missed much. That fellow King proved a great stumbling block."

Charles asked why they had been saddled with King at all. "We really thought you could work the oracle with Winston, you know, Uncle Giles." Sir Alexander King was the civil servant in charge of the General Post Office.

Giles gave a friendly growl, recalling how Kell had arrived, with Charles, seeking immediate clearance to have Karl Gustav Ernst's post intercepted and examined.

Half thinking aloud, and partly for his own amusement, Giles went over the facts of that night.

After hearing Kell out he had immediately telephoned Churchill's Eccleston Square house. After a short delay the Home Secretary came on the line: not too pleased at having been called from his bath. Giles told him this was a matter of national importance, and was reluctantly asked to come straight to the house. "You'll have to take me as you find me," Churchill said. "I have the onerous duty of making an after dinner speech tonight. Clearly, I am tardy with my ablutions."

"I was received by the Home Secretary in his dressing room as he bumbled around for studs and tie," Giles told them. "He was dressed informally—in his underdrawers and shirt, stockings and carpet slippers."

After listening to Giles, Churchill had looked glum. "You realize the Royal Mail is sacrosanct?" he said.

Giles had caught a glint in Churchill's eye. "Come on, Winston. This is a question of the country's security. By scrutinizing this fellow's Royal Mail, we could bag a whole nest of the blighters."

Winston Churchill nodded. "Very well. I'll make my recommendation tonight. But I fear it will take a few days. My order alone will not bear complete weight. To have Ernst's post examined you must get assistance from a man not noted for speed." He spoke of Sir Alexander King.

"Took three days." Kell still gazed at the urn. "Even then he tied us up with red ribbon."

Across the lawns, on the far side of a line of trees, two figures could be seen on horseback.

"My Farm and Estate Manager, Berry," John Railton said, as though this important conversation had little bearing on *his* future.

Charles said that King has been nice enough but played by the book. "It widened the circle of knowledge. Dangerous."

It had worried everyone. King insisted that the sorter concerned had to know, so had a senior member of the Post Office. "Those two are always present when the stuff's opened." Kell turned his attention directly to John. "That's three men in all, if you count one of my people. Too many for something as sensitive as this."

They admitted that it was worth it, though. The first intercepted package contained a dozen sets of hair clippers, complete with leaflets in German on their use. Careful examination revealed a number of more specific instructions mixed up with the leaflets. These included postcards and letters, addressed, stamped and marked to be forwarded. The letters contained minute details of targets for reconnaissance and surveillance.

Similar packages, and bulky letters, arrived at roughly two-week intervals, most of them sent by a Fräulein Reimers, of Potsdam. They all contained cards and letters for forwarding. There were also messages from Gustav Steinhauer, the self-styled paper manufacturer, drawn to their attention during Captain Nicolai's visit to London.

The recipients of the instructions lived in places as far apart as Edinburgh and Exeter; and MO5, with help from the Branch, now ran a full-scale surveillance on the whole ring.

There were thirty agents receiving instructions via Ernst's "post office," and most of their orders centered on gaining intelligence on dockyards and fortifications. The pay, Giles told John, was meager. "Ernst receives about a pound a week for his services."

"And he suspects nothing?" John asked.

Kell shook his head. "All we can do is watch and wait. If any trouble flares up, the whole bunch can be arrested in a matter of hours." Technically they had gained control of the entire German network in the United Kingdom.

"Well, it's certainly—" John began. Then his words were cut through by a terrifying scream from the house.

Charles was on his feet, recognizing the frightening noise as coming from Mary Anne. "Oh my God! Mildred!"

As he turned toward the house, Charles caught sight of two figures running— Vera, the maid, going like a greyhound across the fields, her cap flying off and the black dress and starched apron lifted high, and Billy Crook, following her; catching up fast.

9

In the hall, Sara stood, white-faced, at the telephone. She held out an arm to stop Charles from going up the stairs as she spoke into the mouthpiece: "Yes, doctor . . . as quickly as you can . . . Thank you." Putting down the instrument, she turned to Charles. "Don't go to her. She'll not thank you for it . . ."

"Is she—"

"Mary Anne, Mrs. Kell and one of the maids are with her. Yes, she's in labor—and it does not look good." She took hold of his arm. "You'd want to know the truth. The doctor will be here as soon as possible. In the meantime I've sent for Martha Crook. She's probably the best person to have at a time like this. . . ."

"But—" Charles looked dazed.

"If you've any doubts, I can tell you that Dr. Squierey himself asked. The first thing he said was, 'Have you got Mrs. Crook there?' So she'll be in good hands."

Charles opened his mouth, his eyes blank; but Sara seemed to read his thoughts. "Yes, my dear. If it gets dangerous. I'll see you're with her. Now, please, Charles, stay with the other men. This is women's business."

Giles moved from behind his nephew, taking him by the arm and leading him back to the terrace. There, they tried to continue with some normality, talking about naval policy and the need to build up strength on both land and sea.

But Charles hardly heard a word, though he tried to force his mind onto the conversation.

It was impossible. His thoughts were blurred, running together. Now, suddenly, they became focused by what could have been the cry of an animal in pain.

10

It was no animal. The cry came from his wife, Mildred, propped up, swathed in towels, her legs stretched apart, in their room upstairs.

Sara had seen Martha Crook a number of times since John had told her the truth about the woman. Tall, with graying hair tied in a bun at the nape of her neck, she had an extraordinarily quietening influence: as though she possessed a secret gift for calming inner fears. Her voice was soft, and her hands even softer as she probed Mildred's abdomen, swollen with child. Even Mildred, though in great fear, felt safer on hearing the soothing speech: "There, there, now quiet and gently, my dear. All is going to be well for you both. Don't you fret. Just keep taking big deep breaths when the pain comes...."

"The pain's ... there ... all ... the ... time ..." Mildred gasped, then cried out again at the shears of agony which seemed to be cutting into her. Martha gestured to Sara, motioning her away from the bed to the far side of the room.

Martha Crook's exceptionally dark brown eyes looked serious as she spoke very quietly so that only Sara could hear. "I fear it's bad, Ma'am. Just pray the doctor doesn't get here for a while; otherwise the poor lady'll be gone."

"What?" Sara felt fear of her own.

Martha put a hand to Sara's lips. "Shush, now. I don't know what the lady's doctor has been about, nor if he even knows, but that child in her must be turned. It's a breech birth, and Dr. Squierey cannot do it. I know. I've seen him try, but he has no knack for it. The lady'll be in some pain, but with God and luck I'll turn the child. If I do not, then neither'll live and that's truth." She took a deep breath, glancing at her patient on the bed. "It's a big baby as well. Makes matters more difficult. Now ..." She gave instructions, with no fuss. Clear and lucid. They were to hold the patient tightly by the arms and calves; mop her brow and keep her from looking down. "On no account do I want her to see what I'm doing. You understand? Now, the hottest water I can bear to wash in; and plenty of disinfectant."

For the next hour Mildred cried out a great deal, and occasionally, mercifully, lost consciousness. They held her, firmly straddled on the bed so that she could not move, while Martha Crook talked constantly, working her agile fingers, first around the abdomen and then, slowly, inside Mildred.

Mildred's hair was slick with sweat, and her cries became louder, more agonized, as the life inside her shifted, relaxed, then shifted again. Gradually, the cries became softer as she weakened, losing blood together with her will to continue bearing such intense agony.

At last, Martha Crook stood back, still speaking, then leaning forward to whisper, her eyes fastened, gleaming, on her patient. "Now, my dear; now you have to summon all your strength." Slowly she repeated: "All your strength."

For a second it seemed that Mildred could not hear, then her eyes opened.

Something moved within the eyes, as though fever were being sucked from her. The change was mystical, as a special, uncomplicated bond suddenly formed between her and Mrs. Crook. "*All* your strength, my dear," Martha whispered, and an unbelievable sense of peace crept into the room. "Now, bear down. Bear down; and your lovely son will come into the world. You want that, don't you?"

Mildred gave a small nod; the agony and burning hell of the past hour appeared to have left her, and she did as she was told, without question or sound. The rest was simple; natural and easy. The boy came, gently, with no further fuss, into the world. The babe took two little snuffles of air, as though sniffing the place he had found, and then began to cry, as fit and lusty as any child.

The doctor heard the cries as he came up the stairs. His job was now relatively easy—to make Mrs. Charles Railton comfortable, and give his own instructions, to be certain that no septicaemia set in: though he had seen Martha Crook's work before and knew it to be unlikely.

Sara went downstairs to tell a much relieved Charles that he had a fine son, but Mildred should be left to sleep, as it had been a most difficult birth. When she returned to the room, Martha Crook had quietly disappeared, going down the back stairs and out into the hot August afternoon, returning softly across the fields to the Glebe Cottage.

Mildred slept until late, and Charles saw his new son, and the mother, after dinner. Both appeared to be healthy, and he remarked on Mildred's radiance. Only those in the room during the birth of little William Arthur, named after the General, knew what a miracle had been accomplished.

11

At dinner that night Giles noticed that in spite of the flying he had done during the day and the presence of his friend Dick Farthing, James was unusually silent. He even commented on it to Sara.

"Oh, James, of all people, is mooning over some girl." She smiled, as though passing on a secret. "It's all right, she's very respectable. Old Army family. Lives the other side of Haversage. They call her M-M-M because of her initials, Margaret Mary Mitchel, with one 'l.' Nice girl. James has been like this ever since they met. It's a good job he's off to Sandhurst next month; that'll settle things one way or another. Either she'll wait for him or it'll all fall down."

Giles Railton gave a tiny nod, his lips moving up, then back again in a fast thin smile. James, like Giles' daughter, Marie, was the true family future, and could well see to himself. Though Giles truly thought of himself as the boy's guardian angel.

It was John's gaunt and tired face at the head of the table which really concerned him with his private knowledge of his nephew's health; that, and one other thing—the looks which passed constantly between Sara and the young American flyer, Farthing. Giles knew much about life, and more about secrets. He had seen that look before, just as he could now see the mark of death lying across John Railton's face. He had also heard his nephew speak of the relationship between James, Sara, and the American. "He's like a brother to both of them," John said. In the tone, Giles detected a bitter barb, hidden away among the words like a cipher.

Chapter Ten

1

James had always got on well with his cousin Caspar, so it was arranged between them, then with the authorities, to share a room, and servant, when they arrived at the Royal Military Academy, Sandhurst, in September.

James' only regret was his enforced separation from the delightful Margaret Mary Mitchel—who had almost, though not quite, taken precedence in his affection over aeroplanes. They had met at Lady Dartmouth's Ball during the Season, in London.

Normally, James preferred to stay in the country, where Richard could bring one of the Farmans down, sometimes for entire weekends.

It was necessary, though, to go to London, even in this Season which followed the "Black" Ascot. Young men like James and Caspar were expected to prepare young women to mix with men in society.

He had never been much attracted by women, but at Lady Dartmouth's Ball he encountered Margaret Mary early in the evening, and, not really knowing what was happening to him, reserved every dance—something not usually done.

She captivated him from the moment he set eyes on her. Striking, with a mane of red hair, slim boyish figure, an impish face covered, to her embarrassment, with freckles, and a sense of humor which went with the face. She was unlike any girl he had met until now; not beautiful in the classic sense, but highly desirable.

For the first time a human being, M-M-M, haunted his more lustful fantasies. Yet it was not just the physical side of her which attracted James. This girl could talk about things other than her favorite pony or what it had been like at school. On that first meeting he encountered a mind much aware of things about which he had little knowledge—music, for instance, was a true passion with her.

To James' great delight she knew exactly who he was, and soon revealed that she lived only six miles the other side of Haversage, near the village of

Challow, on the Uffington road—not far from the undulating hills, and the White Horse, a place where James had often been taken, when younger, to toboggan during hard winters.

She was also part of an Army family, her father being Sir Bertram Mitchel, former Colonel of the Royal Artillery, who had known the General, though more by reputation than any social contact.

James learned later that Sir Bertram preferred life at Challow Hall; mainly for the sake of his frail wife, who had contracted one of the more unpleasant forms of malaria during the Colonel's term of service in India.

His daughter, however, was far from frail. Together, the couple began to climb into each other's minds. James listened to Margaret playing Chopin, while she came over to Redhill to watch the flying.

From friendship their feelings blossomed into that indistinct, and blurred, relationship; unspoken but clear in each other's eyes and gestures.

On the weekend before he departed for Sandhurst, James walked Margaret into the woods and there kissed her; once tentatively, then, as she returned his kiss, several times. They remained, lost in each other, for a good hour, speaking of their feelings, neither of them truly comprehending what was happening, yet both sure that they wanted to spend the rest of their lives together.

So it was with mixed emotions that James finally arrived at the Royal Military College. This was a long-awaited moment; yet so much had been added to James' life in the last few months—the flying, a new and closer relationship with his stepmother, and now this extraordinary passion for a girl, from whom he resented being parted.

The couple decided they would make no public announcement. Margaret Mary knew that the wait cold be long and difficult, depending on which regiment finally claimed him, but she remained unconcerned, being as determined as she was striking; and, while both young people imagined their passion to be secret, the families were well alerted to the true way of things. Sara's words to Giles, during the weekend at Redhill Manor, about Sandhurst being a make or break time for the couple, were echoed at Challow Hall, where Margaret Mary's parents had both taken to James.

If anything came of the relationship, the families would not stand in their path. Only the Army, or a sticky patch in the Empire's history, could do that.

James and Caspar quickly settled into life at the Royal Military College. It was, they soon discovered, less taxing than being at school, and it depended on the individual on how much time remained idle.

For those who were at Sandhurst during the two years spent at that establishment by James and Caspar Railton, the requisite subjects included French, German, Mathematics, Military Engineering, Military Law, Tactics, Musketry, Drill—naturally—Topography, Gymnastics, Fencing and Riding.

James was puzzled for a long time after the Commandant's interview; for this senior officer insisted that James should continue to fly regularly—as "an outside sport." More bewildering was the Commandant's directive that he should especially continue his studies of French and German with, as he put it, "renewed vigor."

James threw himself happily into the routine. On most Saturdays he went over to nearby Farnborough to continue flying when the weather allowed, and, eventually, taking his Aero Club Certificate.

At least once a month he could make the relatively easy journey either to Challow Hall or Redhill Manor. So he was fully and happily employed, living a pleasing life which combined all that most interested him; and the feelings between James Railton and Margaret Mary Mitchel deepened rather than diminished.

2

"I'm not given to bad language, but I'm bloody furious!"

"Tell me, Vernon. Tell me the whole thing." Giles Railton stumped along beside Kell in the late-afternoon mists of Regent's Park.

It was November; cold, both men wore greatcoats, mufflers and overshoes. The paths glistened with moisture, while here and there a soggy leaf, gold a week or so before, lay like a vandalized butterfly. Giles Railton had eagerly agreed to the meeting.

Kell started to tell the story.

In mid-October two of Quinn's men had arrested a suspect in Portsmouth. Quinn traveled down to the city, followed by Kell and Charles Railton, who remained in the background to avoid any public identification.

The arrested man confessed to everything, admitting that he was a German national—Siegfried Helm. Yes, he had been sketching the Portsmouth harbor defenses. He identified his own notebook and the sketches.

Then, of his own volition, Helm told the Branch interrogators that he was an officer of the Imperial German Army—a lieutenant of the 21st Nassau Regiment.

Helm was immediately charged under the Official Secrets Act. "I was overjoyed." Kell sounded less than happy now. "Like a fool I even thought this might bring about a withdrawal of the barber's shop network from the country."

The case was complete—with corroborating evidence from two British officers. Both had seen Helm at work, sketching searchlight and gun emplacements.

The trial was at Winchester, under Mr. Justice Eldon Bankes. Sir Rufus Isaacs, the Attorney-General himself, prosecuted for the Crown. The case was unanswerable, and Sir Rufus obtained an easy conviction.

Then came the bombshell. "A farce," Kell said. Before the judge's summing up, Rufus Isaacs had raised a point of law and strongly stressed the limitations of the Act under which Helm was being prosecuted. It was the first time such a case had been heard, and there was little doubt in Sir Rufus' mind that an act of espionage, carried out by a foreigner in *time of peace,* did *not* constitute a serious offense in the law as it stood. Nevertheless the jury returned a verdict of guilty.

Mr. Justice Bankes, taking into account that Siegfried Helm had already spent four weeks in prison, bound over the prisoner and ordered his immediate discharge.

"That all?" Giles did not look at him.

"All? Sir, the Official Secrets Act has *got* to be changed or the German Intelligence people active in the United Kingdom will have a field day at our expense."

Giles grunted, looking at the rapidly closing mist. "Agreed. I shall lobby everyone. We'll get an amended Act onto the statute books."

"I sincerely hope so."

Until this Helm business they had all been confident that MO5 had the German agents working in Britain wholly under their thumb. Now Kell voiced serious doubts. Watchers were doubled; the letters, instructions and cards which moved to and from Karl Ernst's shop were subjected to greater scrutiny, checked by top cipher men—brought from the DID's office at the Admiralty—and not allowed to pass until either Kell or Charles Railton gave the word.

Until the law was changed, a sense of bitterness hung over MO5's offices.

At Christmas there was a new name on some of the presents under the Christmas tree at Redhill Manor—another William Arthur Railton, son of Charles and Mildred.

On Boxing Day morning, the hunt met as usual, and James, looking splendid in uniform, rode beside Miss Margaret Mary Mitchel of Challow Hall—another fact to be much commented on by family, servants and townsfolk alike.

So 1910 came to an end. Happier than it had started; but with some troubled minds in secret places.

3

Two years later, just before Christmas, 1912, James, now officially a second lieutenant of the Hampshire Regiment, was married, in Haversage Parish Church, to Margaret Mary Mitchel.

Both young people had matured, and took their devotion for one another with an amused seriousness. As some older members of the family commented, it was good to see two members of the younger generation who did not spend all their time at house parties or dancing the night away.

In fact, James and Margaret Mary reveled in each other's company. When they were apart, they wrote letters daily. James, under his wife's guidance, had begun to enjoy books outside of those called for by his profession; he was also beginning to taste the delights of serious music. In some of his letters he wrote poems. One read:

> Across the hidden places of my heart,
> You search me out;

Following the tracery of my daily life
So Death can never conquer
The secret generations of our souls.

The newlyweds spent a happy three weeks in Paris, giving up three days to Marcel and Marie Grenot—though Margaret Railton, as she now was, knew nothing of the sealed package James passed over in private to Marie. Much lay behind the delivery, not least the great turning point in James' own life, which had certainly paved the way for their marriage.

It had happened very early in 1912, just after he had returned to the Royal Military College.

James was aware that many changes were afoot. Over the previous Christmas Andrew, now promoted to Commander, had been beset by questions concerning the sudden, controversial appointment of Winston Churchill as First Lord of the Admiralty.

Churchill had arrived, like a strong breath of sea air, at the Admiralty, as First Lord, in October 1911. His Navy Board was announced in November, and stories concerning new plans and proposals began to run like wildfire.

"I don't suppose my old chief will last for long," Andrew told Giles, John and Charles. "Come to that, there's talk about giving the Intelligence Division a new title. Instead of a DID we're to have a Director of Naval Intelligence. And you know he's appointed old Jacky Fisher as his adviser?"

"I had heard," Giles said dryly. "So Fisher's himself again, and given up growing roses?" Then he chuckled. "We shall see great changes when Winston's at work. The man's a human engine."

James overheard this conversation, and more, though he was not prepared for change to touch him quite so quickly. In January, within a week of being back at Sandhurst, he received a personal message from the Commandant, waxed and sealed, asking James to call on him at the unusual hour of ten in the evening.

He arrived at the Commandant's quarters, and his superior beckoned him into his small, private study; showed the young man into a chair, and offered him both a drink and a cigar.

Finally, the Commandant settled himself and began to speak. "I'm sorry about the lateness of the hour, young Railton," he began, "but it's for the best. There are reasons why our meeting should be kept quiet."

Puzzled, James waited for more.

"First"—the Commandant gave him an unusually benign smile—"I should tell you there's no question concerning your commission. You'll be gazetted in the summer. Now, I presume you've some preference regarding a regiment?"

James sipped his brandy. "There's been talk of a Flying Corps, sir. That's what I really want."

The Commandant smiled, then bluntly suggested that he should apply for a commission in the 2nd Battalion Hampshire Regiment.

James opened his mouth, and was about to say that he did not see himself in the Hampshires, when the Commandant cut in. "My own regiment actually. Now, listen carefully. The Hampshire Regiment would welcome you, though I'm not certain that you'll actually ever serve with it. I can say no more. Perhaps it *will* be this Flying Corps; or something else. My invitation to you comes from a special source. It will have side benefits which should interest you even more. Still keen on marrying old Mitchel's gel, are you?"

"Very much, sir."

"Good. The first proposition is the Hampshires. The second has a more urgent bearing. If you take your commission with the Hampshires, this summer, I can promise that you'll be posted back here, to the staff of the Royal Military College. Now that," he spoke slowly, "would make me effectively your Commanding Officer, and I'd gladly give my immediate blessing to your marriage."

"I would be an officer on the staff here?"

"We think a lot of you, Railton. Mull it over. Be grateful if you could let me have your decision before the week's out."

James did not have to give the matter any thought. That, he imagined, was the end of it. Marriage at Christmas, with his commission, and a wonderful posting to Sandhurst.

All this came to pass; yet, beneath the surface, other things began to happen. A few weeks after his conversation with the Commandant, James received a letter from his uncle. The letter was disarmingly simple.

> My dear James,
> I know that you can arrange to be free on most Saturdays, and I wonder if you would be good enough to visit me, in London, on Saturday next, to discuss some rather important family business.
> It would be best, under the circumstances, if you did not come to Eccleston Square, or my club. So I would be grateful if you would meet me, at twelve noon, outside the Duke of York's Theatre, St. Martin's Lane.
> Please do not reply to this. I shall wait for you until 12:30 P.M., and trust you can be there.
>
> With all best wishes,
> Yr. Affect. Uncle,
> GILES RAILTON

4

James had too many of the Railton characteristics not to be intrigued by Giles' letter. A hundred armed guards would not have stopped him going to this meeting. On the appointed day he even arrived outside the Duke of York's Theatre ten minutes early.

There was no sign of Giles. People passed by; the traffic flowed in its orderly chaos. Then, on the stroke of noon, a cab drew up and two well-dressed men alighted.

One remained by the cab door while the other came straight over to James. "Mr. Railton?"

"Yes."

"Mr. James Railton?"

"Correct."

The man produced a small card which he quickly handed to James, barely giving the young officer cadet time to read what was written on it in Giles' more legible hand:

> James—Trust me. Go with these men. They will take you to someone very important. Listen well to what he says. Yrs. G.R.

The man almost snatched the card back, saying, "This way, sir," and taking James' arm.

As James allowed himself to be led to the cab, the second man moved around the vehicle, to the far door, so that once James was in, he found himself restricted: sandwiched between the two.

The blinds were quickly pulled down, and they rumbled off, fast, the cab taking constant twists and turns. The first stranger apologized for the blinds being drawn and the uncomfortable speed. "It's not really advisable for you to know where we're going. For your own sake. In our business we have to do many peculiar things." He had a flat, unaccented voice betraying no particular class.

They rode in silence for the best part of an hour, and when the cab finally came to a stop it was suggested that James remain quite still, in his seat.

The second man got down, leaving the door open. In a moment he was back, giving an "All clear."

The first man addressed James. "When you leave the cab, move quickly. There's a house directly in front of you. Go up the steps and through the green door. We'll be with you all the time."

James did as they told him, seeing a large gray house to his front. There were railings and area steps, while a further six broad steps led to the green-painted front door, standing slightly ajar.

The door closed behind them. They were in an uncarpeted and virtually undecorated hallway.

"Right. Up the stairs, please."

"May I ask—" James began.

One of the men merely gave him a friendly but firm nudge. "There's someone waiting to see you. Can we go?" Then they took him through the house, along corridors and across bare rooms, until they stood in another, wider, passage, with a large door to their right. The first man tapped at the door, and a hearty voice called, "Come."

"Mr. Railton, sir," announced the leading man, and James found himself in a pleasant room, facing a man he judged to be about fifty years of age, seated in a comfortable leather chair behind a large, military-style desk.

"Good. Well done, lads." The man behind the desk beamed up at James' two guards. "You may leave us alone. I'll signal if I need you." He motioned for James to be seated on an old stuffed armchair.

The man was big and friendly, dressed in an elegant gray suit. The round face was slightly weather-beaten, as though at one time or another he had spent many hours facing wind and weather. James privately identified him as Royal Navy. He had that clear-eyed confidence observed in many of his Uncle Andrew's colleagues.

"I would like some kind of explanation, sir," James began. "My uncle—"

"The admirable Giles Railton." The naval man gave a gentle laugh. You could feel the charm ooze from him. A great hit with the ladies, James thought.

"Giles Railton," he continued, "put me on to you. I'm looking for chaps with spunk and spirit. Men with a taste for adventure."

"Sir, with respect, before we continue might I ask to whom I am speaking?"

"I'm *so* sorry." He appeared genuinely mollifying. "Just call me C. Most people do. I assure you, young Railton, your Uncle Giles, who happens to be a good friend, would not have put me on to you if he thought our meeting a waste of time. Now, do you object to a few questions?"

Rarely, James later discovered, did anyone resist this mystery man. He was used to being obeyed, yet had a knack of quietly charming that obedience. In spite of the friendliness there was a distinct touch of steel beneath the velvet.

C began to go through James' academic training, his background, time at Sandhurst and the arrangements for his future.

"You appear to know all about me, sir."

C gave a full and hearty laugh. "I *should* know all about you. I more or less arranged the Hampshire Regiment business and the posting to the Royal Military College in the hope you'd fall in with a little plan of mine. Now, your French and German...."

They established James' proficiency in both languages, then C smiled warmly, saying that he understood a marriage had been arranged.

"In confidence, sir. If all goes well, we're to marry at Christmas."

"Capital. Now, what about the flying?"

They talked on for a good hour and a half, C quizzing James about things such as his view of world politics, the ins and outs of military tactics, then switching to flying and the possible uses of aeroplanes in war.

At one point he said, "You've a fertile imagination. Let me put this to you. Assume we are at war. Suppose there is information to be had by dropping a spy behind the front lines. That a possibility?"

"As long as you pick the right place. Somewhere quiet where you can land and take off with some degree of safety. And not get spotted, of course."

C nodded, looking pleased, and they continued to talk.

At last C sat bolt upright in his chair. "Right, James Railton. Let me tell you that I like the cut of your jib. Sorry about all the deception in bringing you here, but we have to be careful in our trade. We've had our eyes on you for some time now. After our talk today, I can tell you that we'd be glad if you served with us. I'd like to offer you an appointment. We can use you if you'll come to us."

"Sir, who exactly are you?"

C revealed that he was in control of all intelligence matters outside British territory. "I deal with agents and possible agents—spies, if you will—in all foreign countries."

"The Secret Service?"

"If that's what you want to call it. Yes, you could say that I'm head of at least part of the Secret Service. James, I'd like you to join us. Do a spot of training first of course."

So James was quietly and painlessly introduced into what was to become his life's work. He returned to Sandhurst, was commissioned that summer and suddenly discovered a shadowy world just under the surface of normal life.

At a moment's notice he would receive orders, usually by hand, which took him into what would become the new reality for him, a twilight place with a different set of values and a fresh language.

He learned codes, wireless telegraphy, methods of surveillance; he studied street plans of all the great European cities and was taught about methods of communication.

It all sounded exceptionally simple: almost like a child's game. The truth, as he was soon to discover, was very different.

On his honeymoon, when he handed the package to Marie Grenot, James was carrying out his first assignment for his new Commanding Officer, C.

Giles Railton, unknown to James, had need to pass information quietly to his daughter, who had been officially warned off seeing her German Military contact in Paris.

So, between the first pleasures of his married life—the delicious bouts of lovemaking, and pillow-talking, James Railton was blooded into the hidden world of his family.

5

And, in Berlin, Gustav Steinhauer retained his desk at the Wilhelmstrasse, but was a constant visitor to Number 8. There, he often saw the beautiful young woman who had been introduced to him on his first visit. His experience in matters clandestine suggested to him that the girl was being prepared for some other dark operation spawned from Nicolai's furtive imagination—certainly the new Chief of Intelligence appeared more concerned with devious plots than the day-to-day running of his Military Intelligence officers.

It was now that Steinhauer felt the moment was right to send The Fisherman into action—to put him "in place" as the next generation of the trade would say.

It took five days to brief him. The docks and naval bases would be his first concern, though there were also other things.

"Never stay in the same place for more than a few weeks at one time," he cautioned the big man. "Keep moving, remain in touch, using all the methods we have taught you."

Steinhauer had received the descriptions of the way The Fisherman had axed the Irish traitor to death. He could never admit it, but Ulhurt frightened the bowels out of him.

The Fisherman traveled by various routes to England. He then went to Scotland for two weeks, renewing his acquaintance with Mrs. MacGregor of Invergordon before moving south to London. He absorbed background. In the event of hostilities, Hans-Helmut Ulhurt would be fully operational.

Chapter Eleven

1

The man whom James Railton knew as C was, of course, the naval officer Captain Mansfield Smith-Cumming, in charge of the new Intelligence Service's Foreign Department, eventually to become the Secret Intelligence Service, or MI6, just as his opposite number's—Vernon Kell's—department would be designated MI5.

Giles Railton was in constant contact with these departments and shared many secrets with them. Both were passing through the fledgling stage, learning their trade in a somewhat leisured fashion. By recruiting men like James, C was preparing himself against the day of possible war.

The seasons of the following year, 1913, ran their usual course. By midsummer it became known among the family that James and Margaret Mary had lost no time. There was to be yet another Railton.

In the world of the secret trade, Patrick Quinn had retired, his place, as Head of the Branch being taken by the astute Basil Thomson—a professional of military bearing and ruthless instinct, yet a man who could charm when necessary. Also, to Vernon Kell's particular relief, appropriate changes had been made in the Official Secrets Act.

It was during the summer of 1913 that Giles again turned his attention to his daughter-in-law, Bridget, in Ireland, deciding to visit her and meet in the most clandestine way possible.

He knew the risk, and conveyed it to Smith-Cumming and Vernon Kell. They were all three aware of the precarious situation surrounding their agents working in Ireland.

Parliament was set to push through the Home Rule Bill, but division within Ireland itself appeared to become more clear cut as each day passed. In Dublin, the Bill's third reading in the House of Commons was hailed, in January 1913, as a great national triumph. In Ulster, however, it was a different tale. Nine months later, almost a quarter of a million Ulstermen were to sign a "Solemn League and Covenant" in their own blood, swearing to resist Home Rule at all costs.

"It's only a matter of time," Giles told Bridget. They met, at the corner of a wood, near the ancient beauty spot of Glendalough. It was five-thirty in the morning, the sky a soft pearl heralding a beautiful day.

Only Giles knew that three of Vernon Kell's men, who had traveled independently, watched from safe vantage points. He had brought a heel of bread and some cheese which the pair ate as they talked.

"I know it." Bridget lived in fear, and Giles was aware of it. Her bravery sometimes staggered him.

"Neither side appear to have arms in quantity as yet. But it will happen, and soon. Then there'll be much killing."

"The Unionists have the means, or so the people who talk to me say."

"True enough. People like Carson and Craig can ship arms into a hundred different places. But your people—the old Irish Republican Brotherhood— have their ways also. You're still seeing them? They suspect nothing?"

"If they do, nobody shows it." She did not smile; the subject was too dangerous for smiles.

Giles considered the terrible plight of the double agent. "We must find some genuine information for you to give them. Something that will make them even more confident about you."

They talked for another half hour—Bridget passing on names and addresses of Fenians she knew to be active; Giles going over new possibilities of communications. He wished it were Malcolm and not the girl, but Malcolm did not even know Giles was in Ireland.

"Soon," he told her, before leaving. "As soon as we can plant something genuine, I'll let you know. Take care of yourself, and watch them, every single one of them."

At home, as the year drew to a close, Margaret Mary Railton gave birth, on November 20th, to a fine son—Donald Giles. James was a father at the age of just twenty years, and like a child himself at the very idea of it.

Christmas passed at Redhill, with most of the family present, all but for the Grenots, and Malcolm and Bridget. Almost before they were aware of it, the year crept to its end. The Railtons, wherever they were, heard the bells toll midnight on December 31st, and knew they now lived in the year of Our Lord Nineteen Hundred and Fourteen.

Nobody realized they were moving closer to blackness and terror.

The old ways were as good as gone. A new era had dawned.

2

Padraig O'Connell sat by the roadside, in the early morning of a new day: June 28th, 1914. The sun had just tilted over the horizon, spreading light down over the Wicklow Hills, touching the outcrops of stone, bringing the fir trees to life.

Somewhere, up to his right, a deer moved, fleetingly, against a copse. Then he saw his contact, coming on foot across the fields.

They greeted one another as strangers who might be passing on a summer walk.

"Well, so." Padraig's head turned toward his contact; still as stone.

"Well?"

"How much has been passed on? What do they know in London from their officers in Dublin?"

The contact looked him steadily in the eyes. "They know what all Ireland knows. That the Ulster Volunteer Force is now well armed to the tune of some forty thousand rifles."

"Nothing else? No secrets?"

"Only rumor. They've been told that arms have been purchased in Germany and will be on their way to the Home Rule Volunteers within the month. The rumor is that Casement is behind it and that they'll be landed somewhere near Kingstown."

Padraig smiled to himself, for this last was a piece of nonsense he had hoped would be accepted as truth. Sir Roger Casement and his friend Erskine Childers had bought arms for the Home Rulers to defend themselves against the Ulstermen. But they would be landed a long way from Kingstown. "And that is all? Everything that's gone?"

"Everything."

"You swear to me?"

"I swear."

"Well, you take care now. If anything else is passed back to London, let the boy know and I shall be with you quickly."

"I'll keep my side of the bargain, have no fear of that."

The contact began to move away, then stopped and faced O'Connell. "I do this for one reason only. I love my wife more than country. I want her left alone and in peace. I want her safe."

"And you run when I tell you to run." Padraig O'Connell gave him that twisted leprechaun smile. "You can run for me over this business of rifles for the Brotherhood."

Malcolm did not respond, making to move away again. O'Connell called, as if he had gone farther back up the road, "It would be for your own benefit, and remove all suspicion from you, *Mister* Railton."

"Yes?"

"Oh yes. You're after having the confidence of many officers in Dublin, so."

"Some."

"Then if I give you the date and place of the landings—for the guns and ammunition, I mean—you could pass it on."

"Defeat your own cause?"

"Not if I give it to you a shade out of true, like a few degrees out. Enough for the soldiers to arrive, near the right place, and an hour late."

"I see."

"Do you now? Good. Then that's what we'll do. The date, my friend, is to be July 26th. Next month. In the small hours, and at Howth. You know Howth?"

"Just north of Dublin, yes. In the small hours, you say?"

O'Connell wagged a finger. It was not a gesture of fun, but rather almost obscene in its warning. "I'll give you a more precise time nearer the date, but it'll be a couple of hours late, so don't be taking liberties, *Mister* Railton. You'll be the only outsider to know. Your stock with your Dublin officers will be high enough for being almost right when the police and Army arrive just too late to catch the lads. You follow me?"

"Oh, I follow you." Malcolm felt the bile in his own mouth.

O'Connell still smiled as he watched the tall, loping figure disappearing up the road. The English can be such fools, he thought. Both of them—the Irish Railton and her English husband. Both working for him and the cause, and neither knowing what the other did. If one tried to be clever, or false, the other would almost certainly give it away, and if that happened. . . . He cocked his head, closed one eye and leveled the forefinger of his right hand at a stone, the thumb back like the hammer of a revolver. Jerking the thumb forward, Padraig O'Connell made a noise like a small pistol shot.

3

On the same day—June 28th, 1914—except for Marcel, Marie, Malcolm and Bridget, the Railtons gathered at Redhill Manor, having come for a whole week.

Charles and Mildred had come with Mary Anne, who, even after her Coming-Out, was still pestering to become a nurse.

Giles arrived quietly.

Andrew and Charlotte were alone, for Rupert was at sea; Caspar with his regiment; and Ramillies in London—now a junior member of the Foreign Service, he was required for duty. On instructions from his grandfather, Giles, he had not told his father exactly for whom he was working.

Andrew spoke a great deal about the possibility of going back to sea before long. There was much talk in Admiralty circles of a new DNI, the favorite being Captain Reginald Hall—known to all as "Blinker" because of a slight tic which manifested itself by a constant blinking of the eyes. Hall was later promoted to rear admiral, and eventually gained a knighthood.

Churchill was still blowing a gale through the hallowed Admiralty, and Andrew had been right in thinking the First Sea Lord—Bridgeman—would not last. His tenure had run for barely a year, and Winston was organizing, and reorganizing, with characteristic enthusiasm.

As for James and Margaret Mary; well, they knew what they were there for; and the new baby could be cosseted by all.

It so happened that on the previous evening James' old friend Richard Farthing had telephoned, asking if he could drop in for the day. Nobody objected, though Sara did not seem overpleased.

That morning John Railton awoke with a slight headache. He bathed, dressed and went down to breakfast, quite content, for the morning was beautiful and appeared set fair for a perfect summer day.

Someone suggested a game of croquet later.

John mentioned Dick Farthing's visit and Sara frowned.

Andrew said he wanted to laze.

James and Margaret Mary slipped back upstairs, undressed, locked the door and laid themselves on the bed again. Margaret Mary took his hands in hers and began to kiss them, placing each finger by turn in her mouth. James found this highly arousing.

4

"I think I shall take a walk," John Railton said as they finished breakfast. It was a little after ten. "Anyone coming? The rose garden?"

"I'd love it." Sara wanted to please him. John Railton had done so much for her; living at Redhill Manor had really changed her life and broadened her perspective.

James and Margaret Mary reappeared and said they would come out shortly. Both Andrew and Charlotte caught the look which passed between the young lovers. Privately each wished for their own youth once more. Not that they complained about being more mature lovers. To be alone at Redhill Manor, without the ties of their brood, was stimulating.

Sara took John's arm and they left, following the route out through the drawing room.

The roses looked beautiful: great crimson miracles, like blood among thorns of greenery. It was the best part of summer, John said. June was the best month. He even quoted a single line from Browning: "All June I bound the rose in sheaves." Then he picked a perfect bloom and handed it to Sara.

She said it was lovely, and John told her that it paled against her own beauty. "You've been the light of my life, Sara."

"Oh, John—you've pricked your thumb."

"It's nothing." He sucked the blood away and laughed. Then they heard the sound of a motor. "Dick's new toy coming up the drive."

Dick Farthing had just bought a Ford "Tourer," of which he was immensely proud.

"Let James and Margaret take care of him," Sara whispered. "It's nice to have the rose garden to ourselves. Lord, the air is so sweet." She took a deep breath, through her nose, smelling the grass and roses; the corn from the upper meadow; and the freshness of the morning. "There's no smell like an English summer," she said. Then: "Oh damn—I wanted to be alone with you."

John Railton looked up and saw James and Margaret Mary, hand in hand. Then he spotted Dick Farthing, the young man's brown eyes, and the lopsided smile on his face. "Hallo there," Dick called.

"He's come in his motor," Margaret Mary laughed as they approached.

John Railton raised an arm in greeting. Then the pain struck across his chest. Far away he heard Sara cry out, and arms went around him to stop the fall. He could not get his breath, and everything tilted, blurring around him, as they gently lowered him to the ground. "I'm . . . sorry," he tried to say. "All right . . . in a minute."

James knelt beside his father, and Dick moved in close to Sara, who was on both knees, cradling John's head in her hands.

"Nothing . . ." The pain clawed at his chest. He wanted to say it was nothing; that in a moment it would pass, but the breath would not come.

Through the pain he also smelled the sweetness of the air: the soft, gentle scent of the dark night closing in.

He did not hear James' almost strangled cry, "Pa! Pa! Dick, get someone. Get the doctor, for God's sake," and James saw Sara's face, eyes widening as she looked down at his father, not believing what she knew.

The body was completely relaxed, the jaw slack in death and all the blood gone from the face.

Sara began to cry, softly, half-whispering John's name, as Andrew and Charlotte came running into the rose garden.

"Leave him here, in the sun, for a while: until the doctor comes, anyway." Sara spoke slowly, desperately trying to control herself. Then: "Oh my God, no! No! Not John! No! No!"

But John Railton, Member of Parliament for Central Berkshire, heard nothing, lying dead in his rose garden, by the heart attack he had known must come.

5

The General's death, a little over four years previously, had signaled change for the Railtons. John's sudden passing brought crisis, but like some minor irony built into a Greek tragedy, for there were two more deaths on that summer day which brought supreme crisis to the world at large.

They took place some one thousand miles southeast of Haversage, in the Balkans. The Archduke Franz Ferdinand, with his wife, the Grand Duchess Sophie, did not even want to be there, in the town of Sarajevo, Bosnia. He hated the area, but the Emperor had commanded that he attend the maneuvers in both the provinces of Bosnia and Herzegovina.

First there was the small official reception, then a short drive in Count von Harrach's car to the Town Hall. On the way someone threw a bomb at the car, but it exploded under the vehicle following them. So, when they reached the Town Hall, the Archduke insisted on being taken to see the injured, in the hospital.

The procession drove on, but near the Appel Quay the leading cars turned in the wrong direction. Count von Harrach shouted to his driver to stop, and the Archduke looked about him, wearily. He saw the name on the building. It was a shop: SCHILLERS STORE. Then he saw the deep-set blue eyes and the long hair of the young man walking boldly to the car. After that, he heard the shots.

There was very little pain, and he was more concerned about Soferl and the noise around them. His lips felt wet, and he saw Soferl's face above his, and heard her voice, just for a second, saying, "For God's sake! What has happened to you?" Then, with horror, he saw her eyes glaze over as she slipped down, her face dropping between his knees.

Oh my God, he thought, knowing the worst and summoning strength to speak. "Soferl, Soferl, don't die. Live for my children."

A long way off, von Harrach's voice came. "Is Your Highness in great pain?"

"It is nothing," he said, feeling little, yet knowing he could not move.

Then he repeated, "It is nothing," and said again, "It is nothing," and again, and again, each time softer until the blood welled into his throat and the floating darkness crept quietly in.

The car drove very quickly to the Governor's residence, the Konak, and they were made as comfortable as possible.

The Grand Duchess Sophie died first.

A little later she was followed by her husband, the Archduke Franz Ferdinand, heir apparent to the Hapsburg Empire, the prospective follower in the footsteps of the great Emperor Franz Joseph.

Murdered. Sarajevo, in Bosnia. June 28th, 1914.

It was the one act, among so many others, to be signaled out as the great moment when history changed direction in the twentieth century. The Dark Ages were about to return. Hope was gone for millions, taken away by a bullet that severed the jugular vein and lodged in the spine.

PART II

To Ply a Trade
(July 1914–December 1915)

Chapter Twelve

1

Two weeks after the assassination of the Archduke Franz Ferdinand, and the coincidental death of John Railton, Giles sat in the General's Study at Redhill Manor.

John's funeral had taken place one week to the day after his death. Now, Giles returned to Haversage for serious discussions with Sara—for the will had left the family in a state of crisis. Precedent had been broken.

Characteristically, John had left everything to *My dearest wife, Sara.* The will was perfectly clear and uncontestable. John had looked upon her as a Railton, so it did not make any difference if she remarried. Her name could be changed at any time, which meant that the ancient lands, tenancies, houses and estates of the family had passed out of their control.

The General would have seen the irony. Giles recalled a day of wind and rain, when he was about fourteen years of age and his brother home at Haversage on leave. They had walked together up onto the Downs, the General—a captain then—talking of the Roman legions which had passed this way. He spoke of the hard training given to Roman soldiers, then, in a sudden change of mood, had stood, rain blowing into his face, an arm describing a great half-circle as he mocked traditional parental standards. "One day, my boy," he shouted against the wind, "all this will be yours." And on the way back he had said that of course it would never belong to Giles, because he, William, would provide strong sons to carry on the line.

Every ploy had failed. Even the idea, against Giles' secret nature, of bringing Malcolm back to help run the Estate fell on Sara's deaf ears.

"Though the last thing I wish is to keep the Railton heritage from the hands of true members of the family." Sara looked pale from shock and grief. The meeting with Giles was not easy. "You've only just told me that you believe we're on the brink of war. The men will be needed elsewhere, for a time anyway. It is better that I should stay here and run things. For the moment at least."

She had been angered by his suggestion of trouble if she chose to marry again— "John's hardly cold in his grave. I find all this offensive, Uncle Giles. . . ."

"Please, Sara, call me Giles. I—"

"No. How could I think of marriage to anyone?"

He tried to interrupt again, but she would not be stopped. "If, at some very distant date, I *do* decide to remarry, then I shall consult the family and the solicitors. As it is, I must continue here. Please, just leave me alone; let me get on with the things that matter to all of us."

There was no point in arguing further, so Giles, disgruntled, capitulated.

Over dinner on the second night he studied Sara with more than usual interest. It was as though the fact of being part of this family had given the young woman a new kind of resolution. Not every girl in her situation would opt for running a huge estate, which was more like a vast family business.

They spoke of the family now: Giles asking after James, whom he had seen only briefly at the funeral.

"Sad, of course, but he's divinely happy with Margaret Mary." Sara smiled. "Not that I really understand what he's up to. He does appear to spend a great deal of time in London, and even abroad."

"Really?" Not even Giles' eyes gave him away. He knew exactly what James was up to. "Abroad, eh? Yes, I think I did hear something about his being off on a trip a few weeks ago."

Sara had never noticed that Giles' eyebrows were so frosted with gray until he raised them now. "He spent a whole month in Germany. What would an Army officer be doing at the Kiel Regatta, Giles?"

"Looking out for his own." He did not have to lie directly. James had been there as a military observer; just as some naval officers went along to watch military maneuvers. "The delegation to Kiel was rather special. Mr. Churchill was there—"

"And half the senior officers of the Royal Navy. Andrew seemed quite annoyed because he was not invited."

"Andrew's only a commander. Hardly a senior officer. Though the whole business of Kiel is quite incomprehensible. Either Mr. Churchill's very naive, or more than usually Machiavellian." Giles gave her a thin smile. "Churchill has some idea that we should pool all military and naval information with the Germans—particularly naval. The First Lord, it seems, feels that a frank exchange of information will do away with any spy mania."

He paused to sip the excellent Pouilly-Fumé which Sara was serving with the trout before adding, "Much good will it do now."

"You honestly think it's that serious?"

"Very. All trust is ebbing away. I'd never trust the Imperial German Navy with my laundry, let alone the battle order of the Grand Fleet."

"Especially now that you have a grandson with the Grand Fleet."

Sara, Giles thought, was not given to being arch, but the way she spoke of Rupert was as near as damn it. "Rupert." He nodded. "Yes, Andrew's very proud that one of his sons has followed in his footsteps. Rupert's in *Monmouth*."

"Yes, I *do* know." She laughed. "I've heard Andrew preening about it. Rupert's obviously very much the family favorite now he's in an armored cruiser."

Sara turned the conversation to her plans for the Estate and the Farm, but a section of Giles' mind strayed into the area of family secrets, and like a scribbled note in his head, there was a nudge of frustration over Bridget's latest piece of intelligence.

His daughter-in-law had reported the details of a landing of arms for the

Home Rulers near Dublin. Giles duly passed it on to the Military, who in turn told him that their people, on the spot in Dublin, had an informer of their own. The details were similar to those Bridget had given, but not quite the same. They were convinced that their own man had the correct information. He would have wagered on Bridget.

Giles was to recall the thought a couple of days later when Ramillies came into his office with news that the police and a detachment of the King's Own Scottish Borderers had failed to foil the landing of arms. "They were landed at three A.M., near Howth," Ramillies said. It was exactly as Bridget had reported, and the military information was that the landing would be at five in the morning at Malahide. Two hours late and a few miles out.

2

Padraig O'Connell drained his glass, grinning at his comrade, Fintan McDermott. "Sure we had 'em by the knackers. Confusion and consternation, Fintan. The boys were grand. Worked like true soldiers of the revolution."

"And the police, with the bloody British Army, ended up only nineteen rifles to the good." Fintan spat loudly onto the bar floor. "The bastards go for our lads, but never a murmur when the Ulster Volunteers had their weapons handed to them on a plate, so."

They were drinking together, in a bar right on O'Connell Street, and, almost as Fintan spoke, the sound of loud jeering came floating in from outside. Padraig nodded toward the door. "Something's up. Let's take a look, then."

Outside, along the broad Dublin thoroughfare, they could see an approaching crowd—a shouting mass of drab men, women and children capering and dancing in the middle of the street.

"It's the soldiers," Fintan muttered as the khaki uniforms came into view between the crowd, surrounding and marching with them.

Padraig nodded. "King's Own Scottish Borderers. Some of the bastards that were out last night."

His companion grinned. "Come on, then, let's have some fun." Together they moved toward the crowd.

It was a small detachment of some twenty men, a sergeant and a young officer. All looked tired after their night chasing around Malahide and Howth, ten miles or so north of the city. But the men marched with set faces, only the young officer occasionally glancing at the people who milled around them shouting, "British out . . . Home Rule now . . . Go home now . . ."

The men marched toward the bridge over the Liffey, and the crowd grew. From time to time the Sergeant murmured words of encouragement: "Steady, lads. Soon be back at the Castle." But the chorus became louder, more violent. The Sergeant could not see his young officer starting to twitch—a slight tic of the facial muscles.

Padraig and Fintan ran alongside, enjoying the spontaneous taunting.

The detachment turned into Bachelor's Walk, a small quay running alongside the river, and, as it did so, the chanting reached a pitch: "Home Rule NOW ... Home RULE NOW ... HOME RULE NOW!!!"

The young subaltern's nerve finally cracked. With an unexpected command, he swung the squad about, and, before his Sergeant had time to do anything, the order was given.

Too late, Padraig realized what was happening. Even he could hardly believe his eyes as the officer heaved out his heavy Webley sidearm. The troops turned as one, the front rank dropping to their knees. Padraig yelled, "Fintan! Down! Fintan ..." He thrust out an arm to push his comrade to the pavement as the fusillade crashed out.

The bullet that killed Fintan McDermott nicked O'Connell's arm before splattering his friend's throat.

The crowd turned, some screaming in panic. There were other shouts—of the wounded; of women and children caught in the hail of lead. Then the sobering order from the cool, experienced, Sergeant: "Cease fire!"

Padraig saw a woman, her shawl covered in the blood waterfalling from her mouth; and another man lying on his back, eyes wide with the wonder of so suddenly meeting his Maker. Around him, the wounded lay groaning—a boy of about twelve years crying out, "Mammy ... Mammy," and the sound of the people crushing and cramming their way back toward O'Connell Street; while the troops were moved away at the double.

O'Connell cradled Fintan's body in his arms, the hatred washing over him, so that he shouted mindlessly, not even hearing his own voice, "You bastards! Bastards! Murdering bastards!"

There, on the pavement of Bachelor's Walk, with three people lying dead, and over thirty wounded, Padraig O'Connell made a vow. His soul would not be quiet until they were driven for all time from his country—from Ireland, which had been so cursed by English rule.

3

All Europe basked in sunshine, and for those many thousands on holiday in England there was little thought of war. The assassination of the Archduke had taken place hundreds of miles away—just another example of extravagant Balkan bloodshed.

By July any concern was centered on the latest business in Ireland. Three dead and thirty-eight civilians wounded in the center of Dublin by a section of the King's Own Scottish Borderers. The British newspapers and public-house politicians brooded, prophesying civil war across the Irish Sea.

Most of the British government were also on holiday, though keeping in close touch as the situation moved from bad to worse. They fought until the eleventh hour to avert the crisis, but pessimism prevailed.

For most people, when it came, war arrived like an unexpected thunderclap—sudden, and unconnected with anything that really concerned them.

Toward the end of July, James and Margaret Mary Railton arrived at Redhill Manor.

They had agreed to stay for a week, but as the days passed, Sara became more concerned by the way that James would hardly leave the vicinity of the house. She wanted to show off her plans for the Farm and Estate, but James had no inclination to move farther than the rose garden. Margaret Mary had no excuses to give.

"We do a great deal here for the local community," Sara told her as they walked across the upper meadow, "but I feel we could be more practical. The Farm, the Estate, can be made to pay handsomely. It's no sin to make money out of one's land."

Margaret Mary nodded, her mind far away. Much as she liked Sara, she hardly shared James' stepmother's tastes, her real interests lying in the arts: music, literature and the theater. She was an accomplished pianist, and, as James, given half a chance, would tell anyone, better read than most men of her age and class.

But, as she walked the Railton land on that hot afternoon, Margaret Mary's mind was a long way from Sara's vision of a future profit-making Estate and farm; or even her beloved books and music. Distractedly, she dwelt on her husband and the future. Though James tended to play the bluff, hearty soldier, she knew that underneath his military manner lay something more sensitive. Theirs was a relationship of sensuality on a cerebral as well as physical plane. Sometimes she felt that James was almost embarrassed by this, and recently his protective shell appeared to have grown thicker.

During the drive down to Haversage, his eyes fixed on the hot, dusty road ahead, he said quietly, "It's going to happen, and there's precious little the statesmen, priests, lawyers or even hired assassins can do about it."

"War?" A sense of cold in the pit of her stomach. Nobody—she thought—knew what to expect from a modern war. "Surely not! England doesn't have to be involved. It's not our quarrel—the Balkans: Serbia, Austria, Russia. And the damned Germans. . . ."

"Events make it our quarrel." He went on to explain the delicate situation: how the Austro-Hungarian differences with Serbia, together with those between Germany and Russia, had merely been waiting, as though in storage, until some opportunity presented itself to bring their rising hatred to the point of violence. "We're certain the Kaiser sees the Archduke's assassination as an opportunity not to be missed," James shouted above the engine and rushing wind. "They've played it very close. A long game as Uncle Giles would say. Kaiser Bill continuing with his sailing trip around Norway, while the Emperor remained in the Tyrol. We suspect they were planning all the time. Now the good old Kaiser's turned up in Potsdam. There's talk of doing some old-fashioned bartering over France and Belgium, but the government isn't going to wear that. I fear we'll be at war within the week."

"Who are *we,* James?"

"Who . . . ? What . . . ?"

"You said . . . *We* are certain . . . *We* suspect. Who are *we?*"

James glanced at her, then back to the road ahead. "Military people." Then, flatly, with no feeling: "Maggie, you must have some idea of the kind of work I do."

"I find it odd that a Sandhurst instructor's always dashing around Europe. You disappear for weeks on end." Somewhat cooly she added, "I have no reason to believe you keep a mistress . . ."

"Maggie!"

"Well . . ." The laugh came back to her voice. James loved the laugh. "Well, you service me enough when you're at home—and I'm certainly glad of that. My girlfriends tell me they come off rather badly in that department when their husbands find a little actress or a tart to play with."

"Good God—do you all get together and discuss your—"

"Sex lives," she supplied. "Yes, I think we do. The silly brainless girls I'm forced to mix with seem to think they should provide the stud references in case they play musical beds at one of their idiotic little house parties. I suppose it's really quite healthy, Jamie."

"Don't call me Jamie!" he snapped. He disliked the diminutive for himself, though called his wife Maggie without turning a hair.

"Then don't treat me as though I was one of those idle, pretty ladies who haunt country houses at weekends. I'm asking plainly enough: what *do* you do, James? Tell me straight."

He stopped the car by the roadside, leaving the engine ticking loudly. A horse reared up in the field across the hedge; then, snorting, cantered away.

James looked her full in the eyes. "I'm under instruction as an intelligence officer. When I go away, that's part of it."

"And when you go aboard?" He sensed she was very still, like someone in church, at prayer. Some doves cooed from a copse on the far side of the road. You could hear them, all mixed up with the low growl of the idling engine.

"Sometimes it's a test. Twice it's been to find out things, and talk to people. Now, you must promise not to tell a living soul, not Sara even. Certainly none of your friends."

She gave a little nod. "You're a spy."

He said that no, it wasn't that easy. "Like talking about the world situation, it's an oversimplification. Spy is not a word we—"

She laid a hand on his arm. "It's all right, darling James. I know. I've suspected for some time. You Railtons are such a secretive bunch." She remained silent for a moment. "Funny, everyone's been so full of that business in Dublin and the possibility of civil war. We should have been looking further afield."

She held on to his hand, nails digging into his palm. "Thank you for telling me. I worry. I love you so much, you see, and if war does come, then I shall worry a lot more. But I won't ask anything, I promise."

He moved, as though to begin the drive again, but she would not let go of his hand. "Turn the engine off."

He did as she said, and she took him by the hand, into the field where the horse now stood a few hundred yards away. There, behind the hedge, she laid herself on the grass, lifted her skirt and took him. It was exciting for both of them, out in the open, with only turf under them, the warmth of the sun on their bare flesh, and the possibility of discovery adding a piquancy to the experience.

Now, as she walked with Sara, Margaret Mary recalled the moment so vividly that she could almost feel James within her. Sara's voice shattered the daydream. "Oh Lord, what's this?" Billy Crook was galloping toward them on Mr. Marconi, one of the big grays. He pulled the horse up close to the two women, touching his cap. Billy was a tall, good-looking lad of almost seventeen now. He spoke directly to Sara. "Mr. James sends his compliments, Ma'am. He asks if you'd do him the honor of going back to the house as quickly as possible."

Sara thanked him, noticing, not for the first time, that he had inherited the Railton nose and eyes. Something really would have to be done for Billy.

"What on earth can James want..." Sara began, then saw the look on Margaret Mary's face. "Oh no? You don't think they've let things get that far? Not war?"

"I have to get back to town." James was calm. Margaret Mary simply asked if it was the worst.

"I fear so. The Austrians have bombarded Belgrade. Half Europe appears to have mobilized, and the German Imperial Army seems to be preparing to move through Belgium. Ultimatums and notes are flying about like confetti."

Within the hour they were walking out to the car.

Sara watched. James had gone through a great change. She felt that his marriage had probably helped, but there was something else—an inner reserve, giving off an almost monastic feeling. There was a part of him which Sara could not reach, and she wondered if Margaret Mary was able to penetrate it.

4

In Berlin, as matters became clear, Steinhauer was at work day and night. If it really were to be war, he would have to visit other countries right away. First, though, he had particular work to do.

One of his priorities was to send a series of messages to six spies in England. There were various ways he could do this: by courier—a neutral sailor or the like, who would post the messages to certain addresses by wireless, using the link now established via the Embassy in Washington, which was able to relay coded signals to England and France. Or by a simple personal letter, taken out and posted in Switzerland.

Before the Fisherman had left, Steinhauer carefully set up three new "post offices," unknown to Naval or Military Intelligence. One in Scotland, another in the British Midlands and the third on England's south coast. The Fisherman would call at all three, making the journeys once a month.

He sent six letters to six different names. Inside was a one-word order, hidden in ordinary pieces of correspondence, plus the designated code for each agent. These spies were Angler, Dust, D12, D14, Brewer and Saint. Only Angler and Saint were real—the same person, Ulhurt—the others being "ghosts," so that the number might confuse Steinhauer's superiors. The key word in the letters for Angler and Saint was *hook*. That one word meant that the Fisherman was to begin his sabotage work.

5

In London the whole family knew that it was only a matter of days, maybe hours. Caspar telephoned his mother, Charlotte, to say that he expected movement orders soon. She must not worry if she heard nothing for a while.

Mary Anne—who had got her way and was training at St. Thomas' Hospital—came home full of the rumor that the student nurses there would be asked to take up some form of active duty immediately after they qualified.

Andrew was now sleeping at the Admiralty, just as Charles spent all his time at the—considerably enlarged—MO5 offices.

Giles, with his grandson Ramillies in almost constant attendance, rarely left his suite of rooms in the Foreign Office. It was there, at roughly the moment James was returning from Redhill Manor, that the first Railton family catastrophe exploded.

The telegram came quite normally. Ramillies even recognized the name, but could make nothing of the contents. It was brought over from one of the many convenient addresses Ramillies had come to know well. He had taken it in to his grandfather immediately.

As Giles read the piece of paper, Ramillies saw the change in his face, as though, in a second, he had come to his true age. There was shock and bewilderment in his eyes; lines appeared where none had been a moment before, while a terrible tremor overtook his hands.

"You all right, sir? Is—"

"Go, Ramillies." The croak of an old man. "Go. Just for a few minutes. I need to be alone."

When Ramillies had left the room, Giles Railton stared back at the paper, reading it again: MRS JUNO LEFT PARIS UNEXPECTEDLY THIS MORNING WITH THE BLUE BOOK STOP INEXPLICABLE STOP PLEASE ADVISE SIGNED MARTHA.

He needed no code book to decipher the message. In plain language it read:

MDME GRENOT LEFT PARIS SUDDENLY THIS MORNING WITH KLAUS VON HIRSCH I NEED YOUR INSTRUCTIONS SIGNED MONIQUE.

Giles' own daughter, Marie, had turned coat and run off with the Assistant Military Attaché to the German Embassy in Paris, leaving her husband and children: betraying country and family. Giles ran a hand over his head, as though feverish. How in God's name could this have happened?

6

Possibly Giles Railton had not wished to read between the lines of Monique's regular reports from Paris. Certainly she had given him many hints that all was not well.

For the best part of four years now, the young girl, trained by Secret Service experts, had kept a close watch on Marie and Marcel Grenot, and become established in the area, living quietly in her small apartment above the Bistro Abbeaux, almost directly opposite the Grenots' Paris home. Monique was, to use the later trade argot, "part of the scenery."

After Marie had been advised to close down her activities because of the French authorities' suspicious, near paranoid, attitude, Giles had seriously considered pulling Monique out of Paris. But that extra sense, acquired through years of walking the secret corridors, told him to leave things as they were.

Later, when the first shockwaves of Marie's disappearance with von Hirsch had settled down, Giles admitted, with no reluctance, that all the signs had been there for some time. Despite the plea for caution; despite the two Grenot children; despite her former protestations that she was a loving wife and mother, nobody, least of all her own father, had taken into account that unstable phenomenon: love.

When it had all started, some years before, Marie was happy enough, with her growing family and a devoted if humorless French husband. In those days the General was still alive, and, together with her father had convinced her that a liaison with the handsome Attaché was for the good of her country and very much within the arcane and military tradition of the Railtons.

Only a few months before his death, the General had said to her, "Your father has entrusted you with a secret mission. You are one of the first Railton women to act, under orders, as a soldier." He had given her that particularly charming smile. "This assignment is a soldier's job."

Once the relationship between her and von Hirsch was established, Marcel had to be constantly soothed and reassured: lied to even; and at last Marie had found it necessary to give herself to the German. And very pleasant it turned out to be. So pleasant that Marie returned to him again and again. What she failed to comprehend—just as her father had failed—was that the affair, while well-faked by her in the early stages, began at the most dangerous time for any married woman: almost fourteen years into her marriage to Marcel.

Though she was not conscious of the fact, already, back in 1910, Marie had

become disillusioned with her husband. He was developing pernickety mannerisms; those irritating habits of a man rapidly becoming set in his ways; a
passion for order, born of his work. Marie suffered, like so many women, from
a sense of sameness settling her into a pattern of daily family life. Their mutual
passion was spent, for neither of them had the experience to inject new excitement into the intimate side of their marriage.

There was a more disturbing aspect within the Grenot ménage. Because of
the rigid way in which Marcel ran their family life, a strange barrier of diffidence
had grown between Marie and the two children—Paul and Denise.

The first oddity, reported to Giles by Monique, was the announcement that
Klaus von Hirsch had been retained for a second tour of duty at the German
Embassy in Paris—an unusual circumstance in diplomatic and military circles.

Secondly, Marie continued to see the German officer long after the embargo
on her work for the Intelligence Service: a fact known to Monique, and passed
on to Giles, who was also aware that his daughter now saw the German under
increasingly clandestine circumstances. He disregarded the signs. Danger to
his beloved daughter was nothing compared to the prize of access to any German
High Command moves concerning the von Schlieffen war plan. It is not likely
that young von Hirsch had any inkling at this time that his mistress was passing
information back to London, though the possibility can never be completely
ruled out.

The realities of the situation were there from the start. True, she went to
the first assignation with eyes open, trying to regard it as a duty to her country:
the wound received on the field of battle. Yet no wound could have been more
joyous or sweet than this, for Klaus injected new elements into lovemaking—
things she had dreamed of in feverish, guilty moments.

He would recite poetry as they made love, bucking to the rhythm of the
verses of comic songs; or take her suddenly, unexpectedly, against a wall or
across a table.

They would dress up to titillate each other; act out fantasies; and, most of
all, they would laugh when performing the act—something quite alien to her
previous experience.

During the first two years of their affair, and even later—when she knew
she was lost and hopelessly in love—Marie stuck by her word with loyalty both
to country and family, milking Klaus von Hirsch of all useful intelligence. Yet
this in no way prohibited her enjoyment or the eventual full-flowering of her
feelings.

By 1912 Marie was suffering agonies at the thought of her lover's imminent
departure for Berlin: for it was in the spring of 1912 that von Hirsch was due
to complete his tour of duty at the Embassy.

The couple had by this time become obsessively careful about their meetings,
though they met two or three times a week, usually at an apartment which
Klaus had rented under an assumed name near the Tuileries Gardens.

So it turned out, on a bitterly cold afternoon in early March 1912, that

Marie made her way by a circuitous route to the apartment. The freezing weather, combined with the bleakness of the trees against a muddy sky, seemed to reflect her private misery. This was to be their last meeting, and Marie, usually so resilient, seriously wondered if she could bear the parting.

On reaching their trysting-place, her hands were so cold that she had difficulty taking the key from her bag and turning it in the lock. Once inside the little set of three rooms, she leaned back against the door, immediately conscious of Klaus' presence. Invariably he arrived before her.

Seconds later he appeared in the doorway leading from the small sitting room to the bedroom. He was in his shirtsleeves, one shoulder propped against the jamb, a glass in his right hand, which he raised, smiling at her over the rim.

"Welcome, Liebling." There was laughter in his voice.

For a second she was angry. How *could* he be happy on a day as sad and tearing as this?

"Klaus! It's no time for laughter . . ." Her face crumpling.

He put down the glass and walked over to her. "Oh, but it is. It is a day for much laughter, and for love—even for champagne. A day for everything, my English prude. . . ." He had called her "Prude" since her reaction of sharp, mock-modesty to one of his more outrageous suggestions during their very first bout of lovemaking.

She opened her mouth, then closed it again as he enfolded her in a great bearhug. "I am *not* going," he whispered. "Not going back to Germany. Not going to Berlin. Not even on leave of absence. They have allowed me more time here in Paris. Another term of duty."

At first she could hardly believe it. But he continued: "And I'll tell you something else, Liebling. When I finally do go back to Berlin, I'm taking you with me."

Marie protested the impossibility of this last suggestion; yet, by the end of the afternoon, she knew it would be just like that. When he left Paris, she was going to be with him. Nothing was more certain.

Later, Marie Grenot could recall, at will, everything that had happened during that March afternoon when her future was sealed. Often, in the weeks, months and years that followed, she saw again the rimed, clutching branches of the trees in the Tuileries, glimpsed from the bedroom window; she would summon back the taste of the hot chestnuts which Klaus went out to buy from a street vendor—their flavor rough and sweet against the dry champagne. She could almost bring back the particular feel of him, deep within her, as she lay on her side and he penetrated her from behind, his long hands cupped around her breasts, fingers and thumbs rolling hard on her nipples, stomach pressed against her buttocks as he recited some German nonsense about the train going choo-choo-choo and whistling in the tunnel.

It was the detail of that day which she always remembered, especially later when the bad times came.

Before going home, Marie stood by the parlor windows, looking over the rooftops of Paris, the cold mist rising with chimney smoke, and the lights coming on across the city like a shower of sparks. The memory would stay with her until death.

7

During the next few weeks Marie Grenot battled with guilt as she started to examine her father's true motives for the first time. It began with the realization that it was her father who had manipulated her first meeting with Marcel Grenot. Together, her father, and her uncle, the General, had overseen the flowering of that romance: guiding and maneuvering them toward marriage. And why? The answer was clear now—so that she would be in Paris and therefore of use to her father's work. There had been no thought for her personal or lasting happiness. Together with Marcel Grenot, Marie was a chess piece in the secret diplomacy of nations.

Once she reached this conclusion, the first germs of bitterness took root, flowering into plain malevolence. Her own father was responsible for what had happened—and what would happen. Be it on his own head.

At home she became morose, biting and snapping at Marcel. Happiness could be found only with Klaus, whom she had also betrayed—using him as a source of intelligence. Marie's confusion deepened. Yet the whole devious intrigue of a father using his daughter for diplomatic ends revolted her, to the extent that when the day of decision arrived she had no qualms or second thoughts about going to Berlin with von Hirsch.

July 31st, 1914, the day in question, was hot.

Marie was well aware that the diplomatic attempts to avert war were losing ground, so was quite prepared to face what was to come. You could not live in the same house as Marcel without realizing the gravity of the situation. Also, her father had been openly in touch from London. As Europe trudged inevitably toward doom, Marie faced her own prospects. Her son, Paul, was now, at the age of nineteen, an officer cadet, serving in the Fifth Army under General Lanrezac, an old friend of Marcel's family. Denise, a year younger, was at home, school having finished for the summer. But Marie, now looking to her future, had long since kept a valise, packed with essentials, at the apartment near the Tuileries.

On that day, she was due to meet Klaus at three o'clock in the afternoon, but the call came much earlier.

They used the safest possible method of contact—personal notes, passed through a romantically inclined French housemaid working in the German Embassy. In turn, the girl gave them to her younger sister, who always delivered them into Madame Grenot's own hands, telling the servant who opened the door that the message was personal and from Madame Grenot's close friend, Madame Grise.

The housemaid's sister arrived on the Grenots' doorstep just before ten in the morning. Marie left the house within the half hour, going straight to the apartment.

There was little conversation.

"Are you coming with me?" Klaus asked.

"Of course — if that's what you truly wish."

"Yes. You know it's what I wish. But, Prude, you have to understand everything. It will not be easy in Berlin — particularly since we are not married, and your husband is who he is — let alone your father's position in London. There will be war within a matter of days."

"There is no hope?"

"I doubt it." He shook his head. She did not notice that through this whole conversation he never once looked her in the eyes. "There is to be an ultimatum to Belgium — to allow free passage of the Imperial Army, which can mean only one thing. At the Embassy the feeling is that Belgium will foolishly resist and Great Britain will not stand idly by. You *must* understand what all this means."

"I don't care what it means, Klaus. I only want to be with you; to stay with you. When do we leave?"

"The Embassy has already begun to send staff back to Germany. I leave at noon: in an hour." There were two suitcases standing beside the door.

Marie walked straight to the bedroom to get her valise. In less than an hour they were at the Gare du Nord, which was stifling, crowded, and with the hint of calamity in the air. For a second, as they crossed the large concourse, Marie unaccountably thought of the *Titanic* disaster two years before, for in the babble and crush there was despair.

Nobody questioned them as they boarded the noon express for Berlin. In turn, they did not notice the young woman who stood close as they reached the platform barrier — close enough to see that they were both boarding the Berlin train.

As the engine gave its shrill, almost feminine, whistle, and pulled out of the station, Monique turned away, frowning as she hurried back to the rooms above the Bistro Abbeaux to get her message off to Giles Railton.

By the following morning, Marie was in Berlin, and the news had reached her husband who — hurt, angry and bitter — immediately forbade his children ever to speak to their mother again. This he did by telegram to Paul, and by word directly to a shaken and sobbing Denise who — at Giles' request — was being sent to London.

8

In the wider world, events steamrollered toward Armageddon. As Klaus had predicted, Belgium failed to answer the German ultimatum, and on the morning of August 4th, German troops entered Belgium.

The British government responded with its own ultimatum — that Germany should respect Belgian neutrality. This was due to expire at eleven that night—midnight in Berlin.

Giles Railton was at the War Office, in a room he was allowed to use on a permanent basis, that afternoon, when he learned from the Royal Marine Captain, Maurice Hankey—Secretary to the Committee of Imperial Defence—that the War Book had already been opened almost a week previously.

Before the day was out, Britain was at war, and Giles Railton did not return to Eccleston Square to prepare for the journey to Dover to meet Denise Grenot until the small hours of the morning.

Chapter Thirteen

1

Barely ten days after the outbreak of war, a very tired Charles Railton looked out of a railway carriage window onto the flat, beautiful landscape of Norfolk.

Until that morning Charles had no idea that he would be on the train to Norfolk. It was the last place in which he expected to find himself. Yet nothing could have suited him better.

On the final day, when they all knew war to be inevitable and only hours away, Charles was called to Vernon Kell's office.

Kell had announced that it was time to take action, and that very evening Charles Railton was among the group of officers which visited the Caledonian Road shop to arrest a surprised Ernst.

As things turned out, Karl Ernst, himself, managed to persuade the Bow Street Magistrate to release him on what was a virtual technicality. But, by the time he stepped onto the street a free man, officers from the Branch had been at work sifting evidence from the shop. Ernst was immediately rearrested and was due to stand trial later in the year.

In the meantime, Charles spent much time with members of the Branch as they rounded up those people connected with the Barber's Shop Network. Within the first twenty-four hours of war, twenty-one people were detained. Since then, both Railton and Kell had sat in on hours of interrogations.

Then, in the midst of this flurry of work, Charles was sent off to Norfolk.

He had gone into the office normally, having spent his first night at home for weeks, to find a message waiting for him. Vernon Kell wanted to see him urgently.

Kell's office was like a general's tent in the midst of battle. "Odd and ticklish job for you," he began. "Probably nothing in it, but, as you'll see, the request comes from a fairly important source." He unlocked a drawer and removed a piece of paper. "This is an edited copy, of course. One would not expect to get either the real or the whole thing. You haven't even seen it, mind you—if you follow me. Mr. Churchill came over late last night from the Admiralty. Now, this *has* to be treated in the strictest confidence."

Charles' brow furrowed as he began to read. It was a letter from the young Mrs. Churchill—a personal note to her husband, the First Lord.

Charles replaced the copy on the desk. "If I were Mr. Churchill, I'd have had this around here almost before I'd finished reading it."

Mrs. Churchill was still on holiday, with the two children—Diana and Randolph—at fashionable Cromer, on the Norfolk coast, and the note contained a serious warning. She had been told of a rumor, emanating from confidential sources, that a German plan was already in operation to kidnap her. The plot— Kell said—had been revealed to Mrs. Churchill by "a most trustworthy and well-informed person"—"That's what Winston told me; and I have to believe him. I pressed for more information, but he just repeated that the intelligence was almost one hundred percent accurate, having come from this particular source. . . . "

Charles reflected on the situation, thinking it all sounded a little like a William Le Queux novel. Then he asked Kell if he believed it to be a genuine threat to Mrs. Churchill.

Kell grunted. "Let's say that Winston believes it. He certainly did when he came to me last night."

"And she believes it." Charles indicated the letter. "Believes it, has some details—kidnap by aeroplane; ransom being one of the Navy's capital ships. And she is very brave." He quoted, verbatim, from part of the copy he had just read: "'I have no intention of allowing such villainy to succeed. You must not sacrifice the smallest, or cheapest, submarine, or even the oldest ship. If you gave in to the ransom, I could never live with the unpopularity it would undoubtedly bring. If I die unransomed, then I shall die a heroine, and you will be hailed as a spartan. . . .'"

"I think that's the bit which rattled Winston." Kell gave a thin smile. "Anyway, he was quite clear. She is not to know that we're keeping an eye on things. Thomson's kindly put a couple of his lads down there, and I'm sending you on a watching brief."

"If you say so." Charles disguised his delight.

"I need someone I can trust. If we ignored this business, and something happened, there'd be the very devil to pay. I want you on the afternoon train to Cromer."

Detective Inspector Brian Wood, with whom Charles had already worked on the Ernst surveillance, was waiting at Cromer station.

"I somehow thought Mr. Kell might send you, sir. I've only got DC Dobbs here and we've been going it from the moment we arrived." He ushered Charles into a waiting cab and indulged in small-talk until Charles had registered at the Queen's Arms, an old and respectable public house with five bedrooms. At the southern tip of the town, on the Norwich road, overlooking the North Sea, it was an ideal headquarters, of which Charles approved.

"What d'you make of it?" They were in Charles' room, and Wood had opened the door, taking a seat where he could see along the passage as a precaution against them being overheard.

Wood was a careful, well-trained officer, who seldom took chances even with the simplest of jobs. "Hard to say. We arrived on the first train this morning, so we still need time. The Guv'nor got us out of bed at dawn. I've checked out the house where Mrs. Churchill's staying. *That's* not an easy situation to start with: there're three entrances to the place—"

"Just her and the children?"

Wood shook his head. "'Fraid not. Mrs. Churchill; the two children; her sister-in-law, Lady Gwendeline Churchill—Lady Gwendeline Bertie as was—with her young lad, John; two maids; a cook and a butler."

Charles groaned. "And what's the good news?"

"The staff are in the clear. The maids're local; they go with the house, and have served the family before. The cook is Lady Gwendeline's cook, and the butler's another family retainer."

"Local police?"

The DI grimaced. "Felt it best not to bother 'em yet, sir. Get settled in first."

"Nothing suspicious, then?"

"I wouldn't say that. No, sir. But I shouldn't be surprised if we get ourselves arrested by the local law. There's a positive spy mania going on hereabouts—or so they told me in the bar, with a lot of meaningful looks an' all. We're strangers, and strangers're definitely treated with some caution. There are tales of lights flashing in the night, and the sound of aeroplanes, low overhead."

"Well, the terrain's right for dropping in. Plenty of flat open spaces for landing near the town."

Wood agreed, but seemed concerned as he said, "If this really is a problem, then you do realize we're very shorthanded?"

"That's nothing new. Your other man—Dobbs, is it?—has the Churchills under watch?"

Wood nodded, preoccupied. He was a tall, tough young man who looked as though he should be farming instead of being involved in police work—a ruddy complexion and the hard hands of one who worked the land. "I wonder," almost to himself, "I wonder if we should talk to the local force? Have to get the guv'nor's say-so, of course."

"It's essential to contain the knowledge. Heaven knows this is a delicate one, but I think we should do something—without giving the facts, of course." It worried Charles that other people might have to be called in. You could never completely trust local police. They were good, efficient, knew the area in which they worked, yet this was sometimes a drawback in matters secret.

Locals talked to locals. Inevitably the circle of confidence widened. "We'll have to cook up some story, particularly if it becomes necessary to use them for surveillance."

They agreed that nobody from outside should be brought in on watching the Churchill family itself. "That's far too risky." Wood frowned. "Even if the three of us have to work around the clock. That part must be kept close as skin to flesh. I'll telephone the Guv'nor and suggest a story. Knowing him, he'll come up with something better."

Within the hour they were on the way to Cromer Police Station with a concocted tale about anonymous letters concerning aeroplanes in the area, and lights seen signaling at night, leaving out any mention of a threat to the wife of the First Lord of the Admiralty.

Superintendent Dove—a name which belied his nature—was already expecting them. "The Assistant Commissioner, Crime, telephoned me." He spoke of Basil Thomson, whose duties included overseeing serious crime, naturalization and the Convict Supervision Office, as well as the Branch. "Asked me to cooperate, which I shall if possible." He was a pompous, heavy man, with a walrus mustache and slightly protruding eyes. Now he glared at Charles. "Told you're not one of us. An oddity, what?"

Charles coldly said he did not follow the Superintendent.

Wood tried to come to Charles' rescue. "Mr. Rathbone holds a rank senior to your own, sir. But no, he's not in 'The Job.'"—The Job was the way most policemen spoke of their profession; Rathbone was Charles's name "in the street," as Vernon Kell would say.

"Like to know what I've got on my patch, actually." Dove's eyes began to pop when Wood mentioned rank. "Don't really hold with civilians messing around. Don't know the ropes; unfamiliar with the form. Particularly important in a place like Cromer, where we entertain a large number of special people— foreign royalty; many titled folk. Have to take care, you understand."

"I think you'll find I'm *very* familiar with the form." Charles tried out the Railton charm.

"Have to see about that," Dove puffed. "I've got to cooperate, so I'd best know why you're here."

Charles took the lead. "The Branch and my own department work very closely—" he began.

"Rather hear it from one of our own, I think."

He could only presume that Dove did not really know how offensive he could be. Wood looked highly embarrassed. "Well, sir, Wood took over, giving Charles a quick sideways look, "there is an emergency, and this is emergency business: wartime business—"

"Ah!" Superintendent Dove gave a quick smile. "Don't see why that should worry us too much. Whole thing'll be over by Christmas. Had that from an unimpeachable authority."

"With respect"—Charles bit out the words one at a time—"whether this damned war is over by Christmas or in twenty years' time is of little consequence. We are concerned, Superintendent Dove, with the possible nefarious activities of enemy aliens. Even the probable fact that German intelligence agents may well have already been landed on this part of the coast."

Dove's eyes bulged to bursting point. "Here? On my coast? Most unlikely, I'd say."

"We've had reports of signal lights flashing and aeroplanes flying low at night over this part of Norfolk." Charles turned and spotted a pair of stand chairs. Motioning to Wood, he spoke with all the command he could muster. "I think we'd better sit down, Superintendent. This could take time. And, having spoken to Basil Thomson already, I'm sure you must realize that we come here with a good deal of backing and authority."

Once seated, he continued, "Now, Mr. Dove, we need to know how many of these incidents have been reported to you or your officers since the declaration of war."

"Well . . . Well . . ." Dove floundered. "I know there've been some, but it's mostly rumor or vivid imagination."

"All reports *have* been followed up, I presume?"

"Lot of tittle-tattle goin' on, of course. Lot of rumor. Spy mania and all that . . ."

"Spy mania or not"—Charles raised his voice—"it is of national importance that all rumors and reports are checked. For every couple of hundred red herrings there may be one genuine article. If so, then the two hundred rumors have proved useful. Now, sir. All reports. All follow-ups."

Dove muttered something about "getting the officer concerned," rose from his desk and stamped angrily to his office door.

Charles raised his eyebrows at Brian Wood, almost laughing aloud at this pompous comic-opera policeman. They could hear him talking to the desk sergeant outside: "See if Detective Inspector Partridge is in and send him to me immediately. If not, locate him and get him here double quick!"

"Doves? Partridges? Place is full of bloody birds," Charles whispered.

"Not of a feather, I hope," Wood replied as Dove returned.

"Naturally you have my full cooperation." Dove was trying not to look concerned. "If any reports have not been followed up, I'll want to know the reason why."

"So will we." Charles maintained a gritty hostility. "And so will those whom we represent. As I've said—" A tap on the door announced the arrival of Detective Inspector Partridge, a very different kind of man, whom Charles immediately recognized as professional, ambitious and careful. He proved to be a mine of information, and it soon became most apparent that Partridge got on with the work, filed the reports and tried not to concern himself with the self-importance of his superior, whom he almost blatantly regarded as a stupid and overbearing poltroon.

"The tales come in by the dozen." The DI had an easy manner and was not put off by Dove's presence. "Mainly false leads, but we have a couple of interesting possibilities. Oh, by the way, we were informed about both of you, and your DC Dobbs—"

"Dobbs? Who's Dobbs?" blustered Dove.

"One of my men. Here with us," Wood said crisply, immediately turning back to Partridge. "You've talked to Dobbs?" Only Charles caught the fragment of concern in Wood's voice. The DI would be worried lest Dobbs, a slightly less experienced officer, had been indiscreet about Mrs. Churchill and the true reason for their presence in Cromer.

Wood shook his head. "Not personally, but the beat constable chatted with him—saw his warrant card. He didn't mention you. Claimed he was here on leave, but my fellow reported the incident: a new face on the seafront, you know. My lads can spot holiday-makers. They also sniff people who seem out of place. Your Mr. Dobbs was very obviously not on holiday. Also, the Queen's Head reported two new guests yesterday and another who joined them today. People around here have become very suspicious."

"No bad thing." Charles was impressed. "You mentioned a couple of possibilities?"

"Our old friend the flashing lights, sir. From the area around the golf links just down the coast, near Overstrand: and a waiter at the Hotel de Paris." He pronounced it "Hotel Dee Paris." "The man's been there about a year now; registered last week under the Aliens Restriction Act as a Dutch citizen, though we know he talked about taking out papers of naturalisation when he first came."

Wood briskly asked the man's name.

"Sklave. Joost van Sklave."

"*Von* Sklave, I'd wager." Wood rose. "May I use a telephone? Sklave is German for 'slave.' Better check it with Naturalisation and the Alien Central Register."

Partridge put up a hand to stop him. "Please, just hear me out. Friend Sklave does not know that I've had a man watching him. Not full time, of course, but mainly on Sklave's days off and sometimes after work. Two things about him. He visits Norwich every other week, where he sees a woman called Hilda Fox. The Norwich people've helped me there. She arrived about five years ago. Real name Hilda Fuchs."

"I'll check her as well." Wood moved another two paces toward the door, but was again halted by Partridge.

"That's not all. Sklave is in the habit of taking long walks, late at night, as far as the links near Overstrand."

Charles leaned forward. "You caught him at it?"

"All new to me. Why haven't I been informed?" Superintendent Dove obviously felt left out of things.

"With respect, sir, you have. All in the daily reports." Partridge answered his superior first, before returning to Charles' question. "We've caught him at nothing, sir. We do know that he is in possession of a powerful signal light. Any of this help, sir?"

"It might." Charles turned to Wood. "Brian, you'd best see if the Register really has everything about Sklave and Fuchs. If not, then I suggest your Guv'nor get someone onto the Fuchs woman. You have an address, Mr. Partridge?"

The DI nodded.

"Right. Then I think we should mount some kind of operation on Sklave, here and now. Brian, when you've finished talking to your Guv'nor, I'll have a word with my chief." At last he turned back to Dove. "Superintendent, I have to remind you that this is highly confidential. I have to ask you to speak to nobody about this conversation—not even your wife."

"Mrs. Dove is—"

"The soul of discretion, I've no doubt." Charles stood up and went to the door, following Brian Wood.

2

A warm, airless night followed the heat of the day. Dobbs, after a short break, covered by Wood, was back on duty, watching the Churchills' rented house; and Charles, together with Wood, Partridge and four local plainclothes officers, began their surveillance of the waiter, Sklave.

The quartet of locals was told it was a routine watching assignment. In reality they were being kept in reserve, posted at strategic points near the Hotel de Paris, along the road to Overstrand—some two and a half miles up the coast, and at good vantage points on the golf links, nearer to Cromer.

All had specific orders to do nothing unless summoned by three quick whistle blasts from DI Wood, or "Mr. Rathbone."

Charles took up his post near the hotel, strolling along the seafront, conscious of the heavy Webley revolver tucked under his coat. His mind was on the protection of Mrs. Churchill and the family, though occasionally it strayed to his son William Arthur, whose fourth birthday was next week. The boy was a sturdy little fellow now, and Charles wondered if this job could be completed in time for him to be at the excitedly planned birthday party.

Both Wood and Partridge were close at hand—Wood with instructions to stay well in front but in sight of Charles; while Partridge was to keep to the rear. Sklave, Partridge said, was not devious. "Not yet anyway. He has no reason to think we're on to him, and he behaves like a creature of habit. If he *is* going to take one of his walks tonight, he should leave by the staff entrance a mite before eleven."

As it turned out, that was exactly what he did.

Partridge—the only one of the three able to make positive identification— stayed back, on the inland side of the road. As various members of the staff emerged from the rear of the hotel, Charles would glance across, in the dimmed street, waiting for Partridge to light a cigarette: the signal that it was their man.

Just before eleven a slight figure walked quickly across the road from the hotel, and Charles saw the match flare. From then on he concentrated on the man he now knew was Sklave. They had certain details about him from the Central Register. He had declared his age as thirty-two, born in Amsterdam, unmarried son of a café proprietor. In London they were already crosschecking the facts; just as they were also looking into the background of the Fox woman.

Sklave, Charles considered, was ideal espionage material. The reports said that he was well-liked in the hotel: quiet, helpful, unassuming, thorough—a perfect waiter. And very useful, as he spoke his "native" Dutch, together with French, German and Spanish.

True to Partridge's word, Sklave set off at a steady pace toward the golf links near Overstrand.

Charles wore heavy, rubber-soled boots and moved silently behind the man.

Sklave stepped out, looking neither to left nor right, nor, indeed, over his shoulder. What was more, he wore studded boots which clicked on the pavement, allowing Charles to fall back slightly. The noise factor also meant that Wood could place himself even farther forward, so their quarry could never catch sight of him. As a suspect, Sklave was almost too good to be true.

It was a good three-quarters of an hour before they reached the links. The moon was up, and all who watched could see the small figure walk upright across the broad, open land, taking up a position toward the sea, near the fourth hole. Charles was not the only one to immediately realize that Sklave had chosen the ideal part of the course: roomy, flat and uncluttered.

It was there, on the fourth green, that Joost van Sklave sat down and waited.

Earlier in the evening, the moon had been a great silver ball tinged with red, low in the sky. Now the light dwindled; soon there was total darkness and a silence broken only by sea noise and the occasional sound of a predatory bird or animal. Once Charles heard a screech owl and wondered if this was natural so close to the sea. He was used to hearing them at Redhill Manor, but city and townspeople, he had discovered, were superstitious and held the sound of an owl in a heavily populated area to be a sign of death.

Slowly, the watchers' eyes adjusted to the darkness, and they became as cats; seeing and hearing, moving with a stealth which comes only through training and experience. Charles sensed someone nearby and slipped the Webley from its webbing holster set under his jacket, high against his ribs. It was Brian Wood, crawling through the grass to whisper, asking the MO5 officer what he thought about the situation.

"He's either wise to us and out to give us a lesson; or he's waiting for something; or he just likes it here."

He saw Wood nod. They continued to wait—until almost four in the morning.

Then it came without warning. Straining his eyes constantly, Charles hardly stopped watching the small dark mound he knew was Sklave. Quite suddenly the mound moved, and the waiter's body became silhouetted against the sky— now the color of sun-dried, tilled soil. Both Wood and Charles half rose, Charles realizing he was still clutching the Webley.

Sklave stood like a scenting animal, head cocked to one side. Then he lifted his right arm, holding it stretched in front of him: Charles saw plainly that it was pointing toward the sea, raised at a roughly forty-five-degree angle. Then the light came on, like a blast of contained fire flying upwards from a magician's fingers: on-off-on-off-on-off. Then darkness.

Not complete darkness, for Charles caught a tiny gleam in the sky directly ahead of them—there and gone in a second. Then another; and, as he looked, Sklave signaled again, the beam pointed in the general direction of where Charles had seen the pinpoint glitters of light.

When the noise came, he found it difficult to identify—a flapping sound like the wind slapping against sail. The noise grew louder, and then he saw it, almost at the moment when he recognized the sound—a flying machine, coming in low, without power. The pilot must have flown in high over the North Sea; then, navigating by the stars, cut his engine, to glide in toward the coast, finally lining up with Sklave's signal light. It was no mean feat, and Charles wondered how many times the pilot had done it before—all these thoughts telescoped into a fraction of time.

The wind made a great humming noise in the rigging wires between the wings, while the slapping sound was air, banging against the fabric, as the aeroplane fought to stay aloft in the final moments of its controlled glide. Then, with an audible bump and rumble, the thing was down—on the golf course—speed slowing as the tail slewed from side to side, and, finally, right around so that the craft faced back in the direction of its approach.

The machine itself seemed close enough to touch, now that the sky was turning from dark gray to pearl, as the first signs of dawn streaked the horizon. A big black two-winged bird, square and ugly as a box, with great slabs sprouting to left and right, and a large snoutlike beak ending in a propeller. An Aviatik BII, Austrian built, with a crew of two, speed of almost a shattering seventy miles an hour, and four hours' endurance—just enough to make it over the dangerous waters of the North Sea and back. Charles understood now why Kell insisted on his officers studying and learning everything to do with Britain's potential enemies—including how to immediately recognize German and Austrian aeroplanes, ships, uniforms, insignia and badges.

Now Sklave stood by the fuselage, helping someone from the rear cockpit— first some kind of suitcase, then a figure climbing down.

Sklave and his new companion from the clouds moved with the kind of precision you expect to see on a parade ground. Wood whispered, urgently and a shade too loud, "Now, sir? We get them now?"

Charles reached out a restraining hand, speaking low. "I'm not interested in getting the pilot. Give them some rope. Let them go. See where they lead us."

One of the figures, it was impossible to tell which, had moved to the front of the aeroplane. You could clearly hear the breath come out of his lungs as he heaved twice on the propeller. Then the engine fired with a roar which, Charles thought, must surely wake even the dead in Cromer cemetery.

Under cover of the noise he drew closer to Wood. "Can you find Partridge?"

Wood nodded, his face clear in the half-light.

"Get to him, then. I want the visitor followed. Both of them followed. I need to know what they're up to. Reports every half hour or so. Tell Partridge to be prepared to follow them on whatever transport they use."

Wood nodded. "And you?"

"I'll be back at the Station—Police Station. Arrest only if things get difficult."

Wood nodded. The aeroplane's engine rose in a roar. The machine quivered, started to trundle forward, then bumped and rattled over the grass until its tail lifted and the slim, spoked wheels left the ground as it took to its natural element.

The noise died away as the machine grew smaller, tilting, then climbing, setting course for home.

Charles was so fascinated by the thing that it took the sound of voices to bring him back to reality. Joost van Sklave and his companion trudged through the grass, coming almost directly toward him. He flattened against the ground, face so close to the earth that the scent of damp, dew-drenched grass filled his nostrils, reminding him of early mornings with Mildred, when they had first visited Redhill Manor as a newly wedded couple. Twice, during that wonderful time, they had crept from the house, out into the meadows on fine summer mornings, to make love at dawn in the long, damp grass—naked, unrestrained and as near to nature as they could imagine.

But that was long ago, and he was pulled back to the harsh reality of the present as Sklave and the newcomer passed close to him—Sklave speaking in rapid German.

3

The police stations of England were noted for their tea. At half past seven in the morning, after a night spent lying on the grass at Overstrand golf links, Charles Railton found the tea as refreshing and stimulating as he would normally have found bed, a superb meal or a glass of good champagne.

But tea could not remove the anxiety.

Charles had left the links only when he was certain that the others had melted off into the dawn—positioning themselves so that the two hurrying figures were covered from all angles as they unsuspectingly walked back along the Cromer road.

It was some time since he had risen from the grass to begin his return journey. Now it seemed as though he had been waiting at the Station for an eternity.

At eight-fifteen Brian Wood returned, his face breaking into a tired smile as he greeted the MO5 officer. "You'll never believe it—" he began, then, seeing the duty sergeant, followed Charles into one of the charge rooms.

"Cheeky buggers," he said once the door was closed.

"Come on." Charles tapped the back of his own hand impatiently.

"Our visitor registered as a guest at the Hotel de Paris just after seven-fifteen. Sklave left him about a mile from town and went off across the fields on his own. The German chummy just loitered around and ended up at the railway station. He waited until the milk train came in, then walked off, bold as brass, to the hotel."

"We checked the registration?" Charles was unsurprised.

"David Partridge's going in about now." Wood hauled on his watchchain, pulling out a handsome half-Hunter. "Says they're used to him wandering into the hotels first thing in the mornings to check the registers. Knows most of the night staff. Nothing wrong at the Churchills' place, by the way. I looked in on Dobbs."

Partridge did not keep them waiting for long. "Big surprise," he announced. "The person who landed from the Boche aeroplane—"

"Well?"

"You'd have sworn it was a man, wouldn't you, sir? And you'd be wrong. Long coat, masculine sort of hat. We all assumed too much. The visitor's a woman."

"Well I'll be damned." Brian Wood shook his head. "But I was there. I saw—"

"With respect, you didn't see. You heard. You heard P. C. Roberts give me a report that the suspect had gone into the Hotel de Paris. Young Roberts was acting as a sort of long stop. I had a man much closer: Findlator—very good at getting close. His uncle's the best poacher in Norfolk. When I got to the hotel he gave me the whole thing."

Findlator had been near enough to see the suspect cross the road and stand looking at the sea. She had then put down her suitcase, taken off the hat, unpinned and shaken out her hair. "Long blond hair, he said it was. He also described her as a 'corker,' if you follow that, sir."

Charles gave a bleak smile. "Oh, even MO5 officers have been known to understand what a corker is, Mr. Partridge."

The girl was registered under the name of Miss Madeline Drew, of 35 Chelsea Mansions, London. "The Hotel de Paris has had her booking for over a month," Partridge told them. "She's supposed to be a governess on holiday. I've got one of my fellows in the place now."

Charles gave Wood a satisfied look. "Could do with Mr. Partridge in the Branch, Brian."

Wood nodded. "Have to see what can be done when we've finished with this. How'd y'like it, David?"

"Very much." For a second he sounded like a schoolboy being given an opportunity to be in the First Eleven. "Give anything for a chance, sir."

"Point is"—Wood looked placidly out of the window—"what's to be done now?"

Charles sighed "As ever, we wait and take orders from on high."

Later in the day Wood telephoned Basil Thomson, while Charles talked to Vernon Kell. Sklave and Drew were to be given as much rope as possible.

On the third day there was a slight flurry of anxiety when the Drew woman called at the Churchills' rented house.

"There on the off-chance of a governess' job," Partridge reported. "Mrs. Churchill actually saw her, it appears."

"Even if no job is forthcoming, her face will be known to the household." To Charles, the whole thing looked to be professionally planned. Something would take place soon, he thought. Others were not as certain.

"Best of the moon's gone now," Wood mused. "You won't get the greatest pilot in Germany to take on that night ride until sometime next month."

"And the Churchills are to return to London at the end of next week," Charles reminded him. "It's my guess if anything's going to happen it'll be very soon. Maybe even tonight. I personally think we should risk taking Drew if she goes near the Churchills' place again."

Wood thought for a moment. "If she did manage to abduct Mrs. Churchill, how would they get her away?"

"Ever heard of the sea?"

Nothing happened that night. Nor the next. The alert came on the following afternoon. Partridge reported that Sklave had broken his routine. It was the waiter's day off, and a fortnight since he had been to Norwich. Today he failed to make his usual visit. "Stayed in his room all day."

Charles sat on the front, gazing out at the gray-blue water of the North Sea. In his bones, he felt as if the whole thing were about to blow up in his face.

By late afternoon he had talked to Kell, and further plans were laid. A section of infantry, training near Great Yarmouth, were to be brought up and bivouacked quietly on the other side of Overstrand. It was all done with care: the men were issued with live ammunition; the officer in charge told only what was essential. By six in the evening a telephone call from London assured him that the troops were in position.

The next alert came at just before ten o'clock that night. Sklave was reported to be out and about—walking aimlessly, it seemed, in the general direction of Overstrand.

Just before eleven Charles, on post near to the hotel, saw Drew come out and stroll along the seafront, toward the Churchills' rented house.

Wood had been sent off to shadow Sklave, and Charles could plainly see Dobbs in his usual position. Walking quickly, on the other side of the road, Charles overtook the girl, getting to Dobbs before she could reach the house. "You have all the authority," he panted. "If she so much as puts a hand on the gate, you pull her in."

He had hardly spoken when they saw that she intended to enter the Churchills' house, walking almost casually toward the iron gate leading to the steps up to the front door.

"Go! Now, Dobbs! Now!" And they were both away, dodging across the road to head her off.

Her hand was just touching the gate when she saw them and looked around, her face suddenly alive with surprise. Incongruously, Charles realized for the first time what an attractive girl she was. Then, as they came near, she did the only thing possible—carried on opening the gate, unconcerned, obviously prepared to bluff it out.

Dobbs reached her just in time, placing himself between her and the steps leading to the door. "I'm sorry, Miss, but I can't allow you to go any further." His attitude was deferential, almost avuncular.

"I...I...But why ever not? What's wrong? Who are you? Who are *you* to stop me?"

Charles came up quietly behind her, watching as she tried, surreptitiously, to dump a small purse into the flowers of the garden fronting the house.

"I am a police officer, Miss," Dobbs continued.

"But I have to visit this house. I—"

Charles retrieved the purse from among the roses, speaking for the first time. "I'm sorry, Miss Drew, but you have to come to the Police Station."

She turned. The eyes were startling—a light hazel, almost green, while her hair was a pale gold, glittering and soft. "Come to the—" The laugh seemed, on the surface, to reflect the girl herself—musical, not a silly giggling tinkle, nor a bray, but more like the middle-range notes of a cello.

"And I suppose you're a policeman also." The tone was almost haughty. "Well, you should know that I've come here to find a rather valuable brooch which I think I lost when visiting Mrs. Churchill the other day...."

"We can discuss the brooch in private, at the Police Station, I think, Miss Drew."

As he spoke, Charles studied the girl. Her English bore no trace of an accent; her clothes were stylish—an expensive-looking gray summer dress with white lace trimming and a short cape. Her nose was slightly tilted, and she seemed to have a habit of pursing her lips, more a look of amusement than irritation. Unaccountably, she reminded him of a girl he had met and bedded in Deauville years ago now, before his marriage. By a quirk of the mind, seeing Miss Drew had now blown away the mists, taking him back to the hotel room, the sweet smell among the rumpled sheets, and the long-ago girl's hair straggled, like fine golden cobwebs, on the pillow.

"Well, I've always kept the law, and you appear to have the law on your side. . . ." She gave a small shrug. Her poise and confidence were remarkable, retaining an enviable dignity even after they reached the Police Station. Dobbs stayed with her in one of the small interview rooms while Charles went in search of a woman Reservist.

Before returning to the room, he examined the purse. It contained a small bottle of chloroform and a number of cotton wool and gauze pads.

In the interview room, Dobbs stood by the door with the woman officer. Charles sat opposite the girl and began to talk.

"I have to tell you that I am *not* a police officer. My name is Charles Rathbone, and I am a member of a department of Military Intelligence. However, while I do not have the right to bring any charges against you, I have the authority to question you, and I warn you that eventually the police will charge you under the recent Defence of the Realm Act." This piece of legislation—known usually as DORA—had become law only four days after the outbreak of war.

The girl looked bemused. "But why should I be charged with anything?" In other circumstances she would have been plausible. "I'm here on a short holiday. I was on my way to see if my brooch had been found at Mrs. Churchill's house. What's the crime in that, Mr. Rathbone?"

"Your full name, please."

"What's the crime—"

"Your name, please."

After a moment's pause she answered in a half-whisper, "Madeline Letitia Drew."

"Address?"

"Bloomsbury—35 Chelsea Mansions."

"You have an occupation?"

"I'm a children's governess. Governess to Mr. and Mrs. Hatney-Crawford's son and daughter. Their London residence is 35 Chelsea Mansions."

Charles supposed that she imagined the story would hold up for a while. Brian Wood had checked the address. The Hartney-Crawfords lived at 35 Chelsea Mansions, and there was a governess called Drew.

Charles passed the paper across the table, telling Miss Drew that she had to sign it as a formal declaration that this was her true name, address and occupation. It looked most impressive, but she did not waver, signing with a steady hand.

He took the paper back; then, looking the young woman in the eyes, calmly tore it in two. Turning to Dobbs and the woman officer, he asked if they would leave the room.

It was only after the two officers had gone that Charles was certain of a slight change in the girl's attitude—a worm of concern stirring in the eyes and an uneasiness in the way she sat.

He leaned back in his chair, still looking her full in the eyes. "Miss Drew, I've destroyed your declaration in an attempt to help you. If I placed that document before the authorities, with the already existing proofs, there's no doubt that one morning quite soon you would end up either on the scaffold or in front of a firing squad."

He then gave her the facts—her observed arrival by air; the association with Sklave; the constant surveillance; their knowledge of a plot against Mrs. Churchill; the things found in her purse; the fact that she was not the Miss Drew employed by the couple who lived at 35 Chelsea Mansions.

When he had completed the recitation, her eyes did not meet his.

"I imagine Sklave's waiting for a submarine. Yes?"

She sat with head bowed and hands on her lap. Slowly, Charles counted to thirty before speaking again. "No matter," allowing his hands to rise a few inches from the table, then drop to his sides. "There are plenty of police officers and troops out there near him. He's been under watch since before you were flown in. They'll get him—alive or dead—before the night's over. That's why I'm offering you a way out. Believe me, we know it all. And if you persist in saying that you are Miss Drew, and all the other nonsense, then there's nothing I can do to help you. But, if you use your sense, and cooperate, then no harm will come to you. I mean it."

She neither moved nor spoke. Charles rose, starting toward the door. "I fear the next people who question you will not be so gentle." He looked at her gravely. "Cooperate now, Miss Drew. Tell me everything. But you must do it *now.*"

He thought he had failed. His hand was on the doorknob before she spoke softly. "How can I be certain?"

"Certain of what?"

"That you will not simply take all I have to tell you, then hang me—or shoot me?"

Charles shook his head. "There is no way of being certain. You can only trust me. It's now well past midnight, and there is no possibility of you saving Sklave. Cooperate, and I swear, as an officer and a gentleman, that I shall do everything I can to help you."

A minute seemed to stretch into a lifetime. Then, suddenly, the poise left her. She raised a face which, he now saw, was stained with tears. "I'll tell you everything." A sob. "God help me." It had turned out as Charles hoped and planned. Silently he thanked his Uncle Giles for recommending him for this operation.

She began to talk—so rapidly that Charles was forced to hold up a hand, speaking to her in the way he had so often talked to Mary Anne, to comfort or soothe her when his daughter was much younger. "If you're really going to tell me everything, it's essential that you first give me all details of the present situation, here in Cromer. If you tell the truth about that, then we shall know you can be trusted. You'll be cared for, looked after and protected."

It took over half an hour for her to calm down. It would be a long night. If she *was* going to tell everything, the heart of her information would spill out in a great gush. After that it would be a tedious business, taking weeks—filling in detail, some of which would possibly have to be wrung slowly from her. Guilt would follow the first confession.

As he listened, Charles realized that he was already quite captivated by the girl. Since the birth of their last child, things had not been well between Mildred and himself, and he imagined passion to be buried. But, as he looked at Madeline, the familiar broth of lust began to boil within him, grow and bubble into the need to bury himself within her. This unprofessional emotional confusion worried him.

He heard everything, but was aware of the old sensations—how would her skin feel to the touch? What words could be conveyed by those eyes? Was the fair hair silky to the touch? Would her kiss burn, and her tongue flick inside his mouth like a small pink animal? He imagined her breasts and thighs, and wondered what it was like between them. Men, he thought, are capable of such mental folly. We always wonder what lies in the secret places of a woman's body. We know, we've touched and seen, and felt the spot, yet each time, with every new woman, it is as though we expect to find a novel, magic thing—and sometimes, occasionally, the quest reveals just such a joy.

Charles dragged his mind back from the edge of fantasy, to listen and do his job. Yet the pictures were already firmly planted in his mind. Would she respond, enjoy, screech with pleasure as they mounted to their ecstasy? Would she possibly share his own lascivious pleasings? Already he knew it was going to happen.

Within half an hour the full scope of matters regarding Sklave and the kidnap plot were out. The plan was to take Mrs. Churchill off in a submarine. Sklave waited on a secluded part of the beach—an inlet near Overstrand. They had also bribed a cabdriver to help convey her, unconscious, to the rendezvous.

As "Miss Drew" had not kept the meeting with the cabdriver, it was now certain that Sklave would be getting anxious. The odds were that he would signal the submarine to abort the mission.

With this information, Charles summoned the woman officer, instructing her to arrange for food and tea for the subject, while he rapidly briefed Dobbs. It took about twenty minutes. Then, telephone calls were made—instructions to the troops, and an alert to the Admiralty, so that a frigate could be dispatched in an attempt to catch the lurking submarine.

Dobbs went off with specific orders for Wood and Partridge. Sklave was to be taken, but only at the last possible moment.

When all this was completed, Charles returned to the girl and patiently heard her out.

The real name was Hanna Haas, and she was twenty-six years of age, the daughter of a German businessman and an English nurse. Illegitimate, of course, but her father, Frederick Haas, had been a man of some considerable honor. Mother and daughter were taken to Germany, and the girl was initially brought up among pleasant surroundings in Berlin. At the age of fifteen, with a reasonable education behind her, she returned to London, working for some six years first as a nursery maid, then a governess, to a family in Highgate. In 1909 Haas summoned her back to Berlin, where she found her mother seriously ill. For two years she nursed the dying woman, and when it was over, Frederick Haas helped her. This experience led her toward nursing. She studied and eventually qualified. It was during and after this period that she came—through her father—into contact with military people.

Hanna Haas now found herself being wooed by the Intelligence Branch of the Military High Command. At first this surprised her, but she soon succumbed to the possible glamour of the situation. Until the training and briefing for the present mission, she spent much time under the direct command of Walter Nicolai, and her instructions after this mission were to remain in England and set herself up in some job which would give her access to military or naval information—not a difficult proposition for a girl with her skills and ability. She had been provided with a whole range of espionage techniques, and was familiar with the names of personalities within the German Service. Also, she had observed the workings of that Service at close quarters. There was no doubt of the small gold mine of intelligence in Hanna Haas. She was a source which, if used properly, could be tapped and manipulated as an agent, working for both sides in England.

"Do you truly feel great allegiance to the German cause?" Charles asked after three hours' talking.

She did not hesitate. "I felt trapped once they got me back here—into England. To be honest, Mr. Rathbone, until then it was just a kind of game. Unreal. Then, after I was flown here, there were many moments when I simply wanted to run straight to the police. Yet I was very frightened of what they would do; or of what my German superiors would do, if I became a traitor to them." She swallowed hard. "I feel more English than German. That is the truth, so help me God. It's also natural. The only real relations I have are here, in this country." She spoke of an aunt in Coventry and another aunt and uncle in London. "Mr. Rathbone, I *am* English, and I feel so ashamed at what I've done."

Wood, Partridge and the others returned to the Police Station around dawn. Sklave had obviously warned off the submarine—they had even seen it surface, half a mile or so from the beach, and Wood gave orders for the German agent to be taken. The moment he was challenged, Sklave produced a revolver and, following a swift exchange of shots, died from two bullets fired by Wood himself.

"I'm sorry." The Special Branch man was upset. "Tried to aim low, but the light was bad, and he was moving."

As for the cabdriver, the local police arrested him in the early hours on the road between Cromer and Overstrand. Eventually he would be quietly interned—under DORA—for it was essential that no suspicion should fall on the Haas girl.

Just after nine that morning Charles had a lengthy, guarded, telephone conversation with Vernon Kell.

At first Kell had thought that the best form would be to hand her over to C's people Then he said, "Look, Charles, she's in your charge. Keep her close and take no chances with her. Get her to London as quickly as you can. We've a house you can use to complete the interrogation, then we can decide what's best to be done—how to use her when she's had time to settle down."

It was exactly what Charles Railton wanted, and so, later that morning, he boarded the London train with Brian Wood and the demure, pretty blond girl.

4

Through his own sources, Giles managed to get copies of Charles' report and the interrogation transcription.

Now he pondered on them as he moved siege forces on a simulated "war ride" of the Black Princes' through Aquitaine during the Hundred Years' War.

Life had changed very rapidly for Giles since the arrival of his granddaughter, Denise, from Paris. At sixteen the girl was incredibly mature, and almost miraculously like Marie—in both looks and temperament. It took little time for Giles Railton to discover that her heartache was over the loss of her mother. Her father hardly entered her mind, and in many ways he detected that she was relieved to have been removed from him and his pompously stern regime.

For the first time since the death of his own wife, Giles had to adjust to having a woman sharing his home, but the pair got on well, and quickly established a working relationship, with Denise slowly starting to run the house.

As he moved foot soldiers, cavalry, wagons, mangonel, cannon and siege equipment toward Poitiers, Giles thought about the Haas girl. Vernon Kell wanted to use her as a lever, to feed misleading information directly into the German Military Intelligence Service.

As Giles' model siege train made its bloody progress across France, other things were happening in the world of secrets. The man they called The Fisherman was already on his way to London, carrying a letter, received with special instructions, from Steinhauer. This letter was to be delivered under a great cloak of secrecy, for it originated from Walter Nicolai, Chief of German Military Intelligence. Nicolai had entrusted it to Steinhauer—though he had no idea how the devious spymaster would have it delivered. The letter was but the first stage in the great web of deceit and manipulation which could only end in betrayal and treachery, both of which were meat and drink to Nicolai and Steinhauer.

5

"I don't care what your hillbilly folks like Natter or the precious Mr. Berry say, I—"

"They're *not* hillbillys." Sara gave a look suggesting grave offense, then giggled.

"Well, what do you call them over here? Country bumpkins?" Dick Farthing feigned irritation. In other circumstances he might have been taken for drunk, but a few glasses of wine over dinner, and some port, were not enough to affect Dick's cast-iron capacity.

They sat in the dining room, alone now that the servants had retired, with only the decrepit butler, Porter, hovering outside the door to be sure that coffee was served as soon as they went to the drawing room.

"Anyhow," Dick continued, "there is *no* possible chance of this damned war being over by Christmas."

The smile left Sara's face. "Perhaps you're right."

He had arrived, uninvited and unannounced, but for the telephone call from Haversage, to say he was there and would like to visit Sara at the Manor.

"I'll give you British that"—looking into her large eyes—"you're not cowards. Once the ball begins to roll, you people can't be stopped."

"Oh, don't you believe it. There're plenty of men shaking in their shoes, ready to avoid fighting." She sighed. "But Mr. Berry wants to go; and poor Martha Crook's in a terrible state—Billy just disappeared, leaving a note to say he's taken the King's shilling. She has no idea where he is."

Dick looked sheepish. "To tell you the truth, I was about to join up if they'd take me. But our President, the inflexible Mr. Wilson, seems hell-bent on keeping America out of it."

"Then why don't you? Join up, I mean."

"That's really why I came down to see you, Sara. Look, can we have coffee? Move out of here?"

"Of course." A hint of unaccountable alarm sounded in her voice. Since John's death she had seen Dick only three times—all been very proper, with Dick behaving perfectly. Today, though, there was something different in his manner.

Porter arrived with the coffee, asking if they required brandy or anything else. Sara said that it was all right; they would help themselves. Porter looked disapproving, but, with grumbles under his breath ("In the General's day . . ."), accepted Sara's advice that he should go to bed. "I'll make sure everything's locked up," she told him with a smile, in the manner of one of his housemaids. Porter would never adapt to taking orders from her, so she played a game of her own with him.

"Oh dear. Poor old Porter—he just will not give up." Farthing seemed not to have heard her. "Dick?"

"Who? Oh . . . sorry, Sara. I was daydreaming."

She poured the coffee, her hand trembling slightly. In the back of her mind there was a picture of leaves in autumn being blown over the surface of the lily pond behind the Great Lawn. Then she asked about his daydream.

"Oh, that? It's a recurring dream—awake or asleep, my dear." Though he sat across from her, his hand moved as though he could reach out and touch her. "Sara, you must know that I dream about you day and night."

The picture of the lily pond changed in her head, a vivid recollection of the night they had almost made love taking its place. That was her own recurring dream.

"If I could, I'd ask you to marry me now—I mean as soon as you're out of mourning; after a decent—"

The mist of silence stretched between them, and the pictures in her brain altered, shuffled clearly—Richard Farthing and herself: in this very room; before and after John's death; of times together with words not spoken; the Downs and watching him teach James to fly; his aeroplane wheeling over the house at dawn; the muddle of emotions this tall American seemed to leave behind him.

She asked what he meant by "could."

He took a deep breath. "I came to see you . . . to say goodbye."

Sara had not expected her reaction to be so violent. He spoke harshly, and for a second it almost took her breath away.

As though he detected the shock, Dick hurriedly added, "Oh, not forever. I was on the point of joining the Royal Flying Corps. They'd accepted me. Then I had an urgent cable. My father, and my uncle—the Senator— both want me home fast. They seem to think there's a special job I can do. 'A duty for your country' is how the old man put it. As I see it, my duty's to the survival of mankind. If I have my way, you'll see me back here again in a matter of months, if not weeks. Sara, you know I've loved you almost from the first moment. I know there was a time when you felt the same, because—"

"Because we very nearly did something exceptionally foolish."

"Yes."

"My dear, dear Richard. Of course I care for you. But . . . Oh, after what happened that night . . . Well, I suppose it was a kind of guilt. I felt—"

"That you had to support John. That you loved him more—"

She put her cup down slowly, rose and came toward him, stopping his mouth with her hand. "Yes, I suppose that's partly true. But not wholly. You've never been far from my thoughts since that night." Her brow creased. "I'm not running away from decisions, and things, Dick, but I ask you not to talk about it now—not yet. It's difficult, I know. But, please, remember one thing. If I ever marry again, then I hope it will be you."

He made as if to speak, but Sara overrode him, raising her voice slightly. "Dick, you have to go away. You tell me that you'll be back. While you're away I'll be thinking about you—about us." She wondered at her own control, for half of her mind thought of the bed, upstairs, and Richard's body, the church in Haversage, with orange blossom and the tall, handsome man standing beside her as she promised to love, honor and obey him. "Please, Dick, don't ask me to commit myself now, at this moment. When you come back—if we both feel the same, when a little more time has gone by—then we'll talk. But not just yet."

Dick Farthing remained silent for some time. He did not look at her when he spoke. "If that's what you want, Sara, so be it. We won't speak of it until I return. But I will not change." His face turned toward her suddenly; the old, confident, dazzling smile enveloping her. "Believe me, when I get back, I'm going to ask you to marry me." The grin broadened. "Unless you've found somebody else."

She kissed his cheek, whispering, "Thank you. You know that I'm not going to find anyone else."

Slowly, after another long, tender kiss, she disentangled herself and he stood up, crossing to the table, asking if he could help them to brandy.

When the glasses were filled, he raised his. "To my return?" —looking full into her eyes over the rim. She nodded, feeling more content than she had for weeks.

Then, keeping to the bargain and not talking about their personal futures, he asked about James: "I haven't had a word from him."

"Margaret Mary says he's away most of the time—here, there and everywhere. She knows he was in Antwerp, during the siege, and she gave me the impression that he's off on special duties for most of the time. He's like you—turns up, like a will o' the wisp, out of nowhere, sleeps for forty-eight hours, then spends a day cosseting his loved ones before disappearing again. She says he's changed."

"The war's going to change a lot of people. The papers don't tell us much, but things are not going well for the French, so God knows what's happening to the British Expeditionary Force."

Sara told him that the family appeared to be more worried about Caspar than anyone else. "He's out there somewhere, with his regiment. Belgium, I think."

He nodded. "And what about the twins? Is it Rupert? And—"

"Ramillies."

"Yeah . . . Ramillies. There are so many Railtons, and I guess I'm not too good with names."

"Rupert's safe enough. In *Monmouth*. The ship's an old bucket, but she's an armored cruiser, and Rupert's with eleven of his old friends from Dartmouth. Andrew says he's safe, and well out of it, off South America."

"And Ramillies—what's he up to?"

She gave a humorless snort. "By my reckoning, Ramillies is the darkest of horses—and the most brilliant. Got a flair for languages—like his cousin

James. He's also far away from any danger—trailing in the wake of the enig-
matic Giles. Ramillies is acting as his aide, and, I should imagine, it will be
Ramillies who'll eventually be the *éminence grise* of Whitehall."

Dick pursed his lips. "Never really figured out what Giles Railton does at
the Foreign Office."

"You're not alone in that, dear Richard. Soon after we were married, I asked
John what Giles did. You'd probably be surprised, but John could be quite
poetic at times. He said, 'My uncle lives on the far side of the moon, and
comes down to earth in the most unlikely places, and in a hundred disguises.'
Then he quoted what he said was a Russian proverb: *The moon shines, but it does
not warm.*" She laughed, without humor. "If I were a true Railton, I certainly
wouldn't have told you that. Uncle Giles is a secret moon man and plies a
hidden trade. Enough!"

He shrugged, as though to imply it was not enough, and Sara half-smiled.
"I'll add one thing. I wouldn't trust Giles Railton an inch. Not with anything—
family property, family ties, country, secrets . . . even life."

Dick, catching her mood, quickly changed the subject. "And Andrew? He
was hoping to go back to sea: his own ship."

"No such luck. Chained to the Admiralty. He's happy enough, though. So's
Charles for that matter, even if he never speaks about the job he's doing. They're
a very secretive lot, my Railtons."

"Yes . . . *my Railtons,*" he echoed. "You're very much one of them now. If I
do get to marry you, I've no illusions as to which family I'd be joining."

By mentioning marriage again, Dick had crossed into mutually agreed forbidden ground, and a silence shouldered itself between them. For a while they
sat separated by their own thoughts. Then Sara suggested they should take a
turn outside. She led the way to her own favorite place, the rose garden.

"You can bear to come here now?" He remembered that terrible day, such
a short time ago, when John lay near these very bushes, gasping his sudden
last breath.

"I come here a great deal. There's peace here."

The moon was high, and the roses almost all gone now, leaving only the
scent of other flowers—night stocks, and a hint of rosemary, mingled with
the clear, clean smell of country greenery. He did not have to look at Sara to
know she was smiling.

"John's peace?" he asked.

"I like to think he found peace here. Does that sound sentimental?"

"It might from any other woman." He turned, his arms enfolding her.

Sara, in spite of her good intentions, found herself returning the embrace.
Her eyes stayed open, staring ahead into the darkness, aware of the stars pulsing
through the universe, and the great shadow that was Redhill Manor, looming
in the moonlight.

Dick saw it as well, and shivered involuntarily as he recalled what Sara had said of Giles Railton. Other words came to him—Shakespeare, out of context, yet seemingly right: *Let us be Diana's foresters, gentlemen of the shade, minions of the moon.*

The kiss was not passionate, by their own choice, though it lasted long. Sara, with her own brand of romanticism, allowed herself to imagine it as some physical, shared, prayer: *Oh God, let the peace of this place be echoed through the world. Let peace come, and let the slaughter of battle not take place.*

Deep inside, she knew the impossibility of what she asked.

6

"If the damned Military would only listen!" Giles sat, weary, in front of C's littered desk. "We warned them of the buildup; that it was going to be a copybook offensive: the von Schlieffen plan with a few modifications by Moltke."

Smith-Cumming grunted. "Not your fault. If anyone's to blame it's the French, and then our own senior military people. You do not meet an offensive battle plan as they, and the French, have done."

Giles was past listening. "We told them well in advance. We even managed to warn the idiots about the size of the German army that would be passing through Belgium. But no! They'll only believe it when the forward units are wiped out. How in God's name do we make them understand?"

The Head of the Secret Service gave a grimace. "We do our best to go on providing good intelligence. In the end, perhaps these antiquarian strategists of the General Staff may see reason. Our kind of work is only as good as the use military commanders make of it. What we have to do—" A knock at the door put an end to what could have been a lecture on the military value of intelligence.

It was a messenger with the latest dispatches from the headquarters of Sir John French—Commander-in-Chief BEF—which, when read, only brought more concern.

As Smith-Cumming read the flimsy pages and then passed them to Giles, both men grew more somber—though Giles Railton quickly allowed his near despair to burst into the thunder of fury. "After all we've provided for them, they still fall into the snare! God knows how many lads'll go to their graves because of this folly!"

Giles had the right to be bitter and angry. He had spent hours going through the fine detail of all he knew of the von Schlieffen war plan. The Committee of Imperial Defence could not have been better, or more thoroughly, briefed. Giles' plea was that the whole General Staff should know everything and share it with their French counterparts long before the crisis got out of hand.

And now the trap was sprung, just as the dead von Schlieffen planned, and his successor, Moltke, had reshaped.

The main German thrust had moved, with great strength, curving through Belgium, cutting a great swath, like some giant scythe, toward France. The

German strategists had banked on the French counterattacking heavily in the northeast. This was the core of von Schlieffen's plan—for it was how the French could be caught, pincered and crushed, while the forces moving through Belgium would envelop and rape Paris itself.

But the closed minds of the Allied military commanders of the Entente Powers appeared oblivious to the warning.

"Even when we had aerial evidence of the size of the advance into Belgium, they would not accept it." Giles spoke almost to himself. He had experienced battle, and knew the horror that was now taking place only a few miles across the Channel.

Smith-Cumming found the ability to grunt out a laugh, even at this grim moment. "They wouldn't even accept my agents' information of five hundred and fifty troop trains crossing the Rhine bridges each day. Well, they know now."

The dispatches lay on Smith-Cumming's desk, silent witness to the awful truth. Sir John French, with the one-hundred-thousand-strong British Expeditionary Force, had come up against the forward units of the German First Army near Mons. Now the BEF was in retreat.

Giles was still angry. "Someone has to pay for this."

Chapter Fourteen

1

The Sergeant pointed at the wooden signpost set at a fork in the road. "Right, my lads, that's where you're goin'." The signpost said LE CATEAU 6 K.

One hundred thousand regular soldiers had crossed the Channel with the BEF. The whisper was that casualties were now incredibly high. Sergeant Graves sadly looked at the platoon in his charge. Schoolboys in uniform, he thought.

"Why we goin' to this Lee Cat-ee-ow place, then, Sergeant?" The rake-thin lad called Lofthouse (and well nicknamed Lofty) had to shout to make himself heard, for the hot road was crowded—horse-drawn carts, French and Belgian civilians, old men, women, children, trudging along the grass verges, while the road itself was clogged with troops.

"You are reinforcements for Two Corps, lad. Commanded by General Sir Horace Smith-Dorrien." Sergeant Graves pronounced it "Smith Doreen." "You'll be part of the 14th Infantry Brigade, with the Second Suffolks." In his mind he said "and God 'elp you." "Now, let's see what you learned at Aldershot. I want you fresh, and marchin'."

A squad of infantry went past in ragged file, the men hardly turning their heads to look at the platoon—their eyes dull, and many limping from the blisters of miles.

"Strikes me we're goin' the wrong bloody way," Lofty Lofthouse muttered to the young private marching beside him. "They're all coming *from* this Lee Cat-ee-ow place. What you reckon?"

"Dunno." The tall boy next to Lofthouse had about him the look of the country, and he could not keep step properly, as though used to a different pace—behind the plow perhaps.

The air was heavy as lead, with thunder in the distance—not that they would be able to distinguish thunder at the moment. Ever since they had landed at Le Havre, the sound of guns, far away, had been background music for their journey. As for the clogged roads, they were the reason for the march to Le Cateau, for the transport on which they had traveled from Le Havre had been forced to a halt by the retreating Belgian, French and British troops, combined with the endless stream of refugees. Khaki figures could be seen in the fields, while ambulances, and men hobbling, bandaged and gray with pain, spoke of fearsome work ahead.

As they marched toward Le Cateau, Sergeant Graves worked out the possibilities. Unless troops were really in rout from the enemy, the time always came for them to turn, stand and fight. This, according to all the elementary strategy he had learned, usually meant that a stand had to be made in order to buy time for others: so that an army, corps or division could regroup, rearm and take up a defensive line.

Lurking in the back of Sergeant Graves' mind was the unhappy notion that, possibly, they were heading toward II Corps because II Corps was going to buy that much-needed time for the British Expeditionary Force.

Though the Sergeant's thinking was accurate enough, nobody knew, at this moment, as the little platoon of reinforcements plugged along the dusty road, that any covering action would be fought at all. In fact, only now, in the late afternoon of August 25th, had the bulk of II Corps arrived, under pressure from the enemy, in the Le Cateau area.

They had fought their way slowly back from the Mons battlefields, in harness with I Corps. At this moment, as the Sergeant's half-trained, untried reserves broke into a bawdy song, the men and artillery of II Corps were skirting the forest of Mormal, to the northeast of Le Cateau, and the clutch of villages which lay between it and the town of Cambrai to the northwest.

Sergeant Graves' orders had been less specific than he allowed the recruits to know. Yet, to all intents, this tiny band of raw boys was destined to join their allotted units in the field of battle and move back the way they had come—under the fire of German rifles, machine guns and artillery.

> *Four-and-twenty virgins came down from Inverness,*
> *And when the ball was over there were four-and-twenty less;*
> *Singing, I'll do ye this time,*

I'll do ye now;
The lad that did ye last time, he canna do ye now.

The young civilians in uniform sang with gusto, but all Sergeant Graves could think about was the countryside through which they marched.

The roads suddenly became clearer, less crowded, but the sound of sporadic gunfire was closer to hand by the minute. They marched through bleached, dry, slightly undulating ground—bare but for the occasional tree, and without cover except for the odd ditch in the hard-baked earth. Bloody 'ell, Graves thought. It's like soddin' Salisbury Plain without the trees. Graves did not relish the thought of having to stand and fight in this place.

Nor did General Smith-Dorrien, but later that night he would be faced with no alternative.

2

"Young officer, Mr. Railton, needs a batman. One volunteer." A sergeant, Martin by name, stood in the doorway of the barn, on the outskirts of Le Cateau, making the request sound like an order from God.

Sergeant Graves had handed over his "children," as he called them, to a sergeant-major of the 2nd Suffolks, just outside Le Cateau itself at exactly five minutes past six, as the stormclouds began to gather and the air seemed to thicken like soup.

"Children, Sarn't? The children of this regiment have become old men in the past week. Same'll happen to these lads—those that're spared." And the men were quickly and efficiently split up and sent in twos and threes to those platoons now understrength from casualties suffered during the grueling cross-country chase from the Mons battlefields.

Three of the reinforcements sat in the barn with hardened campaigners, nineteen and twenty years of age, who told them stories of the fighting, exchanged cigarettes, ate bully beef and drank hot sweet tea, brewed up in mess tins and billy cans.

As the new arrivals heard of the bitter fighting around the Mons salient, one of them, goggle-eyed, asked, "What's it like? What's it really like when the shooting starts?" half in fear and half excitement and anticipation.

"Noise, blood and guts." A corporal from North London, still young enough to have acne scarring his face, drew on a thin cigarette. "It jus' 'appens, see. One minute you're scared shitless; the next you don' 'ave time to think. Not till after, like."

"And them bloddy Gerries—" Another man, a fat, red-faced private, spat on the stone floor. "You don' 'ardly ever see them; but when you do it ain't 'alf strange. Like gray ghosts, they are, in them uniforms, and the 'elmets, wi' spikes on 'em, like a London copper."

There was muttered agreement, and a short silence. Then an older man, around twenty-three or four—neat as a bank clerk even in the dusty, stained uniform—cleared his throat. "Funny." He looked up at the beams in the barn's roof. "It's funny. We were in this village—don' ast me the name of it. Odd name it had. Well, we was there all morning, and Gerry, he kept on coming in waves, like; and we just went on shootin' at 'im, and forcin 'im back. I know I killed my first man that morning—saw him slide down like he'd had too much plum duff and cider. Round dinnertime it went all quiet, an' the Sergeant—'awkins—you remember 'awkins, copped it last night, other side of that big wood; them trees; that forest. . . ."

"Mormal—I heard an officer call that forest Mormal," from someone sitting well back in the corner.

"Yes, the forest. Well, Sergeant 'awkins says as how half on us can stand down. It was all quiet, and the sun shining and everything. I went off and sat on a doorstep. Didn't think no people was left in the place. Then out comes this kiddie, 'bout four or five years old. Bright as a button, and not frightened or nothing. She starts to jabber away in her own lingo, then comes and sits on my knee. Well, eventually she finds this whistle." He reached for the top right-hand pocket of his tunic, bringing out a silver police whistle on a chain. "Me mum give it me: use to be my uncle's, him in the police force. Died of pneumonia, 1910. Always keeps it here," patting the pocket. "Never know, do you? Anyhow, she gets hold on it and puts it in her mouth, then starts blowin' and blowin'—makes one hell of a din, but she was so happy; so happy blowin' away." He seemed to take a deep breath to control himself. "First time I was ever homesick that was. First bleedin' time. Funny."

There was a violent crash and roar, echoing around outside, shaking the barn, but only the newcomers flinched.

"Said we was in for thunder." The man with the whistle nodded. "Been sayin' it all day." He looked at the suddenly startled eyes of the newcomers. "No, it's only thunder. You'll know all right when it's the Gerry guns."

And it was at that moment the Sergeant came in demanding a volunteer to be young Mr. Railton's batman.

Billy Crook did not think twice. He stood up and ambled over to where the NCO stood. Sergeant Martin looked at him as though he were deformed. "Ho yes," with a humorless laugh. "And what makes you think you can be a batman, an officer's servant, then, Sunny Jim?"

Billy Crook's voice was cloaked in a Berkshire burr. "Use to work for 'em, Sergeant."

"Work for who?"

"Railtons. Haversage way."

"And where the hell might Haversage way be?"

Billy genuinely thought the NCO was joking. "Come on, Sergeant, *everybody* knows Haversage. Haversage, and Redhill Manor—that's where I worked and lived.

"That's enough of the dumb insolence, lad." The Sergeant peered closer at Billy Crook, his brow creasing. Strange, he thought. This lad had a similarity to Mr. Railton, but he could not quite put a finger on what it was. The eyes, perhaps? Or the nose? "Mr. Railton was related to the late General Railton, did you know that, lad? General Sir William Railton?"

"I was at the Manor when he died." Billy stood, unperturbed by the Sergeant's suspicious gaze. "They sent me down the hill, to the Vicar, that night. First time I ever saw the Vicar, close up like that, the night they sent me, the night the General died...."

"All right, lad. Get your kit and come with me."

3

At twenty years of age, Caspar Railton looked thirty. Tall, like his father, he had already grasped the nettle of confidence. Everyone could detect natural leadership within five minutes of being with him. The striking blue eyes were now filmed with fatigue; his hair, usually blond and lank, was dirty and sticking to his scalp; while the characteristic nose twitched, much in the way his late uncle's, the General's, nose had moved at the scent of trouble; a fox; the enemy; or a pretty woman.

Caspar had seen to the platoon first, making sure his Sergeant found them a good billet for a few hours, then issued the ammunition, followed by rations. He gave special orders concerning any replacements and said he would be around to see the men himself, shortly. Asking Sergeant Martin to get him a new batman was almost an afterthought, just as he was leaving to join the other platoon commanders in the old stone house, once the home of some peasant smallholder.

Evans, the man who had been with him ever since he joined the regiment, had caught a piece of shrapnel in the spine late in the afternoon.

Now, Caspar shaved out of a mess tin, peering at his face in a tiny cracked piece of glass that hung against the stone wall, next to a highly-colored painting of Christ. The Saviour's finger pointed to a radiant bleeding heart projecting from his chest.

A heart just did not look like that, Caspar thought. He should know, having seen one about a week ago. Some poor fellow with a great rent in his chest from a hunk of shell, and his heart literally in his hands, still pumping the life from him. The heart did not look like Jesus' heart at all.

A sharp rap at the half-open door announced Sergeant Martin. One of the other subalterns, also carrying out his ablutions, called for the NCO to enter, and Martin barked out, "Private Crook, sir. Volunteer for batman, sir."

Caspar hardly looked up. "Know your duties, Crook?"

"Not yet, sir."

"Right. You look after my kit, and always have your own near at hand—especially your rifle. In the field, you stay close to me. You'll have to be sharp and keep your eyes open. You'll be my runner when there's action. Oh yes, and you'll help the other officers' servants with meals. Up to it, you think, Crook?"

"I reckon, sir."

At last Caspar lifted his head and looked at the young soldier. "Don't I know you, Private Crook?"

"Billy Crook, sir. Martha Crook's son: Redhill Manor. Known you, on visits, all me life, sir. Rode with you an' all. . . ."

"Good Lord!" Caspar's face split into a wide smile. "Billy Crook!" The sight of the lad brought back a flood of happy memories: Redhill in high summer, and in the winter. Heavens, young Billy had swiped apples with them, and—as he said—they had ridden together. "Good to have someone from Redhill here, Crook. Now, clear up that stuff, would you," waving toward his shaving gear, "then go and join the other servants in the kitchen. Help get some food ready." He turned to Martin. "Platoon settled in, Sarn't?"

"Sir! All settled down nicely."

"Right. Use the time to rest, but make sure all weapons are cleaned. Carry on, Sarn't."

"Sir!" There was another great clap of thunder, almost overhead, as Sergeant Martin left the cottage.

Billy got on with the work, washing and drying his officer's badger brush and the cut-throat razor—stowing them away in their velvet-lined box.

Then, taking his own pack and rifle with him, he went through into the little kitchen.

The other two officers' servants greeted him like an old friend, accepting him at once. They appeared to get on well, though they were as different as chalk and cheese. "Dasher" Dance, a regular soldier, around thirty years of age, knew the ropes; the other, Donald—Billy was never to discover his surname—was short, with pudgy hands, thick lips and a slight lisp. Donald seemed fond of touching both Dasher and Billy—on the arm or shoulder most of the time. Dasher did not seem to worry, mainly, it seemed, because Donald was such a good cook: "Makes hardtack and bully beef taste like it come out of the Ritz Hotel," Dasher said.

Donald was certainly a dab hand with the rations. "Foraging's the first thing you have to learn, Billy. Even when Gerry's around, and all hell's breaking loose, you keep your eyes open. Anything that'll come in useful, you grab. Like these spuds. Dasher pulled them out of a little garden last night, when the shells were falling all around. Keep the peepers open—you'll soon catch on."

As well as the potatoes, they managed to find onions, and Billy also discovered that both men carried numerous small tins in their packs, containing all kinds of things used to make the rations more palatable—saffron, cloves and an inexhaustible supply of curry powder.

That night Donald concocted a kind of hash out of the potatoes, onions and bully beef, while Dasher's contribution took the form of liberal sprinklings of curry powder.

Billy thought the result to be most tasty, and the officers approved heartily of the hash.

"Congratulations," Caspar Railton called out. "Excellent meal, though I detect Dance has been at it with the curry powder again."

The thunder rumbled over the plain during the evening, and later the rain came—a deluge, sweeping in from great towering black clouds, driving down on the old dry roofs, creating small streams in the cobbled streets.

Just before midnight, Second Lieutenant Railton called Billy in and told him to prepare the kit for a quick departure. It was while Billy wrestled with the buckles, webbing and leather that one of the other officers returned from inspecting his own platoon: soaked from the sudden summer storm.

"Company Commanders' meeting with the CO in ten minutes. Be our turn next." He shook the rain from his trench coat. "Don't like the way things're shaping up, Caspar. The General's been here in Le Cateau and up on the ridge, by the Roman road. Don't like the sound of it."

"They don't like the sound of it," Billy repeated to the other two when he was back in the kitchen.

"Nor do I." Dasher spoke from the pinnacle of his long military experience. "Don't like Generals clambering about the countryside in Gerry's direction. Don't like it at all."

Billy shivered. "What you think, then?"

Dasher shook his head with the gravity of a man who expected to hear only bad news. "I think there's a chance we'll be told to stand fast. That I do *not* like. We're outnumbered and out-bloody-gunned."

A couple of minutes later the three young officers were shrugging into trench coats. Caspar Railton told Billy to get back to the platoon and tell Sergeant Martin that he wanted them standing by in half an hour. "Take my kit up to the barn with you." He looked serious. "And your own, of course."

Billy asked what was happening, and Caspar gave him a friendly grin. "That's what we'll find out, Crook. Either we're moving back or we're staying here to meet Gerry head-on"

Back in the barn there was a lot of activity, which appeared to become more frantic after Billy Crook delivered his message to Sergeant Martin. Half an hour later, with the platoon in battle order and rifles loaded, "Safety catch on"—the Sergeant went to each man just to be certain—Mr. Railton appeared, his map case slung at his side, face set, with a slight crease in his brow, accentuated by the strange shadows flung around the barn from the oil lamps which had been lit as soon as darkness fell. They had hung what looked to be old blankets over the doors and the one small window to prevent the light from spilling out into the pitch black. The rain had stopped and the air seemed fresher than before; yet still, in the distance, thunder fought its own battle among the clouds.

Caspar told them to carry on smoking, then began to speak.

In a couple of minutes they knew the worst. "Two Corps is to make a stand around the old Roman road running between Le Cateau and Cambrai—southwest of where we are now," Caspar began. "For those of you who tend to get mixed up with compass bearings, that's roughly off to the left of here." There was some nervous laughter.

"We're leaving very soon," Caspar told them, "and, together with the King's Own Yorkshire Light Infantry, we'll be guarding the right flank. We'll have artillery support from at least three batteries, while the Thirteenth, Nineteenth and remainder of Fourteenth Brigades will be to our rear. The job is to kill the enemy and hold up his advance for as long as we can. Then we shall also withdraw—leaving him with a bloody nose, we hope. Gerry's had it his own way for long enough, according to General Smith-Dorrien. Now we have to give him a little surprise." Billy had a feeling that Caspar Railton did not wholly believe what he was saying.

"Now . . ." Caspar scraped some lines on the wall with a piece of stone, improvising a map. "You've all had a look at the kind of country we'll be fighting in. Bloody flat and without much cover. There's higher ground to the east, and we might be ordered to move up there. But the plan is for us to get out of Le Cateau itself as quickly as we can. It's in a hollow, as you know, and therefore damned dangerous. We'll be moving off around dawn. Any questions?"

The men looked at one another and muttered, but nobody spoke up.

"I have just had a thought," Railton went on. "It's the 26th August today, and that's the anniversary of the Battle of Crécy, when our forefathers won a victory in France against great odds. Those of you who believe in omens should take heart, because I can't pretend the morning's going to bring easy soldiering. Gerry'll be tired, but he's out there in strength, with a lot of artillery."

4

They moved off just after five o'clock, before dawn, climbing the slight rise to the left, above the town, boots and puttees soon becoming soaked in the wet grass.

At about half past five, in the gloom of the early morning, the various platoons began to form up on the near side of the straight gray road running between Le Cateau and Cambrai. It was already getting light, but the heavy rain of the previous night had brought down a thin, almost eerie mist, which hung low across the fields and the crossroads to their left, chilling the bones. Billy Crook, keeping close behind Caspar Railton, sniffed the air with a countryman's instinct. The mist would thicken a little when the sun came out, then it should lift into a brilliant day.

Gerry could come over the fields, and they would probably not see him until he was less than a couple of hundred yards away.

Sound carried, even in the damp early air, and Billy heard the rattle of harness and the metallic sound of the artillery pieces being set up behind them. The occasional whinny of a horse brought back memories of mornings like this at Redhill, and he wondered if young Mr. Caspar was having similar thoughts.

At last, Caspar Railton stopped, ordering Sergeant Martin to see that the three sections of his platoon fanned out to take up positions close to the crossroads themselves. To his surprise, Billy saw that Sergeant Graves was with them. Graves caught his eye, giving him a friendly nod.

The ground on their side of the road sloped down into a small ditch, and from where Billy stood—as Caspar gave his orders—you could make out a fork to the right, and, behind that, the town of Le Cateau, just visible in the thin hanging mist.

As the men of Caspar's platoon began to line the ditch, Billy saw the same thing happening at intervals along the road to his left—on the other side of the crossroads—as far as the visibility allowed. That would be the right-hand section of the King's Own Yorkshire Light Infantry, he reasoned. Their own platoons, toward Le Cateau, were lost in the mist.

"Right." Young Mr. Caspar turned to him. "We'll have to place ourselves somewhere towards the center of the platoon. Over here, I think." He pointed, starting to walk toward the ditch as he did so. "Not much cover. Bit of a natural parapet. You'll have to dig yourself some kind of hollow, but keep near me, Billy. The Company Commander has his headquarters about a hundred yards down the road on our left. I might have to send you back there if things get difficult. Oh, and remember—if I catch it badly or get killed, Sergeant Martin'll take over. If that happens, you whiz off straight down to the Company Commander. Understand?"

Billy murmured a quick "Sir!", wondering at his officer calling him by his Christian name. Then he went forward, dropping on his knees against the shoulder of the ditch, carefully placing his rifle so that he could easily grab it. Billy at least knew about guns, and was able to shoot as well as the next man, for there had been plenty of practice at Redhill.

He began to dig a small hollow into which he could push his shoulders and so make a natural firing position, scrabbling at the earth with his hands after loosening it with his bayonet. Soon he became aware of Mr. Caspar using a small knife. Without a word, Billy stopped his own digging to assist his officer, working so hard that he was sweating by the time it was done. The rain had made little difference to the earth, baked solid by the previous weeks of sun.

Caspar thanked him and started to walk down the line as Billy continued to dig for himself. It was just then that the German artillery barrage began.

For a few seconds Billy had no idea of what was going on. First, a terrible rushing sound hit his ears — like a train, he thought at the time, looking up, confused by the idea of a train turning into an aeroplane. The rushing sound doubled, then trebled, and he was aware of Mr. Caspar flinging himself onto the ground, face downward into the grass. The great sound above was split, in Billy's mind, by a distant series of noises, like far-off Roman candles.

Then came the solid, sharp and all too dangerous explosions: great crumps which made the earth shake and his eardrums go numb. Out of the corner of his eye he saw a series of brilliant red and orange flashes — from behind — but when he turned they had changed to big flowers of smoke and dust.

"Look to your front," Sergeant Martin's voice, quiet and calm, echoed, with the same words instantly repeated down the line.

Caspar Railton had rolled over and was already running toward his parapet next to Billy. Then came more explosions. There was a reek of smoke in the air, and now the mist seemed to thicken with clouding from the detonating shells.

"Blast!" Caspar was beside Billy again, his revolver in one hand, the lanyard drooping from the butt. "Look to your front!" — his voice almost angry. "Bloody Gerry knows we're here. They'll come straight out of the mist when this is over."

"Wha—" Billy started, his voice drowned by an earthquake of explosions as the German guns poured shells around the position.

Behind, there were cries, and the horrible sound of horses, terrified or in pain. Then, in the midst of the madness, came the solid *Whu-whump . . . Whu-whump* of their own batteries returning fire.

"Buggers're ranging in on our guns," Caspar muttered. "Watch your front, lad, they'll come at us any minute."

But that was for later.

Time ceased to mean anything from the moment the first shells landed behind them. Life was, in a way, suspended, or dropped into an unfamiliar country where death and mutilation were the only currency.

Billy Crook had no idea of how long they waited out there on the road as the constant roar and crump went on and on, and the British guns cracked back. Then suddenly a new noise burst through the din of the barrage: a sharper, less-formidable sound; a crackling, and the unfamiliar *ta-ta-ta-ta-ta* of machine guns. In some ways Billy dreaded this new noise more than the earth-trembling explosions, for the rifles and machine guns were more accurately directed.

At first the small-arms fire came from their left. Then, suddenly, it started to the right, and he heard Caspar breathe, "They're here. Somewhere. Keep your eyes skinned."

The mist was just starting to lift: a pearl background with golden reflected light as the sun tried to break through. Then he saw his first Germans — three of them: dark, fuzzy shapes coming through the haze about one hundred and fifty yards to their front, on the far side of the road. He checked the scale on his backsight, slipped off the safety catch and tucked the Lee Enfield into his shoulder. In the few seconds this took him, the whole front had become filled with growing shapes—a long, ragged line of infantry moving forward, straight toward the road.

"Can I fire, sir?" he whispered.

Caspar opened his mouth, but a volley of rifle shots broke out around them and there was no need to ask or reply. Billy had one figure in his sights. He squeezed the trigger, felt the harsh kick of the rifle against his shoulder and the smell of cordite in his nostrils as the figure leaped into the air—a St. Andrew's Cross for a second—silhouetted against the sky, then falling, and nothing.

By the time his first target had dropped, Billy Crook had jerked at the bolt action and reloaded. He fired again, four times in quick succession, knowing that at least three of the shots found their mark. Then he became oblivious to the sounds around him—the crack after crack of other rifles, the constant pounding of the guns to the rear, the continued roar and crash of German shells.

After the first advance and the hail of bullets put down by the men on the ridge, the shadowy gray figures did not come walking, but crouched or slid, creeping on their bellies, like snakes.

Billy stopped counting after his sixth kill; there were so many of them, rising from the ground only a few yards away or crawling almost to within spitting distance. They came again and again during the morning, and you knew time was passing only because the sun grew hotter and higher in the heavens. The noise, and obvious dangers—the thud of bullets hitting the ditch or sharding the road—became the natural pattern of the day. For Billy Crook, the world was reduced to what he could see over the foresight of his rifle; while the sounds of nature became the chirp of the machine gun, the screech of the wounded, the bark of rifles and the quaking thunder of the guns.

In one short lull, Billy eased himself back and saw that Caspar Railton, who kept talking for most of the time, had acquired a rifle and ammunition from somewhere and was busy reloading. Billy wondered where the weapon came from, then, looking around, saw the decimation of his comrades.

He spotted the remains of Sergeant Martin, spread-eagled on his back behind the ditch. There were men lying, as if asleep, over their rifles, while others moved, adjusting aim or reloading. Stretcher-bearers worked, like scavengers picking over rubble, quickly lifting their treasure of shattered bodies onto canvas litters and hurrying with them to comparative safety.

Billy turned to his front again, spotting three Germans trying to creep along a gully across the road. Sighting quickly, he fired, conscious of his officer's rifle also delivering a shot at the same moment. One of the Germans disappeared with a cry, and the other two ducked down and were gone from sight.

So far the action had been from their front, apart from the heavier gunfire

over them, and from behind. Then, as suddenly as the first attack, there came
a rising wave of fire from the right.

"My God!" Railton said loudly, "they've broken through the town!" As
though to give him credence, a runner, crouched and weaving, ran along the
ditch.

"They're through Le Cateau, sir. Manchesters and Argylls coming up on the
right as quickly as possible. The General says to please hold as long as you
can." Then he was off, carrying his message to the next platoon as another
attack—about sixty enemy soldiers—made itself apparent in the fields beyond
the road.

The artillery were moving. Billy recognized the jingle of harness and rumble
of wheels.

As he fired, recocked the bolt action, fired again, worked the bolt and fired,
Billy heard the sounds of guns being made ready nearby. "Good lads, coming
up in close support," Caspar said, firing as a flitting figure rose from hiding,
fifty yards away, then slipped back to the earth.

The German shelling intensified, and as he slid a new clip of ammunition
into his magazine, Billy had to crouch, trying to bury himself in the ground
as a lucky shell hit the gun—limber, horses, crew, everything—only a short
distance behind them. The noises were unlike anything the boy had ever
dreamed of in his worst childhood nightmares—inhuman, agonizing and dreadful: as though a horde of demons had been unleashed in this normally peaceful
and innocent part of the French countryside.

Without warning, the fighting ceased to their front, as though the enemy
troops had been spirited away. The air fell still around them, and the battered,
ripped ranks seemed to hold their collective breath, waiting for some final,
worse, onslaught which did not come.

"It's not over yet." Caspar crawled back from the ditch, moving cautiously
along the lines of his now seriously depleted platoon.

"It's bad." He shook his head and Billy saw a look of horror deep in the
young officer's eyes. "God knows what's happened to the other lads, but ours
are feeling the strain. Doubt if they'll hold off for long." Fighting was still
heavy far away to their left, while the sounds of even more concentrated battle
came from the far right of their line.

The artillery, mauled in the constant barrage of the last hours, appeared to
be re-forming, shifting their positions in order to help in what seemed to be
developing on the right flank. But around the main standpoint, along the ridge
of the Roman road, only the occasional shell whined overhead or exploded—
stray—in the fields nearby. The odd rifle shot made Billy start, jump and
turn—his rifle ready. But the heavy fighting seemed now to be sparing them.

After about an hour Caspar said that it sounded as though the referee had
blown his whistle for the first half of the match.

"Wonder how we'll play in the second half, sir," Billy murmured, and Mr.
Railton laughed.

"I have to tell you." The young officer seemed embarrassed. "You did damned well this morning, Billy Crook. I've seldom seen anyone as cool under fire."

"Don't know how you work that out, Mr. Caspar." Billy grinned. "You was too busy to notice. Anyhow, what's the point of getting in a muck sweat? We all has to go someday. I came use to it quickly, and with a lot of help."

"Help?"

"The General, sir. Back at Redhill. When I was little he talked to me a lot. Told me how it was when you're fighting; said he wanted me to be a soldier. Said I'd find myself on a battlefield one day. Give me a lot of tips, the General did. You've no idea how he helped."

"Oh, I've got a *very* good idea of how much he helped." Caspar smiled. "He gave me a lot of tips as well. You ever play with his army, Billy? His toy soldiers?"

"I have them, sir. Christmas before he died, the General give his army to me. My prize possession that is. He taught me how to play soldiers, only it was never play. Taught me strategy and tactics."

The fighting to their left and right became audibly worse during the next hour. Worse, and if anything closer to hand. Billy was surprised when Caspar told him it was almost two o'clock in the afternoon. He thought it was much later.

Soon after, another runner arrived. "CO's compliments, sir." He managed an apology of a salute. "You're to withdraw by sections, quickly as possible. CO says there's danger in it, so take care. We regroup at . . ." He fumbled in the map case slung around his shoulder and looked at the contents, reading off a map reference.

Caspar thanked him, consulting his own maps, not looking up as the man trotted away. Then he told Billy that they would be moving back, down the line of the Roman road, to their left, to regroup at a place called Reumont. Billy was to pass down the line, giving the orders for withdrawal by sections. "And warn them they'll certainly have to fight their way back. If we're not careful, some of our chaps will get caught up here on the ridge."

Billy nodded, repeated the map reference and was away, moving low and fast along that section of the road held by the remnants of Mr. Railton's platoon.

It was a short journey, but only now did he take in the full measure of what had happened that morning. He was also suddenly aware of what Mr. Caspar had meant about the possibility of being cut off on the ridge.

A mile or so away, to the right, below him, a vicious series of actions was taking place. From this distance it was like gazing at some painting come to life: small figures fought, lived and died among the savage storm of bullets, grenades and bayonets; while the artillery of both sides kept up its constant pounding.

A long cloud of dirty smoke, breaking up into sinister tendrils, swept over the fields, hovering above the desperate men of both sides. If the Germans broke through, all would be lost for those of them left on the Roman road.

Closer to hand, the carnage was terrible to see—the fields stained in patches with blood; horses, and what was left of men and guns, scattering the place where, he imagined, young men and girls from the local villages had probably come, in summer, to learn love. There was no thought of love in this place now.

Along the ditch where Caspar Railton's platoon had made their stand, things were as bad. The numbers of men were now so reduced that Billy had to search hard for faces he could recognize from the few hours he had spent in the barn.

Some lay dead and broken. Others looked at him, anxious, as though willing him to be a messenger of hope. He saw Lofty Lofthouse, his eyes old and showing no sign of recognition. Sergeant Graves, who had given him a cheerful nod when they first reached the ridge, now met Billy with a glance of tired disillusion.

As he glanced at the unlucky ones, caught forever in a frozen moment and now sleeping for eternity, Billy thought, It could be me. Any one of them could be me. Then, for some unaccountable reason, what appeared to him as even worse: It could be me—or Mr. Railton. . . .

He returned, sweating. "Number 2 section say there's only four of them left, though some lads from another platoon've joined them. And Corporal Lester's only got three of his original lads with him, sir."

Caspar nodded glumly. "Right. Let's watch them go, then we'll move our toes. And be ready to kill any Gerry who tries to get in our way." He stood up, shading his eyes, as the khaki figures began to move away from the ditch. Then, as he turned back, the stray shell exploded less than fifteen yards away.

The blast knocked Billy off his feet. His ears rang, while the right side of his body stung from the blast. He rolled over, shook himself like a dog, then moved his arms and legs. He appeared to be in one piece. "You all—" he began, swinging his head to where Caspar Railton had been.

The officer was sprawled unnaturally, with blood all down one side, where his left arm had been sheared off at the shoulder. The right leg was bent grotesquely at an angle, just above the knee—the lower part of the limb hanging free, attached by one thick strand of bone and sinew.

Within a second Billy was beside him, kneeling in the blood. Caspar's eyes were closed, the fine face suddenly parchment gray. Then he moved his head and sobbed, "Mummy . . ."

The eyes opened and the head turned. "Billy! Billy Crook! Jesus!"

"It's all right, Mr. Caspar . . ."

"No . . . Company Commander . . . Finished . . . I'm . . ." The eyes rolled back, steadied, then closed again. "Finished."

But Billy had not been Martha Crook's son for nothing. Since he was old enough to understand, he had watched his mother as she tended the sick or helped at dreadful accidents among the farmhands or men on the Estate.

"Oh no—you're not finished, Mr. Caspar," Billy almost shouted in fury, ripping off his webbing and tunic, then the shirt from his own back—tearing it from collar to tail.

In a fever of speed, he rolled half of the shirt into a ball, pushing it hard against Caspar's shoulder, moving the body slightly so that the bleeding could be stopped. Then he turned his attention to the leg.

His fingers scrabbled at Caspar's khaki tie, pulling it free, binding it tightly around the thigh, ripping at the material of the officer's breeches to get at the flesh. When it was tight and cutting a ridge into the skin, Billy looked down, seeing the blood running less freely. There was no hope of saving the lower part of the leg, and he looked about, desperately shouting, "Stretcher-bearers! Stretcher-bearers!" as he had heard so many shout that morning. But now, nobody would come. The men who had been with them were well away by this time.

Then he spotted the clasp knife clipped to Caspar's belt. The officer had started to use it that morning to try to dig a firing position. Billy unclipped it from the Sam Browne belt, opening the blade, testing it on his thumb, then cleaning it off as best he could on his own handkerchief.

From just above the knee, down to the foot, the leg was held only by slivers of bone and one strand of sinew and veins about as thick as Billy's own thumb. He parted the way with his fingers, then slid the knife blade in. Taking a deep breath, he bore down and started to saw through the cord.

Caspar gave a half-scream, then lay silent as the strand parted and Billy kicked what was left of the limb into the ditch.

He bound up the stump with the other half of his shirt, then tied his first makeshift bandage, on the shoulder, using the revolver lanyard which he un-looped from around his officer's neck, unclipping the far end from the small swivel on the revolver butt.

Caspar Railton was still breathing, and, as Billy put an ear to his chest, he moved slightly and groaned.

Still working in a frenzy of speed, Billy put on his tunic and buckled the webbing equipment. His clothes were smeared with Caspar's blood; his hands like those of a butcher. He took his rifle, slinging it around his neck, checked that the chamber of Caspar's revolver was fully loaded, then hoisted the maimed body across his shoulders, carrying it as he would lift a sack of turnips. So Billy took his subaltern down from the ridge at Le Cateau.

At a jog trot, he carried the shattered body for over two miles, with only one incident. As he approached a copse, near the fighting below Le Cateau, Billy heard the crack of a bullet passing near, then the thump of its rifle, ten yards away, in long grass on the copse's perimeter. He fired twice with the revolver, and a German soldier half-rose from the grass, stumbling and falling on his face. A comrade stepped openly from the trees, calmly bringing his rifle to his shoulder. Billy shot him, once, through the stomach. A third broke cover, his face anxious and hands uncertain on his rifle. But there was no uncertainty about Billy. Without pausing in his steady run, he fired the revolver again, from across his body. The German did not shoot. Billy had but one thought: Caspar Railton had to be brought safe home.

He did not notice the flesh wound in his own right upper arm, where a bullet—spent and stray—had lodged. And, when he got Caspar to the comparative safety of a dressing station, near Corps Headquarters, he refused treatment until Mr. Railton was seen to.

Even then, Billy would take no rest or food until the medical officer assured him that Second Lieutenant Railton was still alive and they would do all they could for him. Only then, and after being ordered—by a bristling major—to receive medical attention, did Billy Crook leave Caspar Railton.

Chapter Fifteen

1

At a little before six o'clock in the evening, Charles Railton climbed the steps to the front door of the Cheyne Walk house. It was the first Friday in September, and already the leaves were turning to red and gold. Summer was draining away, as were the chances of a quick, decisive victory in France.

It was indicative of Charles' sense of guilt that, on entering the drawing room to find Mildred sobbing, he immediately became concerned lest she had by some feminine intuition delved into the darkest secret on his conscience.

"Oh, Charles..." She ran to him, eyes red, nose running.

For a second Charles was too shaken even to inquire into the reason for this outburst of tears. Gently, he led her to the Chesterfield, and there she told him about Caspar.

"Oh my God." He put his head in his hands. "How bloody awful. Only just twenty. Arm *and* leg?"

She nodded, sniffing in a way she would never have done had there been servants about. "Andrew sent a note from the Admiralty, and I've been with Charlotte all afternoon." She paused, swallowing. "Had to hold myself together with her. Let myself go when I got back here. I keep seeing him as he was at that last dinner party in June."

He gave a small shake of the head, then asked how Charlotte had taken it. The question seemed stupid.

"Desperate, of course. Caspar was such a... well, so active.... He was... so... so..."

"They say he'll live, though?"

Mildred raised her eyebrows, making her face a spoiled mask of tragedy.

"He's out of shock; miraculously there's no gas gangrene. Apparently the signs are good. They're bringing him back tomorrow."

"Poor wretched young man—and he's only one of hundreds." Charles looked away. "Perhaps it would be better if he died. A lad like that crippled for life."

Mildred did not reply, and Charles asked how Andrew was bearing up.

"You know Andrew." Her nose still ran like a village pump. "As always. Strong. Silent. He said at least they did not have to mourn—which, I suppose, gives the lie to you. The casualty lists are terrible: from Mons, Le Cateau, Guise . . . Thank heaven William's only four years old. I couldn't bear—"

Charles continued to comfort her, his mind taking in the reality of the golden Caspar being a cripple for all time.

"The most wonderful thing—" Mildred started.

"Yes?"

"His servant saved his life. His batman! You know who? Martha Crook's son—Billy. Martha Crook, who saved my life, and delivered William Arthur, at Redhill."

"I didn't think that lad was old enough to be serving."

"Old enough? None of them are old enough. Brave enough, though." She told Charles the story of Billy Crook, and how he had brought Caspar down from the ridge. "He's already home. They're sending him to some training depot, according to Uncle Giles, so he can be promoted to sergeant. It's apparently very secret, but Andrew says Billy's been recommended for the Victoria Cross."

Charles could not shake the image of young Caspar from his head, and since hearing the news, he was unaccountably more aware of the guilt nibbling away at his own conscience.

"You're in to dinner?" Mildred asked, and the true reason for guilt rose to the surface of his mind. He hesitated, knowing the time to turn back had long passed, then quietly told her that he had to go out again. She did not question him, knowing his profession of secrecy.

Charles knew what was destined to happen almost before Madeline Drew's arrest, and his life had now become even more secret and dangerous than before.

After their return from Cromer, Charles was summoned, with Kell, to Winston Churchill's office at the Admiralty. The First Lord thanked him profusely. "You have saved my wife from great danger and humiliation." The small, dynamic man's eyes glittered. "For that I shall ever be in your debt. But you have also saved your country from that same danger and humiliation. For that, your country will forever be in your debt. As this is so private a matter, the facts will, alas, never come to public light, yet I shall see to it that you, Railton, are suitably rewarded with some fitting decoration."

Few people, apart from half a dozen members of the Special Branch, and three or four from MO5, knew of the existence of Hanna Haas, alias Madeline Letitia Drew. She had become the secret within a secret almost before Charles, with Wood, had brought her back to London.

Vernon Kell saw no reason for taking Charles off the case. He was to control the girl; become "Father, uncle, brother and priest to her," Kell said, omitting the one relationship which now plagued Charles' conscience.

Kell saw to it that she was put into what he called a "safe house"—a small, pleasant villa in Maida Vale, purchased from the Service's meager funds, and watched over, in turns, by officers under training and men from the Branch.

Charles' briefing had been precise. "She is an important and valuable resource," Kell said. "But we mustn't forget, whatever she says now, Miss Haas *allowed* the German Service to send her on a dangerous mission to England. Until you caught her, she was quite prepared to carry out that unspeakable kidnap plot. So beware. Miss Haas could easily take you for a dupe, promise you the earth and then disappear—or go on working for the enemy. In plain talk, she could lead you up the garden path."

Charles was instructed to spend much time with Madeline. "Get to know her, lure her to our cause. Only when you're absolutely certain she's with us should you let her out into the wicked world. Make her—what's the word I want?—Make her *dependent* on you."

Knowing Kell was a confirmed and practicing Christian, Charles Railton was aware that his superior meant nothing more than mental or ideological dependency, though he knew that a sexual dependence between him and the attractive Miss Haas was both professionally and privately of importance.

It happened almost immediately.

During the first few days in Maida Vale, Charles established the girl's background: questioning her about her father—the German, Frederick Haas; her dead mother; the time she had spent as a nursery maid and governess in England; and facts concerning the aunt in Coventry; and the uncle and aunt in London itself.

The backgrounds of these relations were investigated by Special Branch, in particular Brian Wood, assisted by David Partridge, who had been quickly seconded from Cromer to the Branch.

Within four days of Charles' beginning the interrogation, it appeared that the aunt in Coventry, a Miss Lottie Drew; and the other relations, George and Netta Turrill of Hammersmith, were all good, loyal British citizens. They were, however, embarrassed into a certain reticence concerning Miss Drew's and Mrs. Turrill's sister, who had, as Lottie Drew of Coventry put it, "Gone off, with child by a murdering Gerry." The child would undoubtedly be welcome in their homes, but never classed as a true relative.

Each day they talked, in the prim little Maida Vale house, Charles attempting to make the long conversations as natural as possible, putting the girl at ease, in an effort to know, and understand her as a person, without bias. Behind the innocuous questions, however, were queries designed to draw her out concerning her life in Germany—in particular, her dealings with major Nicolai and his Service.

The Maida Vale house was spruce, tidy, neatly furnished, and looked after by a woman, well-known to both Kell and the Branch, acting as guard-companion. Madeline Drew ate well, was shown every possible consideration, and provided with all things needed to make life more than tolerable. It was in this tranquil atmosphere that Charles sought to build up a genuine rapport.

By the third day of the interrogation, he had discovered that his consuming sensuality was certainly reciprocated. The lithe figure with its small, almost retroussé breasts tantalized him. Her movements, and looks, all gave off unmistakable signals.

He chose his questions carefully that particular morning, and they were at ease, using the comfortable stuffed armchairs, in the small sitting room, looking out onto a trim, well-hedged garden complete with trelliswork, a handkerchief lawn and a tiny arched bower covered with climbing plants.

The first two questions—about her private interests and how the German Intelligence Service had looked after her—had been answered and now, just before luncheon, Charles leaned forward and began hesitantly: "Madeline"—they had been on Christian-name terms from the outset—"Madeline, this is not the easiest of topics, but there is something we must get out of the way now, before going any further. I have to ask you about friends..." Charles paused, seeking the right, inoffensive, words. "I'm talking about close men friends. Do you follow what I mean?"

She lowered her head, sunlight sparkling through the window highlighting the golden hair. Then she moved, turning the full power of her eyes into Charles' face. "I have never had a lover." She spoke softly, the gaze steady, eyes showing only innocence. "I am a virgin—physically at least."

"What do you mean exactly?" Charles remembered the woman companion-guard's comment, "Your Miss Drew has, sometime or another, lived a pampered life." The pouting lip and clear-eyed look gave the comment credence.

"She's been spoiled silly," the woman had told him. "Seldom washes a glass or plate, leaves her soiled linen where it falls. I'm a lady, Mr. Rathbone, not a lady's maid." The woman had been quite sharp about having to clear up after Madeline. Like most of the Branch and MO5 officers, she knew Charles only by his work name: Mr. Rathbone.

"What do you mean exactly?" Charles repeated. A full minute passed, then: "Someone wrote that a virgin is a fine steeple without bells. Well, I am without bells, Charles; yet for some reason they are there, and ringing Grandsire Triples, even though no man has touched my body."

She rose slowly, walking to the window. Charles saw her body move inside her clothes. She must have very long legs, he thought, and a picture of her nakedness flooded his imagination—the legs reaching high to her buttocks, then the gently rounded stomach, and breasts like virgin moons, with upturned nipples. Madeline Drew clambered into his mind, tearing concentration to shreds.

"I do not know what love is." She still spoke low, not moving from the window. "I do not know what love is. I have never known. But if it is a desire to share everything—mind and body—with a man, then I have found love in the last few days." Another pause. A count of ten before she asked, "Or is that forward of me, Charles?" She turned, and the spark passed between them as it was meant to do.

He hesitated, looking at her and feeling the leaping flame. Then, one step took him close against her legs, open wide under her long skirt, his right thigh between them, one hand dropping to her buttocks, enclosing, pressing her close so that she could feel his hardness against her. They searched each other's faces, as though half-debating what should be done. Their mouths touched, her lips opening as though she would devour him, one hand going to the buttons at her throat.

Charles' fingers clamped around her wrist. "No. No, Madeline, not yet."

"When? Please, when?"

He knew they could not be seen by the watchers outside, and the trusted woman was out, not due to return until late afternoon. "Tonight."

She gave a little laugh. "But Edwin will be here tonight."

Charles smiled. It had already become a private joke. The trusted lady, once a great socialite, and with many military connections, was a Mrs. Drood—hence the nickname. "I'll arrange matters. If we go on working this afternoon, today's report can be done. I'll tell her we've lost some time; send her out for the evening. We can have dinner here, and—"

She regarded him gravely. "Tonight, then," disengaging herself.

"You'll have to work hard this afternoon...er..." He wanted to use some endearment, but did not know what to say—long-married people are not skilled in the art of courtship.

During the afternoon she concentrated and cooperated well as he questioned her concerning the instructions received from Nicolai for action to be taken following the kidnap attempt. It was old ground, but Charles felt it necessary, both to test her and to bring possible trivial incidents back to mind. From tiny details larger information often comes to light.

Whatever the outcome of the kidnap attempt, she had been instructed to go to the cathedral city of Coventry. There, she would be contacted toward the end of September. However difficult, the orders were for her to be in Coventry by the end of the month. Nicolai's people were taking no chances. She had nothing from the German Service—no addresses; no names. They would come to her.

Mrs. Drood, a smart thin woman whose every move was one of efficiency, returned shortly after four, and Charles went into the kitchen, where she was setting out a tea service, her face registering disgust at doing the menial duty.

He told her the work had not gone well that day, so he would have to return about eight that night to finish. He would be obliged if she could take the evening off and leave the house when he arrived. Her presence, he explained, tended to distract Miss Drew, making her less amenable. "No reflection on you, Mrs. Drood. You know how delicate these matters can be."

It boiled down to a question of trust between two people. A third party in the house was an added tension to the girl, especially while she was being questioned. "Actually, I put it down to your strong personality, Mrs. Drood."

Back in the other room, he asked a couple of questions and wrote on his pad, *I have told her I shall be back at eight. She will go out.* He gave Madeline the paper, which she read and handed back to him.

Charles left at five-thirty and went straight home.

2

On that first of many nights he left Cheyne Walk just after seven, calling in at The Travellers to pick up a couple of good bottles of champagne, then going straight to Maida Vale, where he stopped the cab on the corner of the road and walked to the house. Mrs. Drood was waiting, in streetclothes. "I'm off to play bridge," she told him, as though this were the greatest intellectual achievement known to man or woman. "You asked for me to be back at midnight, and that is when I shall return. I have left a cold collation in the kitchen."

Madeline, waiting in the larger room, smiled as she heard the front door close on Mrs. Drood. "Why does she call it a cold collation?" she asked. "Why can't she say cold supper like anyone else?"

Charles told her Mrs. Drood's father had been a bishop. Madeline smiled and went upstairs, while he arranged Mrs. Drood's cold collation, trying to make it appear more attractive.

He opened one of the bottles, poured two glasses, then called up to Madeline, who appeared at the top of the stairs dressed in a cream and brown silk wrap, tied loosely with a belt of the same sheer material.

There was a hint of scent in the air, something French, he thought, and expensive, though it failed to hide the other musky smell given off by her body. Charles was experienced enough to recognize the scent for what it was. She had become sexually alive, awake and ready for him.

"Oh . . . champagne!" She took a sip, raising her glass, then put it aside, moving close to him, resting her long fingers on his shoulder, the hand digging in like a claw, the other arm motioning toward the stairs. "I've closed the curtains, and the bedroom light has been on for the past hour." Her eyes searched his face as they had done before the kiss that morning. Then she smiled. "Can we have the forbidden fruit first?"

When he was naked on the bed upstairs, she slid out of the wrap to reveal that she wore pure silk underthings, short and very much of the Continental fashion, with lace and ribbons—black and enticing. Charles was oddly shocked, but also amazed, for the sight of her dressed like this aroused him further. It was a new experience, he realized, for Mildred usually undressed in private.

"Don't try to be gentle," she whispered. "They say it's best done brutally, and I want you so much, dear Charles."

She cried out twice—once when he entered her and again at her climax: a long, almost wolflike call. Later that evening, and in the days to come, he was to hear the sound often, mingled with the words, repeated again and again, "I love you . . . so . . . so . . . love! . . . love! . . . love!"

It was soon apparent that, whatever she had not done before, Madeline had heard the arts of the bedroom discussed at length by well-qualified people. She became inventive in ways for which Charles had often longed, thinking it unlikely he would ever have the advantage of tasting them—for some of the acts between the new lovers were things he had only imagined, and then with a certain furtiveness, followed by a sense of guilt. She became the one lover of his life, and, though he was oddly aware of the happiness experienced with Mildred in their early years, Madeline Drew expunged all past experience from his brain. Sex, like pain, carries no true memory, for the mind recalls only the fact of things exquisite and not the full detail of passion.

During the next week, before Madeline was finally briefed, and sent, well-watched, to the aunt in Coventry, they made love on every possible occasion—even while working.

There was often a sense of danger in it, for the couple could have been discovered at any time. This was something which seemed to heighten the excitement. On two other occasions Charles managed to find excuses to call in the evening, while once they performed ruttishly while the watchful Mrs. Drood sat quietly only a room away.

The relationship bloomed, feeding their minds and bodies, and was to do so for some time to come. It was to Madeline's bed that he was returning on the night of the terrible news concerning Caspar. For once, Charles altered his routine, going to Maida Vale via King Street to offer his sympathy to Andrew and Charlotte.

"I have to admit I'm dreading the sight of him when he's brought off the train," Andrew said as they went to the door. Charlotte hardly spoke. Her face was heavily powdered, as though camouflaged to hide the inevitable marks of grief.

3

On the following night, Giles Railton went, late, to the King Street house, visiting Andrew and Charlotte, to inquire about his grandson Caspar, who had now been brought back to London. Andrew had waited for three hours at Victoria Station for the hospital train.

Giles looked at Andrew as though trying to find a window to his soul, relentlessly asking for details in that cold, precise manner which made men fear him. He knew his son better than most. The calm, often stern and silent, courageous exterior hid a softer, more gentle heart than most people imagined.

To the stranger, and certainly to his subordinates, Andrew was a determined career naval officer, showing only the attributes which went with that profession.

But Giles, who had an uncanny sense of truth, could plainly see how deeply Andrew had been seared by the terrible mutilation of his own child. Giles told them that Denise—his granddaughter by Marie and Marcel Grenot—would call on Charlotte the following afternoon. "You must use her for any help you require." He was almost callous in his treatment of the girl.

Caspar was now considered to be almost out of danger, and lay, well cared for, at the Middlesex Hospital.

"He's so damned plucky." Andrew waved the servants away as he saw his father to the front door. "You know what he said, Father? He said, 'Well, I've got the set now, Papa. One arm, one leg and one arsehole.'"

Giles gave a bleak smile and said that he would visit Caspar as soon as possible. In the event, he could not go to the Middlesex until almost the end of the month.

In the meantime Vernon Kell was directing Charles in the matter of Madeline Drew, unaware of the deep feeling which had grown between them. At the beginning of the last week of September he joined Charles, for hours on end, at the Maida Vale house. Together they took Madeline through her paces, giving her careful contact names; signals to use once someone from the German Service got in touch with her; two addresses to which she could write or telegraph; and one to which she could run in the event of danger.

Mainly to test the small team of men and women who would be watching her, it was decided that Madeline should spend the 26th and 27th of September at the Carlton Hotel, behaving as though waiting for someone. "Or merely passing time," Kell said. She was to go out, act normally, and, finally, take a train to Coventry.

They sat in the same little room where Charles and Madeline had first kissed. In the garden, the trees were now almost bare, and the early bonfires of autumn sent smoke drifting, like the aftermath of battle, across the neat fences and hedges. Kell nodded at her. "Railton here will visit you on the final evening," he said, and Charles saw her sudden glance as his superior made the error of using his true name. There was a sign of recognition, even—he imagined— a hint of concern, rising behind her irises.

The next days were so crammed with instructing, and deploying the team of watchers, that the incident all but slipped Charles' mind.

At a little after seven on the evening of September 27th, the day before Madeline was due to leave for Coventry, Charles arrived at the Carlton, where he had arranged to meet the girl in the Grill Room.

They talked about the war—the latest terrible news that three armored cruisers, the *Aboukir, Hogue* and *Cressy* had all been sunk in the North Sea, five days before, with the loss of sixty-two officers and one thousand three hundred and ninety-seven men.

"It's almost unbelievable!" Like the rest of the country, Charles was stunned. "Three capital ships at one blow."

News from France appeared a shade more heartening, and they soon turned from the harsh tragedies to other matters.

Their short meal completed, Madeline took her leave. Charles paid the bill and left some ten minutes later, taking great precautions not to be observed, slipping through a staff entrance to get to her room on the fourth floor.

They made love as though the world were about to end, for who knew when they would meet like this again? Through it all, Charles spasmodically wondered if this would be the last time he would touch her; the last time their lips would meet; the last time he would hear the endearments; feel the final gush of pleasure between their locked, straining bodies.

The room was almost in darkness, the curtains not drawn, and the dying light of a chill late September evening slowly turned the furniture into menacing shapes across the room. Charles lay on his back, and Madeline, propped on one arm, peered at his face, ill-defined in the darkness.

"Charles?" The questioning tone made him turn his head. "You *will* make sure I'm watched, and looked after won't you?"

"Of course." An arm went up and around her neck. "As long as you do everything we've told you." He moved his body to face her. "Madeline, you won't do anything stupid, will you?"

"Don't be silly. How—"

His hand gently touched her mouth. "I should warn you, my dearest, that my superiors would stop at nothing if you did. I could not help you. They would eventually find you, wherever you tried to hide. I know some of them. If you were abroad you'd end up with a slit throat."

Her hand touched his cheek. "Major Nicolai's people can also be brutal. Don't worry, darling Charles. I want to be safe, for I look to a time when we shall be together for always."

The guilt rose, bile in his throat. He stayed silent, thanking God he did not have to look her straight in the eyes.

"Isn't that what *you* want, Charles?"

"Of course." But he knew there was no conviction in his voice. He was this girl's slave, but would never dream of leaving Mildred.

There was a long silence among the dark shrouded furniture, and shadows around the bed.

"Your real name's Railton, isn't it? Charles Railton, not Charles Rathbone," she said at last.

He agreed. She was not supposed to know. "It was my superior's error, using my real name the other day."

He saw her head nod against the white pillow. "It's only that I've heard the name before."

"Oh?"

Her hand moved to his thigh as she asked if he had a sister or cousin: "A relation, married to a Frenchman called Greenot . . . or Graneau?"

"Why?" Suddenly, her hand, which usually resurrected him quickly after a sexual encounter, did nothing, as though he had become emasculated by her words.

"Tell me. Have you some relation like that?"

"Yes." He told her about Marie, his cousin. "Why?"

"It may be of value. I don't know. But that's where I heard the name Railton before. In connection with your cousin, Marie—was it Grenot?"

He nodded. How? Where?

"Major Nicolai, and others, gave me some of my training: specialist things, inks, ciphers, at a house they have in Courbierrestrasse—Number 8. They always called the house simply *Number 8.* Courbierrestrasse is in the western part of the city. I've already told you about the place."

He remembered.

"The other day, when your Mr. Vernon—though I don't suppose that's *his* real name either—called you Railton I became worried. I'd heard it before and knew it was connected with something very unpleasant, but I couldn't remember what. Then, last night, it all came back. Isn't it funny how the brain holds everything, like a book, only you have to search for the right page?"

He waited, silently, for her to continue. From outside there was the sound of traffic in the streets below.

"There was a man called Steinhauer working at Number 8."

"What about Steinhauer?" All gentleness now gone from his voice, his brain alert to memories of the name Steinhauer, which he knew so well because of its connections with the barber's shop "post office" in the Caledonian Road.

He heard her take a deep breath. "I remember being at Number 8 one afternoon. We were working on maps, then Major Nicolai came in, and he was in a very good mood. When the lesson finished, he asked me if I would dine with him. I accepted, and he said we would go straight from the house.

"We were just leaving when Steinhauer came in through the main door. He must have been quite important, because the duty officer stood to attention, clicked his heels and all that kind of thing. You know how they go on; they're worse than our people."

"Just tell me." He felt as though a thundercloud were about to break in his head.

"Well, Steinhauer said he must speak with the Major, urgently. He was smiling. Triumphant."

"Yes."

"They asked me to sit in the little hallway, outside the room Nicolai used as his office. Only they left the door open and I could hear every word. Charles, it's strange, the conversation meant nothing to me at the time, but when it came back, I remembered it quite clearly. Every word."

He asked what all this had to do with Marie.

"Steinhauer said he had just received great news. Hirsch, the assistant to the Military Attaché in Paris, had been in touch again. He was now certain that if it came to it, Madame Marie Grenot—I know it was that name now—would leave the country with him, and go to Berlin. Nicolai made some remark about Klaus being able to seduce a nun if he set his mind to it; and Steinhauer said the Grenot woman was obviously in love with Klaus Hirsch. . . ."

"Klaus *von* Hirsch," Charles muttered.

Madeline did not pause. "He used a vulgar word—*bumsen*—meaning that Madame Grenot and this man Hirsch had been—you know . . . doing it. Doing it regularly."

The anxiety and apprehension crystallized. Charles' sadness deepened—not now for his parting from Madeline, but for his cousin, Marie, and what had happened: the great family scandal.

Since he could remember her, Charles had been fond of Marie. He recalled her quick Gallic temper, inherited from her French mother; the rather mannish way she would stride into a room, paradoxically at odds with her normal walk, hips swinging, breasts thrust forward. She was almost two years his junior, and Charles had constant memories of the time when he was seventeen. His first fumblings of desire had been with Marie—so often the case with cousins. He could see her now, feeding grapes to him, laughing, with her head flung back as they lay under the great oak—now gone—at Redhill, one of his hands running across her breast, hard under the thin material of a summer dress. He had always found grapes an erotic fruit, and knew why. "Go on," he told Madeline, shocked at his private brand of hypocrisy.

"Well, it was then that the name came up. Nicolai said that this was great news. His next words I know by heart: 'You realize, my dear Steinhauer, that Madame Grenot is a Railton, so you know where that can lead us. *Their Secret Service.*' Steinhauer said something about having to handle her properly, and Nicolai replied, 'Oh, she will be handled properly. I'll handle her myself if necessary.' Then they both laughed."

Fear, foreboding and hope commingled within Charles. Madeline tried to soothe him, sensing in the darkness that in some way her story had alarmed and upset him.

Only on his way home did he fully face the dilemma. By rights the information should be taken straight to Vernon Kell. Such action would bring cross-examination, and, in his state of mind, Charles was uncertain of how he would stand up to Kell's probing. There was really only one choice. A family choice. He should confide in Marie's father, his uncle—Giles Railton. Even so, he allowed forty-eight hours to pass before seeing Uncle Giles.

4

On the evening of September 29th, Giles Railton visited his grandson Caspar at the Middlesex Hospital. His mind was not wholly on the task, as the day had been long and with more than one surprise.

A routine meeting of the Committee of Imperial Defence had been attended by Lord Kitchener himself, together with the First Lord of the Admiralty—both representing the Cabinet.

Winston Churchill had suggested that for many reasons, including the sinking of *Aboukir, Hogue* and *Cressy,* Prince Louis Battenberg should be replaced as First Sea Lord. He, not Churchill, had made an error regarding orders to the ships.

After this, Kitchener gave as clear an account as was possible of the military situation—difficult, as he was the first to admit that matters changed by the hour, if not the minute.

Through September, the German armies had been in steady retreat, but today Kitchener had to report that this flight was now halted. The Germans were now holding a line behind the Aisne River, where they had rallied, dug in and were causing havoc with their artillery.

Giles knew that while Kitchener reeled off the strategic moves and countermoves—talking of armies, corps and divisions—his words in no way described the actualities of war. The somber, dispassionate men seated around the table could have been thinking of the whole business as a game of chess; yet the chess game itself was being won and lost by those thousands of pawns—young men caught in fire, burned, rent apart, desperate and choked with blood and smoke: brave, terrified, cowardly and courageous, in the fields of Flanders or the villages of the Aisne Valley.

Walking back to his office, thinking of the visit planned to Caspar that evening, Giles was not to know he had already lost a grandson. Young Paul, son of Marie and Marcel Grenot—brother to Denise—had died two weeks previously fighting with Lanrezac's Fifth Army near Sambre.

Arriving at the Foreign Office, Giles found Charles waiting to see him. "I'm sorry—I just couldn't turn him away," Ramillies apologized. Giles merely nodded.

Charles came to the point at once. "It's about Marie," he began, and Giles turned his cold eyes blankly onto his nephew.

When Charles left, the information having been passed, and received with a curt "Thank you," Giles sat staring at the wall for a long time. Decisions must not be made in haste. Something had to be done. The shrewd old man suspected his nephew of more dangerous and devious games—why else had he not simply taken the intelligence straight to Vernon Kell, who would have passed it to Smith-Cumming? Charles' tale about it being a family matter just did not wash. His nephew was hiding something. His informant perhaps? On

Charles' part there had been a stout refusal to reveal the source of his intelligence, except that it was "sound." Giles had not probed. Perhaps it was a woman. Giles knew of many cases where intelligence officers had fallen into all kinds of traps set by women. But, at this moment, Giles Railton was jumping at every shadow, suspecting even the most normal action. There were plots in which he was embroiled, plans laid, which could, he knew all too well, bring a bright future—golden glory or dusty death.

After almost an hour, Giles wrote a single name on his notepad, looked at it for a while, then took it across the room, tore off the sheet and dropped it into the crackling fire, watching the words *James Railton* being quickly consumed. He would speak with Smith-Cumming in a day or two.

So, it was with much on his mind that Giles arrived at the small private room in which Caspar lay.

The boy looked terribly young, pale, even against the sheets, dark shadows around his eyes—the legacy of drugs—and the marks of pain engraved on his face.

"Well, Grandfather, this is a pickle, isn't it?" The smile was genuine enough to cause the ruthless old man to swallow hard.

"Pickle indeed, Caspar." He took a deep breath. "So what are you going to do about it, my boy?"

"Get myself a peg leg, I suppose. There's little they can do for the arm. I won't play cricket again, that's for sure."

"Why not?"

"Well . . . peg leg and one arm . . ."

"Just because nobody's played cricket with one arm and one leg before this doesn't mean to say they never will. You could be the first."

Caspar blinked. His grandfather was a gruff, tough old bastard, he knew, but there was some truth in what he said.

"No," Giles went on, "I really mean it—what do you plan for yourself?"

"Haven't the foggiest." Caspar shook his head and asked for a cigarette, which Giles lit for him. "I mean, whatever you say, life isn't going to be exactly active from now on, is it?"

"Don't see why not, lad. You know what I do for a living, do you?"

Caspar did have an idea, but there was an unspoken family rule that it should never be admitted. He shook his head. "Something rather grand in the Foreign Office, isn't it?"

Giles made a noise which came as near to a chuckle as he could ever manage. "Not very grand. I coordinate certain matters—intelligence matters. Act as a watchdog to those who deal with espionage."

"The Secret Service?" Caspar lowered his already tired voice.

"That's about it. You can always be of use there. The Service has employed a lot of odd birds in its history. When you're fit again, come and see me. I'm sure we can find something fairly active. A one-armed, one-legged man could

be of great use. Never think of yourself as a cripple. Will you come and see
me when they let you out?"

"Of course, Grandfather." There seemed to be a new light in the young
man's eyes.

As he was leaving, Giles bumped into Andrew, who was on his way to see
his son. "Charlotte's joining me here. About the only time we get to see one
another these days."

Giles gave his customary curt nod.

"Lot of rethinking going on," Andrew said. "Battenberg's on his way out,
and there's talk of old Fisher coming back. The man's seventy-four years' old,
but he's like a damned hurricane—always popping in and out of the Admiralty.
Won't rest until he's back in harness. What's more, he's got Winston behind
him."

"Good lad, Caspar." Giles changed the subject disconcertingly. "He'll do
well, Andrew. He'll do very well."

"Plenty of pluck." Andrew took a pace back.

"And how's the Admiralty Old Building?" Giles asked. "Room 40 got enough
action in it for you?"

"You amaze me, Father." Andrew had the grace to smile. "How do you know
about Room 40?"

Giles Railton laid one finger alongside his nose. "They're a mite jealous in
the War House." He smiled crookedly. "They like to think they know everything
about codes and ciphers."

5

Andrew Railton, who had only a few years' ago reckoned himself as one of
the world's most contented men, was coming through a depressed crisis in his
life. The blow of Caspar's injuries brought a black mood of disenchantment,
though he was too busy at the Admiralty—as indeed he had been almost up
to the end of August—to become outwardly edgy.

Since childhood he had loved the sea and all things concerned with it, and
often truthfully maintained that his early years in the Royal Navy—particularly
once he went to sea—were the happiest of his life.

The prolonged tour ashore at the Admiralty had, after so long, now become
irksome, and in the months immediately prior to the outbreak of war, he had
constantly approached the Director of Intelligence—badgering him for a trans-
fer back to sea duty.

But the bearded, severe-looking Admiral bade him wait. "Just get on with
this job of gathering information about codes, ciphers and wireless telegraphy,
Railton. You'll be back at sea when their Lordships see fit to send you."

Andrew obeyed orders, wrote his reports and got on with his life. But the
fact that nothing appeared to be done about the many pages he wrote infuriated

him. He became irritable at home, and, to make things worse, following the declaration of war, the paperwork seemed to grow on his desk, multiplying like some terrible weed. The result was that it often kept him from his own bed, causing him to stay overnight at the Admiralty. Andrew really felt that he had been left behind. His experience was more suited to the sea than a desk. Life had become dull and frustrating—an eternal round of forms, letters and reports.

Then, like a sea-change, life became full and interesting again.

Suddenly, the W/T interception station at Stockton began to show a vast increase in the picking up of German signal traffic; and Stockton was now joined in this by the radio stations of the Post Office, the Marconi Company and even private individuals. The bulk of these messages were coded, and he immediately drew the matter to the attention of his superiors.

The DID was more than usually interested, and, a week or so after the declaration of war—around three o'clock one Wednesday afternoon—an Admiralty messenger had summoned him to his superior's office.

There he found his chief deep in conversation with a gray-haired, astute-looking man dressed in an almost dandified manner—a gray suit, with a white piqué stripe in the waistcoat; mauve shirt; and a white butterfly collar holding a dark-blue bow tie, white-spotted and neatly in place.

"Commander Railton," the DID greeted him. "I want you to meet the Director of Naval Education, Sir Alfred Ewing. Alfred, this is the officer I told you about."

"Glad to meet you, Railton." The voice betrayed Scottish origins, and Andrew had the uncomfortable feeling that he was being sized up by an intellectual of considerable authority. For a second or two the smell of chalk and damp serge came back, a memory reaching into the nostrils recalling classrooms and the dog days at school all those years before.

Alfred Ewing smiled. "Understand you've been investigating the business of secret writing—codes and ciphers."

"Sir. With particular reference to military and naval messages sent via wireless telegraphy."

The DNE nodded. "Tell me all about it."

Andrew launched into what could have been the basis for a lecture on the history of codes and ciphers—the ancient Egyptian hieroglyphics; eleventh-century Chinese codes, mentioning in passing the *wu-ching tsung-yau*—"Essentials of Military Classics"—with its method of using code words within poems or letters.

"Then," getting into his stride, "there are the Biblical ciphers, sir—"

"Yes, yes." Ewing flapped a hand. "I know all about those. What about modern codes and ciphers? Do you know the source material? Can you lead me to it?"

Andrew told him yes. There was enough material in the British Museum to keep an intelligent man occupied for years; not to mention the collections at Lloyds and the GPO. "They have a great deal—a lot of commercial ciphers. The War Office still uses the Playfair cipher, of course."

"Of course," Ewing spoke firmly. "You see, Railton"—the Scottish accent became more pronounced—"Admiral Oliver here feels as I do, that there will be little call for Naval Education if the war goes on for more than a few months. I've always been interested in codes, ciphers, secret writing and all that kind of thing, so—"

"So," the DID chimed in, "Sir Alfred has kindly offered to organize a department, here at the Admiralty, dedicated to decoding and deciphering enemy W/T intercepts—the very things that seem to have been bothering you so much, Railton. Now, this has to be kept quiet, but I'd like you to show Sir Alfred where the information's buried. You will be the direct link between this new department and myself."

For the next days and weeks, Andrew found himself spending more and more time with Sir Alfred Ewing, who admitted more than once that in spite of his knowledge he was lamentably ill-equipped to lead any department dealing with the clear reading of ciphered or coded messages.

Together, they mulled over dusty books in the British Museum, went through pages of commercial ciphers at Lloyds and the GPO, and examined recent cipher illustrations with the Marconi Company.

It quickly became clear that other minds would have to be brought in. So, with his particular contacts, Ewing called on a number of men then teaching at the naval schools of Dartmouth and Osborne. They came on a temporary basis, but for some—in particular another Scot, the brilliant Alastair Denniston—this was a new turn in their careers. Soon the temporary duty had become a permanent vocation.

They also needed more space, and finally an office was set aside for this fledgling department—Room 40 of the Admiralty Old Building. Eventually, Room 40 (OB) became one of the most important assets in the secret war.

Andrew obeyed orders to the letter, acting as direct liaison with the DID. But, by mid-October, things were changing at the Admiralty, and it was no surprise when the DID called him in one morning to announce he was leaving to take over as Churchill's Naval Assistant. The new DID would be Captain Reggie "Blinker" Hall—a man of some reputation, and not all of it good.

Throughout this time, Andrew viewed the progress of the war with a cold, professional eye. Many, including himself, had expected a clash between the two Grand Fleets to be inevitable, if not decisive, within the first few weeks, but the clash did not come.

6

Toward the end of October, Andrew became concerned for Rupert's safety. Even though his days were spent with the mathematical experts who toiled to unravel the codes, he was still privy to many of the signals leaving the Admiralty. So he noted with some misgivings that Admiral Cradock's force was now instructed to hunt down the German East Asiatic Squadron.

He did not share his fears with Charlotte, who had enough to concern her, being totally distraught about Caspar's future, which she could only see as bleak beyond words. She continued to believe Rupert was as safe as his twin, Ramillies, settled into a regular routine at the Foreign Office under his grandfather's tutelage.

On Wednesday, November 5th, the bombshell burst.

Andrew, following his usual pattern, had walked over from the Old Building at lunchtime, bringing with him the few intercepts which had been successfully decoded during the morning.

He was approaching the Naval Assistant to the First Lord's room, when Churchill, closely followed by Admiral Fisher, came out of an adjoining office. Both men looked unusually grave—Fisher even seemed to be gray-skinned with worry.

"I cannot understand why Cradock disobeyed orders," he heard Churchill say. "Under no circumstances should he have engaged an enemy force of that strength."

"Unless he was somehow surprised," Lord Fisher replied, then looked up and saw Andrew. "It's young Railton, isn't it?" His oddly oriental face creasing into a half-smile.

"Yes, sir."

"Winston, this is—what is the rank now? Commander?" Andrew nodded. "Commander Railton. Used to be my Gunnery Officer in *Renown*." He stopped suddenly, as though taken ill. "Oh, my dear fellow. You had a son in *Monmouth*? Yes?"

"Yes. Yes, sir. Why . . . What's the—" Andrew felt his heart sink.

"I fear *Monmouth* is lost," Churchill began. "And *Good Hope* also. There are survivors, and we can but hope, Railton. Our prayers are with you." And he was off, shoulders stooped as though the responsibility weighed too heavily.

Andrew stood in the corridor, stunned, his eyes burning, wondering if, or how, Rupert's end had come.

The facts, as they emerged later, were that Admiral Cradock, who had been instructed to find and shadow the German squadron, had sailed straight into a classic trap on the previous Sunday afternoon, off the coast of Chile.

Believing his force to have located the light cruiser *Leipzig,* on her own, Cradock, in his flagship, *Good Hope*—together with *Glasgow, Monmouth* and the armed merchant cruiser *Ontario*—was lured, by constant wireless signals, toward the heavy guns of the armored cruisers *Scharnhorst* and *Gneisenau,* and their attendant cruisers.

Late on a gray, squall-swept afternoon, Admiral Cradock could not have foreseen the danger and was forced to put up a gallant fight, which went on into the early evening with the loss of *Good Hope* and *Monmouth.*

Monmouth—in no way fit for this kind of battle—had limped from the action, under cover of darkness, her decks blazing and an eerie glow coming from the portholes below the quarterdeck. Later, though, with the fires under control, but listing badly, she had been sighted against the moon by the cruiser *Nurnberg,* then caught in her searchlights. It was the end. The already shell-torn *Monmouth,* though given the opportunity, refused to haul down her flag, and was dispatched with a hail of fire from *Nurnberg's* 4-inch guns. It was nearly ten o'clock before *Monmouth* finally capsized, her flag flying to the end.

A full month passed before Andrew and Charlotte, by this time in deep distress, heard that Rupert was safe; though over a year went by before his whole story was pieced together by other survivors.

Rupert had been the only man left alive following a direct hit on the quarterdeck, early in the battle. He had helped to fight the fires raging all over the ship, and in the end was literally blown over one hundred feet into the sea where, miraculously, he remained alive for over two hours, before being picked up by *Glasgow.*

Rupert was back in London before Christmas, yet his state was even worse than that of his brother Caspar—now doggedly determined to master the art of walking on his wooden leg. Rupert appeared as a husk of the young man who had so cheerfully set off to fight at sea. It was obvious he would never live a normal life, and he had a gaunt, haunted look, his eyes staring, as if blind, from their sockets, his expression one of almost permanent surprise. The once alert, fine-looking young man walked, breathed and moved. But he did not seem to reflect life at all.

At first he would not speak to anyone, nor go near water—even to bathe. Then, when some semblance of life did return, the very worst became clear. Following the horror and shock of battle, Rupert's mind had taken refuge in childhood, so that he once more became like a little boy of six years.

"As yet we don't know enough about this kind of problem," a naval doctor told Charlotte and Andrew. "Certain things are obvious, though. The mind has reverted to the comparative safety of childhood. Nobody but God can tell if it will ever return to normality."

7

So, in the space of one year, two of the brilliant younger members of the Railton family had been struck down—one crippled physically, the other maimed mentally, so that Andrew and Charlotte had to employ the old family nanny—Nanny Briggs—to care for Rupert.

It was pitiful to watch the full-grown young man reduced to playing with long-forgotten toys on the nursery floor, talking the scribble language of a young child, showing fear at small things, crying, or flying into tantrums, and having to be taken for walks held tightly by the hand.

Charlotte began to look her age, and appeared to have lost the power to laugh; while Andrew became moody and introspective, pondering for days on end at the futility of what appeared to be happening around them.

Andrew was in his room, next door to Room 40, one morning—in a black and silent mood—when Alastair Denniston came off watch, perky and smiling, as his night's work had been so successful.

Andrew looked blank as the Scot greeted him with a cheery good morning. For some odd reason Andrew Railton was again, for a second, transported to the schoolroom—maybe, he thought later, it was the Scottish accent, like Ewing's. In his head he heard part of a far-off history lesson: a reading from the Anglo-Saxon Chronicles regarding the terrible nineteen years Britain was supposed to have endured during the reign of King Stephen.

Automatically, he quoted aloud: *"I neither know how nor can tell all the horrors they did to the unhappy people in this land . . ."* he began, and Denniston stopped, his face grave with sorrow, for he knew what must be going on within Andrew. "I know," Denniston said quietly.

Andrew continued to quote: *"And they said openly that Christ slept, and his saints."* He looked hard at the other man. "Does Christ sleep, Alastair? Does he really sleep?"

Denniston's usual dry humor evaporated completely as he felt the compassion rise. "If Christ sleeps, Andrew, then He will surely wake again. Until He does, we have to look to ourselves."

Slowly, Andrew Railton nodded. His gloom and depression was to be echoed in thousands of homes and hearts over the next years. The old, somewhat arrogant, British way of life had gone for ever. Before new values could be found, there were horrors and betrayals to be faced all over the world.

Chapter Sixteen

1

James Railton sat in the first-floor drawing room of the Kaiserhof, looking across the outskirts of Friedrichshafen. The coffee was good—almost as delicious as that he had drunk in Switzerland two days before.

In this part of Germany, at least, morale was high. He would tell C that practically every German he heard talking about the war spoke of quick victory.

There were exceptions. He thought of the casual conversation on the previous evening.

He had been taking brandy, after dinner, in this very drawing room, and the man who sat down nearby looked pale and under stress, though he was undoubtedly a member of the Officer Corps.

"You stay here before?" the man asked.

"Once or twice. On business." James was wary and careful with his *Schweizerdeutsch* accent.

"Ach. You are not German." There was no implied criticism.

"Swiss."

"So. You Swiss are best out of it."

"Oh?"

"Well, what do you *really* think of the war?"

James was judicious. "Honor must always be satisfied."

"You think so?" The man leaned closer. "Maybe I'm foolish; possibly I speak treason, but this war should never have happened. I have good friends and some relatives in England."

"So?"

The German smiled. "You say you're Swiss?"

"From Zurich."

He shook his head. "I think not. Don't ask me why. But someday—who knows—I may be of assistance to you. Call on me. Feel free to do so at any time."

James had the man's card in his wallet now—*Major Joseph Stoerkel*, with an address in Elisabethstrasse, Berlin. He had been most careful with the Herr Major, but got the distinct impression that he was anxious to speak with someone who had contacts in England.

James now waited for something new to modern warfare; something he would have preferred to be doing instead of simply observing.

He hoped it was going to happen, as planned, this morning, for this was his second visit to Friedrichshafen in less than ten days, and, while nobody appeared to be in the least bit suspicious, James did not wish to chance his luck.

Here, at the Kaiserhof, they knew him as Herr Grabben, who had something to do with money and engineering. It was assumed that he had connections with the Zeppelin base, less than a kilometer from the hotel. Oddly, in this morning's light, the base could be seen so clearly that James considered you might almost be able to reach out and touch the sheds. There was probably rain about, for that was when the foreshortened optical illusion usually occurred.

At this moment James stared straight out at the sheds and hydrogen plant. He hoped the aeroplanes would come within the next hour or so.

Whatever happened, he would have to leave later that day. It would be unwise to stay any longer than twenty-four hours in Germany. It was all very well to live, as Herr Grabben, here in the hotel; but if some nosy policeman decided to inquire into his documents, the discrepancies would soon be dis-covered. James had not entered Germany via any of the normal methods.

Across the lake, just inside neutral Switzerland—at the Bahnhof-Post Hotel in Kreuzlingen—he was known as Herr Franke, a businessman from Berlin, speaking the precise *Hochdeutsch* of the Prussian upper and middle classes. Here in Friedrichshafen they could hardly understand his singsong *Schweizerdeutsch,* with its dropped final consonants and sentences larded with diminutives. C had given him only a fortnight to perfect the lyricisms of the Swiss dialect.

He looked out of the window again, eyes searching the sky, his mind drifting through the phases of the journey that had brought him to this place. Through shell-strewn France; into Switzerland, on diplomatic papers; then a planned disappearance, reemerging on Lake Constance as Herr Franke from Berlin, seeking a few days peace from his responsible job. A word to the head porter of the Bahnhof-Post, saying he would be away for a couple of nights, walking in the mountains. Then the second part of the venture—the long, dark, night sail, in a tiny fishing boat, taking him across the lake, landing about a mile east of Friedrichshafen; from thence to the Kaiserhof.

Whether the aeroplanes came today or not, he would begin the reverse journey that night.

There were only two other guests in the drawing room, but in another public room someone was playing a piano—Chopin; one of the sonatas, though he could not remember which. It was certainly a favorite of Margaret Mary's, the one, he thought, which had the funereal passage in it.

Home, and his wife, came urgently into his mind. The man who declared that absence made the heart grow fonder was an idiot. Enforced absence was a deadly enemy, for, together with longing, it brought the occasional devils of doubt. Each time he returned home, usually arriving without warning, it took two days to rediscover his wife; then it was time to leave again. If they came through this with a happy marriage intact, they should be able to weather anything.

Recently he had noticed an odd phenomenon. In moments of crisis he experienced vivid moving pictures in his mind, often so real that he thought they verged on the hallucinatory. Now, Margaret Mary was seated at the piano, her bare shoulders and arms moving like those of a dancer. For a second he sensed the indescribable odor of her hair, which so roused him that he loved to bury his nose in it. The fragrance of her hair acted like a powerful aphrodisiac.

He sipped his coffee and once more lifted his eyes toward the sky. If they were coming it had to be soon.

The plan had been well-conceived and carefully prepared, originally at the suggestion of the British Air Attaché in Bern. Earlier that month four aeroplanes were boxed and crated, then taken, together with pilots, mechanics and staff, from Southampton to Le Havre, and on to Belfort, in southeast France. The aeroplanes had then been reassembled.

Already there had been one false start; but, three days before, James was told of a new date—the morning of November 21st. This morning.

Outside, about a mile away, all was bustle around the Zeppelin sheds. He could see a squad of soldiers being marched toward the sheds, their mouths opening and closing in song. They would be singing, he presumed, the same words he had heard in Friedrichshafen on the last visit:

> Fly, Zeppelin
> Help us win the war,
> England shall be destroyed by fire,
> Zeppelin, fly!

It was a distinct possibility, England being attacked, if not destroyed, by fire from the great dirigibles. There could be little doubt of the menace they presented.

He glanced up to be sure that the top of the high sash window was open as usual. If they came, James wanted to be certain the glass would not be shattered by blast. As he raised his head, the piano stopped, and the first explosion echoed, blasting toward the hotel—the dull thump of an antiaircraft gun somewhere out on the perimeter of the field.

One of the other guests, seated in the drawing room, dropped his newspaper and half-rose as James spotted the first aeroplane—an Avro 504, a machine not built to carry bombs, but chosen for its sturdy features.

He could hear the engine now, coupled with more gunfire. The other men in the room, anxious and alarmed, left their chairs, coming to stand beside James near the window.

The shape of the descending aeroplane became more visible with every second—the long wooden skid between the wheels and the curved metal protective bumpers under the tips of its long lower wings.

Dirty black clouds exploded near the machine as it continued to lose height, and the guns began to open up around the whole area. The plane kept coming, and James could see others following. There should, he knew, be four of them. So far only three were visible. Then, the first bombs crashed in a line between the Zeppelin sheds.

The second Avro was now overhead, jettisoning its bombs—only three coming away, the fourth plainly stuck in the release mechanism under the wings. With a great double crunch and a high crimson plume, one of the hydrogen tanks exploded to the left of the sheds. As it did so, a shell burst very close to the aeroplane, which bucked under the blast, its engine note changing, and the nose going down.

Now the third aeroplane skimmed in at about five hundred feet, the bombs dropping away like stones thrown in a cluster by a small boy. They exploded with four dull bumps, rattling the windows, one of them taking away part of the Zeppelin shed, tearing it open like a knife ripping paper.

The second machine was in trouble, unable to gain height, but turning and setting its course for home. James doubted if it could ever get as far as Belfort. The other two were already invisible in the murk of low cloud, leaving behind them at least some damage, a great deal of shock and certainly much disbelief.

James had one more duty before returning to Switzerland—to discover how much genuine damage had been inflicted. Already he knew it could not be very great: probably only one tank of hydrogen, with, possibly, some damage to a Zeppelin if there had been one inside the shed which had received a hit.

But damage to morale was considered a victory also. It was quite amazing, he thought, that at least three aeroplanes had managed to fly to the most highly prized base in Germany—for Friedrichshafen was not only the Zeppelin's birthplace, but also the chief strategic testing center. Over four hundred miles from England, the base was considered perfectly safe from any kind of attack. Yet they had done it—a first in warfare.

Outside, the cold air was filled with a strong smell of smoke, drifting in from the base. People hurried everywhere, some occasionally glancing upward as though expecting the *verdammten englischen Maschinen* to return.

In one of the bars, James drank schnapps with a man who had been on the base. He was intelligent; not the kind who would exaggerate. Several people had been killed, he said, though God be thanked there was no terrible damage done. A week would see things back to normal. "Oh yes." He swallowed his second schnapps in one gulp. "There will be much trouble for the English pilots. One of the dead is a Swiss engineer."

James made the usual shocked noises, but thought callously, Shouldn't have been there in the first place, silly bugger. If a Swiss neutral was in the Zeppelin center, maybe even helping, and got himself killed, it's his own damned fault.

By ten o'clock that night James Railton had made his rendezvous with the fishing boat and lay half-dozing in the stern, perished with cold from the wind funneling down the lake. He thought of Margaret Mary again and of the odd incident which had occurred. When he left the hotel lobby to go down into the street, James had passed through the room where he had heard the Chopin sonata being played just before the raid. Even in his haste he stopped for a moment, for the room did not appear to contain a piano.

He would tell Margaret when he saw her again; though heaven knew when that would be. At the moment his orders were to leave Switzerland at the earliest opportunity and head for Calais to make contact with the nearest MIl(c) officer.

This probably meant a return to Belgium; a quiet sortie behind the German lines. Already, during the fighting around Antwerp, James had spent time behind the German advance, doing the uncertain work of recruiting agents who would report on troop movements—particularly those made by train. The idea was to form a network of local people so that permanent intelligence could be brought out and regular reports made to the field commanders. The network was coded "Frankignoul," after its leading agent, and controlled by an officer, known as Evelyn, back in the English Channel port of Folkestone.

But, when James finally got back to the Bahnhof-Post, at Kreuzlingen, in the early hours of the following morning, a telegram awaited him.

It came from Bern, and was written in clear cipher, requesting Herr Franke to call on Herr Gimmell at the Crédit Suisse in Bern.

Herr Gimmell was C. A call on him at any bank meant that James was to report, in person, to London as quickly as he could get there.

Even if the visit to London was brief, it at least meant he would see Margaret Mary soon.

2

Because James was now away for so much of the time, Margaret Mary had found them a small house, near Kensington Gardens, and it was to this pleasant three-story home, set in a small square behind the bustle of the main shopping street, that James returned three days after receiving the telegram.

It was late afternoon. Foggy, a hint of frost, and the dry characteristic autumnal smell of woodsmoke hanging in the nostrils as soon as you stepped into any London street. Margaret Mary had been sitting idly at the piano in the drawing room, waiting for Nanny to bring Donald down to say goodnight. The curtains were not yet drawn, and, as she paused at the end of a difficult line, she glanced down, giving an almost childish yelp of joy as she saw James' silhouette walking slowly, carrying his heavy case, from a departing taxicab.

He was not as tired as usual, but still fended off her myriad questions, the chatter interrupted by Nanny arriving with young Donald. There was happiness, many kisses, and some tears. Then James went off to take a hot bath and change. It was almost eight-thirty when they sat down for dinner.

James told his wife that by rights he should have reported to his superiors on arrival in London. "So, Mrs. James Railton, not a word. If anyone asks, I did not get here until well after midnight."

"You know what I'm like about time, darling. Can't tell midday from midnight." She put on a funny accent, meant to indicate an alluring German spy. "Zo, your secret iss save wiz me." Margaret Mary had a childlike sense of humor which appealed to James.

"You should really join the Service, my dear," eyes alive with the pleasure of being with her. "I'd say you have a natural talent. They'd plonk you down somewhere in Belgium, and you could vamp all the German officers."

"What on earth does that mean? Vamp?" She giggled.

"Well, I'm told the men use the word to describe eating something. But I have it on the highest authority that it really means to attract men by using your feminine charms."

"Oh!" This time the laugh was more wicked. "Can I vamp you, darling? Soon. It's perfectly safe, the doctor— Oh!"

"What about the doctor?"

"Damn! I was saving it as a special surprise."

"What? For heaven's sake, Maggie Mary?"

Her face blanked into innocence. "We've done it again, darling. You're going to be a father for the second time."

His eyes became brighter than ever. "You all right?"

"I'm fine, darling. You've been away so often, and for so long. I'm over two months now, and Dr. Madingly says everything's in order. I can live a perfectly normal life for the next few months. That doctor's quite a card. He stressed it could be a *normal* life, meaning fun and games."

James gave a mock sigh. "I do find you an oddity, M-M. You look as though butter wouldn't melt, yet you're always craving for... well..."

"Oh, don't be so stuffy. Of course I am. It's not only men who get hot and bothered. I'd understand it if you weren't such a goat yourself."

He rose and walked over to her, his hand caressing her shoulder as he bent to kiss her hair. The smell of it gave him the usual wink of desire, and the hand dropped to her breast. She covered it, pressed and then said, "Go and finish your pudding, James. We'll get to bed sooner if you'd only eat a shade faster."

Later, lying in the darkness of their room, she asked him how long he would be able to stay. He told her the truth as always. He had to see people in the morning. There was no way of telling.

"What's it been like this time?"

"Nothing much. No problems."

They lay in silence for another five minutes. Then she asked, very quietly, "James? Saturday last?"

"Mmmm?" He sounded sleepy, though remained alert. Last Saturday had been November 21st.

"Were you in any danger? Please tell me. I don't want details, but it's important. Last Saturday morning."

"I suppose some might say it was dangerous. Why?"

"It sounds silly. I was in the drawing room. For no reason I began to play— Chopin. I didn't play well; it was that difficult one, the Sonata in B-flat minor..."

"The one with the dead march thing in it?"

"Musicians wouldn't quite put it like that, my darling, but you're learning. Yes, the one with the dead march thing in it. That's the point. I could hardly get through it. I began to play the piece, then I felt you were very close. There was this really horrible feeling that something had happened. It was vivid, like a nightmare, then it went, and I *knew* you were safe. It was so real. You were here, James, in the house, by the piano. I could feel you, almost hear you, as I played."

James stayed awake for a long time, pondering on whether he should tell her about the way he had heard a piano just before the aeroplanes came.

3

James had not seen C since the middle of September, and was puzzled by the odd looks they gave him on his arrival at the house in Northumberland Avenue, where the Service was housed, now under the auspices of the Admiralty.

The duty officer went away, leaving James to cool his heels in the small waiting room; but, when the young man came back, all appeared natural again. James was taken upstairs to the now-familiar office, but it was not C's voice that called "Enter!" at the knock.

The duty officer stood to one side, allowing James to cross the threshold alone. The door closed softly, and, instead of C, James found himself looking into the cold eyes of Giles Railton.

"Uncle Giles, sir. I'm sorry, I was supposed to see the CSS." He used the more formal, and correct, initials that stood for Chief of Secret Service.

"Sit down, James. I fear you'll have to make do with me." Giles' eyes never left his nephew, as though he were searching for some flaw. "You have a report?"

James gave a weary sigh. "Yes." He had risen early to put down all that he could about the Friedrichshafen raid. "Brilliant operation, but I'm afraid they did little more than dent morale. Not much damage."

Giles pursed his lips, muttering a faint damn. Aloud, he said the two pilots who had got back safely were given a heroes' welcome. "The French presented them both with the Légion d'Honneur."

James nodded. "Well deserved."

Giles grunted, leafing through the report.

"The CSS, sir . . ." James began.

Slowly, Giles put down the papers. "C has had an accident. I saw him in hospital last night . . ."

"Oh Lord, not flying?" He knew his chief's passion, like his own, for aeroplanes.

Giles shook his head. "No, not flying. For your ears only, James. The CSS was involved in a bad road accident last month, in France. Tragedy really. His son was driving and lost control. The young man was killed, and C's lost a leg."

James' brow creased in vicarious pain, automatically thinking of Caspar.

"He did something quite extraordinary," Giles continued. "After the crash, he came round to find his leg half severed. Then he heard the boy crying out. You know that damned great knife he carries?" James nodded. He had often seen C brandishing it. "Well"—Giles drew a deep breath—"C took it to his own leg. Carved his way through what was left in order to get to his son."

James winced. It was just the kind of thing C *would* do. There was silence between them, then James asked if his uncle would be giving him the next briefing.

"Yes." No more, no less; so, in an attempt to lighten the conversation, James asked what it was to be: "Want me to fly myself into Prussia and shoot Kaiser Bill?"

His uncle looked at him with Arctic bleakness. "There are some things we don't joke about. Your wife will be pleased. You're going to be in England for a while."

This was the last thing he expected.

"You'll be working hard enough." Giles still did not smile. "I've cleared the whole thing with C. You'll be doing an extra German course—"

"But my German's—"

"Not quite good enough to pass as a born Berliner."

"Well?" James finally asked.

"Well, sir. You know about your cousin—Marie?" Giles' mouth was set in a thin line of petulance.

"Of course. Though it's never discussed—like defecating."

"No." Bitterness hardened in Giles' eyes. "However, the security of this country—and the Service—may be at stake. Listen. . . ." Without naming Charles, Giles told of the latest information—that Marie might have been seduced, with the sole intention of getting her to Berlin, and, somehow, using her. "It doesn't excuse her actions. But something must be done soon. You, James, will be going to Berlin, probably in early January, to bring her out. If you can't do that, then your orders are to make certain sure that she never comes out. Not ever. You understand?"

4

On November 26th the battleship *HMS Bulwark,* anchored off Sheerness, suddenly exploded. Over seven hundred officers and men died in the violent, unexpected carnage.

The Fisherman was fully activated. On the following day he killed again. And that particular murder gave him more pleasure than that given by the hundreds who had died, blown apart by the bomb constructed by himself in the privacy of a guesthouse bedroom. At the time, nobody linked the sabotage with the murder.

His masters were well pleased with the sinking of *Bulwark,* and Steinhauer made a journey to England: not only to congratulate his agent, but also to oversee the running of one of Nicolai's main ploys within the heart of the enemy citadel. The German Chief of Intelligence had, at that time, no idea that it was one of Steinhauer's people who had brought about the sinking of the battleship. The story put out by the British maintained the explosion was an accident. MO5 and the Special Branch began an investigation, but came to no definite conclusions.

5

Kent, Ohio, United States of America.

October 28th, 1914

My Beloved Sara,

    Forgive me for addressing you in this way, but it is the truth, and I would be foolish to deny it. Lord knows when you will get this, as I hear mail between our countries is taking an age.

    As you can see, I am in Ohio—staying with my brother, Joe, who is on furlough from the Army. He goes back next week, but returns for Christmas, which we are all to spend in Washington, with the old folks at home—Dad and Mom hate that expression, but we tease them with it.

The envelope had taken until today, December 7th, to get from Ohio to Redhill, and would have crossed with Sara's hurried and rather frantic letter telling Dick about both Caspar and Rupert.

He went on to write about how the countryside was beautiful in what he called "the fall," and telling her he was doing some test flying as a favor to his Uncle Bradley—the Colonel in the US Army.

Dick also said how much he longed to see Sara, and how he missed Haversage, and Redhill. Then he continued:

    Washington was dreary, though I shall have to take care about what I write. President Wilson is a kind of paradox. He really is more of a schoolmaster than President, though very approachable. He has two dominating thoughts: to keep America out of the war in Europe and help bring about peace, though I am pretty certain he has no way of knowing how as yet.

    The great "Duty to My Country" turns out to be a bit of a farce, and quite impossible as it has some bearing on your family. I know you will understand the riddles.

    When I first arrived in Washington, Dad introduced me to an Army officer, a Captain Ralph van Deman. Van Deman wanted to talk with me privately, and it turned out that he knows all about that "far side of the moon" we discussed at Redhill. The Army Staff do not care for the Captain, or his ideas, but he is tough and will go over anyone's head. He has certainly "sold" his ideas to my father, and we both talked with the President, who said he could take no official side in the business at this time.

    Now, here is the real end of the line as far as I am concerned. Somehow they all know I am friendly with your family—I mean the one you married into. It has been suggested that I return, improve my relationship with the Rs and pick brains. I said I had no intention of using personal friendships to ferret out information. The President was calm; I am sure he understood.

He ended on a very different note:

> *When I last left Redhill, I wanted to return in a matter of hours, to tell you, again, how I feel. You linger in my mind. When I walk around the lanes and fields here, I talk to you in my head and, last evening, when I was flying, I watched the sun setting over the horizon, lashing the fading trees with gold, and I so wanted you to be there to see it. There is so much I want to share with you. You are the first thing in mind when I wake, and the last thing before I go to sleep. Between those times you seldom leave me. So, Sara, I am coming back to you as soon as I can. I shall then do the honest thing and ask you to marry me. I pray you will say yes.*
>
> *Darling Sara—forgive me for being so outspoken—give my best to each and every one, and please write. A letter here will always reach me. I shall be with you as soon as I can get a passage in the New Year. Please be waiting. I need you, and want to be everything to you.*
>
> Yours *in love for ever,*
> DICK.

Sara put down the letter, her eyes moist. She sat at her desk, in the General's Study, looking out across the gardens. The trees were now bare, and a fine, cold drizzle swept from the downland. Soon, in turn, the rain would become snow.

The rain was God's tears, she thought. Tears for the boys in France; for the war had now reached what appeared to be a stalemate, with both sides digging in on a line running almost from the English Channel to the Swiss frontier. This would, she was told, continue until at least the spring, and, if Dick returned before the war ended, Sara knew she could not marry him. Yes, she certainly loved him. His words, in the letter, were almost a mirror of her own thoughts and feelings.

She wanted Richard in every possible way—body, mind and soul—yet, following what had happened to Caspar and Rupert, she had pledged that no man would either enter her bed or take her to the altar until the war was over, finished and done with. She had watched Charlotte suddenly become prematurely gray; and the rocklike Andrew go to pieces because of the war.

She thought of the other members of her adopted family. Her uneasiness with Giles, which still hung on from the time her late husband's will had gone to probate; the friendly camaraderie with Charles and Mildred. There was strain on that marriage also, she observed, having detected the stress beginning to tell on Mildred.

As for James and Margaret Mary, they were happy as puppies at the moment. James was at home until sometime in the early New Year. After that, Sara suspected that Margaret Mary would again be living in that terrifying limbo of unknowing, her waking moments clouded with worry over her husband.

But this was most women's problem, for she saw it all around her. In Martha Crook, for instance, now that Billy—given a hero's time while he was at home—had returned to the front; a sergeant now, proudly, almost arrogantly, wearing the claret ribbon of the Victoria Cross.

She sighed again, looking blankly at the rain. Gladly she would accept Dick's proposal when he returned, but would not agree to an announced engagement, or a marriage, or even opening her legs for him, until the last shot was fired.

A knock at the door brought Vera Bolton into the Study, to say she was preparing the rooms for Christmas, and had put Mr. Caspar in the blue bedroom just at the top of the stairs, on the main landing. "It'll be easier for him to get down from there, Miss Sara." All the servants had somehow taken to calling her Miss Sara of late.

"Well, yes, but why not the pink room a little further along the landing, Vera? The blue is a bit obvious, and I gather Mr. Caspar does not like to be pampered. He's apparently learning to use his wooden leg very well, and his mother tells me he's sensitive about being helped."

Another knock, this time Porter, to say that "Young Rachel Calmer" was at the back door with a note from Mr. Berry. For some obscure reason Porter disapproved of Bob Berry's marriage to the butcher's daughter, and, in spite of the fact that they now had two children, a boy and a girl, he refused to call Rachel Berry by her married name.

Sara completed the allocation of rooms for Christmas—almost the entire family would be at Redhill over the holiday—before asking Vera to show Mrs. Berry in.

Rachel looked flushed, her clothes damp with the drizzle, but her complexion pink and pleasant—unlike the bovine, scarlet face of her butcher father. Rachel, young as she was, appeared to have done Bob Berry a power of good. The man was always happy in his work; meticulous and full of ideas. The only factor which marred life with Bob Berry was his recently constant pleas to be allowed to leave the Estate for the remainder of the war and join the Army.

"Bob asked me to bring this letter over to you, Miss Sara." She tugged a crumpled envelope from her coat pocket. Rachel showed little of the subservience so often apparent in the farm workers, trying to meet Sara's eye almost as an equal. "He had to go down Haversage on some errand, but says there'll be an answer." Sara took the envelope, inviting Rachel to sit down, chatting on—asking about the children, and the farm—while she slid open the envelope with the General's silver dagger, which she used as a paperknife.

Sara scanned the few carefully written lines and heard her own intake of breath. Her immediate reaction was a combination of shock and anger; then, self-control, learned the hard way over the past months, took over.

She gazed at the paper in her hands, trying to marshal her thoughts, for Bob had done the unforgivable in asking her to break this news to his wife.

The letter read:

Dear Miss Sara,

You will undoubtedly be angry when you read this. But for Rachel's and the children's sake, I beg you to bear with me.

I have asked you many times to allow me to leave and join the Army. It seems to me that the more able-bodied men who join now, the quicker it will be over for everybody.

I am an able-bodied man, and I know they are taking the unmarried men first. But now the special appeal has gone out to married men, I am more determined. Miss Sara, I know you will think me foolish, but I cannot live with myself, nor Rachel and the children, unless I can say I went and fought for my country.

There are plenty of men too old to go as yet. You will find no difficulty in replacing me. I know that Rachel will help, and I ask that she be allowed to stay on and give what assistance she can. If you do not want me back when the job is done and the Germans sent packing, then I shall return for my wife and children.

I fear I start this journey to war on a cowardly note, for I haven't the gumption to tell Rachel. I am sorry, Miss Sara, forgive me, but I have always felt we understood one another ever since the day you took that fall, many years ago now. I ask you, most humbly, to understand my motives, and to be as good as you can with Rachel.

Yr. Obt. Servant,
ROBERT BERRY

Sara folded the letter and put it on the desk, her anger subsiding. Gently she reached out, taking Rachel's hand. "My dear," she began, not really knowing how to continue. Then, again: "My dear. I'm afraid I have some very unpleasant news for you."

She saw in Rachel's eyes that the girl had guessed. The flushed complexion turned white. "Oh my Christ . . . I'm sorry, Ma'am . . . he done it. The bugger done it; he's gone for a soldier."

"I'm afraid so, Rachel." Sara had been prepared for tears, wringing of hands, even hysterics. Instead, she saw a pretty she-devil, furious and furnace-hot with anger. It crossed Sara's mind that perhaps Bob Berry had gone for more than the simple desire to serve his country.

"What'm I supposed to do now, then, Miss Sara? How'm I to look after the kiddies, and live, if Bob's gone for a soldier? I never thought he'd have the nerve." A slyness crept into her eyes. "Is it possible they'll not take him? I mean, if you had a word with—"

"No," Sara cut in, hard. "No, I shall not have a word with anybody. They'll take him, Rachel. Lord Kitchener wants more men all the time, and there's been a special appeal for married men. You know he's doing it for his country *and* you and the children. He's doing it for all of us. I refused to let him go, but he was determined. Maybe it'll turn out for the best. In the meantime,

Rachel, I shall help you run the Farm. You're Farm Manager now, and will be until Bob returns. If he felt so strongly about going, and was willing to risk his livelihood, then it's up to us to support him. Tomorrow I have to go to London. I shall seek some advice while I'm there, and when I get back we'll tackle the job together—the Estate and the Farm. If the men have the backbone to go and face the Germans in France, then we must show them what stuff we women are made of."

Rachel stared at her, mouth gaping. "You mean I got to run the farm, do the books, get up at all hours, *and* look after the children? You don't mean—"

"I mean it." Sara spoke with a firmness the General would have admired. "I certainly mean it. We'll give help with the children, Rachel. You'll help me and earn the same money as Bob. There are other women here who will lend a hand, you'll see."

6

Sara's visit to London was a monthly chore, but one she enjoyed. By the terms of John Railton's will, she had to make a brief report—in person—to the Railton family solicitors, King, Jackson & King. Old Mr. King had retired, and his son, Jonathan, a thin, slightly watery young man given to long silences and the steepling of fingers, now saw Sara each month at the chambers in Gray's Inn.

Young Mr. King, who obviously had his own particular preferences as far as the ladies were concerned, treated Sara with great courtesy, but made it plain that the meeting was but a short ritual required by law, therefore binding, but something which could be dispensed with quickly.

Sara usually made sure the appointment was over by midday, and spent the remainder of her time shopping and generally enjoying the city which, at one time, she had been reluctant to leave.

On this visit she had arranged to see both Charlotte and Mildred, for the latest small drama at Redhill had given her the idea of, possibly, involving the other two Railton women—both so harassed by present events—in the running of the Estate and Farm. As she sat in the taxi on her way to the Carlton for luncheon, following her Gray's Inn meeting, Sara thoroughly rehearsed her plan. She would put it to Charlotte and Mildred that, as the men were needed for the business of war, it was now up to the Railton women to see that the most prized possession of the family was kept in good order. She would suggest that each of them should spend one week at Redhill every month, assisting with planning, and even work on the Farm and Estate. She thought it a good idea to put it to them now, giving the women until Christmas to think the matter out carefully—and talk it over with their husbands, if need be. If so many of the London society ladies could be nursing in France and Belgium, it was certainly not above the dignity of Railton women to nurse the land they owned and enjoyed.

As the taxi took her through the busy streets, Sara realized more than ever why Bob Berry had made his decision. The pressure to join up was becoming hard for men like Berry to resist.

Posters were everywhere—YOUR COUNTRY NEEDS YOU screamed from almost every wall, and, as they reached the Carlton, Sara saw that the whole hotel had become a huge billboard: ENGLAND EXPECTS THAT EVERY MAN THIS DAY WILL DO HIS DUTY *** NO PRICE CAN BE TOO HIGH WHEN HONOUR AND FREEDOM ARE AT STAKE *** YOUNG MEN YOUR KING AND YOUR COUNTRY NEED YOU TODAY.

It was as she was paying the cabbie in front of the hotel that Sara saw Charles. For a second she started to get out and call to him, then realized he was not alone. Clinging to his arm as he hailed another cab was a young, very pretty blond girl who looked up at him with adoring eyes.

Sara took time in paying off her cab before walking slowly into the hotel, not knowing, now, how to greet Mildred later, or what to say.

Chapter Seventeen

1

"Vernon, I'm sorry—I've committed the worst sin in your book." So Charles Railton to Vernon Kell, in his office, now in the Old Admiralty Building.

That morning there had been a small ceremony over at what was now exclusively known as the Admiralty. Lord Kitchener came across to pin the medal on Charles, and Winston Churchill wrung his hand, saying how very grateful he would always be for what Charles had done for his dearest Clementine.

The medal was then removed, and "Blinker" Hall—very much in attendance—said that Charles must reveal nothing about the decoration until "probably after the war."

It was immediately after the ceremony that Giles took Charles off to an adjoining office and quizzed him closely about the information concerning Marie having been lured to Germany by von Hirsch. "Right under your hat, Charles"—his eyes like old pennies—"but an operation is being mounted on the strength of this intelligence. I don't want it to go off in our faces."

In Charles' mind the tumblers clicked into place. Once more he heard Madeline's voice, and saw a picture of them together, making love on the floor of the Maida Vale house. "You want to interrogate the source yourself?" he asked.

Giles allowed himself a smile. "Yes, I would like to speak with the source." The smile faded. "I hope you appreciate my coming to you instead of going directly to your superior."

Charles knew that now was the time to be at least partially honest. Giles already had suspicions.

"There are problems about this?" Giles raised an eyebrow.

"I'm not certain. The source is highly active," Charles volleyed back, turning toward the window. It was the first week of December, and the streets were full despite the war. A bus went by, packed to the running board. PEAR'S PURE SOLID SOAP—PEAR'S MOST ECONOMICAL it said on the side of the bus, with a little circle between the two slogans. The circle showed two unlikely pears on a branch. Wash away at least some of your sins, Charles thought. "The source is highly active," he repeated, then: "I have a small confession to make."

"Confession—" Giles started.

"—is most economical." Charles smiled into his uncle's blank face. "The information I passed to you seemed more like a family matter—"

Giles gave him a terrifying stare.

"I was probably wrong. I did not pass it on in my own report to Vernon Kell."

"You're a fool, Charles." It was said without malice. "This is *not* a family matter."

"It concerned my cousin, Marie. Your daughter. We're all a mite sensitive about what happened. I felt *you* should know. Marie's in Berlin. Foreign—not our pigeon, sir."

"But the source is in your deposit account, Charles. You should have told Kell. Learn some diplomacy, man. That piece of intelligence might have brought you something from the Kingdom of Heaven, as they say. It's a Country matter. As far as your Service is concerned, that intelligence was money in the bank—a bargaining counter. My advice is that you inform Kell before I come running to him with requests for the password to his magic cave."

So, immediately after luncheon, Charles went to Kell, ready to pour out his expurgated version of the story.

"The Drew interrogation..." He watched Kell's hands, then his eyes. One hand moved slightly.

"What about it?" Friendly, but with a touch of reserve. Natural enough, for Madeline Drew was beginning to provide interesting facts.

"During the interrogation something came up which concerned my family."

"Yes?"

"You probably know, Vernon. We try to keep quiet about it, but my cousin—"

"Marie Grenot? Yes. Most people who *do* know about it are very sorry. Drew mentioned Marie Grenot?"

Charles told him everything except for his own impropriety with Miss Drew.

When he had completed his version, Charles said he hoped Kell would understand. "It seemed a family matter to me. At the time anyway. I've told Giles Railton that you knew nothing about it. Called me a fool—which I suppose I am."

Kell thought for a long time, not looking at Charles when he finally spoke. "Strictly, I suppose you *were* foolish. It *should* have gone into the report. But you're the only one who can put it right. When's your next contact?"

"Tomorrow. Unless we get a sudden hands-off signal."

"In Coventry?"

"Yes. The usual place."

"Right. Try to get her to London. I'll see to Giles Railton. If he wants to enter the Seagull's nest, he'll have to dance to our music."

Since Madeline Drew left for Coventry they had begun to use elaborate code names for her and everything connected with her. Mr. Rathbone—Charles—was known as Anton, because Madeline Drew had been coded Seagull. Charles had become obsessed by the works of Anton Chekov, having read the recent translations. He had even seen the production of *The Seagull* at the Little Theatre two years before. Hence, the code names. There the connection ended, for the entire watching and collecting business was filed under the heading Rainbird. Information received became known as Gold.

When Madeline went off to her aunt in Coventry, the designated watchers moved in, waiting for the signal that someone had made contact. Nothing happened for almost two weeks. Then one morning when Charles was snowed under with other matters, a message took him quickly up to Coventry.

A hotel room had been booked for him, and Brian Wood was waiting. Wood had been chosen to stay well back from the team of watchers, his job being to liaise with Charles. "This morning," he said cryptically. "Good as her word. Came out around ten-thirty, dropped a glove by the gate as she fiddled with her handbag. A definite signal as arranged."

"You've followed it up?"

"You meet her tonight. Six o'clock. The place is near the cathedral. Bit of a tart's parlor, I'm afraid, sir. Safer that way, and the woman who owns it'll think it's just another married man with his fancy woman."

"Safeguards?"

"Everything taken care of. She has a route to follow. We've had a telephone installed." He rattled off the number. "If the window's open at the bottom, it's clear for her to come straight up. Closed, then it's hands off. Fallback in one hour. If that's no good, she shuts up shop and we try tomorrow."

Charles had never been in a common whore's bedroom before, but this place was just as he had expected it to be. A fair amount of red plush, a fashionable fringe on the mantelpiece cover, a doll in a long white gown, wax-faced, with eyes that closed when you laid it on its back; a dressing table arrayed with ranks of bottles, and a sampler over the big brass bedstead saying HOME SWEET HOME, with a little cottage in the top left corner.

The place had the smell of being used regularly for one purpose, so it was a relief to open the window.

The gleaming new telephone—looking like some futuristic mechanical man holding a club in its one hooked claw—stood, almost accusingly, on the dressing table. It rang at exactly ten minutes to six.

"She's clear," Wood said at the distant end.

Charles sat back in an overstuffed armchair and waited. She arrived at exactly six o'clock. Berlin, he thought, had trained her well.

She came straight to him, her cheek cold against his and her breath warm in his ear. He felt her body push against him, and she whispered, "Oh, Charles, it has seemed an age. I couldn't bear it any longer." Then she pulled her head away and kissed him, expertly and full of physical need, her mouth opening, tongue licking around his teeth, as a small child will devour the last morsels of ice cream from a bowl.

She was like some terrible and beautiful flower, with Charles as an insect victim, unable to resist.

Gasping, they pulled apart, and he asked the most important question—if she had news for him. Petulantly she said that of course she did. Yes, she had been contacted by her people, but all the time she spoke she was undoing her coat, throwing her hat onto the chair, then her blouse and skirt and underskirt, then her bodice, finally revealing tantalizingly short pink drawers.

Charles had no choice in the matter. Like a man rushing to get into a much-needed bath, he fumbled with buttons and studs, then leaped, rather than climbed, onto the bed.

In the afterglow and released tension Charles asked for her report. She smiled at him, dazzling in her satisfaction and pleasure. "Part of our bargain should be that you always make love to me at least three times before I tell you anything."

"It's not safe for us to stay too long. The place is watched. You realized that, of course?"

"That's one thing we should talk about, Charles. The people who are doing the watching. They're inept. Too easily seen. It worries me. If the friend I shall tell you about returns, he is sure to recognize one of them. They have a routine which never varies."

"All right." Charles held up a hand, palm facing her, as though to ward off some spell. "I'll have a word." It worried him, though, and certainly would not have happened in Paddy Quinn's day.

For a time, Madeline would not stop talking about it: "Seriously, darling, it is dangerous. These people have been well-trained in Berlin."

Gradually he brought her to the important matters in hand, sitting opposite her on one of the stuffed chairs.

She spoke low, keeping to facts, painting in details, answering questions almost before they had time to form in Charles' mind.

Two days before, a tall man in a dark coat and hat ("It's absurd, but he looked like all those drawings you see of spies") dropped a card through the door and rapped on the knocker once. He did not wait.

The card was an advertisement for a tea shop. Madeline's name and address was written boldly on the reverse side.

Madeline had subjected the card to heat, as they taught her, and the heat revealed secret writing, probably an ink made with the simple ingredients of lemon juice and formalin, possibly using a well-known brand of disinfectant.

The message read: *2.30 this afternoon. Sit alone.* She went, and sat alone. At about a quarter to three the same tall man came in, smiled and went over, holding out his hand: "Madeline, my dear, how nice to see you. . . ."

"He is dark, with a slightly hooked nose, full head of hair, beard, glasses. Speaks with an accent which is not German. Russian possibly. I don't know. Serbo-Croat origins." He told her they would stay for fifteen minutes only, and she must leave first. "Then he asked what happened in Cromer. I told him the story we concocted and he said a report had to be made. It could take a few weeks to get instructions. I was to wait. Orders would come. He was merely there to get the Cromer story. 'G' is what I have to call him."

G had told her to expect a letter: "But I've a feeling he could come to the house again. That's why I'm so worried about your people. He's no fool." She was getting very nervous about things going wrong.

Would she describe him again? Could she say more about his accent? Try to mimic him?

At last the questions were exhausted, but she wanted to make love again and he could not resist.

2

So Charles returned to London and reported to Kell. Life continued. Basil Thomson, on the evidence of Charles' report, went personally to Coventry and reorganized the team of watchers.

Two weeks later Charles was in Coventry again, performing the same ballet— through the streets and on the featherbed. G had taken the risk of calling at the house to collect Madeline, so the watchers followed. After the pair parted, one of the Branch men trailed Eagle, as G had been coded, and lost him in London, at Euston Station.

As for Madeline, nothing had changed. Orders would come.

The following week there was another contact with the tall man, and this time he indicated that the orders had arrived. She would be expected to spend a large amount of time traveling, mainly in trains, to and from London, and down toward the south coast ports. Berlin wanted details of troop movements. She was provided with a small book giving details of regimental badges, and her work routine was left up to her. G would see her in five days' time. Meanwhile, he provided money, two hundred pounds toward expenses for travel and hotels.

On this occasion, now that they knew her role, Charles made arrangements

for their next meeting, telling her she was to give G some real information—
"millet," Kell called it.

She was to follow G's instructions, but only inform him about selected items
which Charles would provide through the post.

It was this meeting that was arranged for the day after Charles' "confession"
to Kell, and he again took the Coventry train to meet the girl, who dominated
his thoughts.

In the Coventry "tart's parlor" she purred, naked, leaning over him in the
dark. "Do you think I've done well? G thinks I've done *very* well. I've got to
carry on and report to him when he arranges another meeting. Have they found
out about him yet?"

In fact they had, for G was registered as a Russian alien named Muller,
living in Bloomsbury, near Russell Square.

"If they have, I would not tell you, my darling. It's not in the rules—and
you certainly know the rules." Charles smiled.

"Meaning?"

He patted her bottom. "Meaning you are well trained in all the arts of your
craft."

She laughed—which craft was he speaking about? The one he ordered to
sail or the one he sailed in?

She asked if he had an itinerary for her journeys during the coming week.
G merely provided the place-names. It was Charles who controlled her movements.

"How would you like a couple of days in London?"

"With you, Charles?"

"At the Carlton. I can get away for one of the nights."

She squealed like a child. "Oh, and it's nearly Christmas—"

"Wait." He stopped her mouth with his hand. "We'll have one wonderful
night, but you may not like the next day too much. There's someone important
who wishes to see you about Marie Grenot." She must stick to the story she
had told him about Marie; but he cautioned her, "On no account give the
impression that we have anything more than a professional relationship. It could
bring great harm to both of us."

It was, then, on the morning after they had spent the "wonderful night"
together at the Carlton, that Sara saw them leaving the hotel. At that moment
Madeline did not know she was on her way to be interrogated by Giles Railton.
Nor could she know that she was already pregnant by Charles.

3

The village of Ashford lies a few miles from Wicklow Town, in the direction
of Dublin. In one of its six public houses, Malcolm Railton sat quietly drinking
with Padraig O'Connell.

It was ten o'clock at night, in the second week of December.

"So the English think the Fenian movement is dead?" O'Connell looked over the top of his glass, his eyes red in the glow from the turf fire.

"No, I don't think they're that foolish. But they imagine things'll be quiet now there are Irishmen fighting alongside a common enemy."

O'Connell let out a loud, almost drunken, laugh. "Can't the buggers read? Don't they allow them the Irish newspapers in London?" He spoke of a letter published in the *Irish Independent* only a couple of months previously, by the Dublin-born Foreign Service diplomat Sir Roger Casement, urging all Irishmen to fight against Britain and not against the Central Powers.

"Oh yes, but I don't think they take Casement very seriously. He's gone to ground and'll get himself arrested if he sets foot in this country, or across the water."

"Well, you find out how much they know, friend Malcolm, and I'll tell you what *I* know. For some damned reason I trust you, even though you're an English bastard. You'll find out?"

"I'll do my best. You can be certain of that."

"Right, then. Well, here's the latest. . . ." Padraig began to speak softly. At the end he said, "The English will be too busy with their war to notice that the Irish patriots are armed and organized, ready to throw them out of this country once and for all. You'll see."

On the following morning two telegrams were sent from the Post Office in Dublin's O'Connell Street.

One was to Sara, at Redhill, apologizing for the fact that Bridget and Malcolm Railton would not be able to join the rest of the family for Christmas.

The other was to a Mr. Gordon Rainer, in Paddington.

This second telegram—in cipher—told its recipient what he already in part knew: that Sir Roger Casement was in Berlin to recruit and get German assistance for a future uprising in Ireland.

Giles Railton had the deciphered message in his locked desk drawer when Charles showed Madeline Drew into the room.

His usual chilly manner became warm, even pleasant, with the girl as Giles bade Charles leave them. He felt it was always best to be as nice as possible before he put someone to the question. Giles was a Grand Master at inquisitionary techniques.

Six hours elapsed before Charles was summoned to take Madeline away. The girl was white and shaking: "That man is a ruthless, dreadful person," she sobbed.

As for Giles, he looked as though frozen inside an iceberg. Much to Charles' concern, Giles Railton kept his nephew locked from his conversation and company throughout the entire Christmas holiday, while Madeline refused to give any clue as to what had transpired during the inquisition.

4

The riddled and mutilated corpses remained, either buried in shallow graves or lying in the fields, woods and ditches of Belgium and France—that dreadful killing area of the final months of 1914. The trail of dead, from both sides, marked the ground for all time, as did abandoned and shattered armaments.

Before Christmas the Allied armies faced those of the Central Powers, entrenched and miserable, along a line stretching from below Ostend, through Picardy and Champagne, into Lorraine.

Across Europe there was rain. Over the sweeping downland, above Haversage, around Redhill Manor, it snowed.

The whole Railton family, with the exception of Bridget, Malcolm and, of course, the Grenots, gathered for the annual festivities, though much to Sara's chagrin, Giles took over the General's Study, where he remained for most of his visit.

The children, and some of the adults, played in the snow, building snowmen, snowballing or taking the three old toboggans onto Roman's Slope.

Caspar, looking surprisingly cheerful, arrived in a wheelchair, with a snake-slim, beautiful young nurse called Phoebe, who appeared to watch over him like a nanny. He insisted on spending at least two hours each day trying out his peg leg—his courage and determination appearing miraculous to all who watched him.

Only on the final day of this rather somber Christmas did the rest of the family discover that Phoebe was in fact The Honourable Phoebe Mercer, heir to the Lancashire cotton millionaire, Lord Mercer of Bury. They also failed to notice that she put Mary Anne's nose out of joint.

Mary Anne was also in uniform, and scheduled to leave with several Anglican High Church nuns for France in January.

On Christmas Eve she spent some time with her cousin Caspar.

"Sure you're up to it, Mar?" he asked, using her initials as they had done since childhood.

"I passed everything, top of my group. And spent a lot of time in the wards."

Caspar's smile was not patronizing. "Oh, Mar, I hope that's enough. Some of the professional soldiers over there've been shocked at the sheer barbarity of modern weapons. I hope to God you're tough enough."

"I was tough enough when we played soldiers years ago."

"This isn't playing soldiers!" Caspar snapped. Then the smile returned. "Yes, you were quite a tomboy. Uncle Charles treated you rather like a boy, didn't he?"

She nodded. "I think he very much wanted me to be a boy. Well, he's got his heart's desire now; though little William Arthur's a handful, and Father isn't at home enough to appreciate him. I'll tell you one thing, though, Cas. I'll wager young William Arthur doesn't get the beatings I got." She had the same true Railton look as the others—tall, with a good body which showed under her uniform as she moved.

Caspar shifted in his chair, the effort making him contort his face, as pain bit into the stump of his leg. She saw the beads of perspiration break out on his brow.

"You all right, Cas?"

"Course I'm not all right, Mar. Oh Christ!" They were alone, and had been close all their lives, but this was the first time since childhood that Mary Anne had seen him in tears. "How would you feel, Mar? One leg and one arm. Good old Phoebe pumps morphia into me when it gets really bad, and they say that eventually it'll go altogether. It's not so much the pain as the disability. The look of pity I see in people's eyes. I don't want their bloody pity. I want work. I want to kill fucking Germans—sorry."

"It's all right. I've learned a lot of words since I began nursing. You'd be surprised, cousin."

And at that moment Phoebe returned. "You mustn't tire him, you know," giving Mary Anne a look of professional superiority.

Mary Anne merely laughed. "Even in his present condition I doubt if *I* could tire him, Phoebe."

Caspar was quietly amused by the exchange.

On Christmas afternoon, at the giving of presents, Giles seemed his old self, though Charles noticed his uncle's gaze did not once stray in his direction. For the remainder of the time—Christmas Dinner apart—Giles sat brooding in the General's Study. He saw only three people alone: James, Caspar and Ramillies.

Giles saw James on the afternoon of Boxing Day, after the younger man had spent the morning riding to hounds.

When they were seated in the Study, Giles asked how Oxford was going. He had arranged for his nephew to spend time in the University city while he studied the Berlin dialect and learned from maps and photographs the city which he had visited once only in his life.

"Oxford's fine, sir. Old Professor Bucholz and Dr. Meyer are hard taskmasters, and Margaret Mary's not happy, only seeing me at weekends."

"It would be most unwise for her to join you in Oxford."

"Oh, she understands. Still doesn't like it."

Giles offered one of his rare smiles, and James asked after C. "He'll be back in the New Year." Giles sounded oddly put out, as though a tiny portion of his power would be removed. "Very tough. I saw him last week. He's like a warhorse, pawing the ground to get into battle again."

"I get my final orders from C?" James asked.

"Officially, yes. But I shall be present."

"How long have I got?"

Giles did not look at him. "Not long. The actual date will depend on the reports from Oxford. We don't want you in Berlin until we think you'll get away with it."

James grunted. Inwardly he was already excited. "How do I get in?"

"The same way as Friedrichshafen. Only you'll change identities straight off and head directly for Berlin. Identity is the most important factor. You follow me. You must begin to think as a German now. Once there, you won't have time to look back. You must be invisible in that city."

Outside, in the big drawing room, the women sat and talked. When James came out of the Study, Sara told him that Margaret Mary had gone up to rest before dinner.

"And we all know what *that* means," she muttered, watching Porter, who had been summoned and was shuffling away in search of Caspar. Before this interruption they had been talking to Charlotte, trying to help her and understand the nature of her present distress. Comprehension was not difficult—all had seen Caspar's courage and Rupert's heartbreaking condition (he had played with simple toys through the holiday, and had a tantrum in church, so bad that Nanny Briggs had to remove him).

"I'm resigned to it," Charlotte said. "I can live with Caspar's disablement, because he can live with it; and Rupert has no option. Andrew's the true concern. He's so changed since it all happened." Indeed, Andrew, who had been an almost too perfect example of the Royal Navy at its best, was altered beyond recognition, and Sara was shocked at the way he appeared to be drinking so much.

Charlotte had said he had plenty of work to do at the Admiralty: "Though Lord knows if he's doing it properly. He's always half drunk when he gets in at night." Then she asked if any of the other men had mentioned her father-in-law's speech, after the ladies had withdrawn following the Christmas Dinner. There was a general shaking of heads. "Well, I know Andrew was pretty drunk, but, even within the family, he thought his father had been a trifle indiscreet."

She then recounted what Andrew had told her.

After the dinner, Giles had stood at the head of the table, and facing Andrew, Charles, James, Ramillies and Caspar, proposed a toast: "Within our family there are few secrets," he began. "Yet we all know of our particular work. I doubt if there is any other family in the country with as many of its sons working among the same shadows and carrying the same secrets in their heads. We are, gentlemen, members of a unique, and very special, society. We live mainly in a secret world. Be proud of that, and do not listen to any of the military, or political, pundits who say our kind of work is degrading or contemptible: they have yet to understand the true nature of our various callings. In time, both military and political worlds will appreciate what we do now. This is honorable work; patriotic work. We are"—he paused, searching for the right words—"we are a new style of generation. A secret generation. So, I toast us—the secret generations."

James wondered if his uncle had somehow seen one of the poems he had written to Margaret Mary, into which he had put those very words.

5

Caspar was the only member present who could not be truly counted as one who was concerned in this arcane profession. Now, on Boxing afternoon, with weak, snowy sun throwing a pale imitation of its summer glory across the fields and gardens, he was brought by the attentive Phoebe into Giles Railton's presence.

Apart from his small, and private, breakdown in front of Mary Anne, Caspar contrived to keep up a spirit of bonhomie before the rest of the family.

"How goes the Christmas spirit, sir?" he greeted his grandfather. "You wished to see me?"

Giles raised his head, looking at the young officer, the wheelchair and Phoebe, in that order. Phoebe smiled at the unspoken command and withdrew.

"Yes, I wished to see you." He then asked Caspar if he had thought further about the matter they had discussed at the hospital.

"You mean the secret stuff?"

"Exactly."

"I want to kill Germans. Vengeance is mine."

"You'll not do it in the field. So why not at a distance?"

"What on earth *could* I do?"

"A great deal." Giles hunched forward as though taking the young man into his confidence. "The Chief of Service has also suffered mutilation. He's lost a leg. You'd get on well with him, and he has need of a good young military head close to his. I want to propose you as his ADC."

"Yes, but what would I do?"

Giles paused, then lowered his voice—it was an old actor's trick to gain attention and underline the secret nature of their conversation. At heart, Giles was a cunning old actor. "Must go no further than this room, mind you."

"Of course."

Giles explained that, as he saw it, the generals and politicians would soon be divided within the present deadlock. "There will be two schools of thought. On the one hand, those concerned with a war of attrition; battling trench against trench. A siege, conducted on the largest scale Europe has ever seen. On the other hand, there will be those who wish to go around the trenches. They will want some kind of breakthrough instead of frontal assaults. A breakthrough *around* the lines."

"And?"

"And, for a long time, neither faction will really see the true essential in this war. In the end it will boil down to a matter of supply."

He explained about the train-spotting networks behind enemy lines. "You would be of immense use to the Service by collating the reports. That would be a start, surely? When you're truly fit, of course."

There was a long pause, filled only by the crackling of the log fire. "Grandfather, when I'm fit enough might I come on probation, so to speak? It sounds interesting, but I need to see results for it to satisfy me."

A minute piece of the ice in Giles Railton's soul melted.

6

As Sara had suggested to Dick Farthing, Ramillies William Railton was far and away the most brilliant member of the family. He was also adept at hiding the fact behind what was often taken as a reticent shyness. Ramillies had that rare ability of being absolutely unobtrusive—a young man who preferred to watch and listen instead of joining in, and so, by his very silence, could become almost invisible.

When Porter sought him out, late on that Boxing afternoon, Ramillies was mentally apart from the rest of the household, his nose stuck into Gibbon's *Decline and Fall*. Even so, Ramillies, if pressed, would have been able to state, with the accuracy of a skilled navigator, the exact location of almost everybody in Redhill Manor. He was not, then, surprised at being asked to join his grandfather in the General's Study.

"Before we meet in the office again," Giles began, "there is one word I should like to drop into your ear."

Ramillies waited.

"Russia?" Giles said the word quietly, then stopped for the reply that did not come, so that he had to speak again. "Your feelings on Russia, Ramillies?"

The young man never wasted words. "Turbulence. Trouble. Potential chaos. The biggest internal power-struggle in Europe since Attila the Hun. Nothing's worked so far; the revolutionaries—failed once—will make another bid for power. This time they'll be successful."

"Yes."

Ramillies gave a diffident shrug. "Grandfather, what am I to say? Our own politicians wouldn't listen." He paused, as though the next sentence were a prophecy on which he might be called to account. "The Czar's planning to be away from St. Petersburg." He used the old name out of familiarity, even though the city had become Petrograd a few months before. "It's common knowledge that he'll take supreme command of the Army. Once he's left the city. . . . Well, I'd say the upset will happen pretty soon."

Giles nodded agreement. "Quite. A fair digest of the situation. And, yes, nobody here will listen, so *we* must be prepared. My feelings are that the great revolt will not engulf simply Russia, but the whole of Europe. There's much to do when we get back to London, but at the end of January you will be expected to come into the office only twice a week."

Ramillies raised his eyebrows.

"This is just a warning. You won't be idle. Your time will be spent studying the Russian language, brushing up on Russian lore, art, culture and history: not to mention the ways and means of getting around the country."

"I'm to go to Russia?"

"In the fullness of time, I think, yes. You must certainly keep that in mind. I want you to speak like a Muscovite; know the customs and protocol like a diplomat; and their folklore like a peasant."

"I understand."

His grandfather had no doubt that Ramillies understood completely.

                                    7

Alone again, Giles went back to his musing, and the thoughts which had obsessed him through the whole Christmas holiday—thoughts of what Madeline Drew had, under pressure, revealed to him; and what he was bound to eventually pass on to her.

Being long experienced in the more sinister arts of interrogation, Giles had not initially set out to discover anything new concerning the operations and organization of the German Military Intelligence. Already, Charles had performed that task more than adequately. There were further ways in which Miss Drew could assist, for Giles Railton's devious mind played with the idea of compromising German Intelligence officers. What he wanted was a view of the chinks in the armor of people like Walter Nicolai and his cohorts.

Madeline Drew, trained by the Intelligence people in Berlin, knew much of their private lives. Giles required the kind of information normally not spread abroad—who had mistresses, and did their wives know? Who was perverted in one way or another? Who preferred boys to men, or men to women? Who had strange habits, and who was constantly in debt, or feared some secret becoming public knowledge? These were the things he wished to feed to James before the boy went off to Berlin in search of Marie. Giles considered that if anyone knew anything of this kind, it would be a woman like Madeline.

The interrogation which had reduced Madeline Drew to a tearful wreck, and lasted over six hours, began calmly, but built into a dreadful, browbeating affair, thick with threats and heavy with Giles' personal abuse.

Within a couple of hours, he established that the golden-haired, innocent and open girl facing him across the desk was implicated in a multitude of sexual gambolings with high-ranking Intelligence officials in Berlin. From that discovery he had slowly broken Madeline, probing and prying into the most secret corners of her private life while in Germany.

It was only in the last hour that Miss Drew let slip a hint of her affair with Charles.

Giles had spent most of the Christmas holiday deciding not merely how best to use the general information on Berlin, but what to do about this unhappy liaison between the girl and his own nephew, Charles.

Just as dinner was ending that night, Porter hobbled into the dining room. There was a gentleman to see Mr. Charles, urgently.

Brian Wood waited, full of apologies, in the big, flagstoned hall. It was very urgent. Mr. Kell had insisted he should bring Charles straight back to London.

"What the hell's wrong?" Charles was halfway across the hall, ready to arrange his packing and make excuses to the rest of the family.

"Seagull, sir. She's threatened to pull out altogether uless she sees you within twenty-four hours. Something vital's happened and she'll speak only with you."

Charles, anxious and concerned, set about getting away from Haversage in reasonable order.

Within three days he was back in London reporting to Vernon Kell.

"She's been ordered back," he told MO5's Director. "We've got ten days at the most either to pull her away from this contact—Eagle—or let her go."

Kell sat in silence for a full five minutes. Then: "You'd better come with me. Your uncle's holding the fort until C gets back. We need his Service's advice on this one. See if they can run her at long range, inside Germany."

It was with mixed feelings that they set off for Northumberland Avenue and what Charles suspected could be a lengthy—and possibly unpleasant—meeting with Giles Railton.

8

The man they knew as G—or Eagle—had arranged a meeting with Madeline Drew on Christmas Eve. The message was to the point. Berlin wanted her to return. The means for that return—a U-boat—would be available within the next two weeks.

Whatever the dangers, Giles, in C's absence, was decisive. He wanted the Drew woman out of England.

So, on January 5th, 1915, Madeline Drew left Coventry for Holyhead, where she took the RMS Connaught sailing to Kingstown, Ireland. At Kingstown she went by train to Galway.

In the early hours of January 8th, in a secluded bay some six miles from Galway, a small boat picked her up, rowing a mile offshore to the waiting submarine.

By January 24th Hanna Haas—as she had again become—arrived back in Berlin. She was emotional and in a state of confusion, mainly because, following the quickly called meeting with Charles on the day after Boxing Day, they had not allowed her to see him alone again. She was a very frightened woman on that first morning back in Berlin.

A few weeks later, unknown to her, Charles' kinsman, James Railton arrived in the German capital. Herr Franke had come home, though in his memory James carried a picture of his cousin Mary Anne preparing to leave for France to nurse the wounded; and an even more surprising recollection of Caspar in a wheelchair, sitting behind a desk in C's outer office.

Chapter Eighteen

1

Sara appeared to be blessed with boundless energy, and, during the second week in January, a bitter freezing winter that year, she returned from her thrice-weekly visit to the Cottage Hospital to find Mildred and Charlotte had arrived, as planned, from London.

Over Christmas they had spoken at length on how the Estate, and Farm, could now be run. Sara made a list of strong young girls and older men in the district who knew something about farming and were in need of work. The Railton women would each have to play their part. Charlotte, Mildred and Margaret Mary had spoken to their husbands, all of whom expressed their admiration for Sara's sensible plan. They had even spoken to the quiet, nervous Denise who, in turn, had told Giles. Initially Giles wondered if it was some form of intrigue, though, intrigue or not, he felt Sara was doing the right thing by involving the whole family.

Already, the women had each agreed to try to spend one week in three at the Manor to assist in the general running of the place. Later that afternoon they would bring Rachel Berry into their circle. "She's a shrew at heart," Sara said, "but if we handle her properly; allow her to think she's organizing everything, I think she'll be a good ally. We need someone like her who can mix with the girls and old men on their own terms. I think she'll be the whip in our hands."

In fact, when Porter knocked and entered the General's Study, Sara thought Rachel had arrived.

"It's Miss Mary Anne," he told them curtly, for he did not hold with women closeted together on farm business.

"What about her?"

"She's here."

"A flying visit." Mary Anne stood in the doorway. "I have twenty-four hours, and they told me Mama was here. I leave for France tomorrow afternoon."

Mildred rose and went to her daughter, embracing and smothering her with questions. Was she getting enough to eat? Enough sleep? How were they treating her? Until Mary Anne had to push her gently away.

"Mama, I'm fine. I couldn't go without saying goodbye."

"You look tired out. You really have to—"

"Go?" Mary Anne smiled. "Yes. I'm as much under orders as a soldier."

They sat her down and Sara rang for tea. "We can feed you up at dinnertime. At least you can relax now, rest and be with your mother."

Mary Anne signaled a look of gratitude, acknowledging that Sara understood her emotions far better than Mildred.

Rachel Berry arrived soon after, and the meeting continued, with Mary Anne going upstairs to rest. But she talked later when they heard she had been working twelve-hour shifts.

"But that's ridiculous!" Charlotte began.

"War is ridiculous." Mary Anne had changed from the soft—if stubborn— well-bred girl. "Only the men who are out there, and the women who have to care for the dying and wounded, can know how ridiculous it is."

"These Anglo-Catholic nuns—" Mildred began, a distaste creeping into her voice. She mistrusted anything in the Church of England which appeared to ape the Church of Rome.

"Are incredible!" Mary Anne snapped tartly. "Some of them work more hours then we do. They rarely lose their tempers, and even the youngest is wiser than I'll ever be." Then she talked at length and with passion of the war horrors she had already dealt with as a nurse.

Mary Anne's outburst threw them into an uneasy silence; and Charlotte in particular thought much about Caspar and his personal bravery.

2

Caspar was aware they had an agent in Berlin, and that he, or she, was known as Peewit. He had no idea that Peewit was his cousin James. He also knew there was another agent who was presumed to be in Berlin. The code name of this one was Seagull, and Seagull was daily expected to be in contact with one of their men attached to the British Office in Switzerland. The contact was known as Ruby. Peewit's contact, also in Switzerland, was Pearl, and each day C asked if there was news from either of them. Ruby and Pearl remained silent. This did not bother Caspar; he had other things on his mind, mainly what he saw as alarming information emanating from the train spotters.

"The figures speak for themselves, sir." He had taken his wheelchair into C's office. Even C wheeled himself around, and both men practiced using their peg legs at home, in off-duty moments. "Even if our people are exaggerating, the ratio of arms and ammunition being moved up to the German front line is seventy percent heavier than our arms movements."

C nodded. Urgent reports had gone to the Committee of Imperial Defence, and the government. There was much talk of stepping up arms production, but so far little had been done.

"Our troops'll be annihilated unless we get more ammunition to them!" Caspar was excited. "If they collapse, the Channel ports'll be easy meat."

"Exactly what I've reported." C's tone lay on the borderline of anger. "Silly damned fools are so tied up trying to find a way to break in through the back door—Turkey and all that—they can't see how quickly the war can be lost."

In the outer office again, Caspar began to leaf through a batch of new signals. He detached one from the pile and made for C's door. It was a short message from Switzerland—Peewit had made contact with Pearl. A full report would follow.

3

Gustav Franke stepped off the train at the Charlottenburg Station and made his way through the crowd to the exit taking the numbered metal tag from the policeman on duty. The number on the tag was that of his allotted *erste Klasse* cab.

He was going to the Hotel Minerva on Unter den Linden. Herr Franke was returning to Berlin for the first time in years, and his face showed all the nostalgic emotion of a man coming home, with smiles of recognition as he spotted old landmarks from his childhood.

For the past ten years, Herr Franke had lived in Switzerland, his family having moved there for reasons of health. His mother had died two years after the move, and his father followed her last year. Now that Germany was at war, there seemed to be no reason for Herr Franke to remain outside the Fatherland. True, the damage to his leg in a skiing accident three years ago would prevent him from serving with the Army. But his knowledge of the theory of flight and the workings of modern aeroplanes could be of use.

His papers showed he wanted for nothing. He carried a letter of credit for several thousand marks—the bulk of his deceased father's estate. There were no surviving relatives living in the city, so he would stay at the Minerva for a day or two while he looked for a suitable apartment. After that he would report to the authorities and see what service he could be to the Fatherland.

Even in the damp cold of a slightly misty evening, Gustav Franke's heart leaped at the sight of the "Linden," the trees in their winter nakedness, the great buildings and shops just as he remembered them. With the memory came other pictures—his Aunt Irma's house near the Tiergarten, and the fine ladies and gentlemen parading along the Sieges-Allee; the grand marble Monument of Frederick William III, which his grandfather Franke took him to visit some Sundays in the summer, traveling in from their house in Wilmersdorf.

In his mind, he could see the house, with its heavy mahogany furniture, the red curtains hanging across the high windows, the smells of cooking filtering up from belowstairs. He remembered his toy soldiers—Grenadiers, smart in their red jackets and led by an officer on a great black horse.

It was as though these things had really been a part of James Railton's childhood, so well had the professors at Oxford taken possession of his mind.

He felt no fear at being deep within the heart of Germany. "*Be* Gustav Franke," they had told him. "*Be* the complete man, with a past, present and future. Live him. Do everything he would do. Regard your mission as the fantasy."

The Minerva was functioning with the normal efficiency of any first-class Berlin hotel, and, even at this time in the morning—his train had arrived at 7:00 A.M.—a number of guests were about. As at the station there were a large number of uniforms. Only occasionally did the reality creep into his mind— a brief flash of Margaret Mary's face; a sound in the street reminding him of London.

He bathed, shaved and changed. They had given him three addresses, two of people who, while not active agents, were at least known to have sympathies with Great Britain, and that of the house in the Courbierrestrasse where the German Intelligence Service carried out some of its work. James also carried another name and address with him—that of Major Joseph Stoerkel, the disillusioned officer with whom he had talked briefly in Friedrichshafen.

By ten o'clock, refreshed and breakfasted, he was taking a cab to Elizabethstrasse, in search of Stoerkel. The Herr Major, they told him, was not at home. He had already left for his office with the Imperial Army Postal Service, near the Main Post Office on Alexanderplatz.

It was almost eleven o'clock before James discovered that Major Stoerkel was second in command of military censorship. Half an hour later he arrived at the office in which he worked.

A rather surly clerk asked what his business with the Herr Major might be.

"I have his card." James showed the piece of engraved pasteboard. "He invited me to call on him if I was in Berlin. Tell him it is the Swiss gentleman he met in Friedrichshafen." Three minutes later he was seated in front of Stoerkel's desk.

"So, Herr— Herr— Grabben, is it not?"

"Franke." James looked him in the eyes and saw the right eyebrow twitch.

"Ah. My memory is faulty. As I recalled it, you were called Grabben. A Swiss gentleman."

"German." James had decided to be brazen. "I was born here, in Berlin. I have spent many years in Switzerland, where my family moved a long time ago. But—"

"And how can I help you, Herr Franke?"

James did not allow his eyes to unlock from those of the officer. "I have returned to Germany. There is work to do for the Fatherland. . . . I thought—"

Joseph Stoerkel pushed back his chair and stood. "Come, Herr Franke. I usually take an hour or so for luncheon about this time. You know Habel, on the Linden? Excellent for luncheon."

Habel's menu was comprehensive, for the restaurant had an international reputation, particularly for luncheon, and a bowing, obsequious waiter took them through the throng to a table in the far corner of the main room.

The Major was obviously well-known at Habel. The waiters spoke to him correctly by rank and name. They drank the Leberknödelsuppe and ate a main course of Königsberger Klops—meatballs in caper sauce. It was only when the headwaiter brought the Berliner Pfannkuchen that Joseph Stoerkel began serious conversation.

"I always order these. In fact they make them especially for me, even out of season." The doughnuts were traditionally eaten on New Year's Eve, and normally only served between Christmas and Lent. "Now, Herr Franke, what do you wish of me?"

James lowered his voice. "In Friedrichshafen you gave the impression that you were disillusioned with this war."

"That was said to a Swiss businessman."

"Pretend you're speaking to the Swiss businessman." James experienced a surge of fear, as though he had only just realized the risk he was taking. A few words exchanged about the war with a man back from the front were not enough upon which to base trust.

"If I did, how could I be of assistance? The doctors have pronounced me unfit for active duty at the front, so I glance through random letters written by our fighting men, to make certain they are not indiscreet." He gave an apologetic smile. "They may, perhaps, tell the truth about the hell of war."

"There are two things." James could do nothing but commit himself now. He would move straight out of the Minerva and go to one of the addresses they had given him in London. Possibly people there could advise him of somewhere to live—an earth, for a fox. "First, I really should do something to help the Fatherland, otherwise people will take me for a coward or an indolent fool."

"And second?"

"I am looking for an Englishwoman."

"Oh, my dear fellow, aren't we all? Mind you, a French girl would be a change."

James ignored the remark. "She could be thought of as French. Her married name is, or was, Marie Grenot."

"She is in Berlin?"

"I don't know. She left Paris the day before war was declared, with a German officer, Klaus von Hirsch."

"Then she could be Frau von Hirsch, or the Gräfin von Hirsch by now. I presume we speak of the old Count von Hirsch's boy? The one who spent so much time at the Paris Embassy?"

James nodded.

"And you wish to serve the Fatherland by finding this lady?"

"She is English. A distant relation."

Stoerkel gave an amused smile. "Just like the Kaiserine and the British Queen Mary, yes?"

"Yes."

"There are a number of English, French, even Belgian ladies married to German officers. There are even some who are not married, but live in style. I will see what I can do. At the same time I shall inquire to see if you can be employed in any way." James had told him of his aeronautical qualifications. "Where can I reach you?"

James said it would be better if he made contact with the Herr Major.

"Yes? I have a telephone number at work, and at my home. It would be best to call yourself by some fancy name—say you are Baron Hellinger. If I have news I will tell you. The details will be addressed to the Herr Baron at the Alexanderplatz Post Office, Poste Restante. Does this satisfy you?"

"For the time being. I trust we shall meet again."

The Major laughed, then suddenly leaned forward and whispered, "Our Army is about to use a terrible weapon. Probably in the Ypres area, in the spring. It will be an attempt to break through and dash for the Channel ports again. Remember CL2, and COCL2. Soon."

Herr Franke paid his bill at the Minerva late that afternoon and traveled over to Bayreutherstrasse, near the zoo. On the second floor of an apartment building he found Frau Dimpling, a lady who, they had told him, hailed originally from Eastbourne. She had married Herr Dimpling, a young German engineering student, in 1909. Letters, C said, had been passed to him from the Foreign Office.

Before leaving the Minerva, James went to the nearest post office and sent a cable to Switzerland. It was an innocuous message concerning the availability of various consignments of watch and clock mechanisms, together with a request for details of docket numbers. The message was signed by a Helmut Gatti, and the return address was Poste Restante at the Zoo Post Office.

The real message was contained in the consignment and docket numbers, and it was this decoded signal that arrived on Caspar Railton's desk.

4

She had striking red hair and looked as though she were recovering from an illness, her face white above the smart blue dress. She spoke German with a strong English accent, and later admitted to having been a schoolmistress.

"Frau Dimpling, I have to speak with you," James said in German.

"Is it about Wolfgang? Is it?" As if pleading.

Once inside, and certain there was nobody else in the apartment, James spoke in English. "I have to trust you. In London they said you could be trusted. I've just come from London."

She gave a kind of cry, her whole body trembling, and she threw her arms around him, sobbing. "Thank God!"

Wolfgang Dimpling, her husband, had been reported missing, presumed killed, near Antwerp during the battles of the previous autumn. She had no friends in Berlin, her parents-in-law were both dead, so she had written and written to London. Hetty Dimpling, née Fairchild, had waited, going out only for food. Germany had taken away her husband; she was homesick and frightened, so this tall, good-looking young man came as a godsend.

She smothered him with the affection usually reserved for her husband — she drew a hot bath, ran out to the shops after inquiring about his favorite food, and then shut herself first in the kitchen and later her boudoir. Dinner was candlelit and delicious, and Hetty Dimpling became a changed woman: vivacious and attractive, with her hair let down to her shoulders. James marveled over the transformation.

He also marveled later that night when she came to his room, slipping into the bed and moving close to him, lips cool as cucumbers, and passion, pent up for so long, like a waterfall at full flood.

It was the first time that James had been unfaithful to Margaret Mary, but he felt no guilt or shame. The sad-faced, plain redhead saw to that. Berlin, and his assignment, had suddenly taken on new dimensions.

5

"He's made some kind of contact," Smith-Cumming told Giles. "That's all I can tell you. There's no mention of any lead on Marie Grenot."

"Well, at least he's there." Giles showed no hint of emotional involvement.

C mentioned the references to poison gas. "Chlorine and phosgene, my people tell me. The military men do not appear impressed."

"They are impressed only by what they see with their own eyes. The number of corpses impresses me, by God. I understand that the Salonika business is to go ahead, even though the initial Gallipoli landings have not been an unqualified success."

Smith-Cumming shrugged. "Typical of Churchill, though. He fought against that particular way in through the back door. When he lost, to the Gallipoli plan, he adjusted and has put all his power behind it. If it comes unstuck, *he'll* pay for it."

Giles did not appear to hear. "We know Peewit's location?"

"The Zoo. That woman's a shot in the dark, but one of the few we could offer. You ever get worried about your family. Railton?"

"Why should I?"

"Well, Peewit, and his first subject, they're—"

"Railtons, yes. Doing their duty, that's all. It's something we do. Everyone in our position. It'll go out of style soon enough, what with incompetent government and incapable General Staff. We could end up with a bankrupt country and people looking for a new way. We could even lose Empire. Our kind have heard the chimes at midnight, C. We may be the last generation to do so."

"The damned Military'll go on resenting us for a long time to come. I just hope to God someone had the sense to take the gas business seriously."

But nobody would take it seriously, in spite of the special information supplied by Peewit, and later, in the field, by French agents, together with German prisoners under interrogation. Spotter aeroplanes reported no signs of any odd equipment. The commanders in the front line, around the Ypres salient—the most likely spot for the German armies to try to breach for a dash to the Channel—warned company and platoon commanders, for what it was worth, of what they called a rumor.

6

Nurse Mary Anne Railton saw her first gas cases on St. George's Day, April 23rd, at a casualty-clearing station a few miles south of Ypres.

There was no doubt about the battle. For almost a week the ground had shaken, while smoke coiled over the city itself. Mary Anne, who had arrived there on April 17th, separated from the nuns, and detached—with two other girls—from the hospital train in which she had been working, felt she was now as near to the war as she would ever get.

She had also become a hardened veteran. Her first day on the hospital train brought her up against the horror of shattered bodies still numb from the shock of wounds.

Wounded or dying, Mary Anne treated them the same, with as much skill and compassion as she could muster. There, among makeshift, crowded wards, she soon learned the art of detaching herself from the terror and reality.

Then, wakened at dawn one morning, a senior medical officer told her, together with nurses Dora Elliott and Jenny Cooper, that it was "up the line" for them. The trio did not question their orders, saying goodbye to the nuns and clambering into the back of the truck where the same medical officer waited, showing little patience.

She had known the other two nurses since almost her first day of training, and they were, if not firm friends, at least close acquaintances—Dora, short, blond and bubbly, originally of Irish extraction; and Jenny, always in trouble.

It took almost two hours to reach the clearing station, where they were greeted by Sister Price, whose personality would have done credit to a drill sergeant.

"Nurses Railton, Elliott and Cooper?" Sister barked, and the girls, crumpled and sweaty from the uncomfortable journey, looked around, seeing flat ground and four large tents with a small cluster of khaki bell tents nearby, and felt, more than heard the noise of pain and death.

"Well?" Sister Price snapped, and they realized she was asking for their identities. Each answered by giving her name, and the Sister immediately fitted names to faces. Once she had met her nurses for thirty seconds, Sister Price never forgot names or muddled faces. She told them her name, that this was the most forward clearing station; they would see things here they had never seen before; they would work longer hours; they would do as they were told, and use all their skill. "If any of my nurses shows the slightest incompetence, she goes home. Bags packed within five minutes. Now, that tent"—pointing to a small bell tent about fifty yards away—"that is your home. You have fifteen minutes to settle in." She whirled, pointing to the reception area—the smallest of the four long tents. "Fifteen minutes!" And she was away. Three ambulances chugged up the track toward them as if to underline the urgency.

"There's no place like home." Dora stood inside the small tent, looking at its three pathetic "biscuits," lockers, and the metal bar for hanging their clothes.

Jenny and Mary Anne dumped their battered suitcases beside the "biscuits" which would be their beds. "Well, *I* prefer the Gerry shells to Sister," Dora commented.

"It's what we volunteered for," Mary Anne said primly.

"*I* volunteered to get away from my dreadful parents." Jenny tried to tuck her hair inside her cap, but it promptly tumbled out.

"Your hair's dropped again, Jenny." Dora moved to help.

"So've my drawers." Jenny turned away. "Several times. It's something to do with the aging process."

"Well, don't blame me if you get a bollocking from Sister."

"Sister can go and fuck herself."

"Jenny!" Mary Anne looked shocked for a second.

"Oh, come on, Railton. Be your age. If Sister doesn't do it to herself, she won't get it at all. Frigid old crone."

"I don't see how 'language' helps."

Jenny laughed. "Railton's nanny wouldn't like it."

"Railton's nanny isn't going to get it," sniggered Dora. "Mary Anne, it *does* help. It's a safety valve."

"Yes," Mary Anne bridled, "we hear the men use that kind of language, but half of them don't know any better. We're nurses first, but we're also ladies."

"I've never been a lady in my life, Railton. You try living in a Liverpool hovel with seven brothers and sisters. I bet your papa didn't come home drunk of a Saturday night and virtually rape your elder sister in front of your eyes. We're not all ladies, Railton."

"Nurses! Nurses!" Sister Price's strident voice penetrated the fabric of the tent.

Dora looked at her watch. "We've still got five minutes."

"Nurses!" Sister calling again.

"Oh God." The three girls, still soiled by the journey, hurried from the tent. They did not return to it for almost fifteen hours.

Altogether there were three doctors, two Sisters—Price and Beamish—and seven nurses at the casualty-clearing station, and Sister Price stood head and shoulders above everyone. Even the doctors feared and respected her. Martinet though she was, Sister Price's bark was much worse than her bite. Mary Anne soon found the incredible reserves of both skill and compassion within this woman. She also discovered the first frightening effects of gas.

That morning, as they ran to the reception tent, all three girls felt a new anxiety: not exactly fear, but a sense that they were about to confront unknown horrors.

"'A' Ward—in that tent." The Sister pointed. "Gas cases. Do what you can. I'll be with you in a moment."

The sign on one of the flaps told them which was A Ward, and Mary Anne was the first to step inside.

"Jesus!"

There were about twenty patients, brought in by the ambulances. They lay in rows, their noise breaking above the steady rumble of nearby guns. It was like a ragged, frightening, wind in an old chimney—a crackling, forced, gasping noise from the worst nursery nightmare.

The men were full of movement, as though inflicted with a terrible twitching of the limbs, and it took a moment for the nurses to realize that their movements were of desperation as they tried to grasp for air. Their faces were blue, and they panted, fighting nature to relieve the distress of lungs irritated and filling with fluids.

The faces of the other nurses and the two doctors on duty showed that they were appalled. One, a captain who looked about Mary Anne's age, grabbed at the girl. "Nurse, help me with this one—he's drowning in his own lung fluid. Help me."

Together, they propped the terrified man against the wall, Mary Anne bundling blankets behind the patient's back. Together they worked for an hour, trying to give the soldier some relief.

"He's got all the symptoms of acute bronchitis," the doctor said quietly. "If we could only drain the lungs."

Mary Anne, called away constantly, returned to the lad again and again, but they were fighting a losing battle. He died at around five that afternoon, as Mary Anne sat by the bed. *He just opened his poor tired eyes, took the deepest breath he managed all day, smiled and died,* she wrote to Mildred. She did not say that she had cried for him. It was the last time she was to shed tears for the dead or dying.

Of the twenty men brought in as gas cases that day, all but six were dead before midnight. The rest coughed, wheezed and fought their way slowly back to a kind of life. Other wounded were arriving all the time, and there seemed to be a procession of ambulances coming and going.

When they were finally relieved, the three nurses went to the small mess tent, ate a few spoonfuls of stew and staggered to their tent.

In the darkness they could hear the clunk of spades against the earth and knew that the detachment of troops, there to protect and assist, was busy, digging graves.

Mary Anne sat down heavily on her "biscuit" and looked up at Dora. "Fuck Gerry," she said. Dora nodded.

Day merged into day, and night into night. Men came, were treated and sent on, labeled with recommendation for further surgery, treatment or a "blighty"—to be sent back to England. A lot of men came, and went nowhere except into the earth.

Within two weeks the battle, which became known as 2nd Ypres, was over, and men fought simply for a few yards of ground. At the end of the first week, Otter arrived.

He came at night, just after dusk, shambling into the reception tent, blackened, scarred, with caked dirt and blood all over him. He was stark naked except for the tattered fragments of what could have been a vest, and part of his right boot.

Mary Anne was on duty in the reception tent, and, in some ways, was responsible for the loss of any clues about him, for she stripped the rags of clothing from him and threw them into the metal container into which soiled or infected bandages and dressings were placed to be burned.

She cleaned him up, noted that he had two very slight wounds—a scratch across his scalp and another down the right thigh. They needed dressing, which she did by herself. He had the wild, frightened animal look that came with shock, and she talked to him quietly, but all he could mouth was 'Ott . . . Ott . . . Ott . . ." Hence the nickname they gave him: Otter.

"A blighty, sir?" Sister Price asked the doctor who examined him later in the evening.

He shook his head. "No. No, we don't even know whether he's one of ours or theirs. Best keep him here for a day or two. The lad's terrified, and it could be more damaging to move him." It was the kind of compassion none of them could really afford, but the doctor, an RAMC major, had spoken.

When the casualty-clearing station was moved back, and the staff sent to No. 6 General Hospital, Rouen, Otter was still with them—nameless, unidentified, without rank, number or nationality. He was tall, in his mid-twenties, fair and good-looking, and constantly tried to please. He would run errands, help the nurses and doctors with the heavy lifting, bring tea into the wards, smile at everyone and say, "Ott . . . Ott . . . Ott . . ." like some tame domestic pet. Even his eyes had the pleading look of a stray dog in need of love, and his normal gait appeared to be an oddly uncoordinated half-run, taking little steps instead of the firm strides his long legs were obviously capable of making.

At Rouen, nobody questioned him. It was as though Otter had been demoted from the human race for the sole purpose of becoming a helpful mascot for doctors and nurses alike. Nobody shouted at him or gave him harsh orders. But he was quick, and soon even picked up rudimentary first aid.

The staff that had worked together at the casualty clearing station remained together as a team at the General Hospital, and Otter was always with them.

"He'll either get his memory back or some silly devil'll suddenly take him away and put him through hell," the Major told Sister Price. "But for the time being he's walking wounded. And he's our walking wounded."

Otter had a special regard for Mary Anne, as she had been the first to take pity on him. Often he would follow her around like a loyal terrier, and he never had any difficulty understanding what she required of him.

One morning three weeks after they got to Rouen, Mary Anne was dressing a wound when they brought several stretcher cases into the ward. Orderlies helped the men into bed, and presently the Major came around, with Sister Price, to make his observations. Mary Anne went on dressing the wounds—a great gash where shrapnel had taken a bite from a young corporal's right thigh—aware that the Major had reached the bed next to her patient.

"Shrapnel wounds, left shoulder. Lacerations left cheek," Sister Price intoned.

"Mmm." The Major bent over the wounded man.

"Blighty, sir?" Sister asked.

"No. Sorry, old chap, not this time. You'll be up and walking in a few days. We'll see in a week."

"Name, rank, number, next of kin," Sister Price snapped.

"Hunter—Jack—corporal—2-5-4-0-1-0—no next of kin, Ma'am."

Mary Anne looked up sharply. The name and voice stirred something from childhood. She peered at the man on the bed.

Later she went to him. "You're name's Corporal Hunter?"

"Aye."

"Jack Hunter?"

"Yes." Wary.

"Didn't you once work for my grandfather, General Sir William Railton?"

"I might have done. Your grandpa, eh. And who are you? No, let me guess. You're Mr. Charles' little girl."

"Yes. It is you, isn't it? Mr. Hunter? You were Grandpa's Estate Manager, weren't you?"

He nodded, and she thought there was pleasure in his eyes at seeing one of the family again after so long.

But it wasn't pleasure in any normal sense. Jack Hunter had prayed for a time like this. Ever since that stuck-up bitch, Mr. John's wife, had seen him run off the Estate, he had prayed. One day, he thought, a Railton would be alone, and at his mercy.

7

James went out every other day. Nobody appeared to bother with Frau Dimpling, and he explained matters to her in simple terms, even though she was a woman of above average intelligence.

She was twenty-eight years of age, and had met Wolfgang while he was on holiday in Eastbourne where her father was a local bank manager.

Wolfgang, with his degree in engineering, was finishing his education as a student engineer at a motor-car-engine factory near Croydon. His parents— who were both to die in a tragic fire in 1912—were also well-to-do tradespeople. Hetty Fairchild and Wolfgang Dimpling took one look at each other and fell in love. Herr Dimpling, senior, visited her father a month later, and the forthcoming marriage was announced.

Since the news of her husband's presumed death, the lonely Frau Dimpling, fearing for her safety, had dared not write to her parents in case the letters were intercepted: yet, with that odd illogicality of the English, she had written to the Foreign Office in London. James' arrival had been an answer to her prayer.

James of course, gave her only minimal information. She must speak to nobody about his presence in the house; if asked, he was Herr Gustav Franke, the son of an old friend of the Dimpling family, recently returned from Switzerland.

Quickly, he discovered that she was a young woman who needed a great deal of physical attention. It was, he reasoned, his duty to keep her happy, yet at night he often found himself wakened by the soft sound of a piano. The music worried him.

On the third day he went out, traveling by bus and tram to Courbierrestrasse. He then spent an afternoon in the area, lingering as long as possible near Number 8.

There was nothing to see.

He left any further contact with Herr Major Stoerkel for a week. Then he telephoned the home number. A servant answered. The Herr Major was at home, who wished to speak with him? James said it was the Baron Hellinger.

Major Stoerkel came on the line. "Herr Baron, it's good to hear from you. I wondered when you would get in touch again."

"I shall always be in touch, Joseph. Any news from the Alexanderplatz?"

"I was going to leave a message for you."

"Well?"

"The lady you so admire—"

"Yes?"

"I have an address. She is at Number 36 Wilhelmstrasse, almost next door to the Hospiz St. Michael, near the Anhaltstrasse. She lives in Apartment 23, and it appears to be her custom to go out between the hours of eleven and noon, and again between four and five in the afternoon."

"Thank you. You've been very helpful."

"Oh, I can be of more assistance. When can we meet?"

"Soon," James said, and hung up.

That night he rehearsed Hetty Dimpling in what she was to do. "You must appear very natural. Find a shop to examine. Even go inside if necessary, but make sure that you can see the entrance to Number 36 clearly. I will be near but not in the street itself. Remember, there are two things to look for—the woman I shall describe and anything suspicious—people watching."

In minute detail he coached her in the ways the house could be watched: "Watchers will not wear uniforms or badges of rank. *Anyone* loitering—women standing where they can view the whole section of the street, gossiping; men repairing things, painting signs, passing the time of day. Be casual. See if they're watching you. If they are, then don't look back, just go about some kind of business."

He told her to try to show no fear, but if someone approached, she must get away without too much rush and hurry. James then gave her the description of Marie, repeating it several times and making her go over it until she was eye-perfect.

In the morning he saw her off, following at a safe distance, going to a nearby street.

The café where he waited began to fill up, and the waitress kept coming back to see if he had finished his coffee. He told her he was waiting for a friend.

Hetty, wearing a flattering sky-blue dress, with a slightly darker blue street-coat and a saucy veiled hat, came in at a little after half past twelve. Her eyes sparkled, telling it all.

At home, he made her tell the story three times. There had been nothing at all suspicious. Nobody working, or lounging in the street. Yes, for the hundredth time she was certain about the woman—just as he had described. She was with a tall, very handsome officer, in uniform. They walked to the end of the street, then the officer hailed a cab, so Hetty could follow no farther.

"Did the cab appear suddenly or did it look as though it was waiting for them?"

"Come to think of it, darling, yes."

"Yes what?"

"Yes, it looked as though it was waiting near the building."

His senses asked, Why? Did Marie, provided it *was* Marie, want to be seen? There was only one way to find out.

"Gustav, darling," Hetty called, having vanished into the bedroom, "will you come and love me—please."

Later she said that Gustav was better than Wolfgang. He laughed. "How better?"

"Bigger." She giggled. "Bigger and stronger. Wolfgang was like a baby carrot."

"Oh yes?" Did they plan to trap him by making it easy for him to see her? Should he go in the afternoon? View from a distance?

"While you," Hetty giggled, "you are like a large parsnip."

He turned to her, knowing he had to free his mind in order to make a decision. "Butter my parsnip, then."

8

It was Charlotte's turn to spend time at Redhill helping Sara with the farm organization. Andrew had a few days' leave due, and he had come down with her—to rest, he said.

They were at the house, about to sit down to luncheon, when the cablegram arrived.

Sara tore it open and gave a squeal of joy. "Richard Farthing," she said, a shade too loudly. "He's coming back to England. Look," handing the cablegram to Andrew.

"That'll be nice for you, dear. Do I detect the sound of wedding bells?"

"No." Sara's voice, while happy, was quite firm. "Definitely not. Not yet, anyway."

"Oh no!" Andrew said. They both looked at him, for there was despair in his voice.

"What is it?" Charlotte asked.

Andrew swallowed, looked down at the cablegram again and said it was nothing: "Nothing at all." Then he went to the sideboard and poured himself another gin.

He glanced at the cablegram again. It read: SAILING NEW YORK MAY FIRST ON SS LUSITANIA STOP DUE ARRIVE LIVERPOOL SEVENTH STOP SEE YOU VERY SOON STOP ALL LOVE DICK STOP.

Though his mind was cloudy, Andrew, with his knowledge of intrigue, vividly recalled the conversation he had overheard.

Ten days previously he had been waiting in the DNI's anteroom. The main office door was slightly ajar, and Andrew was surprised to hear the voices of both Lord Fisher and Winston Churchill, the First Lord, speaking with the DNI.

"You're certain the Germans know the ship is carrying ammunition?" Fisher asked.

"I'd be surprised if they did not. They certainly know how short of ammunition we have been in France, particularly since the Ypres fiasco."

"So the chances are they know Lusitania's carrying ammunition?" Fisher again.

"I'm ninety percent certain."

"And you are sure, Reggie, that the German U-boats are sneaking their way through?"

"They've issued warnings, sir. And our own wireless interceptions show U-boats operating off Irish waters."

"Well, that settles it." Fisher raised his voice. "Let her come in by the normal route. Withdraw our own ships to a safe distance during the final twenty-four hours, and the chances are they'll have a go. What think ye, Winston?"

"I am horrified by the possible loss of innocent life."

"It'll take more than one torpedo to sink her, and I wager if they try it'll be a nervy hit-and-run kind of thing. Our ships will quickly close in and pick up survivors. My honest opinion is there will be very little loss of life."

"I suppose"—Churchill again—"that everything else outweighs loss of life. A German action such as this will bring condemnation from all four corners of the globe."

"With luck—if it happens at all—it will convince President Wilson, and the rest of America, that they must join the fray against the common enemy." From Fisher. "I'm told there are a lot of Americans already on the passenger list."

"Yes, you're right of course," said the First Lord.

"*Lusitania* must be put at risk. If she is torpedoed, and the Americans are brought in, then this whole wretched business will be over that much sooner. Give the orders, Jacky."

"Aye, aye, Winston." A laugh. "But I'm committing nothing to paper...."

The DNI interrupted: "Leave it all to me, sir. I'll chart her position and call off the escort, make certain she's in the most dangerous place at the right time."

The words echoed through Andrew's head. Dear God, he thought, the concept was understandable—to bring the United States into the war—but he liked Sara and knew she was fond of this young American. She had lost one husband. Now it was possible she would lose the man who could bring her a second chance of happiness.

9

When the late John Railton MP pensioned off Jack Hunter, his Estate Manager, in the spring of 1910, everyone in Haversage and at Redhill Manor knew Hunter had virtually been dismissed. They knew also that Sara Railton was responsible, and that Hunter got the cottage and annuity only because of Mr. John's knowledge of the General's wishes.

In 1910, Hunter was only thirty years of age. He had worked at Redhill Manor since he was fourteen—the General's man; but, said the gossips, the General had strange tastes as well, though not young boys and very young girls like Hunter. Live and let live, that was the General.

Hunter had liked the General. They understood one another, and the old man kept out of his private life. He had taught Hunter many things, and one of them was a certain dignity. Many feared him, and, at the time of his going,

Vera Bolton's mother had said, "Ar, that Jack 'unter be a man of vengeance. His kind'll wait for half a century for revenge."

But, around Haversage and Redhill, nothing more was heard of the man. Hunter took possession of the cottage near Stanton St. John, drank a bit, dug his small garden. But within him, the iron entered his soul, and Jack Hunter could do nothing about it. His existence was lonely enough, and he had time to ponder. The only Railton he had ever liked was the General: the rest were a steaming dungheap as far as he was concerned. Especially the women. Digging his garden, in the springtime of 1911, he cursed them all and swore his own vengeance. Jack Hunter was now low as a slow-worm, and that because of Railton women.

He did not plot or plan, for he knew the day would dawn when one of the Railtons would put himself—or herself—in his power.

Some of the locals knew about Hunter. Those with sense warned their children to stay clear of him; others did not worry. Strange things happened in the isolated communities, but few spoke of these matters, and rarely did anyone write about them, unless it was some scandalized vicar. It wasn't a thing you talked about—at least not until something very bad had happened. As it did in the late summer of 1914, when they found young Emma Gittins, from the nearby hamlet of Forest Hill, not quite twelve years of age, half naked in a ditch, with blood all over her thighs and the blue marks where she had been strangled.

The police came all the way from Oxford and spent days asking questions. They had Hunter in three times, but went away in the end. It frightened Hunter, though he could not remember things that clearly.

Then, one night, just before Christmas, he woke in the dark. He was screaming, and he knew. There was some idea in his head that a little girl who tried to fight him was a Railton and should be done away with. He saw the picture clearly.

The next morning he went off and took the King's shilling. In April 1915, helping to reinforce the new line of trenches along the perimeter of Polygon Wood, four miles or so from Ypres, he had taken the shrapnel in his left shoulder and cheek.

At the clearing station they told him it was a blighty for sure, but now, at the General Hospital in Rouen, the doctors changed their minds. He would be there for about a month, they said. On his feet in a few days. "You can be a great help in the ward," the frigid Sister told him. And Jack Harold Hunter rejoiced, for there, tending him, was a Railton woman. She was older than he liked them, but he would make an exception for Nurse Mary Bloody Anne Fucking Railton. She would squeal when he split her thighs.

So, Corporal Hunter was respectful, pleasant, always thanking her and calling her "Miss." The time would come, sure as eggs were eggs.

10

Few passengers took the notice seriously as they boarded the SS *Lusitania*. They had seen it in the newspapers, and there it was again, beside the official list of departures at the dockside. Dick stopped for a moment to scan it:

NOTICE!

TRAVELLERS intending to embark on the Atlantic voyage are reminded that a state of war exists between Germany and her allies and Great Britain and her allies; that the zone of war includes the waters adjacent to the British Isles; that, in accordance with formal notice given by the Imperial German Government, vessels flying the flag of Great Britain, or any of her allies, are liable to destruction in those waters and that travellers sailing in the war zone on ships of Great Britain or her allies do so at their own risk.

IMPERIAL GERMAN GOVERNMENT.

Much of the talk was of the possible U-boat threat, but most people—including the officers—were sure that no harm could come to a vessel like *Lusitania*. "What would be the point?" said the young officer at whose table Dick Farthing dined on their first night at sea. "The German Navy're only interested in merchantmen, not passenger liners like this."

The others, gathered around the table, at ease, having eaten well, and drunk even better, nodded sage agreement.

"And why are you traveling to Europe, Mr. Farthing?" The man on Dick's left also had an American accent.

"To see friends. Indeed, the lady I hope to marry is English. I'm an aviator and I'm going over to fight the Germans."

"Well done, sir," applauded the young officer.

"Stout fellow," remarked a military-looking man.

The American smiled and nodded, so Dick asked him why he chose to make the journey.

"Fair question. My name's Frohman. Charles Frohman..."

"The theater!" Dick exclaimed. "Charles Frohman, the impresario?"

"Guilty."

"Why, you're famous, you produced *The Arcadians*."

"Guilty again."

Dick, like the others at the table, was fascinated to find they were in the presence of a celebrity.

"And what takes you to Europe, Mr. Frohman?" one asked. "Some big new musical extravaganza?"

Frohman spread his hands. "Alas, the law brings me to Europe." He explained that he was in partnership with the English actor-manager Sir Edward Seymour-Hicks. "We took a lease on the Globe Theatre in London. Unfortunately, I did the renovations and installed an elevator. The landlords have taken exception. It appears I should have gotten their permission. Seymour-Hicks cabled. They're about to sue us, so I guessed I'd better go and get Edward off the hook."

They laughed at his odd predicament. *Lusitania* was just clearing the Hudson: heading out into the Atlantic.

11

Three nights later, in Rouen, Mary Anne was doing her first spell of night duty. She was tired, and pleased to have somewhere to doze—the little office, usually Sister's domain during the day.

Happily, the ward had no serious cases, otherwise she would have been obliged to sit at her desk in the ward itself all night. As it was, she could keep her conscience quiet by making an occasional visit around the beds. The night sister was predictable, arriving on the dot at half past the hour, every three hours.

So, for most of the night, Mary Anne could read, doze or brew a cup of tea on the small stove.

It was four in the morning, and she was half asleep, when she suddenly became alert. The door to the office opened, almost silently, and Jack Hunter slipped inside, using all the cunning he had practiced so often in the woods and coverts of Redhill.

"Corporal Hunter, you shouldn't be in here, you know." She was relieved it was only this patient. She smiled. It was always best to humor difficult patients. "Now then, Corporal, if there's something you want—" Mary Anne stopped short as he clicked the key in the lock and dropped it into his pocket.

"Oh, aye, there's something I want, Mary Anne Bloody Railton...." He laughed, low and unpleasant.

"Corporal!" She had become used to being obeyed by patients. "Open that door and we'll go back into the ward."

He shook his head. "No, *Miss* Railton."

"What is it you want?" Her voice betrayed no fear.

"What do I want, *Miss* Railton? First of all I want what I'm going to get—and it's between your legs."

He moved fast and was on her before she had time to cry out or move. She felt one of his big hands across her mouth, while his other reached down. He was pushing her backward across the desk, and reaching for her long skirt.

She fought, thrashing out with her arms, fists balled, hitting him with all her strength, her mouth working as she tried to bite the hand. Her skirt was rucked up to her thighs now, and she began to kick out with her legs. When he took his hand away from her mouth it was so unexpected that she did not cry out. A second later she was not able to do so, for he hit her, hard across the side of her face with the back of his hand, then again, swinging the other way, with his palm. When the hand was clamped over her mouth again, Mary Anne was only on the lip of consciousness.

She fought through a great wall of fog, yet knew what he was doing to her. This was the most terrifying thing, for all power to resist seemed to have ebbed away.

One hand was tearing at her drawers, and she was unable to stop him stepping between her thighs as he pushed her back down onto the desk, leaving her legs dangling.

The pain brought her to. It was like a great red-hot poker jammed between her legs, a searing terrible agony as he thrust into her, ripping at flesh. She knew then that the wetness was blood, and the pain grew worse as he moved higher into her.

The anguish so wakened her that she was at last able to get her teeth into his flesh and bite. For a second his hand moved and her scream overpowered his curse. He hit her again, and the world became this fearsome, jarring scalding between her legs, a floating darkness, and the knowledge that his hand was now not over her mouth, but around her neck, and that very soon there would be complete darkness. She was going to die.

The agony rose; he smelled horrible and she heard him panting heavily through the mist. Then, over it all, came a tremendous crash, and his weight was lifted from her body so that she slid to the floor. Clearly she heard the words: "Ott . . . Ott . . . Ott . . . Ott . . ." Rising, as though in rage.

The Otter was there, spinning Hunter around, a fist smashing into his stomach, a knee going hard into his exposed private parts, swollen and huge. She saw Hunter double up, but, before his knees buckled, the Otter's fists locked together and he brought them down on the Corporal's neck with a final cry of "Ott! Ott!"

Hunter sprawled forward onto the small floor, and there was the sound of voices and footsteps. The Otter was bending over her, covering her nakedness and making shushing sounds.

Her mind cleared, and she heard him speaking, but it was in German: "Kapitän Ott . . . Ott . . . Kapitän Otto Buelow, Number 5 Battery, Imperial Horse Artillery, at your service, Fräulein. I am your prisoner now, yes?"

She had time to mutter in schoolroom German, "No . . . No . . . You must pretend. You must just say Ott . . . Ott. Please pretend. . . ." Then Mary Anne felt the blood soaking her thighs and lost contact with the world.

12

Andrew was in no position to understand that his very high consumption of gin was doing him harm. Never before had he suffered so many violent changes of mood or such depression. It was probably the strain, he considered. Certainly his duties at the Admiralty brought about the obsessions. The American, Richard Farthing, was a current obsession, and he hardly knew the fellow. Yet Sara knew him, and because of that, Andrew had been like a cat on hot bricks since *Lusitania* had sailed from New York.

On the morning of Friday, May 7th, the concern lifted slightly. It was plain that the Commander of the Royal Navy's base at Queenstown, Ireland—Sir Charles Coke—had been worried enough to send two signals. The first had gone on the previous day: SUBMARINES ACTIVE OFF SOUTH COAST OF IRELAND. This very morning the Admiralty had received Admiral Coke's latest signal: SUBMARINES ACTIVE IN SOUTHERN PART OF IRISH CHANNEL. LAST HEARD OF TWENTY MILES SOUTH OF CONINGBEG LIGHT. MAKE CERTAIN LUSITANIA GETS THIS. Whatever possible intrigues were taking place within the Admiralty, those on the spot were doing their best to see the great liner through.

Lusitania had cleared Fastnet and now turned toward land—taking a bearing on the Old Head of Kinsale.

Dick sat in the great first-class dining room with Charles Frohman. They had taken the second luncheon sitting on purpose. It had been a jittery few days, and during the previous evening, Captain Turner announced that they were now approaching dangerous waters. He had posted double lookouts, imposed a blackout and had the lifeboats slung out. "A precaution only," he told the passengers. "On entering the war zone tomorrow, we shall be securely in the hands of the Royal Navy."

"Well, Dick, you can just see land up there—Ireland, I guess." Frohman paused to order the lamb cutlets. "I was on B Deck just now and we seemed to be making a right turn to sail along the coast. What is that, port or starboard?"

Dick grinned. "Starboard."

The orchestra began to play "The Blue Danube Waltz," and Frohman moved a hand in time to the music. "I guess we're safe now. You going straight to London?"

"Not quite." Dick's plan had been to travel to Haversage. He was about to speak again when the ship gave a tremor and there was the muffled sound of a bump, as though they had hit something. It was hardly an explosion, more of a shudder.

A few seconds before, Walter Schweiger, Captain of the U-20 which had been shadowing the great four-funneled liner since one P.M., had quietly given the order to fire one of his three last precious torpedoes. The time was just before ten past two on a beautiful sunny afternoon.

"What the hell was that?" Frohman asked.

A second later there came a great rumbling noise; the whole dining room shuddered, and the deck under them lurched.

Dick was on his feet. "Something hit us."

"Guess we should forget the lamb cutlets."

It took them less than three minutes to reach B Deck, and all the time they could feel the deck sliding under their feet.

The stately ship was listing heavily to starboard. Toward the bow, a great plume of smoke hung for'ard of the first smokestack; the vessel was still making way, under its own momentum, though the bows were already skewing into the water, the angle of list increasing with alarming speed.

It was all happening very quickly. As they reached the starboard rail Dick, with Charles Frohman, could see there were men and women in the water below. Worse, lifeboats were being dropped. They saw one take the long dive from its tilting davits, smashing into people in the sea below.

"The other side!" Dick caught Frohman's arm and they began to climb the angled deck.

But, on the port side, things were worse. Because of the increasing angle of the ship, it was even more difficult to launch the boats. They reached one boat station and were about to climb up and join other passengers huddled in the frail craft, when the order came down that the Captain had forbidden further launching of boats.

To his amazement, Dick saw a young ship's officer draw a revolver and shout toward the crew, "To hell with the Captain! The first man to disobey *my* orders to launch the boat I shoot to kill."

As he shouted, Dick was appalled to see a sailor knock out the retaining pin. The boat dropped, hit the angled side of the ship, screeching its way down and crushing passengers already in the sea. Farther aft the same thing happened.

Frohman shook his head and they slithered back to the starboard side. Shouts and cries came from all around as the ship keeled over even farther, its funnels now looming over the struggling humans in the water.

Dick turned, scanning the deck. Women screamed, trying to grab at their children while some men helped them with life jackets; others ran back and forth, not knowing which way to go. Only the stricken ship appeared to know its destiny. The bows were well down in the water, and sinking.

Frohman put a hand on Dick's arm. "Seems I can only think of one thing to say." He gave his familiar, almost mocking smile. "Peter Pan. J. M. Barrie. 'To die will be an awfully big adventure.'"

Dick nodded. He felt very calm.

Chapter Nineteen

1

In Berlin, James worried over the problem. He had sent Hetty out twice more to the Wilhelmstrasse. Once in the late afternoon and once in the morning. She described Marie accurately. The woman had left Number 36 again, at the times Stoerkel had predicted. The same man had been with her, and the couple appeared to chat happily. But they went through exactly the same movements—walking up the street and hailing a cab which awaited their signal. The routine did not seem right. James felt Marie was being put on show—a decoy. There was nothing to be done but make a personal identification.

So it was with some misgivings that James set out, early one morning in the second week of May, to look at the situation in the Wilhelmstrasse.

He arrived at about nine in the morning, walking the length of the broad, clean thoroughfare, hardly glancing at Number 36, but trying to pick out the best possible place for him to safely make an observation. On his second pass, coming back toward the Anhaltstrasse, he saw a small café, its window replete with pastries. Inside, middle-class ladies took coffee and a morning slice of *Torte*.

He disappeared into the Anhaltstrasse, walking with purpose until about ten minutes to eleven. "Always move with confidence, as though you know where you're going," they had told him. He was not being followed, and took a route that brought him back to the café. Looking into the window, he saw that a table with a good view of the street was now vacant.

He entered, sat down, ordered coffee and waited.

She came out of the building just before eleven-fifteen, and he would have known her anywhere—the same confident stride, the tilt of the head. Strangely he felt a pang of anger as she took the officer's arm. He noted the fashionable dress and well-groomed, sleek appearance. "If there is any problem, if she will not come out of Germany with you," both Giles and C had said, "then you must be sure she ceases to exist."

Giles put it more plainly at their very last meeting: "You kill her," he said without emotion.

The couple was definitely following a routine—the walk up the street, the sign as the officer raised his hand, and the cab, waiting where James had earlier spotted it, almost outside the Hospiz, moving up to meet them.

He went back to the Zoo and sent another telegram to Switzerland. Then, that night, he made a telephone call to Major Stoerkel's home.

"Herr Baron Hellinger—I have been waiting for you to telephone." The
Major sounded bluff and hearty. "I have the most urgent news for you."

"About . . . ?"

"There is a letter waiting as we arranged. It is of the utmost importance.
You understand?"

James said he would collect the letter in the morning.

2

James used the reflection of the shop window to view the Alexanderplatz
Post Office entrance. The glass was highly polished, and the display of books
inside made it a perfectly natural place for him to browse. A passing tram cut
off the view for a moment, then it cleared and he saw Hetty making her way
up the steps. It was a calculated risk, but he firmly expected her to walk out
of the Post Office, tucking the letter into her bag, which was their arranged
signal.

She had a note, signed by Gustav Franke, giving her authority to collect
anything left for him Poste Restante.

The minutes ticked away. Another tramcar went by, people clicked past
along the pavement, a staff car growled among the traffic. Then he saw Hetty
coming out, putting a long white envelope into her bag, pausing on top of
the steps.

She took two steps down as the car pulled up and four men detached
themselves from the pedestrian crowd, while two more came out of the Post
Office from behind her.

He knew she would crack very easily. Thank God he had told her only
essentials. Rooted to the spot, James watched her being put into the car. He
could not go back to her apartment, and there was only one more trusted
address in Berlin. Stoerkel was out. James Railton, a stranger in a strange, and
enemy, land, was almost on his own.

3

The sinking of the SS *Lusitania* sent a wave of shock throughout the world,
and there were those at the Admiralty who waited anxiously to see if the fact
that at least a hundred American passengers had perished would make any
difference to President Wilson's policy of neutrality.

The first Sara knew was a telephone message from Andrew. He broke the
news, then became emotional and unsteady. "I wanted . . . you should know
before the newspapers . . ."

Sara felt a terrible numbness, and mouthed "Yes," but it did not come out
clearly.

"You there, Sara?"

"Yes."

"Just wanted you to know. Your chum. The American—"

"Yes. Thank you, Andrew." It was why she had made up her mind not to marry Richard yet—in case of something like this. Not marry him. No, and now it could be too late.

"Sara?"

"Yes. I'm here, Andrew."

"First reports are that the casualties're not heavy. Lots of boats got there chop-chop."

"Chop-chop," she said, automatically imitating him.

"Let you know soon as I hear more."

"Thank you." She thought of Andrew's child, Rupert, reduced to a giant boy by disaster at sea. God, not Richard, please not Richard. . . . Replacing the receiver, Sara went off in search of Mildred, who was helping with the Farm and Estate during this particular week.

It was late afternoon, and Vera told her that Mrs. Mildred—Railton wives were always called by their own Christian names, not those of their husbands—had gone over to the Glebe House to see Mrs. Berry.

Sara asked Natter to saddle up her new gray, Boston. "Quick as you can manage, Ted." She even smiled at him. Martha Crook was coming through the field path from the cottage. She waved, but must have sensed something, for her smile faded as she got close.

"Afternoon, Miss Sara." A hand went out, resting lightly on Sara's arm, as though trying to gain knowledge through touch. "What's wrong, my dear?"

Even then, Sara did not cry. "The *Lusitania*'s been sunk."

"Oh, save us!"

"You remember the young American who—"

"Mr. Farthing, yes."

"He was on board. He was a passenger."

Martha Crook moved closer, her hand wrapping itself around Sara's lower arm. Very quietly she said, "And you love him very much, Miss Sara. Yes?"

She bit her lip. Behind Mrs. Crook, Natter was leading Boston out. Martha Crook nodded. "He's fine," she said softly. "Mr. Richard Farthing's alive and well. I promise you that." But Sara was past any belief.

In the west the sun dipped toward the horizon as Sara trotted off toward the Glebe House. Lazy in the last minutes of the day, the fields reflected gold from the blood-soaked sky. He saw that same sun this afternoon, Sara thought. Wherever he was when it happened, that was what he saw; and he can probably see it now.

She was exceptionally calm when she reached Glebe House. Mildred had turned out to be very good at helping Rachel organize their work force; while Rachel could manage even the most difficult man and demanded a very high standard from all of them.

"Had a letter from Bob today." Rachel looked sheepish.

"Well?"

"He's got some leave coming. I think he'd like to see me, and come back here, but he darsn't."

Sara heard herself laugh. "Well, you tell him he'd best come back here. Who's he afraid of, you or me?"

"I think both on us, M'm."

"Well, tell him not to be a fool."

It was not until they were almost back at the Manor that Sara told Mildred about *Lusitania*.

Vera Bolton waited near the door to say that Mr. Charles had telephoned. "Wanted to speak to Mrs. Mildred, urgent."

"Might I, Sara? He'll have heard about *Lusitania*, and be worried for you, no doubt."

But it was not about that disaster. Charles had just been told of the attack on Mary Anne, so now Sara had to help Mildred in *her* pain and anxiety. There were no details. Just that she had been attacked by a patient at the hospital in Rouen and was being brought home on Monday.

"I feel so helpless." Mildred's eyes were red-ringed. "It's stupid. They say she's not seriously ill, but I'm desperate to know what's happened."

Yes, Sara thought, and so am I—desperate to know what's happened to Richard.

Mildred had already decided she should get back to London the next day—Saturday—"to be with Charles."

There was no further news that night. Lord, Sara thought, these Railton women. Am I like that? Mildred had kept up a constant monologue concerning Mary Anne, talking about her childhood and making up possible theories about what could have happened. She knew about Dick Farthing, and that Sara was shredded with worry; yet all she spoke of was Mary Anne. No comfort there.

Mildred left on the early Saturday train, and by evening the panic had grown in Sara's mind. If Dick were indeed alive, he would have been in touch with her by now. She cursed herself. Damn the war; damn everything; damn herself for being such a silly little moralistic prude. She should have married him right away. At least she would have been his wife—or his widow.

She tried to sleep, but no sleep came, and she tossed and turned all night, falling into a light doze.

She dreamed—walking under the sea, oddly, by moonlight, the moon itself rising under the water to reveal a tunnel of twisted metal among the rocks and fishes; then the moon turned to blood, and it was sunset. The fishes changed into men. The men appeared to be alive, beckoning to her, but they were dead, and she knew the beckoning was the effect of the current. One of the men reached out and took her by the hand, as if to lead her through the maze of metal. She looked away, then back, and it was Richard's hand she was holding. He was white in death, his face wrinkled and like bleached parchment, as though it had been under bandages for six months. He walked with her down an aisle of wrecks toward Mildred, who carried the body of Mary Anne. Sara realized that she wore a wedding dress, but it was dirty and stained with great streaks of blood. Dick took her hand more firmly, and began to pull her upward, carrying her to the surface. They broke through, and she was swimming. Nearby, a buoy clanged its bell. She woke, suddenly, and the bell was the telephone ringing in the hall downstairs.

The clock showed a quarter to six in the morning, and the ringing which had broken her dream stopped suddenly. A few moments later there was a knock at the door.

It was Vera, dressed and busy already, her face broken by a broad smile. "The telephone"—she made urgent motions with her hand, repeating—"the telephone . . . telephone."

Her wrap tightly around her, Sara's hand quivered as she tucked the earpiece behind her hair and gave a tentative "Hallo?"

"I couldn't let you know before this. I'm safe."

Sara let out a short moan, part pain and part relief at the sound of Dick Farthing's voice.

4

"Hunter? Jack Hunter? That perverted man your father doted on?" Mildred's brow creased.

Charles told her only what he knew. Mary Anne was in St. Thomas' Hospital. The doctors said she was well.

"The amazing thing is this German officer—Buelow, one of their gunners"— Charles continued, telling the whole story—"there's no doubt he saved her life."

"A Hun saved her? But—"

"It's certain. Kell's been to speak to him, and we have permission to keep him in one of our places once he's fit enough to be moved. Fellow's been in appalling shock. But he saved our daughter, Mildred. We owe him Mary Anne's life."

She wept quietly. "But how much of this terrible story's going to get out, Charles? I mean, what in God's name are her chances in the world? A young girl who's been—"

"Raped," Charles said firmly. "You can't run away from it, Mildred."

"Oh my God, the shame. We'll never—"

He put an arm around her shoulders. "She'll have to appear at the court-martial, and so will the Hun. That'll be kept quiet. I don't think you need worry over much about that. There'll be the civil action, of course."

"Civil? To do with Mary Anne?"

"The police in Oxfordshire want to talk to him. The murder of a child just before the war. Now we can go and see her."

Mildred turned away, looking out the window at the spring shower lightly sprinkling the trees in the street. Softly, she said, "I don't know if I can face seeing her."

5

The clothes he stood up in; a few marks; his knife; the Mauser pistol; two sets of forged papers; and what was in his head: this was James' inheritance from C and Giles Railton. Natural instinct told him to get out, run for Switzerland. But he took a train to the suburb of Wilmersdorf, called in at the nearest post office and sent yet another telegram, then went in search of the last address they had given him.

The contact was a Lutheran minister who had studied at, among other places, Oxford. It was there he had met various men who rose through the years into places of importance in the Foreign Office. Pastor Bittrich received some of these men into his home during the summers between 1908 and 1914. It was during this time he indicated that should there be a war between Germany and England, he would use all his efforts to help the English cause. They even gave him a password should they need his assistance.

The house was a pleasant old place off Gasterstrasse—the street tree-lined, almost rural. James went to the front door and knocked. It was opened by a fat, apple-faced maid, who said the Pastor was out visiting but would soon be back. Would Herr Grabben—James had changed identities again—care to wait for him?

Herr Grabben sat in the parlor, with the baleful eyes of a crucified Christ looking down from a lithograph above the mantel.

When Pastor Bittrich arrived, James rose to greet him. The man was tall, thin, and with a perpetually surprised expression.

James spoke in German. "I have a message for you, Pastor. We have a mutual friend who asks me to tell you that gentlemen in England, now a-bed, shall think themselves accursed they were not here."

The gaunt Pastor turned to look up at Christ on the Cross, and noticed there was mildew beginning to form around one of the Roman soldier's helmets. "And hold their manhood cheap, whiles any speaks that fought with us upon Saint Crispin's day," he replied.

James did not see the color drain from the Pastor's face or the look of genuine fear cross behind the man's eyes.

"You have other messages?" the Pastor asked.

"No. I wish to stay with you. Quietly, and only for a day or two. Until I can make arrangements." He really meant decisions. "I shall be no trouble."

When the Pastor turned he was smiling. "You are welcome." He extended a hand. "You will be no trouble."

6

Caspar now used his peg leg all the time, and there was talk of some kind of a new artificial arm. He sat in C's outer office, going through the information from the network they called *Frankignoul*, and the other one, recently set up by Catholics in Belgium. The latter was known as *Biscops*, but because of its religious connections, C referred to it as the *Sacré Coeur Ring*. It was Caspar's job to mark up points of special interest for C. He also took care of incoming signals, such as the two which had caused so much excitement that morning and were the cause of his grandfather's arrival at C's headquarters.

Giles had paused to talk to Caspar, on his way in, a few minutes before. He had even mentioned *Sacré Coeur*. Giles had a personal interest in that network, for he had shifted Monique, his private agent, from Paris into Belgium, where she now appeared to be successfully acting as a "postman," running information over the German lines into France.

Behind C's door, Caspar's grandfather was hearing of the latest developments—of the signals from sources Pearl and Ruby.

"He's identified the subject then?" Giles smiled.

"You can see for yourself. Even down to the address. She's there, in Berlin, Giles. The question now is what he should do."

"He's *your* man." Giles, having set the business in motion, placed his nephew in the field, was quite willing to let the matter rest. "What of Seagull?"

It was the first they had heard from Madeline Drew, via her contact, Ruby, since she had left England. The message was lengthy, giving details of regiments and divisions being sent from Germany to the Western Front. As Giles remarked, the intelligence contained nothing they had not learned already. The sting in Seagull's message came at the end, for the final sentence, when deciphered, read: HINTS THAT I AM TO BE ORDERED BACK INTO ENGLAND. PLEASE ADVISE.

"And how the devil can we advise?" C growled.

Giles hid his feelings. "Again, she's yours—admittedly run by Kell's people when she was here; but advice is up to you. I'd leave it alone, C. If she returns we'll soon know. What about the real things? Are we performing a useful service?" He did not appear to expect a reply, for he went straight on, changing the question, "And what about this nurse? The Cavell woman?"

Nurse Edith Cavell ran a clinic in Brussels. The clinic served as a lifeline staging post to get both wounded and agents back to England.

"Not one of mine. She's helped get a lot of people out of Belgium, but as far as I'm concerned she's not on the books. I—"

It was at this moment that Caspar knocked on the door. "Another signal from Peewit, sir."

C examined the deciphered message and cursed quietly. "They've got the Dimpling woman. I think the Wilmersdorf contact's safe, but who's to tell?"

Giles rose. "Don't worry. If Peewit performs, he performs."

When he had gone, C stared at the door, wondering at the incredible lack of feeling within Giles Railton. He thought for a few moments, then summoned Caspar. Within an hour a signal had gone to Peewit's Swiss contact, Pearl. When decoded it read: PEEWIT TO BE ORDERED BACK TO LONDON BY FASTEST AND MOST SECURE ROUTE STOP URGENT AND OF PRIME IMPORTANCE STOP C.

7

"I think that's terribly brave—Mr. Frohman quoting from *Peter Pan*. Thank heaven you got away."

"*He* didn't, I fear, Sara."

She had sent all the servants to bed and cooked their meal herself. Sara was becoming more skilled with each day she spent at Redhill.

When Dick had finally arrived, during the early afternoon, she had seen to it that he went straight to bed. He bathed and did as he was told, but asked to be wakened in time for dinner.

She roused him at eight-thirty, and now, over a saddle of lamb, listened to his story.

"Please tell me." She reached across for his hand.

He spoke quietly, telling how, after Frohman had spoken, they had become separated by a crush of panic-stricken passengers. "It really was pretty awful."

In the end, he had begun to climb aft up the now wildly tilting deck. "There was a sailor who had got his legs crushed. He just lay there and knew there was nothing anyone could do for him. He held out his life jacket and said to me, 'Take it, guv'nor. It's a long jump, but you'll stand a chance.'"

Dick had jumped. "Tried to choose a spot well away from the folks in the water, and I thought I wouldn't live through it. But I did. The water was quite cold. I remember getting a long way from the ship, lying on my back and drifting. She was at a really crazy angle, like some toy a kid had thrown into shallow water; the bows seemed to be skewered on the ocean bed, and the screws were way out, in the air. Then she went down. It must have been the boilers that blew, but they didn't go with a bang. It was more like a moan, as though the ship were crying out. Then the sea boiled around, and that was the last I remembered until I woke up in a hospital."

"And you didn't let me know."

Dick said that his one thought was to get out. "I felt well enough. I had all my documents, so I just got up and dressed—they had dried my clothes. I walked out, took a train to Dublin and then got on a boat. I called you as soon as I could."

She sat, silent for a moment, gazing at him. "I can't tell you how good it is to see you. What are your plans?"

He gave a diffident shrug. "I want to fight Germans. And I have to talk to Giles. I've messages for him."

"Oh?" Not angry but cold. "You think *Lusitania* will bring your country into the war?" There was a definite coolness now.

"President Wilson is set against it, but he'll have to bring the USA in sooner or later. Sara?"

"Yes?" Very distant.

"Before I do anything else—see Giles; enlist—there's something more important to me than anything else." He looked straight into her eyes. "The last time I was here we made a pledge. I haven't changed, Sara. I love you. You're the dearest thing in all the world to me, and I want to marry you. If you need me to go down on my knees, then I will. But I'm asking you now. Will you be my wife?"

The pause reached out, tense, uncertain. In his mind Dick heard that terrible rumbling moan as the *Lusitania* had gone down. Then Sara began to speak.

"I . . . I, Oh, Dick. . . ."

"Please," softly.

"I was going to say yes, but not yet. Made my mind up after Caspar and the terrible thing that's happened to young Rupert. I wanted to marry you, because I love you so very dearly, but it wasn't right while the killing was going on and on. But now . . . Well . . ." She pushed back her chair. "Dick, yes. Yes, I'll marry you as soon as you like."

They collided into each other's arms and stayed close for what seemed like an hour. "We'll go up to London tomorrow. Choose a ring, OK?" He grinned at her. "Then we can make some decisions—announcements and things. Isn't that the right thing to do?" He felt very hot, and she was pressing her body close to his.

"We'll do whatever you want, Richard. Whatever. I love you, and I think we should do something about it now—straight away."

Dick allowed her to lead him up the stairs to her bedroom. Rings, dates, announcements and all the paraphernalia of the wedding were swept to one side. The world was reduced to immediate needs, and the basic outward signs of their love, as they exchanged bodies, locked themselves together, becoming as one.

8

The Pastor gave him potato soup and some pleasant kind of stew. They spoke little, and, after the meal, James was shown to a small room under the eaves of the house.

"You will be safe here for a few days at least," said the man of God, and James lay down fully dressed and fell into a deep sleep.

He dreamed of sounds—a piano playing Bach and Liszt. He did not hear the Pastor leave the house in the early hours, nor the men arrive at dawn. The first he knew was someone shaking him, roughly. His hand went to the pillow, but the Mauser was not there.

"You are Gustav Franke?" There were two men, both heavy and with the authoritative, brusque manner of policemen.

Grasping for consciousness, climbing up from sleep, James said no, and that his name was Grabben.

"We think it's Franke," one of the men said.

"You will come with us." The other began to pull him from the bed. James was not allowed to argue.

He saw neither the thin Pastor nor the apple-faced housekeeper as they took him downstairs and out into a waiting car.

Chapter Twenty

1

When Mary Anne first returned from the hospital she was like a mouse, jumping in fear at the slightest noise. Mildred forced herself to put on a brave face, though she felt mortified at what had happened to her daughter. On the second night of Mary Anne's return, Mildred went up to the nursery and found the girl playing with her little brother. She shouted at Mary Anne to leave the child alone. It was as though Mildred felt that Mary Anne was a contaminating influence.

Because Mary Anne had allowed such a terrible thing to have happened, she saw the girl as a kind of carrier of evil, who could pass on the sins of the flesh to others. Mildred's dislike of sexual congress, so marked after her experience with William Arthur's birth, became more pronounced. All memory of how good things had once been now dwindled and disappeared.

She began to go to church more often, sometimes as many as three services on Sunday, and four or five times during the week. If there had not been some dreadful sexual desire within her daughter to begin with, she would never have become a victim, she reasoned illogically.

Then there was the court-martial.

Mildred refused to go, or be any comfort to her daughter. But Charles stood by the girl, traveled with her to Aldershot and sat with her in the closed military court, proud of the way in which she gave her evidence.

They brought Buelow down from London, and it appeared he had learned a little English, though most of the evidence was given through a translator. On the final day, the President of the Court commended Kapitän Otto Buelow for his act, making it plain that he was responsible for saving Nurse Railton's life.

Corporal Jack Hunter was sentenced to a dishonorable discharge and fifteen years' hard labor in a civil prison. Once he was moved into civil custody, the authorities talked with him about other matters.

On their way home, Mary Anne asked her father if he thought there was any way she could see the German, Buelow. "I haven't even had a chance to thank him."

Charles said that he would find out. He spoke with Vernon Kell the following day, knowing they were training Buelow: testing his possible loyalty, using the very same house in Maida Vale where Charles had become entangled with Madeline Drew.

Kell worked on plans to infiltrate agents among German prisoners of war, so that they could be informed of conversations and thus gain fresh intelligence. It had become part of Charles' work to assess and analyze the information. He still thought of Madeline a lot, but took care to inquire only occasionally if they had any news of her. He asked now, during the conversation concerning Buelow.

"As a matter of fact, C *has* had one message from her." Kell told him about the hint that Nicolai seemed to be suggesting her return; then they passed on to Buelow, and Charles returned that night with the welcome news that he could arrange a meeting.

On the following Tuesday, Otto Buelow met for an hour with Mary Anne. Charles was not present, but another MI5 officer sat in, together with the interpreter they were using at the Maida Vale house. MO5 had been given its new name earlier in the year.

The conversation was stilted, but it was obvious that the two young people were very much attracted to one another. Later, Kell spoke of this to Charles, asking if perhaps Mary Anne could be of value to them as far as Buelow was concerned.

Charles held out little hope. In fact, Kell became a trifle concerned. Over-night, Charles seemed to have lost interest in the whole business.

The truth was that, foolishly, in an attempt to draw Mildred back to some semblance of normality, Charles had spoken to her at some length about Mary Anne's visit to thank Buelow.

His wife appeared to take the whole business calmly enough when they talked, but that evening when Mary Anne came down to dinner, Mildred had suddenly begun to rant and rave at her, calling her a lover of Germans, sar-castically asking her if she was granting this Hun Captain the same kind of favors she must have given away in the hospitals. "Women of our class do *not* get themselves raped unless they ask for it!" Mildred shrieked, adding mel-odramatically, "You have brought shame upon us: unto the third and fourth generation."

Charles tried to remonstrate, attempting to defend his daughter against these ridiculous suggestions, but Mildred became wilder. She didn't want a woman like Mary Anne under the same roof; she didn't want Mary Anne contaminating her son, and so on, and so on, hysterically.

In tears, Mary Anne tried to use reason. In the end, the girl lost all patience, slamming out of the room while her father attempted to calm her mother.

By the time Charles had quietened Mildred and gone upstairs, Mary Anne had left. Her old Gladstone bag was not there, and she had taken enough clothes for immediate needs.

He telephoned Kell, who talked to Thomson. Discreet feelers were put out. The Metropolitan Police issued a description to officers on the streets. In the meantime, Charles spoke carefully with Andrew, Margaret Mary, Giles, and, lastly, Sara at Redhill. None of them had heard from Mary Anne. For Charles it was the end. Apart from the matter being embarrassing to the family, Mildred had behaved abominably. He told her plainly that he thought she needed medical help.

Mildred laughed in his face, put on her coat and went down the road to pray for her harlot daughter's soul.

(As a footnote: Hunter was charged a month later with the murder of the child, Emma Gittens. He appeared at the Central Criminal Court in the following April, where he pleaded guilty, was sentenced to death and hanged at Wandsworth Prison on June 26th 1916.)

2

"Well, Richard, I gather congratulations are in order." They sat in Giles Railton's drawing room at Eccleston Square, after dinner. Denise had brought them coffee and brandy. She had not actually served at table, but Dick Farthing felt she might just as well have joined the servants, for her grandfather appeared to treat her as a unpaid housekeeper. Shame, he thought, for Denise was growing into a beautiful young woman.

Dick grinned. "I suppose I really should have come and asked your permission or something." He always found flattery helped with people of Giles' standing.

"I think not." The words came back like a cold shower. "Sara holds the Railton family in thrall, Richard. A very difficult situation for an old established clan like ours. Her marriage will undoubtedly raise legal questions. We can deal with those when the time comes." He raised his glass. "Here's to you and Sara. You'll be taking her back to America?"

"No!" Charm had not paid off, so Dick was quite prepared to play Giles at his own game.

"Oh? Then what are your immediate plans?"

"First, to marry Sara. We've set the day. December 23rd. A Christmas wedding. I rather think Sara wishes you to give her away."

"I see. She plans to be married from Redhill, then?"

"Naturally."

"And after that?"

"Well, I'm applying for a commission in the Royal Flying Corps. Marry Sara; fight the Hun. My priorities."

"Well, you should have no problem with the RFC. I have a number of—"

"Oh, I think I've taken care of that, sir."

"Really? All right, Richard, you wanted to see me—I take it that the meeting *is* about the wedding, provision you are making, provision Sara will have to make because of a remarriage. I would suggest—"

"No, sir, I did *not* come to talk about the wedding. To be truthful, I know Sara's talking to the family solicitors. I guess she'll want to see you as well. . . ."

"I would be most surprised if she did not."

"No, sir. I'm here on official business."

"Official?"

"Mr. Wilson, the President of the United States, has asked me to speak with you."

"I fear you have the wrong man in me, Richard. I'm only a Foreign Office consultant. The President's kind of business goes through the American Ambassador to someone of higher rank than I."

"Not this." Dick held his ground. "I know you liaise and coordinate on intelligence business, Mr. Railton."

Giles' face froze. "Well, you know more that I, sir. Where has this extraordinary idea come from?"

"The President himself, via the Ambassador. You're well-known in the field of secret diplomacy. I've simply been asked to speak with you privately."

Silence. A car outside. Then a dog barking nearby.

"Speak then," Giles finally said quietly.

Dick Farthing began. He talked about the fact that the internal security of the United States was handled by the Bureau of Investigation; that Military Intelligence, as such, was in a shambles, and that the Secret Service was in fact part of the Treasury Department, having nothing to do with espionage.

Giles nodded, indicating he knew all this.

"An officer called van Deman had the President's ear, Mr. Railton. He's reorganizing what is known as the Information Branch of the War College. The General Staff is against having anything like the Services you've built up here. They—"

"They know that if they've the guts to get into this war, we, together with the French, will have to hand them intelligence on a plate. They won't have to work for it."

"You could be right, sir. The President's a far-seeing man. He feels the United States should at least have some people who know the workings of intelligence departments like your own."

"Does he now?"

"He's asked me to speak with you privately."

"To what end?" Giles seemed vaguely amused.

"To see if you would accept, two, maybe three, accredited officers to study the workings of your own intelligence departments, so the United States has a basis on which to work."

Giles seemed to think for a moment, then he rose. "As it is private, and *very* confidential, I can give you an answer to take back personally to Mr. Wilson. When the President sees fit to bring the United States to the aid of Europe, I shall be only too pleased to use all my power on his behalf, and give him whatever facilities he asks. You must tell him to send another emissary when America enters the war."

3

"Merciful heavens, but he's as cold as charity." Dick gave a mock shiver. "I left with rime on my eyebrows."

"Told you so, darling." Sara laughed. "But there are those who can get the better of him."

"Let me guess. You?"

She gave him a cat-who-licked-the-cream smile and nodded. That morning, she had been to see young Mr. King, of King, Jackson & King. She explained to Dick the trouble she had experienced with Giles after John Railton's death. "I'm not a Railton—well, only by marriage—and Giles is scared witless lest I make off with the family fortune. Redhill Manor is the sacred stone in their crown."

"It's been a Railton property since before the Ark. I understand that. But, Sara, you *are* a Railton. You were John's wife." Dick gave a frustrated sigh.

"I bore him no children, but you're right. Mr. King says it's quite clear in John's will. I can marry. I can live there; farm there. My husband can live there and share in any income. He says it's almost without precedent, but if another Railton, like Giles, tried to test it, he'd lose. The only thing I cannot do is leave it to a new husband. I must leave it to James, and so on down the line."

Already she had seen Andrew, and he upheld her staying on. "Called me his little sister, but I think he was a bit drunk." She planned to explain things to the others. "The women are with me, though I don't really know about Mildred anymore, because nobody does since Mary Anne disappeared."

They finished lunch and left the Ritz, where they had been eating, Dick to an appointment at the War Office, Sara to call on Caspar.

As though to further demonstrate his independence, Caspar had left home and was living in a small house he had rented near Bedford Square. Sara had rung his office number early that morning, but was told he had a day's leave. So, now she thought to surprise him.

She arrived just before three and rang the bell. No reply. While she stood fiddling on the doorstep, Sara discovered that the front door was not properly latched, but swung open at a touch. She stepped into the narrow hall and immediately became worried by the sounds from behind the door to her right. They were the noises of someone in pain, struggling and panting for breath.

Not wishing to frighten Caspar, should he have fallen, or hurt himself, she gently pushed open the door. Within seconds she closed it again.

The room was a drawing room, small but well decorated and furnished. Under a high window stood a day bed. Caspar lay on the bed, minus his peg leg and stark naked. A young woman straddled him, riding him as though bent on winning the Derby.

The couple were too engrossed in one another even to notice her, but Sara smiled as she tiptoed from the house. She wondered if another wedding could be in the offing, for the young woman so ardently fucking Caspar was none other than his erstwhile nurse, the Honourable Phoebe Mercer.

Fancy, she said to herself hurrying away. Just fancy. Old Phoeb.

4

Since his message in May, saying the Dimpling woman had been taken, there had been no further contact with Peewit. Silence. In June, a short paragraph in the *Berliner Tageblatt* gave the news that Frau Henrietta Dimpling, an Englishwoman who had taken German nationality by marriage, had been tried for espionage, found guilty and shot. No Franke; no Grabben; no Railton.

"They're not even going to tell us." Giles was convinced that James had died. C noted that for once he seemed upset.

C decreed that Margaret Mary should be told nothing of their suspicions until after the birth of the second child, due in August. Until then, they would wait. Seagull had sent four other messages—nothing particularly startling.

There was still no news of Mary Anne, but Charles had managed to get Mildred to see a doctor. She still haunted the church, but prescribed sedation appeared to have some effect.

So they waited until August before saying anything to Margaret Mary; and while they waited there was plenty to occupy everyone. Charles still monitored reports from their infiltrated men in the prison camps, who now included Otto Buelow. Some of Kell's men worked close to Special Branch officers in France, and in Ireland, where tension grew steadily. "Ireland's like a watched pot," Kell said. "It never quite boils, but one day it will, and maybe we won't be looking that fine morning."

With Gallipoli a shambles, Churchill left the Admiralty, taking the Chancellorship of the Duchy of Lancaster in Asquith's new Coalition. Later in the year he would leave the Cabinet altogether. The drive for munitions was on at last under the silver-tongued whip of Lloyd George, and a new terror struck. German Zeppelins began to attack England, even bombing London. Now nobody felt safe.

On the Western Front, men fought and died for a few hundred yards of earth, and names like Neuville, or Givenchy exploded from the maps that people marked with little pinned flags in their parlors.

"Keep the Russian going," Giles goaded Ramillies. "You'll need it, and sooner than you may think."

On August 20th, Margaret Mary Railton gave birth to a daughter. A sister for little Donald. She was called Sara Elizabeth. A week later, Giles went, with C, to Redhill Manor, and spoke to Sara. They would tell Margaret Mary next week, they said. It was not correct protocol, but they felt, as James' stepmother, she should be the first to know.

The news put a blight on all the happy preparations she was making with Dick, whose commission had been granted. He would not be required for service until the following January. "I thought they were crying out for pilots!" he raged.

"Be thankful," Sara whispered. "I thought you were crying out for a wife." Suddenly she covered her face and gave a mighty sob. "God, I can't believe it about James, Dick. Tell me it isn't true."

But it was Margaret Mary who told them it was not true. Two officers from C's Service went to the house near Kensington Gardens, and Sara contrived to be there, to see the baby at the same time.

They told her, flat-voiced, with sympathy. It was the considered opinion of his Commanding Officer that James had died in action.

Sara moved in to comfort her, and was surprised to see a secret smile on Margaret Mary's lips as she slowly shook her head. She thanked the officers with a steady voice, saw them to the door and went on with her conversation.

Sara suddenly interrupted her. "M-M, my dear. Please, how can you be so sure about James?"

"He's alive, Sara." Her face lit up as she spoke. "I just *know* he's alive."

Sara thought she sounded strangely like Martha Crook.

"But *how* can you be so sure?"

"James and I always know about each other. He's with me when I play the piano. Believe me, Sara."

5

In the village of Ashford, County Wicklow, Padraig O'Connell met Malcolm Railton in their usual bar.

They had talked for about an hour when Malcolm put a hand on Padraig's arm. "I've never seen you wrong yet, have I?"

"No. But I've told you already—I've never trusted an Englishman before. What's the matter with you?"

"Nothing's the matter. But you must know that I have to go to England— for Christmas—and take Bridget with me."

"So, and will you come back?"

"Padraig, it's essential. Family business. A marriage. I *have* to be there; they would suspect if we dodged it."

"Maybe I'll have work for you while you're there. How long will you be gone?"

"A week. Ten days at the most."

"Good. Come back for the New Year, because things will change fast then. How can I trust a bloody Englishman? But you come back. God love us all, Casement's returning, and there'll be fire in this country in the next months. It doesn't take spies to know that."

"No." Malcolm turned away, and caught a glimpse of the sun going down over the Wicklow Hills, with dark clouds hanging as though God were sending a storm in on cue.

Chapter Twenty-One

1

It was in early October—soon after Nurse Edith Cavell had finally been betrayed, and executed in Brussels—that Giles knew his nephew Charles had been compromised.

"Cavell was nothing to do with us," C reiterated for the umpteenth time, as though trying to convince himself.

"We used her, though." Caspar was troubled.

"Of course. She was there, ran a good escape route. Gallant lady. It remains, young Caspar, she was not official. If the public wishes to make her a martyr, all well and good."

Later that same day, Giles was with Vernon Kell and Charles. They also talked about Miss Cavell's execution. "Betrayal, treachery—it's all part of the trade. Terms of our trade if you like."

Giles continued in a monologue: "Take the fellow Buelow. Doing us some good in the prison camps, but a traitor to his own; and the Seagull woman, treacherous to both countries." He paused, trying to gain Charles' attention. "She's sending interesting stuff, so C tells me."

There was something odd about the way Charles stood. A stiffness; an unusual angle of the head.

That evening, hunched over the maps and soldiers, reliving the events in Scotland during "The Forty-five" Jacobite Rebellion, which ended with the carnage at Culloden, he put his mind to work on Charles' possible predicament. A few years earlier Giles had visited Culloden. He was not superstitious, but in that grim place he knew there were ghosts, shadows of the terrible slaughter. He wondered if Flanders would hold ghosts a couple of hundred years hence.

Then his nimble, labyrinthine brain turned again to Charles. Of course the man was worried, obsessed, with Mary Anne's disappearance and his wife's emotional turmoil. But Giles smelled something else, and the only other element in Charles' situation was the woman they called Seagull.

By October 1915 there was hope for Mildred, and Charles knew it. The gleam of hope came unexpectedly. Charles had behaved himself, even though, like any normal man, he missed the company of a woman who could be all things to him. He had taken up his old habit of dropping into The Travellers at day's end. A few stiff gins before going back to Cheyne Walk gave him courage.

It was there that the light suddenly emerged.

The club was not busy on this particular evening—it must have been sometime in the last week of September—when Charles took a drink and a copy of *The Times* to his favorite chair. After a few minutes he became aware of someone staring at him. The man was a short, tubby clergyman with thick pebble glasses, pleasant rosy cheeks, white hair and skin like a baby's.

Charles met his eye and nodded. He had seen the cleric in the club before now, but never met him. Now, the man advanced on Charles.

"Do you mind if I sit here?" The voice contained none of the parsonical inflexions Charles identified with Church of England clergymen. "You don't remember me, of course. You *are* Charles Railton, aren't you?"

Charles admitted he was.

"Good." The man nodded, absently. "Merchant," he said. "Paul Merchant. Vicar of Haddington. You married young Mildred Edwards, Parson Edwards' daughter. I was Vicar of the next parish. We met once at the Parsonage."

Charles searched the files of his past. He could only just recall that rather grim, dark house that was the Parsonage, and his first visits there, with Mildred's father, the Rural Dean, pompous, full of piety and quotations.

"I'm afraid not." Charles tried to laugh.

"Of course not. But I *would* like to speak with you. You see, I knew Mildred, and her parents, for a very long time, when she was a child." He gave a pleasant chuckle. "I am of an age when I cannot tell you what I did yesterday, but can recount the distant past with ease." He peered at his hands.

"I understand you may not wish to talk of this," Reverend Merchant continued, "but I believe it is important."

"Talk of what?" Charles was on his guard. London's clubland never changed, he thought. It was a constant repository of secrets, kept and guarded like the Crown Jewels. Clubland was a village; they knew everything, though would never repeat that knowledge outside the smoking rooms. They would all know about Mary Anne's rape; Mildred's tantrums; their daughter's disappearance; and that Mildred was under a doctor's care. Not one of them would normally admit it, but these matters were known.

"One hears things." Merchant did not look at him.

"Such as?"

"I think it would be wrong of me to repeat gossip. Yet, if it is true, would you listen to a story? It is about something that happened to Mrs. Railton— Mildred Edwards—when she was only twelve years of age."

Worried, Charles nodded assent. "Go on."

"She was a good girl; brought up in the faith; obedient; charming. Is she much changed? Yes, of course she is changed. She first altered after what happened at the Parsonage."

"Happened?"

"It was unpleasant. I do not wish to be uncharitable, but the Rural Dean and his wife did not handle things well. I only know about it because I arrived there at a—possibly—inopportune moment."

He told the story with no further digression: simply stating facts, as a good witness gives evidence.

A few weeks before her twelfth birthday, Mildred had been left alone for an afternoon at the Parsonage. The Rural Dean and his wife had one servant—a housekeeper. On that day, the housekeeper was also away, shopping in the nearby town.

When her parents returned, Mildred was nowhere to be found. It was high summer, and they thought she might have gone into the woods nearby.

They found her, at dusk, wandering in the woods, her clothes ripped and tattered, with blood on her legs. She was quite dazed. "I was there when she was brought in," Merchant told him. "At first it was thought someone had attacked her. The local doctor came over, and . . . well . . . er . . . yes, she had been interfered with. She could give no cogent story. Would not say if it was an assault on her by some man, or if it was, well, childhood experiment. . . ."

Her mother had finally settled on the idea that the whole thing was Mildred's fault, and was backed by the Rural Dean. "The poor child was in some kind of shock. What she needed was love, affection, rest, medical attention. Instead they browbeat her, trying to get at the truth. But, I fear, young Mildred had found the experience so strange—I personally feel she found it pleasant—that she somehow made up her mind to forget the details. She had no answers to give, so the Reverend and Mrs. Edwards found her guilty of this enormous sin. A child of twelve. She was shut away in the darkest room of the house, with bread and water, for two days. When they let her out, she still had nothing to tell them. But by then I should imagine she really had closed off part of her mind, making sure she would never again recall it."

"You swear this is true?" There had never been any hint. Charles' thoughts went back to his wedding night, which Mildred had so enjoyed, and an odd remark came bouncing back over the years. She had become insatiable after the first time, and, in the early hours Mildred, clinging naked to him, her legs wrapped around his body, had whispered, "Wouldn't it be good in the open air? Under trees . . . in a wood. . . ." Could this dreadful childhood experience be responsible for the violent reaction she had shown toward Mary Anne?

"There is a little more," the priest continued. "I believe I should tell you, though by rights I should not. I kept my counsel at the time, and have always felt it was right."

"Yes?"

"About a week after the distressing business, a parishioner came to see me. A wise old man, versed in country lore and the ways of village people. We talked, and he said something which revealed much. We spoke about the sights and sounds surrounding all men and women in remote communities, and he said, 'Trouble is, Vicar, the young folk see the beasts at it and want to copy them. Is that wrong, Vicar? God's showing them. It's natural. But they don't always go about it right, even when they're well schooled. Even Vicar Edwards' young lass and—he mentioned the name of a local boy—I see 'em trying, and they couldn't get the hang of it. . . .'"

Charles thanked the man and talked longer than he intended. The next morning he visited Mildred's doctor and told him the whole extraordinary tale. A week afterward the doctor talked to him at length, saying he had no doubt that Mildred had gone through an early sexual experience which she had found pleasant, though it weighed her with guilt. "I doubt if she'll ever allow herself to remember it. The mind is an odd thing. Memory plays tricks. I think if she could bring herself to recall that childhood experience it would be good for her."

This had not happened by the first week of October, when Charles received the shattering telephone call from Madeline Drew, saying she was back in England. She had to see him immediately.

2

They met, as arranged, in a small café in Knightsbridge, and the moment Charles saw her he knew he was lost.

"What are you doing back here?"

"Charles"—her eyes fixed on him like moonbeams, open, honest, fat with love and desire, deadly as a searchlight to a Zeppelin—"Oh, Charles, I've been so afraid. I've missed you terribly."

"When did you arrive? How? I shall have to make a report, and you'll be looked after. They'll want to question you. . ."

"No." Throaty. "Not yet. It's not safe. I need somewhere to be alone with you; to talk."

It was eight in the evening. Happily for him, Charles never had to explain to Mildred where he was going if called out unexpectedly at night. She had said she intended to go to bed early. Mildred had seen the doctor—Harcourt, a sound Harley Street man—that afternoon. When Charles had left Cheyne Walk she looked tired.

"I know of one or two places to rent." Recently he had spent four days, out and about with another officer, looking for what they now called safe houses, of which they were in great need.

They had purchased three places out of the twelve or so viewed. One of the rejected properties was the second story of a large house in Hans Crescent, going for a reasonable rent, fully furnished and ready to be occupied immediately. The owners, who lived on the ground floor, would remember him, and know his business was official.

They ate a simple meal; then Charles took her to Hans Crescent. The arrangements were made, with Charles paying a month in advance. He stressed the official nature of the rental to the owner, mentioning the Official Secrets Act. The owner, a retired major, veteran of South Africa, understood perfectly.

"This is purely temporary," Charles told her.

"We shall see, darling Charles. Now, please, please, take me to bed before I die."

So he did as she said, and the relief was so great that all thought of immediately reporting the circumstances was placed on the simmering rear of the stove that was his mind. He should have known better, even then. Already Charles had broken all the rules of his trade. By rights he should have marched Madeline to safety and telephoned Vernon Kell the moment he clapped eyes on her. Now every minute was borrowed time. Charles was not just foolish, but plain stupid in what he did. But a man led by the genitals has little conscience.

He bade her not to go out, and visited on the next evening, determined to get at the truth. Nicolai had ordered her back, she confessed, and although she had obeyed Charles and stayed in the flat, it was essential that she should go out the following morning. Her German masters expected her to keep meetings with two men in London. She could supply information to Charles: "It'll be good intelligence about the current number of agents in England and France. I promise you that, my darling. But if you report the source, or the fact that I'm back, all will be lost. They suspect me in any case, and they're good. Darling, they'll hunt me down wherever you hide me. They'll kill me." And her eyes changed, the fear of a child in the dark. "Please, until I've reassured them, don't report to your Mr. Vernon."

So he lay with her, naked on the bed, and felt his manhood and self-respect begin to return.

Mildred was awake in bed when he got back to Cheyne Walk that night. She was friendlier, and even asked if there was any news of Mary Anne. "The doctor seems to be doing wonders for my nerves." A smile, unusual for Mildred. "He's been asking the strangest questions about when I was a child—at the Parsonage. Why should he do that, Charles?"

He shook his head. "Some of the questions asked by doctors are beyond me."

That night Mildred dreamed she was lying under a cathedral of trees, and a young man, with Pan's face, leaned over her, scrabbling at her clothing as she whirled among the earth and leaves, ripping her dress. She awoke to find the top sheet was torn, and she had a broken fingernail.

On the next day, Charles heard that they were still receiving Seagull's messages, sent from Berlin to Switzerland.

"You've been having me on a piece of string." His voice raised at her for the first time. "Madeline, you're still working for *them*. The Seagull signals are coming in more regularly than ever. You fool, Madeline, there's little I can do to save you now...."

"And what happens to *you*, my darling?" There was no trace of threat in her voice. "You've kept me here. I've already passed information to you. They'll have you in prison for assisting the enemy. Probably shoot you. If you had gone to your people straight away, it would have been different. You've left it too late. Don't you see, my darling, we're in the same boat. My masters threaten me; yours will stop you in your tracks."

"I know where my duty lies."

"Do you? We can help each other, and enjoy one another at the same time. Our respective masters can be kept happy. Nobody need ever know. Then, when it's over, we can come to an arrangement."

"Madeline, my dear. I'm a Railton...."

"So is our daughter."

His jaw dropped, and the color went from his face.

Madeline Drew gently explained the situation with the aid of photographs she had brought with her. In a hypnotic horror he stared at the pictures. Even though the child was so tiny, the Railton characteristics were plain for all to see.

When Charles left the Hans Crescent house that night, he did not even see the two Special Branch officers in the shadows across the road.

October rolled into November, and then December. On the Western Front the guns stifled silence. Men died and hung on barbed wire. Villages changed hands. Earth was fought over, won and then recaptured. The uncertain weather that had persisted all summer began to change, and winter was upon them.

On a November night, Giles, his head stuffed with secrets and intrigues, came down from the Hide, where he had been moving Napoleon's forces in the early stages of Waterloo, and saw Denise, caught in the lamplight as she tidied the drawing room. She was rapidly growing into a beautiful young woman.

"Sit down for a minute, my dear." Giles smiled fondly at his granddaughter.

"What do you wish, Grandpapa?" She spoke English well.

"I've been thinking." He smiled. "Are you happy here?"

"Oh yes. I am safe. I have everything I want, and the family are so good to me. Think, Grandpapa, I am to be Sara's bridesmaid at Christmas. It's so exciting."

He nodded. "I wondered..." A pause to the count of six. "I wondered if—say, next year—you might like to do me a favor."

"Anything."

"Would you like to go back to France for a few weeks? Just to deliver some messages to friends of mine?"

"If you say I must."

"We'll see. We'll talk about it again."

3

Sara Railton was married, in the Parish Church of SS Peter and Paul, Haversage, to Captain Richard Farthing RFC, on December 23rd, 1915. In order to show economy, and with a complete disregard for superstition, she wore the dress in which she had been married to John Railton, a fact which caused a deep division of argument among locals and family.

On the night before the wedding, Dick stayed at the Bear Hotel, in Haversage, and had a small dinner party to which all the Railton men were invited. All accepted apart from Giles and Malcolm. They made reasonable excuses, but everyone knew they would be closeted, together with Bridget, in the General's Study for most of the evening. There, though nobody was to know, they came to certain strategic decisions which were to affect the Irish situation during the coming year.

Andrew got drunk at the dinner, and Charles—looking a little peeky, everyone said—had to put him to bed. Charles was to be Dick's best man on the following day, as no Farthings had been able to make the journey to Europe. In his speech at the dinner, Dick said he made no apologies for the fact that James should really have been his best man, and they all remained silent for a minute's prayer and hope that James might still be alive.

Margaret Mary was still convinced of her husband's safety. She was to be matron of honor, with Denise as bridesmaid. It was easy enough to make it a happy occasion, though Sara was a shade cross when Caspar arrived and almost stole the thunder by announcing that he and Phoebe would need a double room as they had been married, in secrecy, the previous week.

Billy Crook and Bob Berry had contrived leave, and the whole town turned out.

Even Mildred looked better, though few had the temerity to mention Mary Anne.

The couple departed from Redhill late in the afternoon to spend their Christmas quietly at an hotel near Torquay. This left the Railtons in command of the Manor for their own traditional Christmas festivities. For the second year running, Giles took over the General's Study and played little part in the holiday games. Yet he also thought much about James Railton.

4

They had kept him in the same cell, in the place where they had taken him immediately after his arrest in Wilmersdorf.

For the first week there had been little sleep. The questioners came in teams, with about one hour's rest between the interrogations. James did as he had been instructed, and told the story about really being Gustav Franke, but working for a Swiss firm under the name of Grabben.

They made no physical threats. He was not charged with espionage. Then, after a week, they simply left him alone.

Every other day they marched him along stone corridors into a yard so that he could walk for an hour. This was always done at three in the afternoon, rain or shine.

James started to learn the art of remaining sane under these solitary conditions. He scratched the days off with a thumbnail on one of the softer stones of the cell wall. He kept to a rigid routine, including modified physical jerks in the small, cold room. Each morning he quoted as much Shakespeare as he could remember. Each afternoon he flew, in his mind, taking an aircraft up from Farnborough and flying precise distances, closing his eyes, and going through the entire business, exercising his thoughts. At night he worked on his German and French.

They would allow him no paper or writing materials, so all things had to be performed within himself. Eventually, he knew, they would come back to question him.

He did not know it was Christmas Eve—though he was aware that the festival was near at hand—when the Judas squint slid open and closed at an unusual time, early in the morning, almost before he was up and about. They had opened it normally only half an hour before.

James was intrigued, memories suddenly came back unheralded, and a scent seemed to have penetrated the cell. It was pleasant, the scent of spring flowers, and he knew it from somewhere, but could not quite put his mind on it.

5

Major Nicolai waited at the prison early that morning of Christmas Eve when the woman arrived. He showed great courtesy, and they had coffee together in a small office before he took her deep into the bowels of the fortress.

It was a damp and miserable place. Later, she thought to herself that it smelled of despair.

Walter Nicolai, and Steinhauer, had both explained what would be done, and they stopped in front of the cell door. She positioned herself directly in front of the Judas squint. When she was ready, she nodded.

It took about three seconds. She nodded again, and the little metal door was closed.

Within minutes, she faced Nicolai—alone—in the same office in the main building.

"Well?" he asked. "You recognize him?"

She nodded. "Oh yes. He's neither Swiss nor German. He's English. His name is James Railton. Does that amuse you?"

Slowly, Nicolai shook his head. "No, but it interests me. We can do much with a man called James Railton."

And in his cell, James sat, quoting aloud from *The Tempest*. There was the scent of English flowers in his nostrils, and his heart shook with fear. His cousin, Marie, had used a scent which smelled just like this. He knew it well.

> A solemn air, and the best comforter
> To an unsettled fancy, cure thy brains,
> Now useless boil within thy skull. There stand,
> For you are spell-stopped. . . .

Hell was about to come down around his ears, and the solitude would have been sanity by comparison.

6

On December 30th, *HMS Natal* blew up, in a great ball of fire, with no warning, at Cromarty in Scotland. The Fisherman had spoken yet again, and was drawing closer to those with whom he would soon become, unexpectedly, involved.

PART III

Terms of Trade
(January 1916–October 1935)

Chapter Twenty-Two

1

It was on Giles Railton's personal instructions—passed by Basil Thomson—that a Special Branch watch on Charles was kept within a tight circle which did not include Vernon Kell. Giles had spent too long among the shadows himself to allow it to become what he would term public knowledge. It was this surveillance which first led them to Hans Crescent.

Unknown to either Madeline or Charles, some of the Special Branch officers quietly forced their way into the rooms in Hans Crescent and rigged up their own listening device—built from telephones and bits and pieces of Army communications equipment. It was rough and ready, but the Military had learned a great deal from the enemy on the Western Front. The Germans had been listening in, regularly, not only to the field telephones, but also by placing microphones near trench breastworks. The latest listening gadget was now concealed behind the metal flanges of the Hans Crescent bedroom's air vent.

It was not wholly successful, but eighty percent of the conversations which took place in that bedroom were heard, written down in shorthand—using several different listeners—and transcribed, again by many hands, into reports seen in their entirety only by Basil Thomson and Giles Railton.

Giles took little pleasure in reading page upon page of these documents. As they came straight from the bedroom, there were, naturally, entries which simply read: *The subjects appeared to be indulging themselves sexually for the following hour. No reliable conversation could be heard.*

But there were some exchanges of immense interest, and one such took place very early on in January.

They were in the bedroom when Charles taxed Madeline over the question of important information. Somehow she did not seem to comprehend the seriousness of the situation into which they had both become inextricably dovetailed.

"I'm giving you all I can—all I know," she complained. "Isn't that enough?"

"Of course it's not. Can't you see? What you're giving me isn't possible to use in these circumstances. You've pleaded for me not to go to my people, and like a fool I've agreed. Now it's too late. I have to go sooner or later. . . ."

As always she became nearly hysterical when he spoke of telling the authorities: "Steinhauer's men will get to me," she sobbed. "I promise, Charles, this is the only safe way. Put me even in the Tower of London and he'll get to me. For God's sake, if you love me, please don't have me taken in!"

"It's both our necks, darling. *Both* of us. They can have you for espionage any time—and they won't hesitate to shoot you—not after the Cavell woman. As for me . . . Well, it'll look pretty bad." He took a deep breath. "They'll have me on toast as well. Dawn, a wall, a post and a firing squad."

"You don't know what Steinhauer's like. He controls all operations in England. He says his men are everywhere. . . ."

"That's rubbish. If we say you've just arrived, and keep you under a twenty-four-hour guard, you'll be fine."

"He'll have me killed." Her voice became very calm. "You've kept your side of the bargain. You know what they're looking for. . . ."

"What they've always looked for: dockyards; troop movements; ship movements . . ." He paused and the listeners heard noises of movement as Charles got out of bed, pulled closed the curtains and lit the gas. "Madeline, I *know* we could keep you safe. Why are you so certain you'd be killed?"

Softly—it was only just audible to the listeners—she said. "Because Steinhauer has a man here in England. He's done it before, and will do it again."

"How do you know? Tell me about this man."

"I just know he's here."

"Who told you? Steinhauer?"

She did not hesitate. "No, Steinhauer's said nothing. I've overheard him talking . . . and listened to others. Some speak openly about him, but he's feared. They call him The Fisherman."

"'The Fisherman'? Why?"

She shook her head. "I don't know—only that's what he's called in Berlin—either The Fisherman or Saint Peter. Because he fishes for souls. Listen . . . you remember there was a ship which blew up . . . when? In 1914? November? Soon after the war began. Yes . . . November. Just blew up. . . ."

"*HMS Bulwark.* Exploded with no warning. Sheerness. Yes?"

"He did that. The Fisherman planted the bomb that made the *Bulwark* explode; others—the one in December, *Natal.* . . . Charles, there are plans for him to deal with other ships."

"If that's true, then he's a saboteur. Yes, he's killed people, but they are naval personnel. . . ."

"He's killed at least two men." There was fear in her voice, as though even talking about this man might bring death.

"Oh?" Charles sounded alert. Unknown to the listeners, he had a sudden terrifying memory. The darkening street in Rosscarbery, Ireland. The blood and the ax. The huge man, limping toward him, on the opposite side of the road. Why? There was no connection. . . .

"I know there was one man in Portsmouth; another in London; and a woman in Scotland," Madeline almost whispered.

"Two men and a woman. No names? Nothing else?"

"Nothing . . . Yes . . ."

There was a pause. Finally she spoke again, "Yes. I know how he killed. All three were strangled. A white silk scarf. That's all I know about it. . . ."

This particular conversation remained intact in the transcript. "I think we should begin to look through the files," Basil Thomson said to Giles.

Giles shook his head. "No. Well, yes, by all means look through the files with the Criminal Investigation Department. But I would counsel no action as yet."

"If it's true: '. . . plans for him to deal with other ships.' We can't risk leaving him loose."

"For a day or so only. I may be regarded a cold fish, but I don't want to see my nephew brought to trial for espionage and treason. Give me a day or so. See if Charles takes an initiative."

"A couple of days, then." Thomson thought the whole business was exceptionally serious.

So did Giles, which was why he happened by Vernon Kell's office during the late afternoon of the day on which he read the transcript, and was present when the first news concerning Mary Anne came in.

Kell always made time for Giles, and the conversation went back and forth for ten minutes or so, then Giles casually asked what Charles was on at the moment.

"Heaven knows"—Kell flung up his hands—"the man never stops. He's got some bee in his bonnet about sabotage now; strange lead; gone dashing off to Portsmouth. Which reminds me—I'll have to get hold of him. A friend of mine in Movement Control had news of Mary Anne. Girl's turned up at her old posting—the General Hospital in Rouen. The RAMC Commanding Officer has asked for the paperwork, which doesn't exist of course."

Giles hardly reacted to what was essentially good news for the Railton family. Instead he continued with his questions about Charles: What was this sabotage business? Where had the lead come from: What was Charles up to?

"Charles is an old hand now—a very successful officer and doesn't need me on his back twenty-four hours a day."

"Well, at least he's taking the business seriously," Giles told Basil Thomson the next day.

"I know." Thomson sounded oddly bitter. "After our conversation, two of my men checked through the files at The Yard. Your nephew had beaten them to it, and the idiots in the Criminal Investigation Department had failed to make any connection between the three murders. All quite obvious, but in different parts of the country, so they're on the unsolved file."

"And there are two men and a woman, as she said?"

"Exactly as she said. A naval lieutenant called Fiske, found in the dockyard, Portsmouth, November '14; a fifty-year-old chemist, in the back of his shop—Camberwell—last July: name of Douthwaite; and a woman of thirty-two, a Mrs. MacGregor, in a boardinghouse, just before Christmas: Invergordon. All strangled; white silk scarf; particular kind of knot; MacGregor'd recently had sexual intercourse—no sign of rape. Someone suggested the work of a naval officer. The white silk scarf, right?"

"You're suggesting that our man *is* a naval officer?"

"Treachery isn't confined to the other side, Giles. If German Intelligence had the wit to plant people on us years ago, then it's likely they've already penetrated the Army and Navy. I want to put one of my best men onto this business. First we have to find exactly what Fiske, Douthwaite and Mrs. MacGregor had in common."

Giles paused, giving the hint of a nod. "You already have Charles working on it."

"Then, with respect, I really think we should haul Charles up in front of Vernon Kell and arrest the Valkyrie of Hans Crescent. Get it into the open."

"Give it twenty-four hours, Basil. Let's see if Charles has really got anything. It could save us time in the long run."

But twenty-four hours was far too long.

2

Charles had told Madeline she was to go out only if her people instructed her to do so. Always she must leave a note, tucked behind the picture above the main room's fireplace, giving him some idea of where she might be. He did not know how long the investigation would take: after all, he was not a trained detective. Yet, as Thomson later related, he beat the official CID and Branch people by a mile.

First he began with the chemist in Camberwell. His death had not been in the chronological order of things, but, as Charles was in London, then he must start in London.

The facts of the case were straightforward. Cecil Douthwaite had lived over his shop—five rooms, one of which he occasionally let out, a practice taken up after his wife's death in 1913.

He ran the shop, which he had bought in 1899, with the help of his wife until her death, employing only a boy to take prescriptions to customers or items to local doctors. Since his wife's death he had also employed a young woman—Dorothy Knapp—to help in the shop. She was the only person authorized to hold the second set of keys. The occasional lodgers were given a single key which admitted them to the side entrance, bypassing both the shop, dispensary and storeroom.

On the night of July 16th, 1915, Miss Knapp had left the shop at her usual time, 6:30 P.M. Mr. Douthwaite gave her a cheery "Good night, behave yourself, don't be late in the morning." Apart from the murderer, Dotty Knapp, who was only twenty-two years of age, was the last person to see him alive.

The next morning, July 17th, she had arrived at 8:30 A.M., to find that her employer was not in his usual place, the dispensary. She was immediately alarmed. It was so unlike the man. The storeroom was locked, so she walked through to the stairs and called. No reply. She went up and found him, in his little sitting room. He was bolt upright in his favorite chair; the face was blue and the silk scarf had been knotted so tightly that his windpipe was shattered.

The police officer in charge of the case had noted that the victim almost certainly knew his murderer or at least trusted him. He was obviously taken by surprise, and there was evidence to suggest someone had been seated for a while in the other, matching, chair.

Using a Metropolitan Police warrant card, a common practice among senior officers of the Department, Charles started to sift local records and talk to people. In a matter of hours he discovered two significant facts overlooked by the police: that the late Mrs. Douthwaite's maiden name was Gerda Erzberger, born Hamburg 1873. Her parents had emigrated, settling in London when she was seven.

Immediately he asked for a check on the parents with the DORA Aliens List, to find that they had both returned to Germany in 1911.

From Dotty Knapp, who turned out to be a pert and cheeky little brunette with large eyes, he learned that, toward the end of 1914, Mr. Douthwaite had a regular lodger. ("He liked to call him a 'paying guest,' though"—she rolled her big eyes—"sounded more genteel.") This man was not there all the time, but kept up regular payments. "Well, he couldn't be at Mr. Douthwaite's *all* the time, could he? Him being a seafaring man, like."

No, she never heard his name. Yes, she saw him often enough. Of course she could describe him—which she did. Charles felt the hairs on the back of his neck bristle. Rosscarbery, and the big, limping man climbed into his head. How did she know he was a seafaring man? She couldn't say. Maybe Mr. Douthwaite told her; she just could not recall.

Charles went off to Portsmouth and looked at the facts against those on file. In November 1914 Lieutenant Alexander Paul Fiske, aged thirty, was waiting to be assigned to a new ship.

Alexander Fiske, Charles learned, had been trained in the normal manner of naval officers—Dartmouth. There was no mention of his previous school on his record, though his service was without blemish.

Both parents were deceased, but the fact which interested Charles more than anything was the reason he was waiting for a new ship. His last one had been *HMS Bulwark*. Lieutenant Fiske had been lucky. He had gone on leave the morning of the explosion.

A shore patrol found his body, on November 28th, 1914, half-hidden behind some oil drums. The scarf used to strangle him was his own.

The other information which Charles managed to cull in Portsmouth was that Fiske had few real friends. He also spoke German.

Charles was about to leave for Scotland when the message came through asking him to get in touch with his wife, and with a Mr. Vernon.

Cautiously, over the telephone, Kell told him about Mary Anne. He also asked Charles if he would postpone his trip to Scotland. He should really see his wife before going any farther away.

Mildred was oddly incoherent on the telephone. Her speech was slurred,

and she seemed to flit from subject to subject like a gadfly. Obviously she was
relieved that Mary Anne was safe, but the conversation was interspersed with
odd and jumpy questions: Where could she have been? Why had she gone back
to Rouen? Last, and rather distressing, could Charles please bring home some
of those nice acidic drops he sometimes bought? Mildred, it seemed, had a
craving for the acidic drops, and she went on about it at length until the thread
of her conversation became so tangled that she just stopped and laughed strangely.
Alarmed, Charles took the first train back to London.

3

The Fisherman did not go out very much these days, but spent his time
waiting for instructions. He already had the primary order—to find another
target and deal with it.

He had been involved in doing this up until the unfortunate affair at Invergordon. Fiske and Douthwaite had been bad enough, though he told himself
they were both necessary. How else do you deal with people who had lost their
nerve? And Cecil Douthwaite did not have much nerve to start with. Alice
MacGregor was different. He had been perfectly safe at her little boardinghouse.
Nobody asked questions, and he walked for miles, observing what vessels were
anchored in Cromarty Firth. The right one would be there eventually, and he
had all the papers, uniform and other documents needed, together with the
explosive, in a safe place.

Alice MacGregor had been lonely, and she liked him. She had proved that
years ago. Safe as could be, he thought, until that night when everything went
mad. Well, he could not return to Invergordon or Cromarty Firth for a while,
so the only possible answer was to sit tight. If nothing happened by the end
of March, he would go up north again.

The note came during the late afternoon, addressed to him and marked
URGENT. BY HAND.

It was simple and to the point. It said: M6, *who is known to you, is likely to
spoil all present orders. Suggest you deal with the matter personally. St.*

Appended to the letter was an address. The Fisherman shaved, put on his
heavy coat and hat, then took a white silk scarf from one of the drawers. He
would purchase another tomorrow.

4

She thought the knock at the door could be Charles, so she rushed to answer
it.

"You?" She smiled.

"You didn't think I'd—"

"No. No, it's not that. Walter said you might—"

"Time to talk seriously. Can I come in?"

"Of course." She opened the door for her visitor and then closed it.

Her back was turned for a moment, and that was when her caller strangled her, there and then, in the hallway.

5

The Fisherman walked carefully around the building. He thought he smelled watchers, and he was right—two of them, concealed in the shadow of a doorway with a clear view of the entrance.

But there was nobody watching the tradesmen's door around the corner— not even from overlooking windows. The Fisherman could always detect watchers, even hidden behind the darkest windows.

The only clues would be footprints in the heavy frost which sparkled on the pavement. They would be gone by morning.

Taking a small jimmy from his overcoat pocket, he broke the lock on the tradesmen's door. There were lights in the main hall, and the sound of conversation came from behind a door.

Quietly, he went up the stairs and knocked. Once. Nothing. He gave it a minute and knocked again. Still nothing. A third time, before he slid the jimmy in. The door gave a sharp crack, like a rifle. He pushed gently, and the door stuck.

Then he saw her legs.

The Fisherman left quickly, quietly, knowing it was time to get out. Send a report and go up north again. Glasgow or Aberdeen perhaps.

6

Mildred looked strange around the eyes, but appeared to be better than he had seen her for some time.

They sat in the drawing room in Cheyne Walk, going through the scant information passed on via Vernon Kell and Giles.

"I'm just relieved." It was the first sign that Mildred's attitude had altered. "Will they allow her to stay in France?"

Charles said Mary Anne had asked for the posting to be ratified. "I gather she wrote a letter to the German, Buelow, at Christmas, telling him that she hoped to be posted back to Rouen and she'd let him know."

Mildred gazed into the fire for a long time and then changed the subject. "I'll really have to see Dr. Harcourt again. Tomorrow. I *must* see him tomorrow."

Mildred appeared to be trembling. Then she seemed to pull herself together. "Yes. Yes, I hope he can see me tomorrow."

In the farthest corner of her mind, Mildred was experiencing strange, vivid and disturbing pictures. They seemed very real to her, as though these were things that had happened only a few days ago. There were trees, and a very young boy. She lay on her back and could feel the boy's breath on her lips. It was all she could do to stop herself crying out at the sudden pain between her thighs. Then Mildred was back in the room, hearing the knocking on the front door.

A maid came in to say that Major Kell and Mr. Thomson wished to see Mr. Railton.

"I was just coming over to the office, Vernon," Charles began. Then he saw the look on their faces.

They were surprisingly gentle about it. "We know, Charles," Basil Thomson told him. "Vernon didn't know until an hour ago. But the Branch have known from the moment you kept your first assignation with her. Technically I have to arrest you under the Official Secrets Act, though I should imagine we'll keep it in the family, eh, Vernon?"

Kell put a hand on his shoulder. "An Enquiry, that's all. We know you meant well. But why didn't you come to me, Charles?"

In some ways it was a relief. Charles expelled a deep breath. "Hasn't she told you?"

He saw the flicker of mingled pain and embarrassment in Kell's eyes, but Basil Thomson answered, "She can't tell us, old man. I'm sorry, but she's dead. Strangled with a white silk scarf."

7

On the first Wednesday of February, Monique, Giles' special agent, now working closely with the *Sacré Coeur* Ring, was stopped, arrested and questioned while passing through a patrol area from one part of Belgium to another.

The German officer insisted on a humiliating body search. They found nothing. Her papers were in order. There was no reason to hold her.

Monique had dreaded this possibility and had therefore taken elementary precautions. She carried the information sewn carefully into the delicate embroidery of her silk, open-legged French drawers.

Eventually the embroidery was transferred onto paper, revealing a map which detailed the German defense system along the Somme area of their line. The map made it plain that already this was becoming an almost impregnable stretch within the five hundred miles of German fortifications. That fact made little difference to the planning and strategy of the generals.

8

They fed James three times a day. In the morning he would get two slices of bread with some kind of grease which passed for butter, and a cup of foul coffee. The middle meal never varied, except in texture—a soup, sometimes watery, sometimes dotted with vegetables, one piece of bread, with a cup of water. In the evening it was usually a couple of potatoes still in their jackets. Occasionally there was cabbage.

Once a week they let him walk around a small courtyard. He saw nobody but the guards, and heard no other prisoners. The interrogation had stopped abruptly, and nobody appeared to be bothered with him. The cell was damp, smelling of mold, and the two blankets were no protection against the raw cold. James wondered if they were just going to shoot him out of hand. It was all too placid.

Just over two weeks passed before anything happened, and even then he did not realize how well they had lulled him. It began late one night after he had taken a more than usually thick bowl of soup. When he began to vomit, James realized they had removed the bucket from his cell.

He shouted and hammered on the door, but nobody came, and the vomiting grew worse. He did not, then, feel particularly unwell, just the unpleasant nausea and finally the retching when his stomach was empty.

He hardly slept: the nausea swept over him in waves, while the tiny cell filled with the stench of vomit. At dawn he began to shout again, but the warders took no notice.

Breakfast was pushed through the flap in his door at the usual time. He cried out, but the sound of footsteps receded.

Weak, tired and hungry, now that the vomiting had passed, James took a few sips of coffee and began to eat the heel of bread. It tasted vaguely bitter. Half an hour later his bowels exploded in a scalding stream of diarrhea. He was doubled up with the pain, and wretched, for he had fouled himself.

The stench in the cell became unbelievably vile, but there was still no sign of the guards. Food was pushed through regularly—and left untouched.

Exhausted, still suffering from diarrhea, James lay helpless on the bed.

By the next morning he was convinced that he had been seriously ill, and by some freak his warders had not heard his cries.

"My God!" The door had crashed open, the oath spluttering in German from a new face—a man who looked, and sounded, like a bullying drill sergeant. His hand was held over his mouth and nose. Behind him, two soldiers clutched handkerchiefs to their own noses.

"You foul, filthy pig!" The Drill Sergeant screamed. "Your cell. I've never seen such disgusting behavior. The Commandant will hear of this!" And he was gone, the door clanging shut.

Half an hour later they were back, placing two buckets, a scrubbing brush and a piece of rag just inside the door. "You will clean up this mess, and your clothes, prisoner. That is the Commandant's order. Everything must be clean by six o'clock tonight.

One bucket contained lukewarm water, the other a solution. Lysol, James thought. For his own protection against further disease he did his best with the inadequate materials, managing to get most of the excreta and vomit off the floor, but incapable of cleansing himself, his clothes caked with ordure.

The Commandant arrived, with the barking Drill Sergeant who screamed at James to get off the bed. He hardly had enough strength to move.

"It is not good enough," the Commandant declared. "See this prisoner is issued with clean clothes and given more materials to cleanse the cell. This is disgusting behavior, even in a prisoner of such low morals as this man."

They dragged James away. He was stripped and thrown into a scalding bath. Then two soldiers scrubbed him almost raw, using thick-bristled brushes and some kind of carbolic soap. When they returned him to the cell, it had been well cleaned.

This time there was a bucket, and more food.

James was ravenous, and knew he must eat and drink to regain his strength. The night was uneventful, but the Commandant arrived the next morning. "It is better," he snapped, "but not yet quite right." Turning to the Drill Sergeant, he ordered that the prisoner should whitewash the cell.

His body was still raw from the scrubbing and seemed touched by fire at every movement. They brought a bucket of whitewash and a brush. Slowly he set to work.

They fed him normally, and it took two days to complete the job. Then life went on as before—for about a week.

Again, it began at night. Too late, he realized that the bucket had gone and that the soup was thicker. Of course—they were feeding him emetics and violent laxatives in the food.

The small hours were the worst, when he was violently sick again and again, his abdomen feeling as though steel nails were clawing within him.

This time the guards did not play games. He was too weak even to stand up when they came in and dragged him along the flagged passageway, throwing him into another bare, larger cell, where they systematically beat him.

Dazed, and almost unconscious, he was propped in a chair and the interrogators began.

What was his name?

Franke.

Wrong. A clout on the head which sent him reeling to the floor.

What was he doing with the Dimpling woman?

Nothing.

Wrong. A fist in the face.

They went on for hours, and finally he was dragged back to the cell. No food came for twenty-four hours.

Time stopped, but he estimated it was about a week later when they came and took him along curved stone corridors, up steps and into what appeared to be the guards' and administrative quarters. Four private soldiers, armed with rifles, escorted him out to a covered van. Inside, it was dark and smelled of sweat. The soldiers got up beside him, someone closed the doors and the van began to move.

In all, the journey took two days. They stopped only to eat, relieve themselves and sleep.

During the journey he tried to recite the whole of *Hamlet,* getting to the end and beginning at Act 1, Scene 1, again. He managed it five or six times before they arrived.

They were in a courtyard, and it was snowing hard; boots crunched and slipped, for the snow appeared to lie on cobbles. Above them, walls rose, and the windows were mainly Norman. James tried to think of the areas of Prussia, or Austria, most likely to contain Norman castles in good condition.

The cell was larger and high up in the building. Again, the walls were of solid stone blocks, but there was a natural dividing line formed by a high arch. This division separated living quarters from a sleeping area, and now he had a more comfortable bed, complete with clean pillows and blankets.

In the living quarters, a table and two chairs were bolted to the floor. For the first time in weeks he sat at the table to eat a reasonable meal—some kind of tasty stew made of rabbit, onions, cloves and potatoes. He was given a small carafe of red wine and half a loaf of bread.

The interrogation began at dawn on the next day.

The first inquisitor was a short man, almost a caricature of a German, square-headed, with cropped hair, a scar down the right cheek. He wore a gray civilian suit, though everything else about him was military. James thought of him as Bullet Head, and they went over old ground: What was his name? Why had he been in Berlin? Why Hetty Dimpling? Why Pastor Bittrich?

James replied to the questions, giving the same answers as before. When it came to awkward things like Major Stoerkel, he denied anything incriminating. It was the Herr Major's idea that they should communicate in a clandestine way. He was simply looking for an English lady called Miss Brown, who had married a German officer when she had lived in Paris. She also had been a good friend of his father's. No, he could not think why the Herr Major wanted to make a secret out of it.

Why, then, had Frau Dimpling collected a letter from the Alexanderplatz Post Office: a letter meant for him? James could only think it was some kind of mistake.

"Frau Dimpling has been shot as a spy."

James showed no emotion, but shrugged and repeated that he did not know a Frau Dimpling.

"Perhaps *you* will be shot as a spy."

James shrugged again, looking unconcerned. "That would be unjust," he said. He was essentially a good German, even though his family had lived in Switzerland.

At dawn the next morning they marched him into the courtyard, stood him against the wall, gave him a cigarette, let a Roman Catholic priest ask if he wanted to make his confession, then brought out a firing squad, who loaded their rifles and waited for the final order.

James felt very composed.

9

In London, Margaret Mary was feeding baby Sara Elizabeth when she heard the Chopin Sonata. Later, she was to say that it was as though someone were playing it in the next room; so much so that she went to see. The piano stood silent; nobody else was in the house—except, she thought, James, who was very close to her.

She continued to feed the baby—she liked to do these things herself whenever possible. At Redhill, or with other members of the family, she was forced to let Nanny do everything, but she preferred to spend as much time as she could with both Donald and Young Sara—as the family called the infant to distinguish her from Sara Farthing.

The piano stopped, but James was close to her all day, even when she went over to see Charlotte—something Margaret Mary did once a week in an attempt to help her sister-in-law.

Charlotte was improving, responding to her visits to Redhill, which Sara had insisted were maintained on a strict rota, winter and summer. She also enjoyed the long talks when other members of the family called on her at home. Charlotte was happy when, toward the end of January, for instance, Caspar announced that Phoebe was going to make her a grandmother.

"I don't really look old enough to be a grandmother, I know," she giggled to Margaret Mary, "but good old Caspar. One arm and one leg, but everything else intact."

"And how does Andrew like the idea of being a grandpapa?" Margaret Mary asked. She was concerned about Andrew. To her, he was the classic fallen idol, the clay of his feet coming to light under pressure.

Charlotte made an uncertain motion with both hands. "He blubbed," she said, as though Andrew had done something disgusting. "Like a baby. It's not the first time. A month or so back he came in, sat in his chair and sobbed for a good hour. I tried to comfort him; asked him what was the matter. . . ."

"Was he drunk?"

"Not more than usual. He kept saying that Rupert need not have been as he is; that it was all terrible. He kept repeating, 'Too late, Charlotte!'"

Though he was often either elated or moody with drink, Andrew was still able to do his job, and the past year had seen may changes. With the advent of "Blinker" Hall, things had become frantic in Room 40. Hall expanded operations, and Room 40 soon became several rooms, while numerous new faces—many of them academics—were seen in the Admiralty Old Building.

Following the *Lusitania* disaster, a new drive and determination was apparent among those who listened, read, analyzed, tracked and deciphered at the Admiralty. Naval Intelligence had a reputation under its new chief which was second to none.

10

"The job," Giles complained to Smith-Cumming, "is to give the Military and the politicos something to work with."

"We *are* providing as much intelligence as we can. Blinker appears to have the edge on us because the work is more immediate. Our problem is getting people to act—we've discussed it a thousand times."

Caspar listened as they droned on, and, not for the first time, wondered if he—minus one arm and one leg—was the only stable male left in the great Railton clan. He had no worries, lived a full and happy life with Phoebe and had begun to enjoy his work with C. But, if the rumors were true, his uncle Charles was in trouble; his grandfather had become obsessive about the world of secrets; and, by the sound of it, new and dangerous ideologies as well. His own father veered sharply between downright maudlin pessimism and a false elation; Marie was off with a German lover in Berlin; James was missing on some escapade; and Aunt Mildred seemed to have gone dotty.

He came out of the reverie to hear his grandfather say that he had another useful recruit, and did *White Lady*—their very successful Belgian network—or *Sacré Coeur* need another courier? C said the more the merrier. "Then I've just the girl for you." Caspar was stunned to hear Giles Railton put forward his own granddaughter, Denise Grenot, Caspar's cousin, as a serious candidate.

11

"Tell me, Mrs. Railton, these daydreams—flashes, you call them—are they to do with your childhood?"

Mildred looked across the desk and could not meet Dr. Harcourt's eyes. "I remember them best after I've had the medicine. If they're important, you should allow me to take some of the medicine home so I would have it to hand."

Harcourt felt a small stab of concern, for he knew what Mildred Railton's plea really meant. He was a conscientious medical practitioner who now found himself coping almost daily with mental problems brought on by worry, grief and the stress of war. Mildred Railton's case had become increasingly interesting after her husband had revealed the story concerning her childhood.

He had talked to many other doctors and had studied the standard works, so he knew that if he could relax Mildred to a point where she would respond to careful questions, there was a chance that she might reveal to herself the hidden secret of her childhood. Once the mind unlocked that traumatic knowledge, she might be successfully brought back to normality.

The main problem was getting the woman to relax sufficiently, and finally Harcourt had knowingly taken the step of using mild doses of laudanum—

just a couple of drops, taken in water before he saw her. The results had so far been good.

The subconscious was obviously working hard, revealing some of her childhood trauma—she spoke of leaves, moss under her, the face of a young boy and occasional pains in the genital area. He was loath to give up treatment now, yet Mildred's suggestion that she be given laudanum to take at home was a clear indication of dependence.

They talked for a further half hour. She was certainly a happier woman than the one who had first come to his consulting rooms, and as a doctor he knew he would be able to wean her off the drug once her mind was clear again.

At the end of the session Dr. Harcourt gave her a prescription for one dose. It would take her through the following day, Thursday, and he would be seeing her again on Friday.

Chapter Twenty-Three

1

They did not blindfold James, but allowed him to stand, smoking a last cigarette. He centered his thoughts on Margaret Mary. He could hear her playing a gigue. Bach, he thought.

He noticed the soldiers looked frightened, and very young. The officer shook his hand and stepped back. James stood to attention. Out of the corner of his eye, he saw the officer unsheath his sword. He heard the first order, then there was a scuffle and a runner came hurrying up to the officer. In seconds the squad was marched away and James found himself being hustled back into the building.

They brought him coffee. Then the second inquisitor came in. James thought of him almost immediately as The Professor. He wore a crumpled suit, needed a haircut, perched steel-rimmed spectacles on the end of his nose and appeared unfamiliar with his duties.

The Professor said his name was Einster, and insisted on shaking hands. He started to leaf through a heavy file, as though he could not find his place. When he finally spoke, it was as if he were reading from the file, but he looked up at James, smiling happily.

"Yes. You're James Railton. Your father and mother are deceased—I am sorry about that. I think I once met your father in London some years ago. He married a second time. Now, what was her name? Anna? Hanna?"

James shook his head. Her name was Franke. It was all in the record.

But the Professor raised his head, giving the same pleasant smile. "Of course—her name's Sara, isn't it? She has been married again, I gather, to an

American. Now, Lieutenant Railton, I'd like to talk about a number of things. And, if you play the game, you will not have to go through the somewhat harsh and final realities of which you had a preliminary taste this morning."

They went on like this for almost two weeks, James denying he knew anyone called Railton, and the Professor nodding, taking no notice as he recited a litany of Railtons: their follies, foibles, strengths and weaknesses.

He knew it all, down to Uncle Giles' real position at the Foreign Office. In the end, James just refused to comment or corroborate.

2

Everyone tried to be helpful to Charles. "We understand about the strain, old chap, but it was a deuced silly thing to do," Kell said. Giles did not see him or speak to him again for some time, but Charles had several visits from Basil Thomson, who wanted to know many things.

The bulk of their first conversations, which all took place in Thomson's office at Scotland Yard, was about The Fisherman and the work Charles had already done on the case.

He was taken to The Yard by car and always returned directly to Cheyne Walk. A plainclothes officer stayed outside the front of the house; another was stationed at the rear. These watchdogs remained in place around the clock.

After four days Kell came to see him again. They wanted to keep it in the family, he repeated, by which he meant within a small circle of people at MI5 and the Branch. "There *will* have to be an enquiry, and I can't promise anything. The worst will be dismissal, the best a severe reprimand. Personally I'd like to keep you on, Charles. I shall do my best. Get yourself well represented. And try not to give *everything* to Thomson."

"Everything about what?" Charles felt numb. He was not sleeping, and his mind roved around the reasons for his being so foolish. He knew the true motivation, but it all seemed so trivial. "Everything about what?" he repeated.

"This Fisherman business. Try to keep some of it back. I'd like us to have a crack at the rogue. Basil's put Wood on it. Friend of yours, isn't he?"

"If Wood's looking into the murders, it won't be worth while my trying to hide anything. Damned good man, Brian Wood; he'll get all I found and more besides."

Kell looked downcast, then said Wood had already come up with something. "Oh?"

"The girl. Drew. Haas. Call her what you will...."

Charles waited.

"Wood doesn't think she was killed by the same person as the others. Something about the way the scarf was knotted."

A tiny portion of the puzzle fell into place. "Is that why Thomson's been questioning me and going through my movements again and again? I'm a suspect?"

Vernon Kell appeared embarrassed. "Well, it has been mentioned—not seriously, of course. You really are in the clear, but you know what policemen are like."

"It's ludicrous."

"Yes. Yes, I know."

"What about the knot?"

Kell failed to meet his eyes. "Fiske, Douthwaite and the MacGregor woman were all found with the scarf tied very professionally behind the left ear. I don't know which particular knot was used . . ."

"Baden-Powell will tell you. He knows the bloody knots backwards—always trying to teach them to his damned Boy Scouts!"

"You wanted to know." Kell gave a humorless laugh.

"I'm sorry."

"The Drew girl . . . Well, the scarf was just pulled very tight at the back of her neck and tied in what we used to call a granny."

After dinner Mildred talked a lot, and none of it made much sense. She went on and on about her childhood, her father and mother, the future, and the course of the war. Mildred had not been told about the current trouble in which Charles found himself, and she did not appear to have noticed the plainclothesmen.

The next day they drove Charles to The Yard again and went through everything. It took a long time, and, toward the day's end, Kell saw him alone, to say that the Court of Enquiry was set for the following week.

"I can suggest a good man to represent you. And, of course, it'll be a private matter—*in camera*. But do you want Mildred to be told?"

"I think not. Why should she be bothered?"

"Just in case."

"In case the Branch decide to take me off and do me for murder?"

"I really don't think that'll happen, but—"

"No." Charles was firm. "No, I don't want Mildred told, and I hope nobody else in the family—apart from my Uncle Giles—is going to get details of this."

"Mary Anne?" Kell raised an eyebrow.

"No!" Charles had not thought much about Mary Anne since it all happened. That night he found himself going over the night she had left Cheyne Walk. How had she managed? And how had she got herself back to Rouen?

3

When Mary Anne ran from Cheyne Walk, in tears, on that July evening in 1915, she had no idea where to go or what to do. She took the old nut-brown Gladstone, filled only with essentials. There was £6.18 shillings in her purse, an inordinate amount of money, but she had been paid in cash only the week before. She did have her bank book though, so was unlikely to go short.

She found a taxicab in Beaufort Street and asked the cabbie to take her to King Street. Halfway there, she changed her mind. It was foolish to run off to relatives. Her answer was to get out of London quickly. She was angry with her mother, and sorry at the same time. Mama, she thought, must be somehow deranged. It was not surprising. The world had gone crazy; the horror of what she, Mary Anne, had already seen and experienced had undoubtedly made her into a harder person, but her mama had never undergone hardship, in spite of her favorite cliché: "Oh, Mary Anne—life is very hard."

She told the cabbie to take her to Euston Railway Station. Dora Elliott should still be on leave. There had been a letter only the day before, wishing her luck—late—for the court martial ordeal. Nobody else had seen it.

There were detachments of troops at the station, and the place was crowded with people. She bought a single ticket to Liverpool and found she had two hours to wait.

There were more delays, and it was not until six the following morning that Mary Anne arrived, armed only with Dora's address.

In the end, her confidence, and heart, failed her. The cabdriver gave her an odd look when she asked for the address, and when, near the docks, he began to slow down, in the narrow street with the little row houses crowding in one on the other, doors opening straight out onto the pavement, Mary Anne told herself that she could not possibly impose upon Dora or her family.

Only then, with a shock, did Mary Anne remember Dora's words, on their first day at the clearing station: *I've never been a lady in my life . . . living in a Liverpool hovel with seven brothers and sisters. . . . Papa . . . home drunk of a Saturday night . . . virtually rape your elder sister. . . .*

"Sorry, driver." She swallowed. "I've changed my mind. Could you take me back to Lime Street Station? The hotel."

He shrugged and the cab drew away.

She felt disgusted with herself. On reflection, Dora had become more than just an acquaintance during the last weeks in France. She was always bright, very intelligent, and fun—treated as an equal by all men and women, including Mary Anne. Nobody ever thought of Dora's background. Dora was simply Dora. As she registered at the hotel, under the name Edwards out of caution, Mary Anne argued that it would not have been fair to bother Dora at this time in the morning.

At two o'clock that afternoon she took another cab, making the driver stop on the corner of the street so that she could walk the hundred yards or so to Dora's drab front door. There were grubby children playing on the pavement, and some of the doors were open, spilling an unpleasant odor of stale food and unwashed bodies into the close air. Women and men lounged in doorways. One man whistled at her, another made a clicking sound with his tongue.

The woman who answered her knock—dressed in black, a tattered shawl around her shoulders—had the look of defeat in face and eyes, and the smell of flesh unused to either soap or water.

She was thin, with a pointed nose and untidy, greasy, graying hair. The tired eyes were wary and loaded with suspicion.

They stood looking at one another for several seconds before Mary Anne asked to see Dora Elliott. Vaguely she was aware of a small child clinging to the woman's skirt, and of others in the dark bowels of the room behind the front door.

The woman did not reply, simply turning her head to shout, almost too loudly for her frail body, "Our Dora! There's a lady to see yer."

It was with a certain amount of relief that Mary Anne saw Dora's face come poking out of the gloom behind the woman's shoulder.

"Railton!" She gave a little gasp. "What the bloody hell're you doing here?"

"Came to see you, Dora. I need help. I—"

"Oh Jesus, Joseph and Mary! You can't come in here, it's crawling with kids, and Da'll be back soon. Wait." And she was gone, the woman still standing blocking the doorway, her eyes warning Mary Anne that she could not cross the threshold.

A few seconds later Dora appeared in her coat, took Mary Anne's arm and propelled her away from the house and down the street, keeping up a running monologue. "You idiot, Railton, a girl like you coming down here. It's safer on the Western Front. If you live here, you're born to it, but a stranger . . . well, you could have been robbed, set upon, or— Oh Christ, I was going to say or worse, but you've had 'or worse.' This is about the roughest part of the city—"

"I've managed in rough places before."

"Rough places? Yes, the Deux Bateaux in Rouen when the soldiers are a bit tiddly—that's about the roughest you've seen, my girl. You haven't been brought up to it, and if Da got back and took a fancy to you . . . Well, Railton, I'd have had to clobber him with a frying pan. I've spent the best part of my leave trying to get the place clean and hygienic. You've no idea. Where're you staying—and what's wrong?"

They went back to Mary Anne's hotel, and over tea she told the whole story to Dora, who turned out to be completely unsympathetic. "Oh Lord, Railton, you upper-crust people'll be the death of me. You manage to get yourself almost murdered, but when your ma behaves like a stupid cow all you do is run away. You're pathetic. You honestly don't know what life's about, do you?" She threw up her hands, almost knocking over the tea service and causing the waitresses to look down their noses.

"I can't be responsible for the whole bloody world, Railton. Anyway, I'm off tomorrow—to stay with my auntie in the country for the rest of my leave." She looked up, smiling. "You come as well. You'll like my auntie; lives in a little village near West Kirby. Cottage, roses round the door, the sea almost up to the front garden, and a husband who can't be called to Kitchener's New Army because he works the shrimp boats. Fresh eggs, butter and milk; fresh air and only the dicky birds to wake you in the morning. You'll feel better for a week there." She gave her cheekiest grin. "And there are some nice boys in the village—or there were. I 'spect they're all in France by now. You be ready. Half past eight. Platform 3. I'll meet you."

They spent an unforgettable week together. Dora's aunt proved to be a plump woman with sun-bleached hair and a complexion like old leather. She accepted Mary Anne as one of her own and, between them, Aunt Mabel and Dora introduced Mary Anne to life as she had never before known it. The weather held and the two girls spent their days walking along the Wirral peninsula, watching the birds, lying on the grass and looking at the sea, with its multitude of changes in color and movement.

As for boys, there were none to be found, for—as Aunt Mabel said— "Kitchener's taken the lot, men and boys."

Toward the end of the week, the girls, who shared a small room, lay, in their nightdresses, on top of their beds. The window was open to cool the room, with only the occasional sound of a predatory bird or night creature overlying the constant sound of sea-change. Restless, Dora sighed a lot, turning one way and another, while Mary Anne lay still, looking at the moonlight pattern on the ceiling.

"Can't you sleep?" Mary Anne whispered.

"Oh, it's hot, and . . . Oh, hell, I have to go back to bloody France on Monday. Sister Price yapping at me all day and saying I'm a disgrace; the CMO having another go—"

"The Chief Medical Officer? Having a go at what?"

"I'm a bad influence. It's only because I work hard and they're short of nurses that I'm allowed to stay at all."

"Why, for goodness sake?"

Dora giggled. "I got caught. With an officer, in one of the broom cupboards. . . ."

"They wouldn't throw you out just for a bit of spooning."

"I'm afraid, dear innocent Railton, the officer in question had his spoon right in when they caught me. It couldn't have been the most edifying sight— Nurse Elliott with her skirts around her waist, and Second Lieutenant Ponsonby-Smythe, or whatever his name was, shoveling into me hard as he could."

"But, Dora, surely you don't—"

"I told you. I know it's not usual, but I also know there's more than one nurse at the General Hospital who'll give herself to help the convalescent lads gain confidence—and have something to remember. I certainly don't regret it. Grief, I could do with one now."

"A man?"

"Well, certainly not an eggcup! I'm sorry, Railton. You had a bad experience, and I don't suppose you think of sex as being pleasant. . . ."

"That's not true!" Mary Anne snapped. "Yes, it *was* horrible. But, well, as we're speaking woman to woman, there's at least one man I know that I'd do it with tomorrow."

"Really?"

They were silent for a time, then Mary Anne asked, "What's it like, Dora? What's it *really* like? Doing it?"

"Come over here and I'll show you," she whispered. "Don't be shy—come on. It won't be as good as with a man, but I can teach you things."

Slowly, Mary Anne slid from her bed. Her knees trembled as she took the two paces towards Dora's bed; then her friend's arms came up around her neck. Mary Anne felt their lips touch and Dora's tongue slip into her mouth. The warmth came bursting into her loins as their bodies touched.

Afterward, in the dark, they held one another close, stroked each other's hair and faces, whispering endearments, and so fell into sleep, wrapped around one another like children.

"It's much better with a man," Dora said the next day. "Only thing is that a man's face is more scratchy. You coming back to the hospital with me, Railton?"

It was the first time Mary Anne had thought of that possibility. "They'll send me straight home. Nobody's given permission for me to go back to duty—I'm also under age for France, though nobody's found out yet."

"And I bet they don't even know you haven't got permission. Look, I have to get my warrant from the RTO at Liverpool. Your name won't be on the list, but that's not unusual—you've got your uniform with you, haven't you?"

"Of course."

"Then come along. Nobody's going to find out until well after Christmas. By then you'll have made yourself indispensable. They say there's going to be a big push in the spring. We'll *all* be needed."

It seemed to Mary Anne that she had two choices: return home and seek forgiveness, and chance entrapment, or risk the wrath of some RAMC colonel in France. She opted for France, and, as Dora had foretold, nobody even realized it until well after Christmas.

4

When the court of Enquiry sat at the end of March, it found Charles Railton guilty of a serious misdemeanor, likely to endanger the country's safety. The proceedings were held in secret, and Giles came to give a personal character reference, telling the court of the mental strain his nephew had been suffering at the time of the incident.

Vernon Kell spoke of Charles' loyalty and discipline. Attention was drawn to the fact that he had been secretly honored with a decoration.

The Branch made no suggestion that he was in any way involved with the murder of his mistress, Hanna Haas, otherwise known as Madeline Drew.

On the sixth day they found him guilty, and there was an unpleasant night while he waited for the sentence. In the end, he got a severe reprimand and was free to return to duty immediately.

"I don't think you'll do anything so stupid again," Kell told him. "How's Mildred taken it?"

Charles looked away. "Mildred does not know. She's ill, Vernon, and that's not just an excuse for remaining silent. It's like living with a dormant volcano. One just doesn't know what's going to happen next." He made a gesture of despair. Then, pulling himself together, he asked what his chief had in store for him.

"Something rather special, as it happens. I'm putting you in to liaise with friend Thomson at the Branch."

"Doing what in particular?"

"Sitting on his shoulder, listening to every word he says, watching every move he makes. Basil Thomson get's all the thunder—we've both known that for a long time, just as we've known he's making inroads into our department. He's asked for a senior officer to assist him, so now he's getting one. You!"

Charles wondered if Commander Thomson knew of the impending appointment. He could not see the man taking kindly to his presence at The Yard.

That night, on arriving home, he embarked on yet another act of folly that could endanger his career.

Mildred was already in bed. "With one of her headaches, sir," the little maid told him. He took a nightcap in the drawing room and was crossing the hall on his way to his own room when he noticed the envelope lying just inside the door. It was plain white, and of good quality, as was the paper inside—a single sheet with neatly printed writing: *Hanna Haas gave birth to your child while in Germany. She is safe but will not remain so unless you do as we ask. First you will show this to nobody. If you do your daughter will die and everybody will be informed. We have all necessary evidence.*

Charles went back into the drawing room and burned the letter. His hands shook so badly that he could hardly pour himself a large brandy. Oh Christ! he thought. The child in the photographs. His bastard child. No! his love child by poor, wretched Madeline. He could have wept for them all.

5

"Giles, you know I cannot use them. You shouldn't really be running private agents, even though they've been of immeasurable help."

"Just thought you should take them over." Giles looked annoyed. He had been trying to pass on his main Irish contacts—his son and daughter-in-law—to C.

"Kell should have them, you know that."

"I trust *you*, C."

"Meaning you don't trust Kell?"

"'Course I trust him. I'd simply feel safer if you had them. They're difficult to handle. Getting more difficult every day."

"Kell, Thomson, or even Blinker Hall..." C sighed. "All three of them have their hands full with Ireland these days. If you ask me, the Emerald Isle will turn red before long: blood red."

Giles shook his head. "Well, maybe Thomson. He's got a lot of people out there, I know."

"It would be better."

Later, when Giles had left, C called Caspar in to go through the latest material received from their train-spotting networks. "Hate to say it, young Caspar." He coughed. "I fear your grandpapa's getting too old for this kind of thing. Going a bit doolally-tap, if you ask me. Getting odd ideas. You'd think he was a bloody revolutionary, the way he talks sometimes. Too old. Too old by far."

Caspar doubted it. Any man who could send Denise, his own granddaughter, out to be a courier behind the lines, as Giles had done, was not too old. Ruthless; singleminded maybe; but certainly not past it.

6

The Fisherman completed decoding the signal. It read: GO STRAIGHT TO DUBLIN AND CONTACT D2 WHO HAS WORK FOR YOU.

It was signed with the familiar *St.* for Steinhauer.

7

"Well, if Kell wants you to be with me, I'm most grateful. We've a lot on our plate." Basil Thomson managed a smile, and sounded pleased to see him.

"I'm under your orders, sir. So fire away."

"You know Brian Wood, I think."

Charles said he knew Wood very well.

"He's still investigating this Fisherman business. Well, you started it all; uncovered it; so best that you see it through."

"Thank you. I appreciate that."

The head of the Branch waved away the thanks. "You won't be on it all the time. Things appear to be hotting up across the Irish Sea. Rebellions; rumors of rebellions. We're working hand in glove with the DNI on that one. Look, take this file out of the office and read it thoroughly. Get to know the fellow backwards, forwards and sideways. We're both going to know him even better in the near future."

He tossed the thick buff file across the desk and Charles flipped it open. The name on the first page was *Sir Roger Casement*.

Chapter Twenty-Four

1

On returning to Cheyne Walk with the Casement file, Charles found there were letters waiting in the little silver tray on the hall table.

One was from Mary Anne in France. She had written once already, and he had replied. Even Kell had not dared tell him she was also writing to the German, Otto Buelow, at a private Department address. The former artillery captain was performing good work for them among the prisoners of war.

Mary Anne's letter was short, thanking her father for not putting any obstacles in her path regarding the confirmation of her posting back to the hospital. She painted a grim picture of the front line in this bitter winter. The daily routine of death and terrible wounds appeared to have been made worse, now, by many cases of frostbite and exposure. She ended by clearly indicating concern for her mother: *Can I yet write to her? I really do worry, but realize she must be allowed to take one day at a time.*

He carefully folded the letter, placing it in his pocket and giving the cloth a fond little pat. Helping himself to a whisky and soda, Charles settled in one of the leather armchairs and opened the file Thomson had given him. The front was specially flagged with warnings: *This File is Secret. Passing any of the contents to an unauthorized person constitutes a breach of the Official Secrets Act. MUST BE KEPT UNDER LOCK AND KEY.*

Then, in smaller, red, letters toward the bottom of the page, the line which always brought a smile to Charles' face: *Anybody finding this file must return it, without reading, to New Scotland Yard.*

He had already been through the MI5 file on Sir Roger Casement, so presumed this would be similar if not exactly the same.

Quickly he leafed through the pages—the usual stuff about the man's birth in Dublin, education and early steps in the Consular Service, and the famous report on the Belgian Congo atrocities, which caused a major diplomatic uproar in Europe. Then his further work involving the ill-treatment of British and other subjects in the Amazon.

This had gained Casement a knighthood, and he became a well-respected figure, not merely in the United Kingdom, but also in the United States. Then, in the spring of 1912, he retired, because of ill health, to settle in his native Ireland.

Charles yawned. He already knew all this—Casement's alliance with the militant Irish Nationalist movement and the Irish Volunteers. Every Tom, Dick, and Harry knew of Casement's dislike of British politicians and where the man's sympathies lay at the beginning of the war.

At MI5 they had known Casement was spending more and more time in Berlin, planning to get the Germans to assist in raising an Irish Nationalist army aimed at driving out the English.

Charles started to fidget, then a paragraph caught his eye. He sat bolt upright, hardly crediting what he was now reading. The file handed to him by the Special Branch contained a whole mass of information which, to his knowledge, had never been passed on to MI5.

Certainly they knew that Casement's name was on the "to be detained" list, under DORA. But, even when Patrick Quinn was working closely with Kell, Special Branch had kept certain actions very close. The knowledge, for instance, that a search warrant had been granted for Casement's London apartment. Nor had Kell or any of the senior staff seen what Paddy Quinn had produced from his search. Yet here it was, page after page of typescript, photograph after photograph of handwritten diaries, plus a copy of a signed statement from a handwriting expert. The diaries were indisputably in Sir Roger Casement's own hand.

Nobody had hinted to MI5 that these diaries contained, among other interesting, possibly treasonable, facts, indisputable evidence that Casement was a confirmed, practicing homosexual.

It was also plain that while Kell's people had not been included within the magic circle of information regarding Casement, the DNI, and his department, were hand in glove with the Branch.

Charles was now wide awake, going through each entry in the file, committing certain parts to memory, ready to report matters to his chief.

There was minute detail of Casement's visits to prison camps in Germany, and meetings with Irish soldiers who had become prisoners of war. Notes on his conversations with these men had the feel of being direct transcripts; and there were pages of wireless intercepts and decoded telegrams—traffic passing through German diplomatic and naval channels. "Blinker" Hall's code-breakers were providing intelligence directly to Thomson: information which was being updated by the week, if not the day.

From what was already here, it seemed highly possible that Casement had arranged for arms to be delivered to the Sinn Feiners so that an insurrection could take place very soon.

The last entry in the file, to date, showed just how soon. It was a decode of a telegram from Count Bernstorff, German Ambassador in Washington. He had just cabled Berlin that an uprising was planned for April 23rd—St. George's Day—and, that year, Easter Sunday. There was also a request for machine guns, field guns, and between 25,000 and 50,000 rifles, to be supplied to the so-called Nationalist Army.

Charles flicked back through the pages. In all, he considered there were over thirty intercepted, decoded messages between Berlin and their Embassy in Washington concerning assistance, in arms and money, to the Irish Nationalists. As far as MI5 was concerned, the file was a small bombshell. Between them, Hall, the Branch, and, to some extent, C's Service, had enough information to scuttle any plot within the borders of Ireland.

The clock on the mantelpiece struck eight, and Charles realized he had not even dressed for dinner. His head buzzed, and the natural inclination was to telephone Vernon Kell at his home. But the Chief of MI5 had cautioned all officers regarding the use of that particular instrument when secret matters had to be discussed.

He left the file on the arm of his chair and hurried from the room. Unless there was a previous arrangement, they always dined at 8:30 sharp, and he had not seen Mildred since the morning, so had no conception of today's mood.

Ready for dinner, Charles returned to the drawing room. Mildred looked up from the chair he had so recently vacated. She was idly turning the pages of the Casement file.

Charles smiled, walked over, kissed her on the forehead and gently removed the heavy file from her knees. Mildred smiled back, her eyes bright. She was in a good humor. If things were bad, her face took on a pinched, nervous look.

"How're tricks today, then, darling?" He placed the file out of reach. "How's Dr. Harcourt?"

Her smile almost reflected her former sense of fun. "Oh, that old bore. Didn't I tell you? I'm going to someone else now. A woman in Harcourt's waiting room put me on to him. A Dr. Fisher. Just round the corner from Harcourt. Wimpole Street. Very good indeed, much better than Harcourt. He's very careful about the patients he takes on. Runs a private clinic, and he's no more expensive than Harcourt."

Charles mentally noted to make inquiries about this Dr. Fisher. At least his proximity to the Branch would be of help there.

They went to dinner, with Charles clutching the Casement file, which he put down carefully beside his chair. He felt that it was burning a hole in the carpet.

2

On the same day, Caspar—on C's instructions—had read *their* Casement file. He did not know that the version kept in the fast-growing Registry was considerably slimmer than the one held by Special Branch. For one thing, a large number of the intercepted signals were not included, nor were the photographs and extracts from Casement's diaries. Everything provided by C's own people was there, of course. They were not to know that the file was, as the Admiralty Intelligence people would put it, degutted.

At the Admiralty, though, the file—a replica of that on the floor of Charles' dining room—was, at this very moment, being updated by Andrew Railton: a very changed Andrew at that.

Just as Charles and Mildred were tackling their entrée, Andrew was dealing with the Casement file in his small office in the center of what was now a veritable warren of rooms which were run under the general title of "Room 40."

The decode he added had already been forwarded to all relevant parties, and it would eventually be regarded as an historic intercept—a telegram from the German General Staff to Count Bernstorff, saying that the requested arms for Ireland would be sent in a small ship, which they named, together with a bunch of code words, including ciphers to be used when Casement sailed for Ireland: when the arms had left; if the mission had to be aborted; if it was delayed; and a dozen more pieces of information.

By now, Charlotte, who had forced herself to take on war work of her own—apart from assisting Sara at Redhill—noticed that her husband appeared to be keeping unusually late hours at the Admiralty. Strangely, she had not associated this with the fact that Andrew had undergone subtle changes in the last weeks. He was more tired than drunk when he arrived home, and his appearance was slowly returning to its previous smartness. If anything, roles had been reversed, for Charlotte was letting herself slip even more.

The cause for the change in Andrew was the appointment of Miss Grizelda Greatorex as his civilian secretary. Miss Greatorex was short, dark, pretty, a good eighteen years Andrew's junior, and the possessor of two great attributes—a flat in Mayfair, provided by a rich and indulgent father, and a stunning figure.

Andrew, at forty-one years of age, was still handsome, distinguished, and, as Miss Greatorex was the first to admit, exceptionally attractive to younger women.

So Charles, Caspar and Andrew carried a hundred confidences in their heads, the bulk of which were of value to the Empire. And Charles and Andrew were also the possessors of personal secrets which could affect both their private lives and England's security. Charles' affair with the late Hanna Haas still contained a time bomb; while, though Andrew was hardly aware of it, Miss Grizelda Greatorex had an unfortunate tendency to be talkative. Unlike the Railton family, the Greatorexes—Banking and Commerce—were all careless with information.

3

The Professor still saw James every day. James remained cautious. It would be foolish to deny facts, and equally foolish to say anything further, so he settled for silence.

This did not appear to greatly concern the Professor. He questioned, got no answer, so supplied his own:

"You are married?"

Silence.

"Her name is Margaret Mary. You have one son, Donald, and a daughter named Sara Elizabeth. Sara after your stepmother, who has also remarried—an old friend of yours . . . what's his name? Yes. Richard Farthing." The Professor did his vague, spectacles-on-the-end-of-his-nose clowning. "That must be giving your Uncle Giles Railton some sleepless nights—family property and all that, yes?"

A shrug.

"Well, let's say yes, shall we? And what about your Uncle Charles? Bit of a dark horse, Uncle Charles."

"What's going to happen to me?"

"Happen?"

"Do I get a trial?"

"Trial? Oh, my dear chap, you don't want a trial."

"You'll shoot me out of hand, then?"

"What gives you that idea? Nobody wishes to shoot you. They have much more interesting things in store. Now, please, James Railton—what about your Uncle Charles?"

Another shrug, so they began to try a new technique. The Professor came each day and questioned for very long periods. At night, though, they did not allow James to sleep. Instead, Bullet Head came clattering into the cell every half hour, with two soldiers who clumped around, swore, made a great deal of noise and left. Nobody switched the lights off.

James tried to go on remembering Shakespeare, quoting aloud against Bullet Head's noisy entrances. Sometimes in his mind he would fly an aeroplane and, after a week of this, he managed to catnap between interruptions.

Some of the time James tried logic. They had caught him, fairly and squarely. They could have no doubt that he was engaged in espionage in time of war. There was one punishment only—death; yet they seemed in no hurry to execute him, which meant they needed him.

He spent a great deal of his time thinking about the reason for this, and what they really wanted from him.

4

Charles used one of his Department's most secure internal postboxes to get a message to Kell. Could they dine together on Sunday? The answer came back affirmative. The next day, though, he appeared to have been banished from the Casement business—for the time being at least.

"Today you're going back onto The Fisherman business again—with Chief Inspector Wood," Thomson told him. "The Fisherman and matters arising, such as the willful murder of one Hanna Haas. That suit you?"

"More than I can say."

So the morning was spent going through the evidence, all of which he knew, apart from the latest investigations on Mrs. MacGregor's death, which had yielded a second description. It matched the one Charles had picked up from Douthwaite's assistant. A large, heavy, seafaring man with a limp.

Charles read through the details, including the new description. When he had heard the same words in Camberwell, the hair on the back of his neck had prickled. It did so again. He had seen the man, years ago: he could not doubt it now.

"Walked with a strange limp," Wood said casually.

Charles nodded. He knew the odd, dragging limp.

"A peg leg, perhaps?"

"Definitely." In his head, Charles saw blood, and the ax.

That was all they had, until just before luncheon, when Thomson summoned them. "Hall's sent me something which might be of interest. They've had it under 'miscellaneous' for a few days. A wireless signal, repeated every hour on the hour for a whole day—last Wednesday. It's a cipher they've used before."

He tossed the transcript onto the desk. The decode read: ATTENTION AN-GLER***ATTENTION ANGLER. GO STRAIGHT TO DUBLIN AND CONTACT D2 WHO HAS WORK FOR YOU. ST.

"*St?*" Charles raised an eyebrow. "We know him, I think."

"Friend Steinhauer," supplied Wood.

"And who's D2?"

"A rolling code name for a Sinn Feiner. All-purpose contact. The Hun's used that contact code a dozen times before, so Blinker tells me."

"So our man's in Ireland?"

"Possibly. Wait events—we've got people there already on the watch. In the meantime we make sure all ports, particularly the Irish boats, keep a lookout for your limping blond giant."

Over luncheon, Charles asked if Brian Wood could "have a peep in the DORA-related files. Name of Fisher. A doctor with consulting rooms in Wimpole Street. Or see if he's got an account with any of your people."

The answer came back before the afternoon was out. Fisher was untouchable. Aged forty-three. Henry Fisher. "Respectable. Well thought-of, if you can think well of a quack who's a soft touch for fashionable ladies who need calming down—laudanum; morphine; cocaine; that kind of thing. Wealthy. Respectable. Something we should know, sir?"

"Don't think so." But Wood did not like the edge to Charles' voice. Later he told Basil Thomson that Mr. Railton sounded "exceptionally worried."

5

They had told Padraig O'Connell to be in the bar near the pier at Kingstown promptly at 8:30. He was there at 8:29, and the big fellow was sitting in the corner, one leg shoved straight out in front as though it did not belong to him.

Padraig got himself a drink, looked around casually, to make sure there was nobody in the place to make him nervous, then walked toward the man, who was wearing boots, dark trousers and short jacket, with a high-necked black pullover.

"Off the boats are you, then?" he asked.

"I work them when I feel like it."

"Ah, and do you feel like it now?" He had changed little, Padraig thought.

"I'll do anything for an honest wage."

Both men were "established," as they would have said among C's people, and did say in Nicolai's training school.

Padraig sat talking for the best part of half an hour. They exchanged drinks, and when he left, there was a copy of the *Independent* on the table.

The big man picked it up and looked at it, casually glancing through the pages. At the bottom of the "In Memoriam" section someone had written in pencil: *Railton. Malcolm and Bridget. Loving husband and wife. Glen Devil Farm, Co. Wicklow. Requiescat in Pace.*

6

"Reggie Hall's too clever for his own good," Kell smiled, bearing no malice.

They had met as arranged, at his own home, and now, after dinner, sat in the Chief of MI5's study. Charles had taken an hour to outline the large amount of information available to Hall and the Branch, which was not on file with The Firm.

"First, I must thank you," Kell continued. "Second, I really don't think it's going to make all that much difference. Hall's got all these special facilities, though I don't know if I can really condone the search of Casement's private apartments. Much good will it do him." Which went to show that even Vernon Kell could sometimes be wrong.

"I just don't trust the Branch or the Admiralty."

"I never have." Kell twitched his mustache. "But, then, I don't really trust C's Boy Scouts either. Must be difficult for you, Charles, with relations littering our secret houses."

"It's my jolly Uncle Giles who bothers me."

Kell grunted. "I always thought Giles Railton was born out of his time. Really should've been plotting for or against popes, helping to run one of Machiavelli's agents out of Florence. Fifteenth century, that's where Giles belongs. You know he's offered me relations of yours in Ireland?"

"Offered—"

"Your cousin—his son—together with his bride. He's been running them privately for some time. C tells me your Uncle Giles appears to be divesting himself of property, mostly personal informants and agents in the field."

"Malcolm?" Charles could hardly believe it.

"And Bridget." Kell sighed. "I'm hauling them in as soon as possible. If they want to stay on as freelance, well and good, but I have no use for them on the payroll."

"Unless Uncle's actually penetrated Sinn Fein."

"He hinted as much—but I'll believe it when I see it."

7

The cold felt as though an infestation of vicious mites had burrowed into his pores. There was no snow, but the ground was like steel under the horse's hooves, and the last light was just going.

Malcolm hoped his wife had at least warm soup in the house, for there had been little time to eat that day, and the weather had made the ride from Dublin twice as long as usual.

He cut off the main road so that he could approach the farm from behind. Long since, they had discussed a whole series of signals when either of them was out of the house, and now, as he came up the rise and saw the white stone building below, Malcolm felt a churning of his stomach.

When he had first come to Ireland, his refusal to become involved in any of his father's work was firm, a decision taken for Bridget's sake and not just his own; only when he discovered the old intriguer had enticed his wife into the web did Malcolm relent. Even the final decision was put off until he discovered that Bridget had, before their first meeting, been on almost kissing-cousin terms with many who were now dedicated Sinn Fein activists.

In the beginning he had wanted Bridget kept out of the whole business, but within months the impossibility became all too apparent. They had worked for a number of years now as a good team, sometimes playing off one another to Padraig O'Connell, their contact, and the faceless men who were Padraig's puppeteers. There were times when they even laughed at the fact that Padraig O'Connell was blackmailing each of them with threats—one against the other.

They had learned as the years passed; learned caution, care and watchfulness. When one or the other was left alone at Glen Devil Farm, the day was punctuated by certain actions which would immediately signal to the returning partner that all was well.

The lamp he could see burning on the rear landing window now should be to the left; it was set far over to the right. In the fast fading light, Malcolm could also see that the churns were still in a row, while the second bedroom shutters were still closed. The churns should have been moved at three that afternoon; the second bedroom shutters would be opened at noon. The door of the big shed to the right of the house was propped open with a large stone. Under normal safety signals it should have been closed by two o'clock.

Over the past few weeks he had taken to carrying a loaded pistol with him. Twice, some sixth sense had given him the scent of danger—a look in Padraig's eyes; a half-heard conversation about armed rebellion. Now he reached down and pulled the Luger 08, a 7.65mm version, from the "poacher's pocket" of his riding coat. Carefully he edged the big gray, Bracken, down below the skyline and tethered him, speaking softly to the horse. Then Malcolm crested the rise again, keeping low, his face suddenly stung by a flurry of sleet.

He knew all the approaches to the farm, having walked them hundreds of times, winter and summer, and chose the western edge of the valley, for it had always been the danger spot—no windows to that side, only the two gables like a great misshapen black *M,* and plenty of scrubby cover on the slope. If there were ever trouble at the farm, Malcolm knew a lookout would have to be posted in the yard itself in order to spot anyone making their way down the western slope.

As well as the incorrectly placed lamp, at least two other lights burned in the house—the one in the hall and another in their main living quarters. Even in the bad light, and through the increasing sleet, he could see the diffused shafts of illumination, blurred across the stableyard. At twenty yards from the house, he automatically pushed his thumb up and forward, taking off the safety catch of the German weapon.

At ten yards, and again at five, he stood for a few seconds, ears straining for sounds, his eyes stinging in the gloom as he searched the ground for movement.

When he reached the cover of the blank gabled end of the house, Malcolm waited again, listening. Something was very wrong. At this time of day there would normally be movement—Bridget had been left that morning with the two trusted farmhands, and there should be sound from the yard, or inside the house, even on a bitter dirty night like this.

As silently as possible, staying close to the wall, he moved along the rear of the house, squirming under the windowline at the rear, and then the far side. He reached the eastern gable, one silent step at a time, moving toward the front of the house. He could see the yard clearly in the light flowing from the door and living room windows. The door was open; still no sounds of life; no movement.

He could hear his heart thudding in his ears, and realized that his breathing was irregular and his muscles tense as wound springs. Fear, he realized as he felt the hair still crawl at the nape of his neck, even in the intense cold.

With his back against the front wall, Malcolm edged toward the first front window, squinting in at an angle. Nothing. Nobody. The table was not laid, the fire smoldered, low, as though nobody had tended it for at least an hour. He squirmed under the window and squinted from the other side. Still no sign of life. He could even see into the unlit kitchen. No shadows, no sign of life. He went under the second window. The same. Then he reached the open door, stepping as silently as he could into the beam of light, the pistol close to his hip, ready.

The hall was empty, the hanging lamp lit, and the small oil lamp burning, trimmed, on the oak table next to the settle they had bought at Norton's last sale in Wicklow Town.

He took a pace into the hall, pistol up, kicking the door closed behind him. The noise seemed deafening, then dwindled. He thought he heard a creak from upstairs, just the slightest noise, like a soft footfall on a dry board. Reaching out with his left hand, Malcolm picked up the oil lamp and, with the pistol ever ready and his body braced for sudden action, he started to move through each room of the house.

It took a long time to cover the ground floor, for he paused every few seconds, listening for sounds, eyes hunting the dark corners for shadows. His intuition told him that Bridget was still somewhere here, and that there was at least one other person lurking in the house. For a second, as he approached the bottom of the stairs, he recalled an old man in Ashford talking about Glen Devil Farm, just after he had bought it. The old man said it was haunted, and, up to now, Malcolm had dismissed the idea with a laugh.

Halfway up the stairs he distinctly heard another creak, this time as though a door had opened. There was light—from the wrongly placed lamp—on the landing, and he stood for a full minute near the main bedroom door, lowering the oil lamp in his left hand, still listening, his back to the wall.

Another creak, from inside the bedroom he thought; then a tiny fluttering which could have been birds in a chimney. Slowly, he unlatched the bedroom door and kicked it open. The hinges squealed in pain as the door swung inward, and from below came another, louder creak—a footfall? The fabric of the house showing resentment at the cold?

A gust of wind, carrying more sleet, hit the bedroom window with a splatter as he stepped into the room, the lamp held high again, casting shadows this time—across the big bed; a shining in Bridget's dressing table mirror, making odd, star-patterned reflections; the huge black bulk of the wardrobe.

He took a step toward the bed, and heard, close at hand, a distinct sound; a settling crack, from the high oak wardrobe.

Lifting the lamp high, Malcolm turned slowly to view the entire empty room, and heard the crack again. He walked to the wardrobe; his right hand, still clutching the pistol, reached out and turned the knob.

The door seemed to hesitate, then bulge. He jerked and it swung open to reveal a moment of unique horror, a nightmare, unreal, unbelievable—Bridget's face, seemingly suspended, glowing a terrible unnatural blue, her lovely eyes now dull, but staring, popping from her head; the tongue which had so often caressed the inside of his mouth protruding from her lips, drawn back in a ghastly grin; and below, a slash of white where her neck should be, pulling her chin up at an odd angle.

Malcolm screamed, stepped back and saw her, standing for a snatch of time, inside the wardrobe, before she began to pitch forward. His right hand went up, as though trying to defend himself, across the upper part of his body at exactly the moment when The Fisherman threw his second white scarf over Malcolm's head.

The scarf trapped his right wrist against his face, and, automatically Malcolm's brain told him to use it to advantage. Stop the silk getting to his own throat.

There were three distinct sounds—the flopping noise of Bridget's body hitting the bare boards of the bedroom floor, the crash of the pistol flying from his hand, knocking the side of the wardrobe, and the tiny explosion as the oil lamp went down to the left.

Then it was all sweat, struggle, smell and fire.

It oddly did not really dawn on Malcolm, until the end, that he was fighting for his life. The smells were a mixture of paraffin oil, burning, garlic, wet serge and excrement (somehow he connected the last with Bridget). Whoever was at his back hauled on the piece of silk with great strength, but Malcolm, stocky like his uncle, the General, and with muscles now strong from the years of labor on the farm, heaved back with the one arm that prevented the material slipping onto his throat.

He felt something hard in his back, as though the assailant had lifted a knee to give himself better purchase. Malcolm allowed himself to be pulled back, then brought all of his weight forward, kicking back at the same time. His ankle hit something hard, like wood, and he felt the attacker begin to falter as though losing his balance.

Malcolm consolidated, kicking again and hooking his outer arm around the silk, hauling forward and then moving his upper body to the left.

He heard a grunt and felt the pressure relax as his attacker began to lose balance. He was aware of the flames now, starting to gain hold on wood and the fabric of the bedroom curtains, beginning to dance and send great awesome shadows over the grim scene. He could feel the heat, and smoke began to reach his lungs. Tiny hands clawed at the inside of his throat.

The white strand of silk slid away, fluttering in the air, almost slowly, and his assailant fell heavily—a big man, dressed in black—half his body rolling into the lapping crimson flames.

Malcolm lashed out with his right boot, felt it connect somewhere near the man's head, heard the grunt of pain and kicked again. The man lay facedown. Still.

For a second he thought of trying to get Bridget from the house, then gave up the idea. The heat was getting worse by the second, and some clothing in the wardrobe had caught, sending up white smoke. *Save yourself.* He almost said it aloud, spotting the Luger right on the edge of the flames, grabbing at it, sensing the pain as he plucked it up, hot from the fire.

As he dashed down the stairs, he thought he could hear the man struggling in the bedroom, but he did not look back or even think of the possibility that more than one person was in the house. The fact of Bridget's death, and the sudden shock, had not yet reached him. In his present condition Malcolm was aware only that somehow the Brotherhood had discovered Bridget and himself as informers. His only object was to get clear, escape, and he had no idea where he could hide. If they found that he had not died, like Bridget, nowhere in Ireland would be safe. Run to Dublin and pray he could make the sanctuary of the Castle. It was the one firm thought in his head as he climbed the rise, panting, half running, aware that the wind had started to howl and the sleet was driving like showers of needles.

Bracken whinnied, on the far side of the rise, and, before Malcolm crested the top, he glanced back to see the sky a dull red, and Glen Devil Farm gushing smoke, with a great plume of blood-colored flame spearing from the roof.

He did not see the big man, coughing and wheezing, stagger from the door, his right cheek seared with a burn and his clothing smoldering. Yet even in this state, The Fisherman stopped for a moment to curse Malcolm; then he lumbered forward to douse his clothes in the horse trough, still cursing—the weather, Malcolm, luck, and his own folly of complacence, and ill timing.

He should not have been so foolish with the woman, he knew now, as the icy water soaked into the serge of his jacket. The sex just was not worth it. It was the same with the MacGregor woman, except that she was a willing partner.

The Fisherman swore again, and, somewhere above the wind and unearthly sound of the fire, an animal howled in the woods.

Chapter Twenty-Five

1

Denise Grenot had become operational. C decided she would be better with the older established *Frankingnoul* network. She was taken to Holland and given what instruction was necessary at one of the network's houses in Maastricht, for most of the reports came into this center directly from Lanaeken, just across the border, in Belgium.

A tram ran between Maastricht and Lanaeken, and this was the main route of the couriers. At the end of January, Denise made her first run, going into Belgium on a Monday morning and returning on Thursday with a large amount of detailed information, both in her head and on paper.

The information she brought back on that particular day was vital to the spring battle-plan. But neither the French Staff nor the War Office took note of it. C even doubted if it was ever passed on to either Field Marshal French or Haig, let alone Lord Kitchener.

2

The Professor still visited James' cell daily and carried on the strange interrogation, supplying the answers to his own questions.

They became quite friendly, and spoke often of music, between questions.

Then, toward the end of January, when the cold had become so intense that James wondered if there would be any end to the winter, the Professor announced that he would be leaving soon.

"Where are they sending you?" James had started to regard their relationship as a friendship.

"They are not sending *me* anywhere." The Professor raised his eyebrows. "It's *you* they've decided to move."

James laughed. He had expected something of the kind for several weeks. Common sense told him they would not keep hammering away at him. It had to end, and James was well resigned to what the ending would be.

"Am I at last to get a trial, then?"

The Professor shook his head. "I've already told you, nobody's interested in a trial."

"I shall disappear, then. . . ."

"You've already disappeared. In London they've given you up for dead."

"My fate, then? A quiet bullet? An unmarked grave?"

Again he shook his head. "You must realize that nobody wishes to see you dead. There are reasons. You have special protection. Go in peace." He sounded like a priest.

3

Giles was in the Hide, with the lamps turned down and no maps on his table. He often just sat and thought these days, like a contemplative monk. But the religion upon which he meditated was one of political ideologies; of society and the vagaries of birth. It was also of intrigues; treachery; betrayal; and where true loyalty should lie if a man's conscience would be clear.

Vaguely, in the distance, he heard a hammering and clanging. He wondered if it was another Zeppelin raid.

Then his man, Robertson, began to knock on his door, shouting loudly, "Sir! Sir! Come quickly, sir!"

It took a minute for him to realize that there was some kind of emergency. Then he crossed to the door, unlocked it and went into the passage.

Looking from the top of the stairs, he did not recognize the figure who stood, dirty, unkempt and ragged, in the hall.

Only when he reached the penultimate step did Giles see that the tramplike figure was his son Malcolm.

"Home is the hunter." Malcolm's voice sounded full of bitterness.

"Home from the chase." Giles sounded unruffled.

Exactly one week later, as the thaw set in, on February 21st, the huge German artillery barrage began around Verdun, smashing all the badly conceived Allied battle plans to shreds.

The dreadful killing season had begun, and no intelligence collected by C, or any other Service, would stop it.

4

The thaw spread over the United Kingdom also, and with it came the news Richard Farthing had been waiting for.

He had hoped to be assigned to a squadron, in France, almost right after reporting for duty, but the powers who ruled the lives of pilots in the RFC failed to post him. Much of his time had been spent at Farnborough, and when he flew it was usually in a flimsy DH-2, which did not please him.

Sara, though, was only too pleased to know that Richard was still in England, flying in comparative safety. Their marriage of only a few months had again altered her life more than she had dared hope. With Richard Farthing as her husband, Sara basked in that balmy sense of true security. She regularly thanked God for the day when James had first met Dick and brought him back to Haversage.

She saw him on most weekends, and found that there was now an emotional stability in her life, centered solely around her new husband. Richard was so different from the Railton men, and without a trace of guile or secrecy in his makeup. His generosity, coupled with what she saw as an incredible knowledge of practically any subject—from engines to the most modern composers, artists and writers—made him unique in her eyes. Indeed, this was the key, she felt, to marriage: partners who saw a uniqueness in each other. It was what James and Margaret Mary had experienced, she now knew; though she doubted if any of the other Railton men and women had even touched the surface of the emotion, with the exception of Caspar, possibly, though Sara had yet to really fathom "Old Phoeb'." The line of thought always led back to James, and she sometimes had a quiet weep about his death, for she was sure they would never see him again, and marveled at Margaret Mary and her unshakable confidence in his return.

Pondering on this always brought her mind to the tiny permanent worry. The one black spot in Sara's life was the constant cloud, no bigger than a man's hand, which seemed to hover in the back of her mind—that one day Dick would be snatched from her.

Their happiness together was apparent to all who saw them. "You can tell as how them two has a good time in bed," Natter croaked to Vera Bolton as they watched the couple ride out of the stableyard one morning.

"Oooh, Ted, you watch what you're saying! You've got a one-track mind you have!" squeaked Vera.

"Ah, and you'm not far behind me, young Vera. I seen you with Billy Crook last time 'ee were on leave, and him so young."

Vera turned scarlet, leaving the yard snapping at him, "I don't know what you're talking about, Ted Natter. You got a nasty mind."

"Daft cat!" Natter responded.

Vera, in fact, knew very well what he was talking about. Certainly there was a matter of some years' difference between her and Billy Crook, but Billy had become forceful and dominating since his medal and promotion. Vera was so much under the eagle eye of her mother, at the Manor, that she had not sampled the delights of womanhood until Billy's leave at Christmas.

The first time was after the wedding; and they crept into the hayloft, above the stables, practically every day of Billy's leave after that. Now he wrote to her regularly from the front, while she had just started to become worried. Usually she was never late. But she had missed her period altogether that January.

As for Sara, she would have given anything to miss, and heaven knew it was not for want of trying, for Dick was by turns tender, passionate, dominating, demanding and altogether the answer to her every sexual fantasy.

His one blind spot was her personal worry about his safety. He was such a good and confident pilot that she knew death in the air rarely crossed his mind. "It's only as safe as you make it," was his watchword. "Which means you *have* to make it safe."

When his orders finally came, he was bouncing with joy, but he grumbled about the fact he would be flying the DH-2 in France. "The German planes are miles ahead," he said on the day his posting came through. "Their Albatros is particularly good. The DH-2's a sturdy little thing, snappy in the climb and very stable in a dive; she's light, stands punishment, but she's no match for an Albatros."

Sara's heart sank and she urged him to take care. "Don't worry about that, my darling." He grinned. "The Farthings are known for their own particular sturdiness. We can take a lot of punishment, and we're also pretty snappy on the turn and in a climb—or haven't you noticed?"

Sara grinned back wickedly. "I've noticed you've only got one forward-firing gun, thank heaven."

"Want to test it out in London?" He put an arm around her. "I guess I should buy some of the new warm flying gear before I go to decimate the Hun flyers. We can do that, take in a show or two, have a grand time. Then you can come over to Hendon and see me off, eh?"

They did it all, saw Hetty King at the Hippodrome, ate more than was good for them, went to Gamages' Aviation Department—where Dick bought a fur cuirass and a new leather aviator's coat—and made love with a concentrated passion whenever they could.

On the morning Dick left, Sara, with one other RFC wife, stood by the edge of the field at Hendon and saw him raise a gloved hand as the little DH-2 buzzed into the sky. To her, it looked very flimsy, but she stayed, with her eyes glued to the two aeroplanes, until he disappeared from sight.

By the time Sara got back to Haversage it was the first week in March, and the rain had set in. All she wanted was to hide in her room and cry, but there were things to be done, and one met her the moment she got into the hall.

Vera Bolton stood waiting for her, asking for a word.

Sara sighed and took her into the General's Study, asking her to sit down— she did not hold with this business of servants standing through interviews, and had a premonition this was not going to be easy. Likely as not, Vera wanted to leave. Already many girls from local houses were going off to be with the men, riding motorcycles, driving ambulances. Dick even told her there were women tinkering with the aeroplanes at Hendon and Farnborough.

"Well, Vera..." she began, then saw the maid was in tears. "What is it? Oh, Vera, what's wrong, my dear?"

Between sobs it came out. "I can't face me mum, M'm. I just can't face her. I'm in the family way."

Then Sara had to forget her own grief and heartache. She had to be kind, considerate and sensible. The father was undoubtedly Billy Crook. "Does he love you, Vera?"

"He said so at the time, M'm, but I gather they all do. He was my first ever. He said so every time; said how he loved me."

"And do you love him? That's really more important."

In a surprising gush of almost poetic speech, Vera said she loved him dearly, that Billy was her meat and drink, her sun and moon, the cobwebs on spring trees in the morning and the shine on fresh apples. Sara had to bow her head and hide her smile, and reminded Vera that she was older than Billy.

"I don't see how that comes into it—not if you love someone."

"Well"—Sara knew it was wrong to suggest it, but it might be necessary— "have you seen Mrs. Crook yet?"

"No! Oh my God, no, M'm. If I can't face me own ma, how d'you think I'd face Billy's mum?"

"I didn't mean about telling her she would be a grandmother." Sara paused long enough for it to sink in.

Vera's mouth opened into an elongated O. "Oooh! Oh no, M'm. No—I couldn't do that!"

"You want to have the baby, then. Very well. I'll do my best to see if we can get Billy's reaction. It won't be easy, but I'll try."

"If he'll marry me, M'm."

"Billy's an honorable boy. Yes, there's a difference in ages, but I personally think you'd make him a fine wife. I think he has to do the decent thing." As she said it, Sara realized how like a Railton she had become. Dick would have laughed to hear her say something like "do the decent thing."

She saw Mrs. Bolton first. It was the deft way in which Sara broke the news, and the plans she laid for Vera and Billy, that softened any blow.

"Well, she's been a wicked girl, no doubt, Lady Sara. I should tan her bottom for her—"

"Oh, I shouldn't do that. I mean, she's a grown woman, and in her condition—"

"It's only her condition that stops me, M'm. Spare the rod and spoil the child." Then she softened. "Our Vera? Who'd have thought it?" And Mrs. Bolton finally went off, smiling and ready to cluck, rather than tut, over her daughter.

She tried telephoning Giles, but Robertson, his man, said that Mr. Giles would not be home until later. So she sent for Martha Crook. She was much more calm and less inclined to be shocked. "She's a good girl, and I think Billy'd be a fool not to take her if he's spared. I'll talk to her and if need be look after her until the baby comes." She smiled to herself. "Well, I can't really blame Billy. There was a letter from him today. He's resting, out of the line, at the moment."

Later in the evening Sara telephoned Giles again. They exchanged courtesies and she immediately sought his help in getting one of his War Office contacts to arrange some leave for Billy: "Even a week'll do."

"I'll try, my dear, but every man's needed there at the moment. Things aren't particularly bonny. If he's out of the line, there's a chance."

As they were saying goodbye, Giles said he was sorry not to have been in earlier. "I had to be out with Malcolm."

"Malcolm? Malcolm's with you?"

"Nobody's told you? You haven't heard? I'm sorry, Sara. Yes, he's been in London with me for a month now. He's better, but it's been a tragic loss to him."

"What? What's been—"

Again Giles apologized. "I can't think why nobody's told you. It's Bridget. Malcolm's come back to England. Bridget died in a terrible accident. A fire in their farmhouse. Razed to the ground, I fear. He's been hard hit."

Only much later did Sara discover that nobody had been told of either Bridget's death, or Malcolm's return, until that very day.

5

On the night Malcolm came back to Eccleston Square, the first cheery greeting quickly evaporated. Within a very short time, he was sitting in the Hide, weeping over the horror at Glen Devil Farm and the loss of his wife.

His father excelled himself in the role of comforter, giving orders for a bed to be warmed and broth to be made, and sending for a discreet doctor.

Only later was Malcolm able to tell him the full story of that night at Glen Devil, and his subsequent attempt to get to Dublin Castle, which had failed, as he had spotted men he knew to be in the Brotherhood set at vantage points.

He lived rough for a few days, allowing his appearance to become that of a tramp, finally stowing away on the Kingstown boat. But by the time he had slipped off at Holyhead, his condition was that of a man who could trust nobody. He had walked, and hidden in railway freight cars, to get to London.

Giles was proud of him. It was exactly what he would have done.

The doctor said the young man was in a state of shock; needed rest and building up. He should be treated gently. As it was, Malcolm slept for forty-eight hours. Then his father sat on the edge of his bed, as he had done when Malcolm was a child, and talked to him, showing only kindness and concern.

"I'm slowly disengaging myself from official activities," Giles said. "We can't all live forever—"

"Oh, come, Papa—you've got a good few years left to you yet."

So Giles hoped. With great luck he might even manage another twenty, into a very ripe old age. There were things he had to do that could take him a long time. He had, first and foremost, to make his peace with the world, and for Giles, making peace was not something that could be done easily. To make peace, he had to make guile.

He told his son that he would be safe in Eccleston Square: "Until you're sufficiently recovered to talk to others. I'm going to give the servants their orders. Not a word about your return must get out yet. Nobody but your nephew Ramillies comes here, and he keeps only specific appointments. Until you're ready, nobody else need know."

And nobody did know until much later.

When Malcolm was fully himself again, it was Giles who invited people to the house to speak with him. Vernon Kell was the first, because Giles knew Malcolm could, if he continued to work, end up under Kell's jurisdiction. Then he had "Blinker" Hall to dinner, springing Malcolm on him as a surprise.

Last, Basil Thomson was given a similar invitation, and between them all Malcolm's knowledge was passed on. With collective information, they were all agreed that The Fisherman was still at large. Probably back in England.

As for an Irish uprising, it was Malcolm's opinion that it could be put down with exceptional speed once the balloon went up.

6

Charles knew nothing of Malcolm's return, even though he still worked close to Basil Thomson. It was one of Giles' stipulations that no immediate family were to know until he was ready. So Charles went on as before, reporting to Kell and doing as good a job as he could with Thomson.

It was not easy, for as the weeks passed, it became more and more apparent that Mildred was a very sick woman. Her changes in mood were now more sudden and even violent.

In her lucid moments Mildred became concerned about herself, for the flashes of memory had returned with a vengeance.

They usually came when she was in need of more laudanum. She was afraid of them, for they had become more than mere flashes. They were things she definitely recalled as having taken place.

As yet she could not fit the entire jigsaw into the chronology of her life, but, deep down, Mildred knew something had happened, at some unspecified time—something so loathsome that she did not really want to know about it.

The result was that she began to take more and more of the drug in order to forget, and push the flashes deeper, out of sight. Dr. Fisher was delighted to supply her with measured quantities—at a price.

Charles anguished at the situation to the extent that he finally told Kell at one of their regular meetings.

Vernon Kell was his usual good self, and suggested a doctor whom Charles could use. "I'll make the introduction, and perhaps you can arrange something—an invitation to dinner, possibly. He's an excellent man. In fact, I believe your uncle, Giles Railton, has used him."

But before such a meeting could take place, Charles received another of the odd messages. This time it lay with the rest of the day's post, on the silver tray.

It had been posted in London, and even the address was printed in the same manner as the previous message. In precis, the note reminded him of his child by Hanna Haas, and told him there were things he would very soon be required to do if the child were to remain alive, and if he wanted the whole business to remain confidential. On no account should he go to the authorities. There followed an address and time. He was to go to this place, following an exact formula, including the method of transport and the route he should take. There, he would meet a contact called Brenner. He might recognize the contact, but he was not to show surprise, and he must use the name "Brenner" at all times.

The time appointed was 6:30 the following evening. It was now the last week of March.

The place turned out to be a nondescript room in a part of London which Charles did not know well. Ladies of easy virtue approached him, and, he admitted to himself, tempted him, in the street near the house. He had a feeling, built from his now not inconsiderable experience, that people had watched him throughout the entire journey.

"Brenner" was certainly known to him. Charles would have said he knew him like the back of his hand, but the realization was only now coming to him that no man can ever have full and intimate knowledge of another. At this moment of meeting, Charles felt the edifice upon which his life had been built begin to crumble. The man he now faced brought with him a sense of erosion.

"Bit of a shock?" Brenner laughed.

"A shock? I can't—"

"Believe it? No, I don't suppose you can, Mr. Rathbone—best we stick to your street name. You call me nothing but Brenner, now is that understood?"

Charles nearly spoke the real name, but quickly fell in with Brenner's suggestion, asking what this was all about. "Are you a blasted traitor because—"

"No. You will refrain from the melodramatic horsewhipping ideas, Mr. Rathbone. We go back a long way, my friend. You must listen to me, because we are both playing a double game. Have no doubts about that. You've been foolish, and all fools have to pay one way or another. This is your way of making amends."

"But these people—"

"These people will probably ask much of you. They will want certain pieces of information. It will be confidential, secret. They will want to know about ships, and troops; about some of the operations being run by the Special Branch. The thing is, they imagine I can control you more easily. All you have to do is obey their instructions. Look up, steal, listen, seek out what they require—for they will always contact you direct. I am but a clearing house. You bring the information to me. Your conscience can be clear, because you should know me well enough to realize that I am not going to give them exactly what you pass to me. They will receive half-truths, and flawed gems only."

"You swear to me that anything I provide will go no further than you?"

"In the main, yes, of course I swear it. This meeting is merely to establish contact. No more. I am supposed to be lulling you into false security. Consider yourself lulled. Don't worry, we'll get them all in good time."

Two days later Charles had another note. Now it was a request. How much did the authorities know about Sir Roger Casement's whereabouts?

Charles had by this time been present at several meetings between Thomson and the DNI. He knew exactly where the man Casement was at this very moment—waiting to be taken to Ireland from Wilhelmshaven.

Dutifully, Charles passed the information to Brenner.

As far as Ireland was concerned, to use Malcolm Railton's words, the balloon was about to go up.

Chapter Twenty-Six

1

It was almost Easter. During the previous week both Andrew and Charles were privy to information which could have a bearing on the rebellion which they knew had been mooted for Easter Sunday.

Charles, now very close to Thomson and reporting daily to Vernon Kell, heard at Scotland Yard on the Saturday before Holy Week: a German ship, the *Libau,* had sailed six days earlier from Lübeck with a cargo of arms and ammunition for the Sinn Feiners. She was disguised as a Norwegian merchantman, *Aud,* and there was no doubt of her intentions. Three days before this intelligence came, they knew Sir Roger Casement himself had departed from Wilhelmshaven in the U-20—the same U-boat that had torpedoed *Lusitania*. What followed caused grave embarrassment to Andrew.

Because the Irish situation was serious, the DNI stipulated that any new important decodes should be passed on to him directly, no matter what time of the day. A set of rules had long been established for this kind of thing. As Head of Liaison, Admiralty Intelligence Division, all confidential signals now went through Andrew.

At the moment that a new, and seemingly vital, decode was produced, Andrew could not be found.

The watchkeepers at Room 40, on Friday, April 14th, passed what appeared to be exceptionally important information to the officer of the watch. His job was to hand this decode personally to Andrew, who in turn would contact the DNI.

It was almost seven in the evening. Andrew had left at five. The officer of the watch telephoned his home and was told that Andrew was not there. Charlotte was puzzled. Andrew had said he would be working until midnight. The officer of the watch said that Andrew should be contactable at his home.

He was at that very moment lying in the arms of Miss Grizelda Greatorex, who was in a state of seminudity, in the bedroom of her apartment in Mayfair.

The real embarrassment was caused by the fact that Blinker Hall himself had decided to visit the watchkeepers, some thirty minutes later, and saw the signal. He demanded to know why Commander Railton had not been informed.

During the evening, Charlotte received four telephone calls, one from Hall himself, trying to contact Andrew. The last gave explicit, tight-lipped instructions for Andrew to report to the Admiralty Old Building at the soonest possible moment.

So, when Andrew returned to King Street, Charlotte met him with a seem-ingly bright, "You must be tired, my dear."

Andrew replied that it had been a devilish day at the Admiralty; that he was sorry to be so late; Hall was in a filthy mood and he had been held up all evening.

Still with an air of sweetness, Charlotte told him that indeed Blinker was in a filthy mood. He had been trying to get hold of Andrew all evening and wanted him back at the Admiralty Old Building as fast as his "Jolly Jack Tar legs" (Charlotte's words) would carry him.

Andrew went gray, turned around and left the house.

On the next morning, the fifteenth, Charlotte went to see a private detective.

The reason that the Room 40 people had become anxious on that Friday night became apparent as soon as Andrew arrived back at the Admiralty. A signal had been intercepted indicating that U-20 was in trouble and had returned to Heligoland. For a time, many people wondered if Casement had abandoned the plot. The possibility was short-lived. Hard on the heels of the information regarding the gun-running *Aud* came the news that U-20 had rudder problems. Casement was now aboard U-19, once more at sea.

"What," Charles asked Thomson, "will be the next move? I realize it's up to the Admiralty—but what happens?" He already knew, from being present at meetings between Thomson and Hall, that any arms shipments were regarded as a priority.

"With any luck they'll pick up the arms boat."

"And Casement?"

Thomson gave him a blank look. "I don't think we need to trouble ourselves too much about him," he said, turning away.

2

Mary Anne was not what you would call a religious girl. Certainly she believed in God, and loved the language of the Bible, but she seldom prayed, though she did like Anglo-Catholic services.

The hospital padre was not, however, an Anglo-Catholic. If anything, he was a shade to the left of Martin Luther, and therefore, when Mary Anne needed religious comfort, she would slip into one of the local Roman Catholic churches in Rouen. She did find an emotional need for comfort these days.

Casualties came in regularly, and they had been told to expect them in very large numbers once the spring was really under way. There was talk of a new offensive to take pressure off the terrible fighting around Verdun. Mary Anne was prepared. But she was also in a dilemma, for her mind constantly strayed to her German savior, Otto Buelow. They exchanged letters in which they shared much of their personal past and views. The German had spoken to those for whom he now worked in England, and there was no problem about the couple meeting if Mary Anne got leave.

That she wanted to see him was without doubt. Her problem was that she now believed herself to be in love with him, and she found herself questioning how this could be. He was still a German, the enemy. Like her mother, Mary Anne remained concerned about what other people thought. When the war ended, her family could well ostracize her if she announced her true feelings for the man. And if she married him . . . ? Yet the feelings persisted.

On the Monday of Holy Week, feeling confused, Mary Anne slipped into the hospital chapel where the padre conducted matins and evensong each day. The lesson that night—the Lamentations of the Prophet Jeremiah—only brought home the horror of what she saw daily in the wards. Words from the lesson echoed through her mind: *I am the man that hath seen affliction by the rod of his wrath.*

On Good Friday she walked down to the little Catholic church in the Place St. Vivien, joining the throng of worshipers as they lined the aisles, moving one at a time to kiss the cross in a ritual act of veneration.

Was God dead? she wondered as she came out into the weak spring sunlight. How could He, if He existed, allow all the slaughter to continue? She did not realize then that the butchery was on the brink of getting worse.

3

"They have Casement," Thomson said cheerfully when Charles came into his office on Saturday morning.

"Well, that just about does it, then."

Thomson nodded with some glee. "Yes. They had him yesterday but the idiots didn't realize it. Shaved off beard and hair, I gather. Hall wishes to keep the thing under the counter. They're taking him to Dublin today. He'll be here tomorrow, which means no Easter holiday for us, Charles."

Charles asked about the reaction in Ireland. Thomson gave a sly smile. "No reaction—because nobody knows, young Railton. You want to be in on the interview?"

So it was that Charles sat in Thomson's office, together with a Speical Branch shorthand writer, when they brought Sir Roger Casement in on the following morning. It was not surprising that they had failed to recognize the man, with his beard and head shaved. Even so, this potential traitor behaved with a dignity that Charles could not but admire.

Thomson, though cool in manner, was slightly deferential. Casement barely acknowledged him, sitting down and glaring at the shorthand writer.

Basil Thomson introduced himself, and then Charles, styling him "Mr. Rathbone of one of our Intelligence Services." Casement continued to stare at the writer.

"You are Sir Roger Casement?" Thomson began.

Casement studiously looked away.

"In the early hours of Friday last, April 21st, 1916, you were landed by canvas boat from an enemy submarine—namely the U-19—at Ballyheige Bay, Ireland. Is that correct?"

Casement examined his own hands.

"Sir Roger, your companions in this foolish, though serious, venture, are already in custody. They have said a great deal. I put it to you that you have collaborated with the enemy; that you have been active in obtaining arms and ammunition in order to foment open rebellion against the King, in Ireland; and conspired to bring about an armed rising and breach of the peace; you have also solicited and incited British prisoners of war to turn and fight against their own country. These are acts of treason."

Still there was silence.

Thomson laughed. "At least say something, Sir Roger. Even laugh at the mess everybody's made so far. They've scuttled the arms ship; and, if that wasn't enough, the man who was supposed to drive you to Dublin took a wrong turning and ended up in the River Laune."

Casement raised his head, speaking for the first time. "I wish to talk with you, Commander Thomson, but I'll say nothing while this fellow's taking down every word."

Thomson hesitated for a moment, then nodded to the clerk, who left the room. No sooner was the door closed than Casement began talking.

"I'll not waste time, sir. Naturally you'll bring charges against me, and I shall refute them all. My main object at this moment is to see the record is publicly put straight, and quickly, before there's any bloodshed. Certainly I came back to Ireland—it's my home—but I came for a particular purpose— to put paid to any planned rising or use of force in an attempt to overthrow the government. For heaven's sake, man. I came to *stop* a rebellion, not to lead one. Please, in the name of God, let me make a statement; let me speak out to the Irish newspapers. Let the Irish people know of my arrest and my true reason for returning to Ireland."

Thomson said, quietly, that it was not within his power to allow what Sir Roger asked. However, he would speak to one who could give a ruling.

"Well, do it now! Before it's too late."

"You don't really think any Fenian is going to do anything now the consignment of arms has vanished?"

"I think it's very likely unless they know why I tried to return." The man appeared agitated and concerned.

"See what I can do." Thomson rose and left the room.

Charles made three attempts to speak with their prisoner, but he sat perfectly still; silent and now composed.

After some ten minutes Basil Thomson returned. When he spoke it was with quiet gravity. "I'm sorry. Your request has to be denied. There will be no statement to the effect that you have been arrested. You will not be allowed to speak to the press."

Casement let out a long sigh. "Then be it on your own heads. I'll answer the charges laid against me in a court of law and nowhere else."

"Why?" Charles asked when he was alone with Thomson.

"Why what?"

"You presumably went to Blinker to get permission for a statement. Why was it refused?"

Thomson appeared to think for some minutes. "I suspect that Hall, like myself, is hoping for the impossible. That they'll be stupid enough to try some kind of insurrection. I feel that Blinker Hall wants nobody, least of all Sir Roger Casement, to tell them to call off any plans. Certainly, I wish they would try it on, because if they do, it can be put down with the utmost severity. Once and for all, these Irish lice can be squashed and hit damned hard. They would be taught a lesson they will never forget."

Which is what happened, starting the very next day, and much to the surprise of most people.

On Easter Monday morning, the rebels, without any deep support from the Irish people in general, seized strongpoints both to the north and south of the Liffey, and cut communications with Dublin Castle. Barricades were set up, trenches dug on St. Stephen's Green and at Boland's Flour Mill, covering the approach road to Kingstown to prevent reinforcements reaching Dublin, if landed at that harbor.

The fighting lasted for less than a week. There was to be no appeasement.

When it was over, the court-martials and executions were secret and brutal, to the extent that Irish men and women throughout the country were repelled by their barbarity. Even the severely injured leader James Connolly was shot seated in a chair. The same squad shot an eighteen-year-old boy, Willie Pearse, simply because he was the brother of the outstanding Patrick Pearse.

One of the many to escape was Padraig O'Connell, who, during the thick of the battle, fought by the side of Michael Collins in the Post Office, scene of horrific and heroic action.

Lying in a loft belonging to one of his many friends in County Wicklow, Padraig, for the second time in his life, swore vengeance on the English. The time would come again, and soon, he considered. Now the bulk of the Irish people were behind them in the cause, and next time nothing would stop them.

He thought about his own contacts in Germany. They would need information about the English secret police methods to enable them to fight fire with fire.

And he wondered what had happened to the big German whom Malcolm Railton had almost killed. Presumably he had got out of the country during the confusion, for his burns were almost healed.

4

Most of the family regarded Giles Railton's quiet withdrawal from active official life with some suspicion. As Charlotte put it, "My father-in-law is not the kind of man to turn his face to the wall at the first intimation of mortality." She also admitted that Andrew was the last of the Railtons she would have imagined of infidelity: and she had firm proof of that—six neatly typed pages from Mr. James Prosser, Enquiry Agent of Beak Street.

Charlotte had decided that the whole question of action over Andrew's now blatant adultery should be kept silent. She was certainly not going to throw away the benefits of being a Railton because her husband had decided to do disgusting things with some little tart.

She would do nothing unless the worst happened, and Andrew was stupid enough to ask for a divorce.

In the meantime she continued to help Sara at Redhill; saw Margaret Mary, worried—with both of them—over poor Mildred's obvious deterioration; and, lastly, made a vow to try to like her daughter-in-law Phoebe, who was disliked by most of the family, the only exceptions being Caspar and Margaret Mary.

The others disliked Phoebe for a whole muddle of reasons. "Bossy and dogmatic," said Sara, and "Unreasonable snob," from Mildred in one of her lucid moments. Charles thought her "Sly"; Andrew hardly ever gave a concrete reason; and Giles was blunt and forthright. "Cotton," he grumbled on the one occasion when Charlotte drew him on the subject. "Cotton means the family's in trade. Railtons've never been in trade."

In reality Phoebe was not nearly as dogmatic as some of the family thought. Her bluntness came from a Northern upbringing; her bossiness from having to stand up to an overbearing father. All of it was really a kind of defense against a deep sense of insecurity. In Caspar she had found the person who could fulfill all her wants and requirements, and the one whom she could also respect, love and admire on equal terms.

Caspar himself had made great progress as far as his peg leg was concerned, and they were now talking about the advances in other techniques regarding false limbs. So he had hopes for his arm. But his greatest achievement had been a mastery of the secret work he performed each day.

C, in later years, was to say that Caspar was without doubt the finest Chief of Staff he could ever want. Caspar rarely needed to look up facts from their many files. He seemed to have acquired an almost photographic memory for names, faces, operations and topography. He would, it was whispered, have been the best man for any enemy to kidnap, for he held details of the secret trade in his head as a genius mathematician holds figures.

Like his mother, Charlotte, Caspar had many suspicions regarding his grand-father's semiretirement. "The old bugger's up to something, Phoeb," he told his wife one night. "I mean, he's been in the game longer than any of us;

knows all the tricks. He's got some poor sod in his sights." After a few moments he muttered, "God, no? No, it couldn't be—" In fact, he had fitted the first clues into place within the jigsaw of truth which was so worrying him.

Later that same evening he made an excuse to visit the King Street house, spending some time upstairs trying to talk with his hopelessly retarded brother, Rupert. While he talked, he searched the boy's room.

Ramillies was out, so he crept into his room also, and performed a similar, and fairly thorough, search.

He said nothing to Smith-Cumming, but Caspar was now certainly worried by at least one glimmering and terrible suspicion. A spare white silk scarf was missing from Rupert's old uniform chest. It had been there a few months previously. Caspar had seen it.

5

Malcolm was "cleaned out," as C called it, by his people, MI5 and the Branch. All three departments prepared files which were eventually put together and issued to all the sections—including Admiralty Intelligence—as the up-to-date dossier on revolutionary action in Ireland.

When it was all over, Malcolm declared that he never wished to see that wretched country again. All he wanted was the chance to do some proper farming. But there was the question of his age and fitness, which made him eligible for compulsory military service.

He still lived with his father in Eccleston Square, and Giles did his best to see if matters could be arranged in the young man's favor.

He had even spoken to Sara about Malcolm taking over running the Farm, but Sara's reaction was merely to say that if Malcolm wished to *help* with the running he would be more than welcome.

In the meantime Ramillies visited his grandfather, at Eccleston Square, at least three times a week. Malcolm was always kept well out of the way during the visits.

During the week before the Casement trial, in May, Ramillies came to the house one night much later than usual.

Giles sat opposite the young man, in the Hide, his eyes friendly, yet never leaving Ramillies' face.

"We will not be disturbed," he began. "Malcolm's tucked away and I've sent the servants to bed. Now...." He started as usual, going through the latest events and gossip at the Foreign Office. Ramillies was now his main source of intelligence from within the corridors of diplomatic power.

It was only three days since they had last met, but Ramillies, whose eyes and ears were sharp for detail, was able to play back almost a minute-by-minute résumé of all he had seen and heard in the past seventy-two hours.

"And what of you, Ramillies?" It was the standard question, and Ramillies

JOHN GARDNER

answered with eyes clear of deceit and a silver tongue which would disclose only so much and no more, even to his beloved grandfather.

"Busy as always. You've taught me so much, sir. I find most of the moves come easily enough. . . ."

"Once you've learned the game, you realize there are few variations." The older man smiled. "Like chess."

Ramillies nodded. "I think I have everything under control. Quiet; possible enemies watched; delicate situations placed so they can never bother me again; and—"

"And the Russian?" Giles asked smoothly.

"I still spend four or five hours a day. I think I'll pass when the time comes, as you tell me it will."

Giles nodded. "Now to the reason I asked you here so late." He opened one of his desk drawers. "Here we have certain details; specific documents," unfolding a dossier. "Can you manage to take two days from the office this week without causing ripples?"

"Naturally."

"Good. I want you to go to Scotland, but there are rules in what I shall instruct you to do. Deviation could bring havoc. . . ."

Just as Giles was beginning to tell Ramillies of the action he wished him to take, Sergeant Billy Crook VC was arriving at Waterloo Station to start an unexpected week's leave.

He had been out of the line when the CO sent for him.

"Spot of leave's come up, Sarn't Crook." The Colonel smiled. All very friendly.

"Leave, sir?"

"Mmm. Not really compassionate, but—"

"Not my mother, sir?" Billy's heart skipped a beat. His mother was looking very well at Christmas.

"No-no-no. But it is, er, someone—your former employer, Mrs. Farthing?"

"Mrs. Richard Railton Farthing, sir." It was old Mr. Giles and the rest of the family who had insisted Lady Sara kept the Railton in. Funny how he still always thought of her as Lady Sara.

"Yes, that's it. She has well-placed friends, Sarn't Crook."

"Sir."

There was a pause while the Colonel shuffled papers. "Well, have a good time, Crook. Collect your warrant. Oh . . . and you're not to hang about in Paris or London. Straight to . . . er"—another look down at the papers—"Haversage, is it?"

"Haversage, Berkshire, sir. Yes."

"Off you go then. Lucky devil. Have a good leave."

What could Lady Sara want? No good thinking about it, or worrying. As long as it was not his ma, nothing mattered. A week at Redhill, in early spring. It would be bliss. No guns. No fear.

He took the underground train to Paddington. Haversage, change at Didcot. Next one in half an hour.

It would have been strange, in the crowd, when he finally walked onto the platform, if he had noticed passing the Chief Petty Officer who walked with a stick, as though he had a peg leg. A big man, broad, with one side of his face heavily bandaged. He wore his Number One uniform, with a Navy raincoat and a white silk scarf.

The Chief Petty Officer was heading toward Platform 2. The Bristol train.

6

"Of course they'll find the bastard guilty, Brian. A traitor. Guilty as hell, and they'll hang him for it. I was there, heard the lies—how he was landed to stop the rebellion."

"But..." Wood considered that Charles Railton was a very different man from the one he had known at the outbreak of war.

"I tell you, Sir Roger Casement will hang!" Charles noticed his hands were shaking. His nerves were in shreds. It was not just the job, being close to Thomson for most of the time, reporting to Kell, becoming involved in the puerile interdepartmental feuds; there were the two other viselike pressures.

Mildred would not leave his consciousness. How could someone as steady as Mildred disintegrate so rapidly? She was getting worse, the moods of elation dropping into deep troughs of despair, and short-fused temper.

During the more placid moments he noticed that each month she asked for a small raise in her allowance. Mildred had always managed her finances like a careful bookkeeper. Now she needed more and more.

Charles could not know that Dr. Fisher had subtly removed her from the laudanum and was "treating" her with morphine. Yet Kell had kept his promise, introducing Charles to his medical man, an earnest, likable and obviously dedicated young doctor called Martin Harris.

They had spent an hour together, with Charles answering questions as succinctly as possible. As Vernon suggested, the doctor was amenable to a small plot— a dinner party seemed best. Charles arranged it. But, when the day arrived, Mildred was suffering from "a terrible bilious attack" and the dinner was postponed. Harris then had to be away, so it would now not take place until early August.

On top of all this, there were the illicit demands for information: munitions output; aeroplane types; recruiting; relationships between the War Office and Admiralty. Hardly a week went by without one of the notes, with a short list of questions.

Because he could trust "Brenner," and knew some complex duplicity would prevent the truth reaching those who asked the questions, Charles did as he had been told. He gathered the intelligence, attended the meetings in the tucked-away house, reported in full to Brenner and tried not to think any more about it.

Somewhere though, on the periphery of his mind, hung a large question mark. He even tried to ask Brenner for more details, but the man smiled, shaking his head. "Holy Writ," Brenner said: "In the fullness of time all things shall be accomplished."

And now, Basil Thomson had asked Charles to discuss the white silk scarf murders with Wood and Partridge.

They waited to take a lead from him, and he cleared his throat, saying that they should look at what they knew of this man whom their enemies called The Fisherman.

Certainly he was a saboteur, and a murderer with at least four victims: "Five if you count Miss Drew..."

"Haas, sir," Wood corrected. The policy was that the dead woman should be named in all documents as Hanna Haas. "And we *can't* count her. The modus operandi is totally alien to the others."

"You mean because of the knot? Then we can't count my kinswoman in Ireland, either, because all they got was charred remains—"

"And the testimony of Mr. Malcolm Railton," Wood corrected again. "It's not simply the knot. There were other indications. Whoever killed Miss Haas did not use the same method. The others were quick professional jobs: a scarf looped around the neck from behind, with the ends crossed and pulled—with a knot added like a signature."

Charles nodded. They knew The Fisherman was responsible for the explosion on *HMS Bulwark,* and that he had orders to carry out similar acts. Couldn't they do a reconstruction? Establish motive?

They began to go through each murder in detail; then the dates and the periods of time when they knew exactly where The Fisherman had been.

Fiske, the first victim—the naval officer—was the easiest. He had been in *Bulwark* and had gone on leave the day of the explosion.

"Let us suppose"—Wood had a sheet of paper in front of him—"The Fisherman could not get aboard *Bulwark*. Fiske was used to take a parcel aboard. If it had happened like that, he probably needed to eliminate Fiske."

Charles nodded. "Yes, I accept that Fiske was the carrier; and the only way to explain the chemist, Douthwaite, and the unfortunate Mrs. MacGregor, is that they unwittingly both made some kind of discovery. And Mrs. MacGregor was his lover," he added.

Which left Bridget and the attempt on Malcolm. And who was responsible for the killing of Hanna Haas?

Wood produced the signal ordering The Fisherman to Dublin. Suddenly Charles realized he was in this room not to help with The Fisherman murders but to share any ideas he might have concerning Hanna Haas' death. Thomson had taken him into the web. Now Wood and Partridge were to question him— for the hundredth time, it seemed. He sighed loudly.

"Look, Charles—" Brian Wood almost invariably still called him "sir," but as a chief inspector, he occasionally lapsed. Now the lapse was timed, carefully, like a comforting hand laid on an arm. *You are among friends,* it said. "Both David Partridge and myself have been through the files. We have access. We know what's passed. You're cleared. Nobody suspects you of double-dealing. Folly and indiscretion, yes. But not murder or treachery."

"So?"

"So, just a few ideas. It hit you hard at the time. Did you have any suspicions that she was in danger?" Yes, of course he suspected. She was scared stiff: terrified.

"Of what?"

Terrified of her own people and his. He told of her horror of coming under MI5's protection. "She said it was too soon." And she gave him the succulent morsel about The Fisherman.

"In your opinion, sir"—Partridge this time, replete with respect—"which of our two sides would have benefited most to have her out of the way?"

"Hers of course—if they knew she was under my protection." How did they know? he thought.

"Quite!" Wood smiled. "She was good. Would have spotted someone playing Wenceslas' page, treading in her footsteps?"

"Yes, she would." Then Charles stopped. "By rights she should have spotted your people as well."

"With respect, so should you."

A little light flared in Charles' mind. *He* should have spotted the watchers. He wondered if she *had* spotted them.

Wood asked him why he said that.

"Because I'm really not sure, now, which side *did* benefit most by her death."

"Who could have done it, Charles? Kell's boys? He carries a few spares, with enough violence in them to do away with someone."

Charles shook his head. "C's pug-uglies?"

"Or the Admiralty. I wouldn't put anything past the DNI, or DID, or whatever he calls himself. Unless she was being run as a double by a Firm other than yours, Charles. C's outfit, or the Admiralty Intelligence Department. Please think about it."

He had thought, and wondered, how the killer had got into the Hans Crescent building without being spotted. How had they missed the killer on those strange listening devices?

7

Ramillies was absent from the Foreign Office for two days.

He took a morning train to Glasgow, stayed overnight at the Central Hotel and then paid a visit to the Bank of Scotland's main Glasgow branch.

The visit took less than half an hour.

He returned on the afternoon train, went home and was back at his desk the following morning.

On that last visit to his grandfather, Ramillies had turned as he reached the door. "No, sir," looking into the hard eyes. "No, it's not really like playing chess. More like draughts—what the Americans call checkers."

His grandfather had smiled, and the ice turned to a white, warm fire of pleasure.

8

The Fisherman found a nice little guesthouse in Bristol which catered to sailors between ships, and each night he followed their last instructions—set up his wireless, tuned it, gave his call sign for ten minutes, waited for fifteen, gave his sign for another ten and waited for a further five.

There was no contact. No orders—and he knew what this meant. Find a good target and destroy it before the end of the year. Soon he would move farther north.

9

Sergeant Billy Crook VC stood, tired, near the firing step, dragging on his cigarette, wondering if it had all been some incredible dream. Now, back among the makeshift life, the cheek-by-jowl existence with death, he could hardly believe it.

Lady Sara telling him that Vera was pregnant, asking him if he loved her or if it was merely lust. Billy had been so startled that he had immediately declared his love for Vera: "Always loved her."

"If that's true, Billy, you'd better go and speak to her now. Ask her to marry you, and leave all the arrangements to me."

And before he knew it, there were special arrangements: a license wangled from the Bishop by Lady Sara, and two days after he got back to Redhill, there he was standing in church, with Will Averton, the blind organist, pumping out the "Wedding March," and Vera coming down the aisle on Commander Andrew Railton's arm, and Ted Natter trumpeting into his handkerchief, and Ken Raines with George Sharp, who had both been to school with him, laughing and giggling their heads off, and old Gregory, the schoolmaster, looking amazed that someone like him—Billy Crook—should be old enough to marry at all. And there was Porter, the old soldier, former servant and friend to the General, now looking decrepit, sad, lonely, pensioned off by the family and given a cottage: but there, proud, at the wedding, wearing his medals and trying to stand straight, as if to say, "I represent the General."

Rachel Berry was what they called matron of honor, while townsfolk and people from Redhill laughed and cheered when they came out of church.

Lady Sara did them proud, laying on a big spread in the Manor and arranging a real hotel in Oxford for two nights, and then the last two in London so Vera could see him off on the train.

As for Vera, she promised to be "A real helpmeet, Billy. A true wife to you—that's my vow." Then she almost devoured him in bed at that Oxford hotel, and when he did her she came like the old Haversage Tramway Company's train whistle, so that he thought everyone in the whole blessed house would hear.

And it went on like that, every night for the whole time, right up to an hour before he had to catch the train.

He smiled grimly as the machine guns began to rattle; having seen the front along their part of the line, Billy did not fancy their chances. Attacking over the top along the Somme was, in his humble opinion, as stupid as walking straight into a threshing machine at harvest time.

10

They brought Roger Casement to trial on June 26th, and even dragged Paddy Quinn out of retirement to be present.

Casement was charged with six specific overt acts of treason, including soliciting and inciting British subjects who were ". . . prisoners of war at Limburg Lahn Camp to renounce their allegiance and fight against the King."

The trial lasted three days, and the jury was left in no doubt of their duty by the Lord Chief Justice. They were out for one hour only. The verdict: *Guilty.*

Before sentence of death was passed, Casement read a long, rambling, vain statement which seemed almost to aim at warping history. Immediately after sentence he lodged an appeal.

There followed a strange incident in which none of the Railtons took an active part. Yet all of them heard the rumors, and wondered on the truth.

The Prime Minister wavered over the death sentence passed on Casement. Public opinion changed to sympathy, and there was much lobbying. One of the many protests was signed by powerful men, including authors like John Galsworthy, Arnold Bennett and G. K. Chesterton. The Americans put Asquith under pressure, and Cabinet Ministers warned that Casement should be allowed to live.

The Branch had been out to nail Casement for years. Now Blinker Hall and Basil Thomson had done it. Also, whatever the truth about Casement's statement—that he wanted to stop an Irish rebellion—Hall and Thomson had successfully kept the press at bay and, almost surely, contributed to that unhappy Easter rising which allowed the Military to inflict ruthless justice.

It is said that Hall and Thomson now inflicted a justice of their own. Alarmed that the death sentence would not be carried out, they dug into the secret hoard originally taken from Sir Roger's flat—the diaries.

Certain pages were copied and backed up with original photographs. The extracts were chosen with care, for they all proved Casement to be a sexual deviant—an acknowledged homosexual. The documents were sent, it is again said, on Hall's and Thomson's instructions, under plain envelope, by messenger. They went to the most influential of those who lobbied for the Irishman's life: to people who could be frightened off by being seen to support a homosexual— still a grave and revolting sin at that time. So, by guile, Blinker Hall and Basil Thomson brought their man to his destiny: or so some say.

Any sympathy for Casement quite suddenly evaporated, and the appeal was dismissed. He was hanged on August 3rd, the day Charles had arranged for the second attempt at getting Mildred to meet Dr. Harris, who came to Cheyne Walk as a "colleague."

11

Mildred was embarrassingly wild and excited, even flirting with Harris. During the meal, and later, Charles listened, noting the odd question dropped into the conversation by the doctor. As the evening progressed, Mildred began to slip into a darker, more nervous mood. Her confidence appeared to dwindle, and at about ten-thirty in the evening she excused herself and went to bed.

Harris remained silent for a few minutes, sipping his brandy.

"She needs to be in hospital, old chap," he said at last. "It doesn't require an expert to see that she's an addict—probably morphine—in an advanced state. You can't just commit her, and we can't even appeal to the medical man from whom she's getting the stuff."

"What happens if—"

"If we do nothing? Charles, I'm sorry. She's far gone. It'll take a long time, with concentrated medical care, to bring her back to normal. It could be impossible. If we do nothing she'll be dead within three months."

12

Denise Grenot, under the name of Jacqueline Baune, boarded the tram at her usual stop, in Lanaeken. For some time she had been doing the run about twice a week, as there was great need for information about German reinforcements as the great battles along the Western Front plunged to and fro, winning or losing a couple of hundred yards here or there.

The Frankignoul network had done more than its fair share to provide accurate and regular intelligence reports, and they followed what was considered to be a foolproof system.

Two members of the organization always made the tram journey into Holland together, one carrying the information, in the sole of a shoe, sewn into clothing, or by some other ingenious method. The other was the lookout. Today, Denise was watching an old Belgian called Paul, who carried the latest figures on munitions trains.

Her job was to make certain that Paul got into Holland safely and made the rendezvous with their contact in Maastricht. She had to be sure the carrier was not followed, then check that she had not been watched. After an hour or so, she would return, with a full shopping bag, to Belgium.

They reached the frontier post, and the German police came on board. It was usually a perfunctory search, yet somehow today Denise detected tension. The Germans hardly looked at anything or anybody. They appeared to take no notice of Paul, who carried a shopping bag which seemed to have been made of a hundred pieces of differently dyed leather, patched together over long winter evenings. Paul was well over seventy years of age and looked frail.

This was an asset to them. Who would imagine an old fool like Paul would have the wit to smuggle information into Holland for onward communication?

Denise became concerned. The police still did nothing, but they were definitely loitering. The tram driver called to them, asking in a mixture of French and German how much longer they were going to be? One of the policemen shrugged and pretended to look under the seats.

She heard the car before she actually saw it—an open vehicle with a long hood: four men packed into the seats. They wore German uniforms, and exploded from the car like a team of comic acrobats, but there was nothing amusing about these men.

One carried a rifle, the others were armed with pistols, and they came straight onto the tram, making a beeline for Paul. He did not even protest as they dragged him away.

Nobody took any notice: there was already enough trouble in their lives. Best not to fuss. Look the other way.

The bell clanged and the tram rattled forward toward Holland and the Dutch border guards. The last Denise saw of Paul was one of the soldiers punching him as they pushed the old man into the car. She thought she glimpsed blood on his face.

Chapter Twenty-Seven

1

They moved James to an old castle, high, among rocks and fir trees, the walls clad with barbed wire like some pernicious ivy. "It is not going to be play here," the Commanding Officer said. "We make you work for your living." The Commanding Officer was an elderly man with many tales of his long and gallant service in the Cavalry.

James believed he was now somewhere in the Rhineland; he appeared to be the only prisoner in this old and drafty castle; and he was still treated with respect. It confused him. Normally all he could expect was interrogation followed by a firing squad.

The Professor's words kept returning: *You have a special protection.* Marie? he wondered. Had she used her influence to make certain that her cousin was kept apart from other prisoners, a secret prisoner, held against the day when the war ended? What then?

All he could do was keep some kind of faith. He recited Shakespeare; flew, in his mind; listened to Margaret Mary playing her piano in their nice little house. There were moments when he even thought he heard the children romping and laughing.

But here they did not leave him alone for too long at a stretch. At the end of the first week James found himself confronted by an English-speaking stonemason for whom he was forced to act as laborer.

Some of the castle's inner walls were in need of repair, and the stonemason instructed him in menial tasks—hauling great slabs of masonry, setting up primitive blocks and tackle.

In the evenings he would dine with the Commandant, who, between his stories of cavalry charges, duels and codes of honor, allowed news of the war's progress to slip out—between the fruit and cheese, like an extra course.

James took it all with the proverbial pinch of salt—tales of huge French losses around Verdun; the bitter fighting on the Somme; and the decimation of the British armies.

"At Verdun the fighting continues day and night," the Commandant told him. "We shall win before Christmas."

It was much later that James Railton discovered the truth—the horrific casualties, the desperate conditions of battle and the problems experienced by Army commanders short of supplies and men.

The year moved on. At least James was conscious of time passing, and a change in the seasons. Then one night—he thought toward the end of August—the Commandant dropped separate pieces of old news. Both worried James. One he considered certainly accurate.

First, according to the Commandant, Lord Kitchener himself had been killed—drowned when the ship carrying him had gone down. Second, back in May there had been a great naval battle. The Commandant said it was now Germany that ruled the waves.

2

Even the men and women in the towns, villages and cities of Britain could have been excused for thinking that Germany ruled the waves, following the Battle of Jutland earlier in the year, for the official communiqué, issued by the government, appeared to be weighted almost in favor of the enemy.

At Redhill, reading the report, Sara was plunged into gloom, telephoning Charlotte immediately.

"I don't see all that much of Andrew," Charlotte said sharply. "But, yes, it isn't good; though he tells me the business was not as bad as painted."

"Have we really lost six cruisers and eight destroyers?"

Charlotte replied flatly that this was so. "I understand over six thousand men died."

Andrew now worked between Room 40 and the War Room at the Admiralty, and even he was not to know the full extent of courage, brilliance and failure which had played a part in the one major naval action of the war.

Only much later did they winkle out the truth about the Battle of Jutland.

It was true that the British losses were great, displaying weaknesses in armor and armament, but by the beginning of June, the German fleet was once more bottled up in their ports, unable to move—as they had been since 1914. The Grand Fleet, in spite of its losses, had been ready for action again within a few weeks. The German High Seas Fleet would never be the same.

Like so many officers engaged in battle from the comparative safety of war rooms, or cipher tables, Andrew learned of the full impact only during the following months. Seldom at King Street anymore, he could usually be found either at the Admiralty or at the fair Miss Greatorex's Mayfair flat. That he was now more sober and fully attuned to his duties became obvious to his superiors. Yet, any who could get close detected a deep unhappiness in the man.

Andrew's current despair stemmed from a disenchantment with his way of life, and, in particular, his relationship with Grizelda Greatorex.

In the beginning the attraction had been intense and purely physical. After a lifetime of steady family life and the careful secrecy of his father, combined with Charlotte's amusing, though serious, running of their household, the attractive young girl was so novel as to sweep him from his feet.

Once off his feet, Andrew also discovered a resurgence of his own virility, which, through the blows suffered within the family, had become nonexistent. The failure had not been his alone, for both Andrew and Charlotte had, in their separate ways, failed to be of true comfort to each other during those gloomy days early in the war. Locked in their own private griefs, they had failed to share. So, when opportunity presented itself, Andrew quickly learned tricks which only a younger girl could teach.

But the honeymoon was over. Charlotte, now fully apprised of the affair, took no action. The relationship between Andrew and Grizelda drifted. Andrew felt torn in two, loath to leave the delights of Miss Greatorex's bed, yet filled with need for the more mature conversation and contact he had so valued in Charlotte.

The matter was resolved by an odd incident which could have cost Andrew his entire future in the Royal Navy.

One evening in June he took Grizelda to dinner at the Savoy. As she prattled on about the terrible shortage of food, the standard of servants and the abysmal quality of current fashions, Andrew's mind, and gaze, began to wander. Across the restaurant he spotted Blinker Hall, dining, deep in conversation with a man in civilian dress whom he recognized as having seen once or twice in the Admiralty corridors.

Half to himself he muttered, "I wonder who the hell *he* is?"

"Who, darling?" Grizelda stopped chattering, quickly glancing in the direction Andrew had been looking.

"Naval officer; captain, over there—"

"You should know him if he's RN—"

"I do. Not the other. I work for *him.*"

"So that's the legendary Blinker Hall, is it?"

"How did you—?" He frowned and she patted his hand.

"You talk in your sleep, silly. No . . . Daddy told me about him. Who is it you don't know?"

"Fellow he's with. Fellow in mufti."

"Oh, *him.* That's easy. He's an American. Met him at a party. Something to do with the Embassy. I'll ask Daddy for you."

Andrew had forgotten what a garrulous creature Miss Greatorex could be.

The next evening, in the middle of a long, dreary story of some girlfriend who had been wounded while driving an ambulance in France, Grizelda suddenly stopped. "That chap you asked about. I found out from Daddy. Name of Bell. Eddie Bell. They call him Ned Bell. Second Secretary at the American Embassy. Thick as thieves with Reggie Hall, Daddy says . . ."

At 10:30 the next morning Commander Andrew Railton found himself in the DNI's office. Blinker Hall looked flushed, and Andrew was not asked to sit down. Then the DNI addressed him formally.

"Commander Railton, you are on intimate terms with a Miss Grizelda Greatorex?"

Andrew, still puzzled at the summons, said he was.

"You also appear to be more than unduly interested in my private life." Hall blinked furiously.

"I'm sorry, sir. I don't follow you."

"Don't you indeed? Did you not ask Miss Greatorex specifically to find out the name of the man with whom I was dining at the Savoy the night before last?"

"Not quite like that, sir, no."

"Not *quite?* Then how, Commander?"

Andrew struggled to find the right words. He was dining with Miss Greatorex at the Savoy where he saw the DNI. "I think I said something idle, like, I wonder who that fellow is—"

"You said, 'That fellow dining with the Director of Naval Intelligence,' did you?"

"Certainly not, sir! I may be foolish about some things, but not about security."

"Indeed." Hall sounded unconvinced. "You know this woman Greatorex's father?"

"No, sir, I've never had the pleasure..."

"No pleasure, Commander. No pleasure at all, I can tell you. The man's an out-and-out profiteer. Into all kinds of schemes in the City, and outside it. Buying up half the decent land in Surrey and Sussex. Talks about putting up what he calls *bijou résidences*. Says he'll make what he refers to as 'a killing' after the war. No, Commander, it's no pleasure. But he happens, by some grievous error on the part of the committee, to belong to my club. I stay away from the blighter, but he struck up conversation with me last night. Said his daughter had been asking after me, and out came this story—that one of my officers had been enquiring the name of the man with whom I was dining. His version—Greatorex's version—is that you had specifically invited his daughter to find out Eddie Bell's name. You deny that?"

"Emphatically, sir."

Hall blinked violently. "I accept your denial, Railton. Accept it completely. Fellow's a bounder. Sit down."

Like the passing of a spring squall, Blinker Hall's manner changed to one of almost avuncular friendliness. "Railton, when I heard all this, I took the trouble to make certain enquiries. Having a rough time at home, are you?"

"Things haven't been good, sir. No."

"Not my business, Railton, but I feel I must give you some advice. Keep away from the Greatorex gel. The map says, 'There be dragons.'"

"Thank you, sir." Inside, Andrew boiled with fury at the way Grizelda had distorted the whole affair.

"Tell you what." The DNI smiled. "Take a couple of days' leave. Sort yourself out."

'Aye-aye, sir!" Andrew saluted and left. Within an hour he had been to Grizelda's flat, put a curt note on the tiny hall table, together with his key, collected what clothes he had left there and was on his way to King Street.

Charlotte wasn't at home, so he made himself comfortable in the familiar surroundings. When she returned, Charlotte gave him a cursory look and headed for the stairs. He called after her:

"Charlotte, I need to talk. . . . *We* need to talk."

She paused, a foot raised to the next stair, then half-turned. "*We?* Who are *we?* The Greatorex strumpet and yourself, Andrew?"

"Grizzle . . . Grizelda has nothing to do with this..."

"You're joking, of course! She has everything to do with it."

"She is nothing; she was never anything. . . . Never anything that mattered, Charlotte. Please, come down and talk. I want—"

"*You* want? You? I can believe it, dear Andrew, because it's always been what *you* want. Not what I wanted, or poor Rupert, or Caspar, or even Ramillies, who hardly speaks now, like a creeping Jesus around the house." But she had started to descend and come toward him.

"I want to change that." His voice remained steady. "I want us to try . . . to try and make amends . . ."

She laughed in his face, close to him, and they began to argue, shout, brawl, until it was done.

"Of course I always knew he'd come back," Charlotte confided on the telephone to Sara later that evening. "We're off to the Ritz tomorrow night, and a show. Quite like old times."

3

Caspar was concerned. First, that afternoon a batch of signals had come in from the War Office. From their contents it looked as though at least one of their networks—*Frankignoul*—had been penetrated by the Germans, while the most recent signals from *Sacré Coeur* had the hallmark of indecision. He waited for most of the day, while C sent for "technicians," as he liked to call them: experts in a dozen different fields, some of them with very shady backgrounds.

It was September, and Phoebe's time would soon be up. "You look like the side of a house—Buck House," he laughed, returning home that night.

"Oh, if only it was as pleasant carrying and pupping as it is in the getting." Phoebe sighed. "I shall forswear fucking when this is over."

"Stop talking like an idiot barmaid, Phoeb. We both know you'll be at it like a rattlesnake soon as the quack says it's feasible. It's me, I know. Too damned attractive by half."

Phoebe saw his attention suddenly wander. He was staring at the fire. "Cas . . . what's wrong?"

A hundred things, he volunteered—no, a million things, and all on the secret side. She pestered, and finally he gave way: it was his brother Ramillies who worried him most. "Never seen him at our end of the street before. He's thick with Grandpa—and I've got a lot of time for that old bugger—but my wretched little brother gives me the creeps. He was coming out of C's office this morning, just as I got in. 'Hello, Ram,' I say, trying to be bright, and all he does is give that bloody smirk and tiptoe past my desk . . ." He stopped speaking, as Phoebe, who had been leaning against the chair, suddenly doubled up with a cry. "Phoeb? What the hell is it, Phoeb?"

"Oh Christ, no!" she gasped. "No—the little blighter's trying to get out. Cas, Christ, the waters . . ."

He managed to get her into the hospital, and she produced a baby boy six hours later. They called him Giles after Caspar's grandfather. It was the first week of September.

A week later, at Redhill Manor, Mrs. Billy Crook went through the same kind of ordeal. This time a little girl—Martha Sara. They sent a telegram to Billy, and received one back: TERRIFIC VERA DARLING CAN WE TRY AGAIN SOON? IN THE PINK. BILLY.

4

Dick Farthing lifted the nose of the little DH-2, seeking cloud cover. The aeroplane climbed well. You just stuck the nose up, opened the throttle and she went uphill like a Norton motorcycle.

This was the bit he did not like, getting home after a photo-reconnaissance. You were always vulnerable in the DH-2, even at the best of times, sitting out in the front, with the great Gnome rotary clattering away behind you and the wind pushing in your face and making it almost impossible to change drums on the one Lewis mounted directly in front. But it was worse with the huge, boxlike camera clamped onto the side.

Now, just as he was approaching their lines again, he saw a pair of Albatros, hunting. He flicked into the cloud, feeling the dampness on his face. When would they send the long-promised Sopwith Pups, with which the squadron was supposed to be re-equipped? Next week, the Squadron Commander had told them. Next week; next month; next year. You would not be so exposed in a Pup, and you would have more firepower; and you wouldn't be doing any photography.

He glanced at the compass, corrected and decided to take a peep below. It should be about right. It was. Ruined church to starboard, and behind that the terrible stained snake of the trenches, great zigged and zagged scars, with the pockmarks and scabs stretching almost as far as the eye could see.

He banked to port and saw the farm, then the copse, and beyond it the field. There were three other DH-2s just taxiing in as he lined up, and he caught sight of an elder, bigger, sister—a two-seater FE-2—parked near the Mess.

Dick was walking back toward the Mess—a tin hut hidden in the trees—when the adjutant called out to him, saying the CO wanted a word. "Got a visitor." He raised his eyebrows.

The CO had flown with them that morning, and had only just got down himself. He sat in a cluttered office, the desk piled with paper, odd bits of flying kit on chairs, and part of an Albatros prop, splintered, nailed to the wall.

"Get the snaps, Dick?" The CO lit a cigarette.

"Yeah, sure. Get an Albatros?"

"As a matter of fact..." Major Stanley Grouse—and there were many waggish comments about *his* name—stopped. "I'm sorry. We have a guest. Captain Farthing—Second-Lieutenant Berry, 70 Squadron."

Dick looked hard, then grinned. "I know you. My God, Bob Berry! Redhill.

You were at my wedding, Bob, but that wasn't even a year ago, and you were a private then..."

Berry rose, stretching out his hand. "A sergeant actually, sir. I didn't want to worry Rachel. I'd almost finished flying training. Been out here since February."

"Well. My God..." Dick really did not know what to say, so Stanley said it for him: "Mr. Berry's come to see you. There's a job for you with 70 Squadron if you'll do it.

"Job? I've got a goddamned job."

"No, Dick. One job. One sortie. Special."

"What do I know about 70 Squadron?" Something nagged at the back of Dick's mind.

"Special Operations, sir," Berry said.

"Oh Christ, yes! Yeah, I do know about 70 Squadron. You do appalling things like landing people behind the lines. No thank you."

"Could you just hear it out, sir?"

"Listen to him, Dick." Almost an order from Major Grouse. "They've come to you for a reason."

"Right."

"You remember Mr. Giles, sir?"

"Can I ever forget?"

"His daughter—the one in France. Paris. You know..."

Dick nodded, almost winking at Berry, who was obviously not going to go into the whole saga in front of Major Grouse.

"She had two children. The boy was killed in '14, the girl's been working behind the lines. Situation's difficult. We've instructions to pick her up, this week. Any morning between six and six-thirty. Our CO's been to London to collect the details. Problem is, they're really not sure if it's her or a trap to get one of our boys on the ground."

He looked Dick straight in the eyes. There were lines of strain around his mouth. "You see, I've never really met her, sir. Not to make a certain identification..."

"And I have." Dick tightened his mouth.

"Quite, sir. You *would* know her, wouldn't you?"

"Of course I'd know her, Bob. Dark hair; looks like a dream walking; answers to the name of Denise." He dropped into a chair and lit a cigarette. "When do we do it?"

"Soon as possible. Tomorrow. Day after."

Dick inhaled smoke. "Day after tomorrow." He nodded. "Give me time to get used to one of those monsters." He meant the FE-2. "I suppose that's what I fly?"

Bob Berry nodded.

"We get cover?"

"We're covering you." Stanley Grouse stubbed out his cigarette. "We'll all have to go over to Abele and have a look at the maps and orders. Going to be a long trip, Dick. You pick her up from a field the other side of Tournai."

"I just hope to God it's her." He did not add that he also hoped he still recognized her.

5

Charles was away. Though Mildred did not know it, he had gone up North with Wood and Partridge on the trail of the Fisherman. But she remembered that he was away the moment she woke, in the darkness of her room at Cheyne Walk.

The shaking was bad, and the craving even worse.

She got out of bed, remembering to put on her wrap, went to the window and pulled back the curtains. There was no moon outside.

Her whole body shook; her skull was full of bees.

She fell once, getting to the desk where she kept the things. It was a thousand years since Dr. Fisher had shown her how to do the injection.

She took one ampoule, then another, in case of mistakes, and carried them, with the syringe, back to the bed.

She had to go and draw the curtains again, because she needed to put on the light. Shakespeare went through her head; it was catching, this Railton passion for Shakespeare: *Put out the light, and then put out the light.*

The flash in her head came just as she was emptying the syringe. Then her head exploded. She thought she had got the stuff into a vein before it happened, but was not sure.

It was real, and at last she knew it had happened. Knew it, remembered it—even his name. Bryden. Young Peter Bryden. Fair hair. Cheeky. Older than her, and knew all about it. But she knew more, because she had read one of Papa's hidden books. They planned it. In the woods. Oh God, no. I'll be punished if I say I loved it; and there was blood. It hurt to begin with, but then it was all warm and nice. She wanted to do it again and again. Now, in the silence of the night, she screamed; and her mind churned with the guilt. Oh God, and then Mary Anne. Forgive! The young face of Peter, over her in the dark woods. The little pain. The big pleasure.

6

Matron did not have the stern look she usually wore when you were sent for.

"Sit down, Railton." She even smiled.

"Thank you, Matron." Something's up.

"I have bad news, my dear—"

"Oh God, not my father. Not Papa, Matron—"

"No, my dear. I'm sorry. Terribly sorry. It's your mother. You'll get compassionate leave, straight away, of course."

But Mary Anne was not thinking about leave. It was horrible. She knew it was horrible, but she felt no sadness.

Far away, there was the noise of the guns.

Chapter Twenty-Eight

The whole of Dick's squadron flew to join him at Abele the next afternoon. By the time they arrived, he had done an hour in the more cumbersome FE-2. Dick considered it noisy and uncomfortable, but managed half a dozen take offs and landings, trying to get the machine in and out using the shortest possible amount of field.

Seventy Squadron's CO—Captain Cruickshank—took him and Stanley Grouse through the essentials of the operation. Denise had been given a code name, "Dot," and was never referred to by her real name.

The field chosen for her pickup was on the outskirts of a village in open country, about ten kilometers east of Tournai. "Very unhealthy country," commented Captain Cruickshank. "We've only used it once before."

If he approached in a northeasterly direction, Dick could taxi almost to the corner of the field. It had the only cover for miles—a small clump of trees. Dot should be waiting in the trees.

"Make an identification, haul her on board and get the hell out quickly," Cruickshank advised, before adding the more unpleasant details. "If it turns out to be the wrong person or if she gets herself wounded on the way to your aeroplane, you shoot her. No sentiment. Orders very much from on high."

"Oh hell!" Dick groaned.

"Best for her in the long run."

Dick nodded gloomily and spent the afternoon studying maps and photographs of the area. Then, before dusk, he took the FE-2 for a final test.

1

Denise had been shopping—not that there was much to buy in Lanaeken these days. After waiting for three hours she had emerged with a cabbage and half a stick of bread.

As she came round the corner of Avenue Sint-Ulrik, where she lived with a married couple, both members of the network, she felt quite happy. They could make soup from the cabbage, and this was the first bread they had seen for ten days.

There were two cars and a horse-drawn van outside the house. Soldiers blocked off the road, and she could just see the couple being dragged into the van. Denise remembered what she had been told, and kept on walking, turning right down the small, unnamed, lane which ran almost up to the church.

She had a little money, and even stopped to count it. It would probably get her to Brussels. At the station she waited for an hour—every minute an agony. The railway station would be the first place they would look. If they had got the couple, they must know about her—Jacqueline Baune.

The train came in, and she found a full compartment. They always said choose a full compartment.

She broke the journey at Leuven. They would be watching for trains direct from Lanaeken, and she had some idea of taking a local. But there were police about, so she left the station and took the bus on into Brussels.

It was almost curfew when she knocked at Marguerite Walraevens' door, in the Rue Medori. Marguerite's house was the receiving office for the *Biscops* network, and there was a wireless there. All agents had been given escape routes. Denise drew Marguerite.

She was calm and very collected, even when she told Denise, almost as an aside, that her description had been circulated, together with another. "Only two of you got out. I think they penetrated the whole network, Jacqueline."

Then she gave Denise the options—to hole up in the cellar, which could be the safest, or to make a run for it. If she ran, they would send an aeroplane. That meant walking, and living rough for two days: "And two nights, in the cold. It's a long walk, and if you don't make it, there's no second chance."

Denise said she would make it. She wanted to go now.

Marguerite shrugged. It would be arranged. She had to pass on wireless messages at 11:45. The answer would be back before dawn. Denise was given maps and shown the best route. "You'll have to memorize it," Marguerite told her. "You can't take the maps with you."

She worked until three in the morning, with Marguerite's assistant giving her the questions and answers. At five, they said it was on. "Start walking about eight," she was told.

The first night was not bad. She made good time and found a barn near a farm. There was straw for warmth.

The second day was not so good. The wind became bitter and cutting, and Denise's joints had stiffened. She plodded on, over open country, sticking to cover.

By dusk she reached the rise which gave a view of the village and the field. Any elation was banished when she saw the two trucks in the village center and soldiers crowding around the cafés.

2

A squadron of Sopwith Pups was landing as he returned, and the Mess was crowded for the briefing.

The Pups were there for support, and the briefing took an hour. There were a lot of questions, and nobody appeared to be happy about the plan. Cruickshank closed the bar at seven, and ordered all ranks to stay on the 'drome.

They took off just before dawn, using gasoline-soaked rags in oil drums to mark the boundaries of the field—a very uncomfortable way of going, as witnessed by two pilots who collided, one following too close to the other. Happily neither man was injured, but the operational strength was reduced accordingly.

Half of the Pups climbed high, with some of Dick's own squadron. The others stayed almost at trench height, putting Dick himself at five thousand feet, with a pair of Pups watching his tail.

The dawn came up with its usual blood-red glow, magnified by the flickering crimson flashes of the guns performing their dawn ritual. Some of the explosions lit the whole sky, and as the sun rose behind smoky dark cloud, the whole familiar map of horror unfolded itself below them: the earth brown, black and sand-colored, gashed and wounded.

They crossed the German lines, and the "archie" began. Dick took evasive action, forgetting for a second that he was flying a slower, heavier machine, so that his first steep turn almost toppled him from the sky.

They appeared to be concentrating on the section above him, and nasty black puffs appeared around the Pups and DH-2s. Dick winced as one of his own squadron's aeroplanes turned too close, losing its tail, hesitating, before it plummeted to explode in an oily fire among ravaged trees.

3

She judged it would take her about half an hour to get to the clump of woodland stretching back from the corner of the fields. It meant staying awake all night and crossing the open ground at first light.

The soldiers below in the village made a lot of noise until the early morning, then things fell silent. Just her, Denise thought, the cold and, somewhere, an aeroplane ready to get her out. As the first signs of day showed in the east, she moved down toward the trees.

The ground was difficult, and she fell several times, cutting a knee and grazing the palm of her hand. It was day now, and she felt naked, afraid, and with an intuition that all was not well.

She reached the road. The trees, and their cover, lay only about half a kilometer ahead, and she began to run as she heard the sound of an engine.

At first she thought it was a German truck, then she realized it came from the air. They were here to get her.

Then the noise changed, and with horror Denise heard what could have been an echo of the aeroplanes' engines. This time she knew it was a German truck.

The trees lay ahead, to the right. She glimpsed the aeroplane, then, glancing back along the road, saw the truck, gathering speed, with men leaning from the back.

The first bullets hit the bank and edge of the road. The next volley cracked over her head, and she flung herself toward the trees. Then there were cracks and thumps, and the *acka-tacka* of machine guns.

4

It took almost an hour of flying by compass and map reference. Dick spotted a crossroads given to him as a navigation point, realizing that he was a mile or so to the right of where he should be. He corrected, looked behind and above, aware of only one Sopwith Pup with him.

He throttled back, holding his turn, losing height, searching for the next reference point. It took an age to come up—a stream crossing his front—and, as he saw it, he also spotted the road at right angles, and the field, ahead.

The aeroplane was obeying him now, like a horse adjusting to a new master. Dick touched the rudder, slewing the nose, then banking to his right, cutting back power, turning to line up for the correct approach.

Down to a couple of hundred feet now, with the field, looking soggy and dew-damp, ahead. He felt the slap of cold as a breeze rustled in, and the nose lifted slightly.

One hundred feet, and the angle of the hedge in line, nose still trying to tilt down and take him barreling into the grass. Then, as he crossed the high hedge, Dick felt the wash of the Pup making a pass to his right, following the line of the road. Even above the engine he heard the stutter of guns.

Christ! Something up. He could do nothing about it now. The aeroplane was near to stallling, the stick almost right back against his stomach. Then the thud, and the rumble of his wheels.

He blipped the engine to taxi at full speed toward the trees, and saw the Pup passing again to his right—the pilot signaling, pointing forward, then firing again. Something on the road.

The trees came up fast, and Dick began to turn, ready to open up the engine and make a quick takeoff, knowing the breeze was now stiff.

Then there she was, dragging a small brown suitcase, a thin figure in a long beige coat and black hat, running from the trees as though hounds were after her—the little fox breaking cover.

He recognized her, but was taking no risks. *"For this relief, much thanks,"* he yelled, and heard the answer strong: *"For I am cold, and sick at heart."*

"Name of the study at Redhill?" Her face was almost level with his.

"General's Study," she panted.

"Your grandfather's study?"

"The Hide. For God's sake, the Boche're just behind!" And she rolled into the cockpit, pulling the case in after her, just as the Pup came straight overhead, firing and swinging its tail, trying to traverse the area behind the trees. You could see the branches leap and dance, or drop as the bullets carved through bark and wood.

As he opened the engine, kicking the rudder to bring the tail around, Dick glimpsed two soldiers breaking from the trees. A second later something hissed past his head, so he banged the throttle open and began the bumpy ride over the grass.

He was leaning forward, trying to will more speed. The breeze clapped him hard on the left side, pushing the nose to the right. He would need more room, more space to reach a safe flying speed. The machine bucked, trembling, hitting ruts in the field, slowing down its forward motion. And all the time there were angry bees zipping past him.

He felt one of the bees sting his leg—just a swift burn, and then a whole full bloom of pain spreading as far as his right knee. He cried out, pushing the leg against the rudder, and finding that the movement produced a rough, grinding agony.

They were never going to make it. The hedge loomed up, and, airspeed or not, he pushed the stick forward an inch. The tail responded, but they were still too slow, the hedge racing toward them at a terrifying pace. He knew his mouth was open in a scream, felt the fire in his right leg and gently drew back the stick. It felt mushy, as though the elevator was not reacting, then there was a sudden pull and, almost in slow motion, the nose lifted. But not high enough, for they were almost level with the hedge. He gave the stick another half-inch, knowing it could heave the nose too high, leaving them sitting in a pile of wood, metal and canvas which just would not fly.

It would drop from the sky, he was convinced, and the entire weight of the Beardmore engine would go straight through his back. But the machine remained stable, groaning a shade, rocking as it clawed for air. They were just going to clear the hedge... only just. Then the main wheels hit the edge of the thick growth.

They seemed to stop for a good five seconds, and he heard her scream above the wind and the terrifying crackle as the wheels were ripped away. They dropped, ten, fifteen feet. He felt the elevator brush the hedge, then by some miracle they were still flying, only a few feet above the ground, with part of the wheel structure banging on the grass below.

Dick held her there, not moving the stick, punching the pedals to keep the nose straight, his right leg now so numb that he could only hope he was moving the rudder. The speed built, painfully. They began to climb, almost an inch at a time.

The Pup came down flying alongside at around five hundred feet, its pilot pointing underneath the FE-2. Dick shouted, "I know! Of course I bloody know, you idiot!"

The whole machine lacked stability, but slowly made two thousand feet, and then he realized how weak he was. The agony in his leg turned to a kind of racking, constant pain, as though someone had taken a blunt knife, cut through the flesh and was now systematically rubbing the blade up and down his shinbone. It also felt very wet when he put his hand down.

The instruments swam for a second, then the horizon tilted. *Concentrate, Farthing, you fool,* he told himself. Two more Pups and one DH-2 had joined him. Together they reached the German line, and he did not notice much about "archie," except there was a lot of it, and he could not take any evasive action.

The smell of cordite was mixed with oil and gasoline, and the heavy aeroplane became more difficult to fly, the stick jumping around in his hands as the wings were rocked and slapped by the explosions.

Then the three Albatroses arrived, and he could do nothing about them except fly on, worry about his course and hope to God the Pups and DH-2 would take care of him. They must have done so, because quite suddenly they were alone. Presently Grouse's DH-2 came up on the starboard side, indicating that he would lead him home. They were almost at the 'drome before Dick realized that the most difficult part still lay ahead. He was flying an aeroplane not known for its easy handling at low level, and near stalling speed. The aeroplane had no wheels, and Lord knew what garbage hanging loose underneath.

Grouse lined him up and waved good luck. Dick began to lose height.

They seemed to have cleared the field for him, and he knew this could not be a copybook landing. Get her down, straight and level, he thought. Just try and let her drift onto the so tempting grass below, and see what happens.

He thought of Sara—the mornings on the Downs above Redhill, when she was still married to John, and had come out to see him land.

For a moment, as the grass came ever closer, he could have sworn she was standing there, over to his right, by the Pups, lined up away from the hangars.

The nose was terribly heavy. It was all too heavy. Shouldn't have put this bloody great engine behind us, he thought. The engine's so damned big that it lifts the nose as soon as you calm it down. The engine was almost completely calmed now, just ticking over, and the nose still went up . . . up . . . up. Stick forward. More you stupid sonofabitch. More and more and more. Get the nose down and keep her level. Don't you want to see Sara again? He was all too aware of that goddamned engine behind him, and he tried to sing, only his throat was too dry.

Like a feather floating down, they touched, lifted, touched again, lifted . . . and the feather became a grinding, crackling, shredding horror of wood, fabric and metal.

5

They took Mildred's body back to the Essex village where she had been born
and had grown up. The Parsonage had changed little, Charles felt. It was about
all he felt, apart from the numbness.

As they left the graveside, he looked up and saw the small patch of woodland
that bordered the Parsonage garden. That's where it happened, he thought.
Where it all began. A little girl, terrified by the thought of sin and the eternal
damnation preached twice every Sunday by her pompous father, comes to sin
like a moth to the flame.

We have heard the chimes at midnight.

"What did you say, Papa?"

"Nothing. We must go, Mary Anne. Little William Arthur needs the two
of us now."

"He's with Sara. We have tonight to talk, Papa." Mary Anne, in her nurse's
uniform, smiled at him, and his face lit up. For a moment it was as though
all the cares of the world had suddenly been lifted from his shoulders. "Doctors
and nurses."

"I beg your pardon, Papa?"

He laughed. "Private joke."

When they finally got home, there was another message waiting which he
opened in private. They wanted full details of the damage inflicted on the
Grand Fleet—apart from those ships sunk—at Jutland, or, as they called it,
Skagerrak.

Andrew had not come down to the funeral, but he was dropping in with
Charlotte that night. They would talk.

6

Giles still had much influence, and a War Office motorcar was put at his
disposal. He drove to Redhill in style and broke the news quietly to Sara.

"I thought it better than to telephone."

Richard had been wounded, he told her, and when she became distraught,
he hurriedly had to say that it was not serious: "Well, not very serious, though
he might not be able to fly again. His leg. Right leg, smashed by a bullet,
and then broken badly when the aeroplane crashed.

"Dear God!"

"He was doing something very brave." Giles eyes were, for once, Sara noticed,
almost warm. Watery.

He thought of Denise, lying in her room, upstairs, at home, her eyes
blackened and one arm broken. Even C had visited her. At night, of course.

"Probably a decoration," he said. Then Sara wanted to know everything: did he swear that it was not serious? That he would not die?

Giles said Richard would be home soon.

7

"You are certain this information is being used wisely, and not given to the enemy in any way it can hurt us?" Charles asked "Brenner." He always asked the same question, adding, "Swear it to me."

And Brenner always told him that the intelligence would not be used to hurt his country in any way.

Charles passed on all the details: "I would have thought they'd have known the Fleet was ready for action again by June 2nd. Obvious the damage was slight."

He went to The Travellers after that, uncomfortable in the knowledge that his daughter was with a bloody Hun that very evening. Otto Buelow was now allowed complete freedom.

The couple dined in a small café, and Mary Anne asked Otto what he planned to do when the war was over.

"I have no doubt we will win—I mean the British, the Allies. I have become an honorary Englishman." His mastery of English was awesome, for he spoke it perfectly, and with what was known as an Oxford accent. "If we do not win, then my real countrymen will probably shoot me."

"But *when* we win ...?"

He seemed unwilling to share a possibly unpleasant fact of life. "I am only an honorary Englishman. My country is still at war with England. When it is over, I fear my true country will need men to help rebuild it. I must go back and help."

Mary Anne felt it was not only wise, but right.

There was a long silence as a very old waiter brought some not very good coffee. It was not only coffee in short supply. The food situation was frightening if you stopped to think about it.

"I should like—" they both said together.

"Please." Otto waved her to continue.

"I should like to see your country. . . . That was what I wanted to say. Your turn, Otter."

"Ha! You still call me Otter. What a long time ago that seems now." He looked into her eyes, reaching forward and placing a hand over hers. "I was going to say the same thing. Only we cannot talk of what I really wanted to ask. It would not be right."

She did not help him. So, eventually, he continued: "I hoped you would come with me, back to my country. Know it is in my thoughts. Please, I am not asking yet, but I would like you to return with me. As my wife, perhaps?"

She smiled as though happiness had at long last defeated constant doubt and despondency. "That's what I want, Otter. It's what I want very much; but you are right. We must neither say nor do anything about it until the war is won."

"And lost," he added.

(Mary Anne and Otto were, in fact, married, after the war, in 1920. They went off to live in Germany, and in the Family it was called "The Elopement." But that is another story.)

8

This year of 1916, autumn did not turn imperceptibly into winter. Winter came in with the lash—the longest, coldest in memory. The following April, there was still snow in England. Troop movements were impeded, fighting iced up, weapons so affected that rifle bolts could not be moved.

It took the hospital train bringing Richard Farthing back to England a full four days to make the journey, but Sara, warned the day before, managed to get to London and spend the night there before setting out, with Charlotte, to meet the train at Charing Cross.

As they approached the great archway, once known as "The Gateway to the Continent," Charlotte pulled Sara to one side. "Not through there," she mouthed. "It's considered terribly unlucky." And she pulled Sara around the station so that they came in on the Brighton line entrance.

The train arrived at 8:00 P.M. It was the last week in November, already bitterly cold and raining hard.

He climbed down from the train with the aid of a nurse and two sticks— his right leg a gray-plastered appendage—and Sara almost burst into tears when she saw him. Dick Farthing seemed to have shrunk and become rake-thin as he hobbled down the platform. Then he saw her, and the light came back into his face so that she knew he would be himself again if she were allowed to care for him.

"Home, love and comfort are the best things for this young man," the MO said at the Receiving Hospital. "He's to come and see us in six months, and we'll review his case. The leg was pretty smashed up, and it's impossible for us to tell what kind of a life he'll be able to lead."

They would send an official notice regarding his medical board. The next morning Sara watched an orderly pack his kit, and then walked with him— he wanted no help and insisted on managing his two sticks—to the taxi, and thence by train to Haversage and Redhill.

Already there was snow in the air, and you could see the relief on his face when she finally got him to bed.

She leaned over and kissed him. "Giles said you smashed your leg doing something very brave."

He gave a weak smile. "You know what a liar Giles can be. Tripped over a flying boot."

Within a month, things were happening in the country. Lloyd George became Prime Minister and announced his new Cabinet—"substitution of dynamite for a damp squib" they called it.

The winter was now well set. By the time spring did eventually arrive in 1917, there were many adjustments to be made. Kitchener was already dead, Britain had a new government, Hindenburg and Ludendorff had taken over the Imperial German Army; Joffre was out; the Emperor Franz Joseph was dead; and though few said it aloud, the Romanov dynasty was ailing. Many Russian prisoners noted for being revolutionaries were being released by the Germans and sent home.

That winter there was a new depression. The fact of the war dragging on, the slaughter and lack of movement, seemed to chill everyone to the marrow, dulling the senses, just like the icy weather as it swept over Europe. A new, pessimistic weariness embraced the country like some medieval plague.

At Redhill they managed a full house and a moderately happy Christmas. Giles did not come, for once, but Andrew and Charlotte were there, now proud grandparents and on better terms with Phoebe; Charles, looking lost, lonely and a shade desperate, came with Mary Anne, who spent a lot of time with Nanny Coles and young William Arthur. Margaret Mary, Nanny and the two children were very much in evidence. ("She still believes totally that poor James is immortal," Charlotte said, and Caspar chimed in, "And so he jolly is, Mama. You'll see!") Rupert had made no progress, and Ramillies went about with secrets in his eyes. As Billy Crook was still at the front, they asked Vera to bring her baby in, on Christmas afternoon, to get her little present from the tree.

On Christmas Eve there was a telegram for Dick. He stuffed it away after reading it, and Sara had to nag, in front of the others, before he handed it to her.

She took one quick look and squealed with delight, bidding everyone to listen to Dick's news. "He's got a Christmas present. They've awarded him the Distinguished Service Order." She held up the telegram and read: "For conspicuous gallantry against the enemy, putting his own life at risk in order to save others."

Everyone cheered and clapped. Then Denise, who had come with Malcolm on Giles' instructions, stepped forward and whispered, "Thank you. Thank you so much," and kissed Richard hard on both cheeks, hugging him fondly.

Sara frowned. "Now why did she do that?"

"French blood. Emotion of the moment," Charlotte muttered, and Caspar, who knew, hissed for them to shut up. "One day he'll tell you, Sara dear," Caspar said with a smile.

9

Another ship—a frigate—lay off Cromarty that Christmas. Work went on normally. Men came and went.

On the morning in question, the officer of the watch paid no attention to the Chief Petty Officer with a limp and a scarred face as he came aboard, saluting the quarterdeck.

Later, when the watch was changed, the new officer of the watch did not give the CPO a second look as he went ashore.

Thirty minutes later, with a great roar and a white flash, the frigate exploded, killing all on board at the time.

At Redhill Manor, Charles received a telephone call from Basil Thomson. Within the hour, he was travelling to Scotland with his old colleagues Wood and Partridge.

As well as the explosion, a young girl had been discovered, in an isolated cottage. She had been strangled with a silk scarf, but, by the time the men from MI5 and the Branch reached the area, The Fisherman was on his way back to London.

Chapter Twenty-Nine

1

When the long, dark winter ended, several events had reshaped both the future of the war, and, though they did not know it, the Railton family's fortune.

First, Giles Railton's greatest wish was granted. C's Service, now usually spoken of as the Secret Service, was placed under the direct control of the Foreign Office. Never again would the diplomats be left in the dark as far as major intelligence was concerned.

Second, The Fisherman was given instructions that would lead to a head-on collision with the Railton family, though there was no way he could ever have suspected it.

Hans-Helmut Ulhurt had been directed to establish a base in London, to carry out delicate work for Steinhauer who, as had so often happened in the past, was using his agent to assist the now promoted Colonel Nicolai.

The Fisherman went about his tasks with his normal professional efficiency. Then one morning he received new orders. Twice a week, at a particular hour, he walked a specially laid-down route. It was while performing this routine that an envelope was thrust into his hand by a small rabbit-faced young man who contrived to bump into him as he limped from the Holborn Post Office.

On returning to his rooms nearby, in the house of a Mrs. Blacket, who imagined him to be a wounded NCO, The Fisherman removed his code books and deciphered the message, which read: MOST IMMEDIATE. URGENT YOU LEAVE LONDON WITHIN THE HOUR. FIND NEW TARGET. ACT AS BEFORE.

As though sensing danger, The Fisherman was off like a scalded cat.

Last, but far from least, America entered the war.

Later, Blinker Hall claimed, in a cable, ALONE I DID IT. Certainly his devious footwork and cunning choreography played no small part, though Room 40 had much to do with this, the saving factor of the war.

Not even Andrew, who was the Railton nearest to both Hall and Room 40, had a whiff of what was in the wind, and it was many years before the full story emerged.

It is enough to say that the code-breakers of Room 40 unbuttoned a telegram sent by the German Foreign Minister, Arthur Zimmermann, to Count Bernstorff in Washington. The Zimmermann Telegram has since become legend, for it proposed, in effect, to assist Mexico to reconquer Texas, New Mexico and Arizona, should the United States enter the war.

Blinker Hall's difficulty was to make the Americans see the telegram as an authentic document. This he managed to do in a complicated manner, using many people—including his friend Ned Bell (the US diplomat who had caused Andrew much trouble)—and much information gleaned in the past years, in particular the fact that the German Embassy in Washington was breaking a trust by using the United States Government Wireless Station on Long Island.

When the full shock of the telegram was laid on the pacifist President Wilson, there was no alternative.

After some flurries of cables and certain Congressmen trying to throw doubts and discredit the message, Zimmermann himself admitted its authenticity.

By the first week of April the United States of America was at war with Germany, though it took almost a year for the American Expeditionary Force to build up in France.

It took only three weeks for Richard Farthing's uncle, Colonel Bradley Farthing, to arrive at Redhill Manor.

2

On the Western Front the slaughter continued. The armies, now swollen in size, constantly heard the cry "The Yanks Are Coming," but the fact that they were not yet there, fighting and assisting as yet, except in the air, did little to hearten men who still lived, fought and died around the now familiar placenames—Bapaume, Vimy Ridge, Cambrai.

Like his chief, Caspar now found his mind drawn to new matters, further east, for the cracks in the Russian Army, and their country as a whole, appeared to be widening. He became more and more conscious of the presence of his brother, Ramillies, moving in and out of C's inner sanctum with disturbing regularity.

He was also soon to meet another Farthing. The fact of Dick's uncle's arrival in England had flashed through the bush telegraph of the Railton family. On the whole, the Railtons had begun to behave as though Sara's husband's family were some rare species, needing particular and close examination.

3

Charles, and his team, in the meantime, had made a small amount of progress. By a fluke they caught the scent of The Fisherman in Holborn. A Mrs. Blacket, owner of what was styled as a private hotel, had cause to report some small items of silver missing.

The local police took note of any guest who had left suddenly. One such was an ex-serviceman who had lost a leg on the Somme. His departure had been sudden, and Mrs. Blacket had not yet let his room. The locals searched, and, behind a chest of drawers, discovered a notebook. It was empty but for two pages containing notes in scribbled German. Even they could make out the word *Natal*. The book was passed on to the Branch, and, eventually found its way, by early summer, to Charles.

Charles appeared to be recovering from the traumas which, with Mildred's illness and death, had previously surrounded him. Only occasionally, Wood noticed, did he appear to be not his usual self. The detective could not know that these lapses coincided with secret orders to pass more information to "Brenner."

One such request had come in the spring for all information on new types of tanks, their dispersal and armament. Brenner was unsympathetic when Charles went to him and bluntly said he saw no reason to carry on the charade. Now, *he* wanted more information *from* Brenner.

"My dear fellow, don't you understand that this is a necessary matter? What we are doing is for the British cause. You *must* continue this fiction" —thus Brenner.

Now Charles prayed there would be no more demands, for at last The Fisherman was in their sights.

From Mrs. Bracket, they knew he had been posing as a wounded senior NCO. They even had a name—Sergeant-Major Willis. Soon they also discovered that the man Willis had used an ex-serviceman's pass to gain a cheap railway ticket to Scotland. The Fisherman was getting careless, and the three-man team decided to follow the trail. What better place to look than Cromarty again?

They left London late on the afternoon of July 9th. As their train was pulling out, news was just coming through of yet another act of sabotage. *HMS Vanguard,* a battleship, had unaccountably exploded with the loss of seven hundred lives.

4

They did not tell James about America's entry into the war until the end of June, and then casually, as though it were a matter of little importance. He was weaker, and certainly thinner. The previous winter had taken its toll and the Commandant had appeared concerned on the two occasions that James had suffered severe bouts of bronchial trouble.

The diet was not helping, and by January they were reduced to the most meager rations. Even when spring finally arrived, the food improved only slightly. To James it was an obvious sign that the blockade of Germany was having a profound effect. The Commandant still dreamed of his cavalry charges, yet, one evening in mid-June, after an almost inedible dinner, the old man suddenly started to speak of the terrible butchery on the Western Front. James said nothing, but thought he was learning a great deal as the aging officer rambled on at about the way tanks were playing havoc with the infantry, and how poison gas, bombs from the air and the grappling struggle of trench warfare was taking the very heart of Europe's youth.

James realized, not for the first time, that he was living a dream. He had no idea of what the battles were like; nor could he divine the true situation. Only the news that America had entered the war cheered him.

5

Colonel Bradley Farthing was the youngest of Dick's father's brothers. The family likeness was uncanny—the same constantly amused expression, a similarity in build and features, while Bradley was, of course, a Farthing name. Dick's second youngest brother, now training with an infantry battalion in Texas, was another Bradley Farthing. Colonel Farthing, though, was, Sara thought, incredibly attractive, barely fifty years of age, and with a charm that would probably make sour milk drinkable.

He pronounced her name "Sar-rah," making two long syllables and refusing to alter this quirk even after Dick pointed it out to him.

Redhill he found delightful. "England as I imagined it," he said, and Sara twinkled, telling him that she understood France and Belgium had changed a little. He might not find them as pleasant.

"I guess I won't be seeing much of France." He scratched his head. "I can promise you that our doughboys'll be over soon, making mincemeat of the Hun, but our General Staff doesn't really see me as a commander in the field."

He did not have to add anything. Sara already had a shrewd sense of why Brad Farthing had come over with the advance guard, but for the moment she did not care. His arrival had brightened Dick, about whom she was becoming deeply concerned.

He had certainly become disturbingly depressed, his old sense of fun vanishing into a morose silence, returning only in flashes after his uncle arrived.

So far there had been two medical boards, and both had ruled there should be no return to duty as yet. But Sara thought she knew her husband. He wanted to get back into the air and fly, even more than ever now that his own country had joined the battle.

Dick did not know that she watched him regularly each morning, for he would slip from their bed and try to get to his dressing room without disturbing her. The first time it happened she took a full fifteen minutes to discover what he was doing. Then, looking from the upstairs windows, she saw him in the rose garden, first stumping back and forth without the aid of a stick, and then sitting on one of the low, gray stone walls, his legs thrust forward, the stick jammed between them. He would push hard, first with his left foot, and then his right, going through the physical motions of flying an aeroplane.

On the next evening she deliberately set out to goad him. "You're homesick," she accused, as they went up to prepare for dinner.

"Rubbish. This is my home now, Sara. *You* are my home."

"Then why, Richard, do you suddenly become a different person when your uncle arrives in *my* house?"

He laughed. "My darling, *your* house? The sinister Giles would probably tell it a different way . . ."

She opened her mouth, a sudden squall crossing her pretty face. Dick went to her, stopping the outburst with his lips before it had a chance to explode. "I jest, my dear Sara," locking eyes with her.

"Well, tell me?" She was still on the verge of anger, though secretly pleased that he had come to her. In the past weeks it had been Sara who always made the moves.

"Tell you? Tell you what?"

He had been limping around the house like a lame duck, she told him, looking dour; bad tempered; edgy. Now, as soon as Uncle Brad arrived, he was a changed man. "I even heard you laugh this morning, Dick. Do you realize how long it is since you actually laughed?"

"Yes." He spoke so quietly, and with such an odd timbre, that Sara turned to look at him. He was shaking, pale, and propped with one hand against the table. "Yes, I know."

Then he began to talk. He told her from start to finish about the operation to rescue Denise—right up to the moment he lost consciousness in the crash. Through it all, Sara detected something she had never yet seen in him. He spoke of fear; of terror as they approached the German lines; the need to vomit as he got Denise on board, and then of the blind panic during that terrible takeoff, when pure luck had got them airborne.

"I've never been so frightened, Sara. And hope never to be like that again. I . . ." A stammer. "I befouled myself." He looked away. "Yes, I shit myself with fear. And why? Because your good, kind, diplomatic Uncle Giles—"

"Not *my* uncle—"

"Adopted Uncle Giles put that child out behind enemy lines. He had her running intelligence through from Belgium to Holland. Ten of her fellow spies were shot."

"How do you—?"

"Caspar told me. Told me at Christmas. Giles could have seen his grandchild shot in a field, and—"

"And it's his job—or was. I gather he's retired."

"His kind never retire. They carry suspicion to the grave. I don't blame him for what happened to me. Yet, for the first time in my life I was afraid—like I'm afraid now."

Uncle Brad had brought with him a piece of Dick's past. "Just him being here's made me feel better, because he's familiar and through him I can remember how I used to be. He gives me a morsel of my old confidence. Oh, Sara . . ." He was in her arms, and she had never thought to see a man weep like this, sobs shaking his body as if bullets were hitting it. She made out some of his words: "Still frightened . . . Don't know if I can do it again. . . ."

"You almost certainly won't have to, darling Richard. . . ."

"No, not fight . . . I don't even know if I've got the guts to fly an aeroplane again. I've become a coward."

She shushed him and made soothing noises. He was shivering and moaning, muttering that he was a fraud to have taken the medal—"They're for heroes"— when she got him into bed. She locked the door, stripped and climbed in beside him, lying close, trying to will her own small strength into his body, telling him he had nothing to reproach himself for. "It happens to a lot of men, darling. It's a kind of fatigue. . . ."

"And they shoot them for it—for being cowards. . . ."

"No. You're not a coward. Dick, remember yourself before the crash, before the flight. You say Uncle Brad's made you think about how you were. You *can* do it again, though nobody's going to make you; and you *are* a hero, I promise." And he relaxed, becoming calm, tenderness returning with the tranquility, then fire ravaging his loins so that she first took him in her mouth, and then into her body, and when it was over they slept.

They missed dinner, and wondered what Uncle Bradley must have thought, but then Sara said it just did not matter what he thought. At midnight she crept downstairs, and the great old house was silent, breathing its history, the stones and wood recalling other people who had admitted to being cowards, yet were full of courage for admitting it.

She prepared a simple cold meal and took it up, so they ate it like children having an illicit dormitory feast.

The next day Uncle Brad went up to London. He would be back within the week.

6

Colonel Farthing had been given plenty of official introductions, as his main duty was to examine liaison with Security and Intelligence. So Brad Farthing was taken first to meet Reginald Hall at the Admiralty. In passing, he was introduced to Andrew: "Been staying with Richard and the lovely Sara," Brad boomed, almost wrenching Andrew's arm from its socket.

He talked long with Blinker Hall, who gave little away, and certainly let the American nowhere near the men and women of Room 40.

Farthing's meeting with Vernon Kell and the people from MI5 turned up little except technicalities.

Charles Railton was still in Scotland, attached to the Branch, so Brad Farthing did not meet him. On the fourth day of his London visit he did however meet Caspar when calling on C—a visit which was arranged with all the trappings of secrecy.

They talked for the best part of a day, for other matters were becoming an increasing concern to C's Service—and to the men at Military Intelligence also—not only simply important, but also exceptionally worrying.

Earlier in the year, on March 16, Czar Nicholas II of Russia had abdicated. A provisional government under Prince Lvov had proved ineffective. There were stories of an imminent rebellion in the Russian Army; of shortages of food and supplies, and—only a day ago—the collapse of Lvov's regime.

Returning prisoners, and Bolsheviks who had been hiding in Switzerland, swelled the revolutionary ranks. The situation was confused, and the latest hard information was that a revolt in Petrograd—formerly St. Petersburg—had failed, yet had caused the setting up of a new government, Socialist-orientated and led by Lvov's former Minister of War, Alexander Kerensky. C and many of his colleagues could only see Bolsheviks around every corner. "If they're going to act successfully, this is their time," C had told Caspar, who now understood why certain known Russian-speakers and experts had been haunting C's headquarters—not least of all the ghostly figure of his brother Ramillies.

At the end of the week Brad Farthing went back to Redhill Manor to find Dick vastly improved. His worries, on first seeing his nephew, must, he thought, have been unfounded.

"Charles may be coming for the weekend," Sara announced brightly. She had received a telegram from him. "In Glasgow, of all places. You never know where Charles will pop up next."

"Let's hope he pops up here." Uncle Brad swallowed his whisky. "I'm looking forward to meeting Charles. That fellow Kell's told me a lot about him."

7

It was Vernon Kell who was initially responsible for Charles' return to London. The two men had spoken on a number of occasions as Charles, with Wood and Partridge, had continued to follow The Fisherman's trail in Scotland. Now, as they seemed to have reached a dead end, Kell decided he could use Charles in better ways. He informed Thomson and telegraphed Charles to return. Charles was to report to the office on Monday. It was now Thursday afternoon. Wood and Partridge labored at Police Headquarters; Charles was at the railway hotel next to Glasgow Central Station. He rang London immediately on receipt of the telegram.

"There's a train in an hour or so," Charles told Kell, "but I'll leave it and come down on the night sleeper. Prefer it."

"As you wish. See you on Monday around lunchtime."

Charles telephoned Wood, breaking the news that he was being returned to normal duties and would travel back that night. The trail had gone cold.

Then he put in a long-distance call to Redhill Manor and spoke to Sara, confirming that he would be coming for the weekend. Only if he brought Mary Anne and young William Arthur, she said, but he could not promise. Mary Anne was now working in one of the London hospitals, and William Arthur had his schoolbooks. Nanny Coles was patiently coaching him.

Charles packed his bag, placed it on the bed for the porter, automatically checked the cumbersome Webley revolver he now carried everywhere, and went down onto the station concourse to book himself a sleeping berth on the night train.

At the ticket office, the man in front of him was also trying to book a sleeper. Charles had long since become wise to the ways of a good agent. His eyes were seldom still, his head turning in a natural manner, constantly on the watch, and his ears alive to sounds and conversations.

"Harker," the man booking the sleeper told the ticket clerk, spelling out the name, as though the woman clerk might find it difficult. "H-A-R-K-E-R. Harker."

And Charles turned his head in the direction of the concourse, saw that one of the platform gates was open, with passengers already moving through for the afternoon London train, and with disbelief, laid eyes on a tall man, walking with a heavy limp. The man turned slightly to show his ticket at the barrier, and Charles saw the rough, pitted red skin of the terrible burn scar down the right side of his face. It was quite visible as he lifted his head and the light struck below the broad-brimmed hat. The Fisherman was there, within his grasp. In one of those strange mental visions, he again saw him in the Ross-carbery street. This was overlapped by the cottage interior. Warm blood dripped down a framed photograph.

But I, that am not shaped for sportive tricks....

Charles stepped forward and bought a first-class single ticket to London, then turned and moved with gathering speed back to the hotel. Within four minutes he had settled his bill, while a porter was dispatched to bring down his small bag, and headed back onto the station concourse. He had fifteen minutes, and knew this was one occasion when he would have to resort to that part of his work he most distrusted—a disguise.

In the gentlemen's lavatory he delved into the bag, bringing out the so far unused tin containing a few small devices for use in emergency. The hair had been chosen to match his own, and the spirit gum held the neatly made walrus mustache in place so that even he, peering closely in the glass, admitted its seeming reality. The spectacles, added to the mustache, completely altered his appearance to the extent that he looked at himself a little too long.

Then he set out for the afternoon train, pausing briefly to buy a newspaper. In his mind there was one picture—the man going through the barrier; the man in Rosscarbery; the man who killed and maimed with explosives; the man who strangled with a white silk scarf.

And that so lamely and unfashionable
That dogs bark at me as I halt by them;

Charles sauntered casually along the platform, glancing sideways into compartments, as if looking for one that was suitably empty, and seeing everything—from the uniformed soldiers going back off leave, to the nervous, thin girls escaping from their Glasgow homes to what they believed to be brighter lights and golden opportunities in London.

Around him, middle-aged lovers hugged and kissed farewell, while in more than one compartment similar lovers studiously avoided each other's gaze, lest someone arrive who would recognize them and carry back tales of illicit weekends in faraway cities.

He reached the center of the train, and the second batch of first-class coaches. A group of young officers, slightly tipsy, with bottles poking from baggage, prepared to summon up courage for a return to the front by making the journey at least memorable. The train was by no means crowded: a compartment which contained a hard-faced woman with a small boy who looked miserable; two businessmen, gold chains curving over their waistcoats, cigars misting the compartment, settled down to put the financial world to rights. Then:

Unless to spy my shadow in the sun
And descant on my own deformity.

The rest of the compartment was empty, while The Fisherman, Charles' quarry, sat, newspaper open, propped in a window seat. Now he had him: hook, line, sinker and gaff.

He continued to walk the length of the train, counting the coaches and boarding it at the last moment—climbing into the most forward carriage as the whistle blew and the stationmaster waved his green flag.

Then, as the train swayed out of the station, Charles slowly made his way back toward the carriage in which he knew The Fisherman sat, oblivious to the danger that was upon him.

At first he thought that perhaps he had miscounted. There was no sign of the man in the compartment. Charles continued, walking the length of the train, toward the rear, passing through the restaurant car in the hope of seeing him there; pushing past men and women crowded in the third-class corridors until he reached the far end of the train, with its scaled-off guards' van.

Once more Charles walked along the tilting, drunken corridors as the train began to build up speed. Again, no sign of the big, scarred man with the stiff leg.

At last he was sure. The Fisherman must have been flushed from the train. He was certainly not here now. Charles knew of an agent's sudden anxieties, the intuition that bids him change his mind, play safe, move. Trust nobody. Weave. Duck and dive. Always look as though you have purpose and confidence. Change plans at the last possible moment.

Charles sensed the frustration of the hunter who suddenly loses the deer he has stalked all morning.

Resigned, he found an empty compartment in an almost deserted carriage and settled in for the lengthy run to London. He would report to Kell on arrival, so that Wood and Partridge could be alerted.

They were coming up to Carlisle when the carriage door slid open. Charles looked up and his stomach rolled, for there was the man, the schoolboy's comic drawing of a spy, in his black coat and brimmed hat. All the details, including the Mauser automatic pistol engulfed by his huge paw.

For a man of his weight and bulk, The Fisherman was exceptionally agile. The door slid open, then closed again with a click, the Mauser's eye never leaving Charles as the man's other arm moved swiftly to pull down the three blinds over the windows which looked onto the corridor.

Then, still smiling, The Fisherman slowly sat down opposite Charles.

Plots have I laid, inductions dangerous...

They went through Carlisle and on into that long open run before Manchester.

"Mr. *Charles* Railton, I believe?" The voice had no guttural inflexion, no foreignness.

Charles stared at him, his eyes wandering between the pistol barrel and the face with its dreadful map of fire, the cartography produced at Glen Devil Farm.

"I'm afraid you have the advantage of me..." Melodramatic, but he needed to play for time. "My name is Rathbone. Leonard Cyril Rathbone."

"Really? I think it's Railton—in fact I *know* it is"—The Fisherman was calm, the voice reasonable—"and I should know it. You've been following me all over Scotland, and I've watched you at it. I even watched you in the hotel this morning."

Charles' face must have shown a twitch of surprise, for The Fisherman continued: "Don't they teach you that a disguise is no good unless it's complete? The herringbone pattern of your suit, Mr. Railton; the cut of the jacket; the hat. A mustache and spectacles alter the face, but the clothes make the man. The clothes and the shoes."

Charles remained silent, holding The Fisherman's eyes in his, then breaking his silence with an acknowledgment of the weapon. "Not your style, sir. Where's your white scarf today? Or your explosives? Or the ax you used in Ireland, all that time ago, when I first saw you?"

The Fisherman's laugh was not unpleasant. In fact, he was almost likable in manner. "I might ask you the same thing, Mr. Railton."

"Oh?"

"Our mutual friend, Fräulein Haas. She went with a white scarf, but I did not do it. What about you?"

"Not guilty, as you must know."

"Mmmm."

A pause as the train clacked over some points, the rhythm changing. Then Charles asked if he were to be shot.

"By me?" Again the laugh. "I doubt if I need to do such a thing. It's my understanding that we're on the same side. Those are my instructions, but, as you seemed intent on disguises and the chase, I felt we should at least talk."

"About what?"

And The Fisherman began to tell Charles more than he even knew himself. He spoke of Hanna Haas, of Marie and von Hirsch, and, not least, the information Charles had passed to Brenner. The Fisherman laughed again. "You know the joke in Berlin? They call you 'The Brenner Pass.'"

Because of what the man knew, and what Charles knew of Brenner, and other duplicities, it slowly dawned on him that he could never win any round. If he killed The Fisherman and owned to it, Brenner would know, and Charles' own situation would be intolerable. He saw clearly how the plot was woven, though could not think why, for there was no motive. He wondered if there were time to rid himself of this man, and decided there was—just. So he allowed The Fisherman to talk on, steepling his fingers and shifting his body so that when the move came it would be natural.

The Fisherman went on, and now began to ask questions. Did Charles imagine his own treachery would, in the end, bear fruit? What were his real motives? Hatred of England? Disillusionment? Fear of what would eventually happen to the Empire and the country?

"Cigarette?" Charles asked, his hand dropping casually toward his right thigh.

"Why not?" The eyes mocked, and Charles kept his gaze locked as he propelled himself forward, across the space dividing them, avoiding the pistol hand, his chest hitting The Fisherman's chest, but, for a second, clear of the Mauser as he tried to pinion his victim.

He later recalled little of the struggle, except for the man's enormous strength

and the one moment when they grappled for the Mauser as he tried to bring
it to bear. He did remember his own right hand desperately scrabbling for his
Webley, feeling the butt, trying to drag it clear, and then, pressed hard body
to body, the shot, and the sudden sense of a human being alive one moment,
dead, sagging and belching blood the next.

Somehow he caught the Mauser before it reached the floor, and saw The
Fisherman's hand opening—not closing—to reach out, in his last spasm, as
though to staunch the blood. He also knew about pulling the trigger a second
time. The second bullet must have hit the heart, but The Fisherman was dead
before his fingers, in reflex action, even touched the wetness.

Charles moved with exceptional speed, catching the folds of the man's jacket
and using them as a trap for the blood, his eyes automatically searching the
seatback to be certain one of the bullets had not passed through the body.

The train swayed more violently, and he had a little difficulty in opening
the door, which smashed back, driven by the train's slipstream. But there was
no problem in disposing of the body. He waited, braced in the doorway, the
corpse dangling and rolling half in and half out of the train. As they passed
over a small bridge, Charles kicked. He thought afterward that it was true,
that a man did have twice his normal strength when faced with a matter
concerning his own survival. What The Fisherman had told him left Charles
in no doubt about the necessity of avoiding suspicion in this business. The
body flopped out, curving spread-eagled, and he saw the peg leg flap up like
an obscene appendage as The Fisherman, with some irony, fell into what
appeared to be a swift-flowing stream.

In the deep bosom of the ocean buried.

With abnormal care, Charles cleaned and tidied the compartment, putting
his bag next to The Fisherman's valise. There was a little blood, but he thought
most had been soaked into the man's clothing.

Then he went down the corridor, to the lavatory, and cleaned the blood from
himself and his clothing as best he could.

At Euston he booked into an hotel near the station, retaining his disguise,
and there went through The Fisherman's valise, uncovering all the secrets.
Charles' own name, and Brenner's, appeared in several messages and documents,
which he burned. He sat, awake, all night, leaving the hotel in time to return
to the station, and make certain the night train was in, and that neither Wood
nor Partridge was on board.

He then visited the "Wash & Brush-up," as it was quaintly called, removed
the mustache and glasses in a private cubicle, retrieved his dressing case from
the bag, shaved and took a cab to Cheyne Walk.

There, in the privacy of his own room, he packed a larger case, placing the
suit he had worn at the bottom, planning to burn it at Redhill, for the scorch
marks from the Webley would never be hidden. He took another holster, cleaned
the revolver, reloaded it and went down just in time to see a delighted Mary
Anne about to leave for the hospital.

He told her he was taking William Arthur to Redhill for the weekend, and sent word to Nanny Coles.

Brenner, he thought, would wait until Monday. Sleep on it. Think on it. Somewhere there had to be an answer.

He could not get *Richard III* from his mind. *As I am subtle, false and treacherous.* Not since he first spotted The Fisherman, yesterday in Glasgow.

Chapter Thirty

1

Charles traveled to Haversage late on Friday afternoon. It was a golden day, warm and with an incredible sunset, viewed by Sara, Richard, Charles and Colonel Bradley Farthing from the top of the rose garden.

Sara then went up to see Nanny Coles and William Arthur. In the meantime the men sat outside with their drinks.

Brad Farthing was particularly interested in Charles, asking questions, it seemed, under the guise of finding out how MI5 operated. Charles neatly fielded some of these queries and, after about half an hour, excused himself, went indoors and, from the General's Study, put in a long-distance call to Vernon Kell's private home number.

Kell came on the line and, as soon as Charles spoke, asked when he had got back.

"I'm speaking from Redhill, Vernon. Got into London this morning. I told you I was coming on the night train."

"You weren't on it, Charles." The voice was cold; more hurt.

"Of course I was on it. Not under my own name, naturally. Not with everything that's been going on."

"What name, then? You weren't under Rathbone."

"Vernon? What the devil is this?"

"What name, Charles?"

"Picked it out of a hat. Harker. Mr. C. Harker."

"What was it you wanted?"

"I'm at Redhill, and a mite worried. Dick has his uncle here. Colonel—"

"Bradley Farthing, yes?"

"That's him. He says he has authority to investigate our security and intelligence methods."

"That's true enough. Nice chap. Seen him myself."

"Just wanted to know the official line, that's all."

There was a long pause before Kell told him to be careful. "Stick to generalities. Technique. Don't go into specifics. Don't name names or quote cases. Right?"

"All I wanted to know. See you on Monday, Vernon."

Kell did not reply, neither did he mention—then or during the following months—the discovery of a body, lying in shallow water, a mile or so from the railway line, in open country well north of Manchester.

On the following Monday Charles reported to Kell and was put on general duties, which meant he was effectively confined to desk work over the next few months.

2

About the same time as they sat down to dinner, on that Friday evening in July 1917 at Redhill Manor, Giles Railton was entertaining his favorite grandson, Ramillies, at dinner in Eccleston Square.

Denise took her meal upstairs in her room, for she had been constantly nervous and in need of rest ever since her return. Malcolm by this time had left—now with a commission in the Royal Navy.

After the meal was over, Giles and Ramillies retired to the Hide. They were there for almost four hours. During that time Giles talked. Ramillies answered questions.

"In all your dealings," the old man told his grandson, "do not forget that I have met them, spoken to them all at length: Ulyanov, who now prefers to be called Lenin; Kerensky, Trotsky, Sverdlov, Zinoviev and all those who follow in their wake. Take care, everyone of them is like a shark, and leadership can change in a second."

As the young man left the house, his grandfather said, "Now, it will be quite soon, Ramillies."

"Yes, sir."

"You're as prepared as you will ever be. If, by chance, they send you quickly, and I do not see you again, good luck. Follow my advice; do as I have said; and the future is secure."

In fact, Giles was to see Ramillies many times before C sent him on the mission for which Giles had prepared him. Certainly Ramillies spent more and more time moving between C's office and the Hide at Eccleston Square.

Now, at C's headquarters, a very large segment of time was now being taken up with events unraveling themselves in Russia.

Already, the fears of the collapse of both Kerensky's government and the Russian Army, the inevitable descent into open rebellion, and of a path made clear for the Bolsheviks, were fast becoming a reality.

C, in close collaboration with the British government, made gallant efforts to shore things up. Agents—including Somerville, in reality William Somerset Maugham, who had worked for C in Switzerland—were dispatched to Russia

with funds for Kerensky. Maugham, in fact, carried a personal message back
to the Prime Minister, and prepared to return to Moscow. But by November
1917 Kerensky's government was a thing of the past.

The British Embassy staff was evacuated early in 1918, its place taken by
an unofficial mission headed by Robert Bruce Lockhart, who sacrificed a brilliant
diplomatic career—and almost his life—in order to provide intelligence regarding the Bolsheviks, and, incidentally, place agents within their ranks.

In London, there was almost as much chaos regarding intelligence as there
was political uncertainty in Russia. The Bolsheviks had moved their headquarters to Moscow, and now Ramillies waited daily for orders to leave. As he
pointed out on many occasions to C, he had been hand-picked for just such an
eventuality. But C failed to deliver the orders.

Several agents were tipped into the confusion. Many disappeared. There were
attempts on Lenin's life, purges in which counterrevolutionaries perished, and
Bruce Lockhart was finally arrested, escaping execution only by diplomatic
moves in London. He arrived back, with other members of his mission, in
early October 1918.

Two days later C called Ramillies to his office.

"Well, my boy, you've been pestering to go. Now it's time. Our official
people are out, but we've left several agents in place, and there's some liaison
with the White Russians. Before you get your full orders, there's one man I
want you to meet. Bit of a rogue, adventurer, undisciplined, inclined to carry
out private and complicated operations of his own. Likable enough, and you
may well run into him again because like as not I'll be sending him back.
Name of Sidney Reilly. He'll give you certain pieces of information which may
help."

Indeed, Reilly seemed to Ramillies a charming, tough man, but it was
difficult to tell the fact from fiction with him. Reilly spoke of the minefield
Ramillies would be going into. "Trust nobody absolutely," he said. "The shift
in events can be so sudden that a friend becomes an enemy overnight." It was
much the same as his grandfather had taught him.

They gave Ramillies three names and three identities; papers; gold, which
he carried in a belt; a German pistol and a knife; and made him commit certain
contact names and addresses to memory. His job was to get as much information
as possible regarding the aims and intentions of Lenin's Revolutionary Committee. He was to be taken in by way of Helsinki. Once in Russia, Ramillies,
or Vladimir Khristianovich Galinsky as he was to be called, would make for
Petrograd. He was a student, politically literate, from Moscow, who had been
displaced by the earlier fighting, wounded slightly (C had arranged this
with the medical people in February, and Ramilies was confined to a hospital
bed for a week) and now making his way to assist the comrades in the final
struggle.

"That's your story. Your grandfather's given you a lot of help," C told him.

"We can get you in. We can provide you with the means to get information out. The rest is up to you."

Ramillies thought, *The rest is silence.* Which, in many ways was true, for less than twenty-four hours after he left England, his grandfather suffered a seizure.

Denise, worried that her grandfather, a man of habit in household matters, had not come down to breakfast, sent Robertson to Giles' room. The servant found him, part-dressed, lying on the floor.

His speech was slightly impaired, but the doctors thought, with rest, he might even regain that. He was as strong as the proverbial ox and could outlive them all yet.

3

Ramillies entered Russia on October 14, 1918, and it took him nearly two weeks to make his way to Petrograd, where he found lodgings near the Smolny Institute. On the morning of October 29th he loitered at the end of Gorok-hovaia. He had the Railton build, slim, tall, though the fair hair was covered by a fur cap, the face by a thick beard, and his body by a sheepskin jacket with leather trousers tucked into heavy boots. In his right hand Ramillies carried a simple workman's trowel. His way of moving, and that certain stillness which seemed to show even when he walked, could never be changed. But neither Andrew nor Charlotte would have recognized him.

Petrograd was in chaos. There was occasional shooting, and fighting around Vasilievsky Island, and in the Malaia Okhta District, for elements of the White Garrison still appeared to be active. Yet nobody knew who was in power or even in charge.

The Revolutionary Committee, and its plethora of offshoots, had decamped to Moscow, its varied and generally incompetent second team being left in Petrograd. You could get sense from nobody. Officialdom had vanished overnight. Few would take any real responsibility.

On the first evening, Ramillies walked the dangerous streets, aware of the small bands of young men and women who seemed intent only on looting, and, possibly, burning things.

Some women stood in lines by shops, hoping that a miraculous consignment of food would arrive; others went out of the city, using initiative and plundering farms or barns.

People were generally to be found in small groups, huddled together, with the strongest taking leadership, though half of them were really political vagrants.

He fell in with one of these groups, who accepted him and led him off. They passed old and young sitting around fires in the streets or arguing in houses where doors had been ripped off to provide fuel.

The disorganization, the leader of Ramillies' group—a big student called Peter—maintained, was the strength of the revolution. "We can now exchange ideas in the open." Though Ramillies could not for the life of him see how this helped.

They had taken over a house near the old Finland Station, in the Vyborg District, and they sat talking and arguing all night. Two claimed to be Anarchists; one was, she said, a Menchovik, the others claimed Bolshevism.

One of the men found wine in the cellars of the house, and the arguments were fired by alcohol. Two of the men fought in the hall, one ending up with his nose smashed, while another took a young girl upstairs. Everyone laughed when they heard the steady bumping above them.

At last they slept, and at dawn Ramillies crept away. Men and women still hung about the streets, young men, armed to the teeth, went by trying to look important, which probably meant they were trigger-happy and needed watching. The lack of control by some central authority was all too obvious. Ramillies still carried his trowel like a badge of office.

Perhaps it was too like a badge of office; or, possibly, they mistook it for a weapon. Or was there yet another reason why the three young Vechekists approached him, asked for his name, then wanted to see his papers. One took the trowel, and it seemed as though he were threatening Ramillies with it.

"You are Vladimir Khristianovich Galinsky?" the leader asked.

"Yes."

"You are from Moscow?"

"Originally, yes."

"Why are you not there now?"

Ramillies told his story, and the three men huddled around him, exchanging glances, passing the papers from one to another as though something were wrong. Eventually their leader said that Galinsky must come with them.

"Why? I've done nothing. Where do we go?"

"Just down the street. Number 2. Headquarters of the Vecheka. A few questions."

At five o'clock that afternoon they took him to the railway station. Four of them took him, and they arrived in Moscow two days later. October 1918 was not the best time to travel in Russia.

In Moscow things seemed quiet enough, but there was a strange atmosphere, a commingling of euphoria and tension.

"Where are we going?" Ramillies asked.

"Not far. To the new Vecheka Headquarters, Bolshaia Lubianka, Number 11. Near the Kremlin."

They took him straight in, hustling him up stairs and then to a large office— bare but for a table, chair and one man sitting behind a desk.

The man was engrossed in reading a document and he muttered, "Sit down." They pushed Ramillies forward, and the man behind the desk said they were to be left alone. He still studied the document.

At last he looked up, cold, quizzical, almost amused eyes below a high forehead, down which a lock of hair strayed. The mouth was firm, the mustache curving at either end, and the goatee beard neatly trimmed. There was something hard, uncompromising, about the man.

Then he gave a smile which chilled Ramillies almost as his grandfather's cold moments froze him. "Ah, welcome. Mr. Ramillies Railton, I understand." It was not a pure Russian accent. "We have been expecting you. My name is Feliks Edmundovich Dzerzhinsky, and I believe we have much to talk about."

The rest is silence, Ramillies thought again. Feliks Dzerzhinsky was the all-powerful supreme leader of the Revolution's Secret Police.

He was correct. There is no further official record of Ramillies Railton.

4

When Charles returned to the office after the weekend at Redhill in the summer of 1917, he did not at first take kindly to the desk work.

After a month or two he relaxed, for Brenner did not call him for any further meetings.

If, during that period, Charles realized he was being placed in a restricted situation within MI5, he did not show it. Vernon Kell remained friendly and saw him often.

The bombshell burst upon him over a year later, in late October 1918.

Though the accusations against Charles Railton were never made public at the time, the family connections, and privilege, assured that an individual knowledge of what had occurred was given to relatives within twenty-four hours.

Reactions within the family were predictable. The somber news of Charles' arrest came in the wake of immense rejoicing. In September Sara had given birth to a son. Even Giles had managed to write a note from his sickbed, indicating that, while she had brought new blood to herself, the family regarded her, and hers, as Railtons. "The ultimate accolade, Giles being what he is," Sara declared.

There was also a sense of the advent of peace, though few realized it was less than a month away. When the news about Charles reached them, each reacted in a different manner. Then they closed ranks. All were stunned, and Andrew seemed to speak for the whole family when he said, very privately, "If it's true, then Rupert and Caspar fought in vain; Mary Anne went through her hell for nothing; Dick Farthing's situation is meaningless; little Denise has suffered for nought. Come to that, if a man like Charles, with his family, education and background, can be guilty of this, then, God knows, those thousands of young men on the ground in Flanders, France, the East—and those at sea and in the air—have all probably died for a spit in the eye."

Few would deny that today, though Charles' case was hardly worthy of such a melodramatic and damning statement at the time.

On the morning it happened, Charles arrived at his desk, as normal at about 9:30. According to the record, he was his usual self, and at 9:46 showed no surprise when Granby, the Department Quartermaster, entered his office, flourished a document and asked if he could have Charles' personal weapon, a Webley revolver, "Just for the usual routine checks. Get it back within the hour, old boy."

Charles continued his paperwork. At 10:05 Miss Wedge came in to ask if he would go up to Colonel Kell's office.

"You wanted me, Vernon?" The door was closed behind him by Partridge, who then placed himself on Charles' right, while Wood closed in on the left. Basil Thomson stood directly in front of Vernon Kell's desk.

Kell muttered, "Sorry, Charles."

Basil Thomson addressed him: "You are Charles Arthur Railton, of Cheyne Walk, London?"

He still did not appear to understand the gravity of what was going on. "What the devil is this? Course I'm Charles Railton, Basil. What's—"

Thomson cut him off and formally charged him. "I have a warrant for your arrest, under the Official Secrets Act, in that between March 1916 and July 1917 you contrived to pass information of a secret military and economic nature to the enemy, in full knowledge of its sensitive nature—the information being handed to one Hans-Helmut Ulhurt, an agent of the German Secret Service."

"This is— What . . . ?" Charles' hand went to his throat, and Wood snatched the arm away.

Basil Thomson had said earlier they had best get a statement quickly: "Very quickly. He mustn't even be given time to think."

"Who the devil's Hans-Helmut Ulhurt?" Charles asked, looking bewildered.

"Charles"—Thomson became the old comrade—"Listen. Everybody knows there are probably extenuating circumstances. We know some of it. Give us the full strength, eh?"

The pause was like a long intake of breath. "I don't know what you're talking about. It was supposed—" He stopped dead.

"It was supposed to what?"

Charles simply shook his head, lowering his eyes and moving his head constantly from side to side, until Kell spoke.

"You can be tried in the civil courts. In the Central Criminal Court." Kell rose. "We would all appreciate it if you elected to be court-martialed, *in camera,* of course. It would be *in camera* at the Old Bailey, naturally; but a private court-martial would not only save your family from the press, but allow us to keep it in *our* family."

"You do what you like." Charles suddenly appeared to pull himself up to his full height. "I have one request. I want to see my uncle, Giles Railton, and I wish to see him in private."

A sense of embarrassment filled the office. Basil Thomson coughed. Then, quietly, Vernon Kell said, "You haven't heard? Nobody's told you?"

Charles didn't answer, staring blankly at them, eyes becoming wilder, looking from solemn face to solemn face.

It was left to Kell. He offered Charles a chair. "I think you'd better..." So Charles sat down and Kell broke the news.

Denise Grenot had gone to her grandfather's bedroom on the previous evening and again found him half out of bed.

"Oh Christ!" A sob in Charles' voice. "Oh Christ... not dead?"

"No, not dead. A second seizure. He's paralyzed and lost his speech. He cannot communicate."

Charles' reaction shocked everyone. He laughed, and it was no sudden fit of hysterics, but a dry, sober, controlled laugh. "Trust Giles. Cannot communicate? Give the devil his due." Then he suddenly became calm again. "I still want to see him—alone, and quickly."

Thomson advised that he should make a statement now. "We've got a mountain of evidence. It'll be best for everyone." But Charles said that they could talk until they were blue in the face. He needed to see Giles Railton.

The doctors said he could see Giles, but not for at least forty-eight hours. The old man was at home, being cared for by a series of nurses; they did not expect him to live for long—a couple of months at the most, a few days more likely. Two doctors called daily. Churchill, now Minister of Munitions, had seen him, and the family were at this moment each spending a few seconds with him. What, they wondered in Kell's office, could the accused possibly gain by sitting for a few minutes with a dying man who could not converse? Charles then made his second demand. He must see his Uncle Giles alone; he wanted nobody present.

In turn, they each tried to convince Charles that he should make a statement now. "After all, the stuff you gave them wasn't all that serious. It's the reasons we're after."

"At least tell us why," Wood pleaded.

No. No, and no. He would see Giles, and then—well. Who could tell? He was not a guilty man. He didn't know the fellow they talked about. No!

"The evidence is there. Damning." And that was the last Thomson had to say at this stage.

Charles seemed visibly torn by the accusations. Then he shut his mouth and refused to speak. He even resisted friendly conversation when it was offered. He would see no other members of the family, though Mary Anne had already been brought and told the seriousness of the charges, and offered to see her father. Like the other Railtons, she did not believe it. "Yes, there was some funny business with an enemy agent, but that was different. Not treason!" Yet, in the quiet, reasonable portions of their minds, each must have wondered, citing the strain of the months when Mildred was so ill, and the terrible battles he had been called upon to fight in that private life. What could he have hidden among the other skeletons?

So they decided: Give him a small piece of rope; let him see the old man, that doyen of their trade; then they would face him with the whole weight of evidence; produce his confession. There was no point in bringing the man to a court-martial, or trial, unless they had a confession. Too many odd things might come out of the woodwork. There would have to be lawyers present, whatever happened—and you know about lawyers, they tend to talk, at The Garrick, or The Wig and Pen, or wherever. Nobody wanted to look a fool.

5

The arrangements were made, complicated and near military, with Thomson's men being allowed to search the sickroom, and identifying that the only exits consisted of the main door and the two front-facing windows, which were immediately jammed shut. They also removed all objects with which the accused could possibly inflict harm on himself. "Don't want him doing anything silly," Thomson grunted.

They took away several pens; a paperknife; Giles' shoes from his wardrobe, presumably because of the laces, his ties; belts and scarves (Charles was kept in gym shoes without laces, while his own tie and garters had been taken away). Anything heavy, pointed or with cutting capability was removed. In effect, the room was almost stripped. The large men were watched by the weak patient, whose alert, frightened eyes followed them as the ritual continued.

They would even have removed the big Bible, with its thick, wide, leather marker, from the bedside table, but Giles began to grunt in an agitated manner. "There's no harm," the nurse said, not quite understanding what was going on. "He won't let anyone move that for a second. It seems to be a comfort, bless him." So the Bible remained, and the Branch men were posted: outside; at every possible exit; near the door of the room itself; and on the stairs.

The doctors said Giles' best time was early afternoon. They had visited him then, and it was the period when he always appeared to be most alert. One of the doctors, in fact, spoke to Charles when they brought him to the house, telling him to expect nothing in the way of movement or speech. "He can make only grunting noises, and gets rather frustrated. If there's any way of communication, it's with his eyes. The mind is quite obviously unimpaired."

They were gentlemanly about the whole business, putting Charles on his honor to call nurse, or doctor, if he thought Giles was becoming worse.

He entered the room at eight minutes past two. As the Branch man closed the door, he saw Charles pull a stand chair up beside the bed so that he could sit near the old man's head.

Charles emerged at three o'clock and was taken straight back to a safe house which Kell shared with C's Service in the center of London. Both C and Kell were present, as were Thomson and a nominee of the DNI's office.

Kell began, somewhat nervously. "We've kept our part of the bargain. Now, will you talk to us?"

Charles Railton looked at them, then slowly shook his head before speaking very quietly. "I shall be making no statement to you, either now or at any later date. If you wish to conduct a trial, please do so. I do not wish to be represented; I shall not put in a plea; there will be no defense."

They thought he was just being difficult, though something had changed in his eyes. Later, Wood was to describe it as "a hardening."

So, as Charles sat at a desk, impassive and certainly unspeaking, they trotted out the evidence—every man becoming his own expert now. First there were the decodes, several of them, beginning in the spring of 1916 but emanating from an earlier source. "We had occasional messages, going to and fro. The Angler file, we called it. Commercial code, with a few odd bits and pieces to make it difficult. Instructions came in, and various short messages went out. We also knew that we were not picking up all of them. Some came and went via a shortwave wireless, almost certainly to an offshore submarine. The suggestion was that they were to and from a German agent operating in Britain."

The Angler file was obviously connected with The Fisherman. The content of the messages proved to be obscure. They even trotted out the one ordering him to go to Dublin. Their first prize appeared to be a short, outgoing signal concerning the death of another agent, coded M6. M6, the expert said, was undoubtedly the woman Hanna Haas.

There were also several incoming signals which appeared to be lists of questions. One of these signals contained the code name "Brenner."

"Our contention will be that *you*, Charles Railton, are Brenner." Charles did not even smile.

The messages were fragmentary, disputable, but certainly pointed to the fact that Angler received certain orders, including lists of intelligence questions to be answered by his contact, Brenner. Because of their fragmentary nature it was also obvious that Angler—after a time they reverted to using "The Fisherman"—was receiving instructions by hand, and almost certainly getting replies out by way of a friendly neutral postal service.

Next, they came to Hans-Helmut Ulhurt, whose body had been discovered in the early hours of that July morning, following Charles' return from Glasgow to London.

They produced statements from ticket collectors and guards employed by the London, Midland and Scottish Railway Company, which in any court would have been damning. Charles had claimed to have returned on the night train as a Mr. Harker. They not only had descriptions of Mr. Harker, but a statement from the man himself. Railton would certainly have had to be a master of disguise, for Harker was barely five feet one inch in height and built like a small barrel.

They also had descriptions of the man, later found dead in a stream, some miles north of Manchester, and statements that he had boarded the afternoon train; also statements about a man with a thick mustache and glasses, wearing a herringbone-patterned suit—identical to the one Wood and Partridge had seen on Charles. This last man was of Charles' build.

The evidence went on, it appeared interminably: Hans-Helmut Ulhurt was undoubtedly The Fisherman, and he had been shot, presumably by the man who had been detailed to find him—Charles Railton, who had gone out of his way to hide the fact. Odd, they said, for the Master of the Hunt to be coy about the kill.

Then they brought Wood on, and he told of his examination of the body, and how, on unpicking the lining of Ulhurt's jacket, they found a waterproof packet in the lining.

The packet, and the papers it contained, were placed on the table. There were maps, printed on fine-quality, thin paper, marked up for rendezvous with, presumably, U-boats; there were also codes known as one-time codes; and a small, thin notebook in which were recorded various, seemingly jotted, remarks. They were written in German, and most had little meaning to the examining officers. One, however, was the key to their case. Scribbled in the corner of a page were the words *Brenner: M6's Lover.* As far as they were concerned, the case was clinched. M6 equaled Hanna Haas, and Charles Railton had already faced an inquiry regarding his relationship with Fräulein Haas. QED.

But they had been painstaking. At night, officers from the Branch had visited Redhill Manor. Among some garden rubbish they found pieces of a half-burned herringbone-patterned suit. Charles was told the evidence was enough to condemn him. They were prepared to bring forward officers who would testify that Charles Railton had "pumped them" on matters.

Last of all—and this surely shocked Charles—they laid out certain financial evidence: of an account opened in the name of George Brenner at the Royal Bank of Scotland in Glasgow. Four amounts, each of £1000, had been paid out. They had all gone, by the direct-transfer method, through the post, to Charles Railton's private account at Coutts in London.

Charles said nothing. In fact he looked unimpressed with this weighty file, which could lead him to a wall facing a firing squad.

The protagonists retired, leaving the accused under the eye of Chief Inspector Wood.

Give him a week at Warminster, they suggested. A combination of Kell's and C's confession experts would squeeze him like a lemon. The pips would drop out.

The role of the rambling mansion—shared at that time by both MI5 and the Secret Service—was in its infancy; and it lies, not in Warminster itself, but seven miles away, off the main road at Knook, near the village of Chitterne.

They took Charles to this Georgian pile—with ugly Victorian additions—and started work.

He remained silent; was calm; ate normally; did as he was told, but did not speak. It was as though, after seeing his silent, dying uncle, he had taken the vows of a Trappist monk. They tried everything except violence, but to no avail. Then fate took a hand.

In the spring of that last year of war, "Spanish influenza," emanating from the Near East, hit the Navy in Scapa Flow and troops in France. The disease grew, crossing England in three distinct waves, the first in mid-July, dying out and striking forcefully again in the first week of November, and reaching its peak the following February. During that period a total of 151,446 people died of the infection, mainly civilians.

Every single Railton in England, apart from Giles, was affected. Only one died. Charles contracted the disease at the end of the first week in November. The doctor in residence at Warminster was called, but watched helplessly as his patient's temperature rose and he became delirious.

Those whose job it was to pry the truth from him stayed by the sickbed, and, as Charles sank lower, becoming weaker with the fever, they noted some of his ramblings. "Uncle... Uncle..." he repeated one day. Then, "... Uncle Brenner!"

They sent for Mary Anne because he began to ask for her, and listened as he croaked at her, sure that she was Mildred: "Sorry, my dear... Sorry... One favor... Please... Madeline, a child, a child in Germany.... Please, when it's over... when... take care of the child... or let Sara... Sara... take care of the—"

At the very end he reverted to the true Railton style. Charles' last words were, *"If we shadows have offended, Think but this, and all is mended."* Quoting Shakespeare to the end. He died, without more fuss, on November 12th, the day after the war ended. Mary Anne could not be consoled. Whatever else, she had loved her father dearly.

Giles was still alive, and there has always been conjecture in the family regarding what would have happened if Charles had lived. For the events which followed, and led to the private mythology, which is the full knowledge of truth within the Railton family, could so easily have unbuttoned Charles Railton's lips and changed the official story.

Yet the extent of the betrayal did not become known until the final acts of those days had been completely played out. The beginning of this end took place in Germany two days before Charles died at Warminster.

Chapter Thirty-One

1

Margaret Mary knew on the morning of November 10th. She opened her eyes and felt a sudden relief, as though something incredible had happened overnight. A fountain of happiness came bubbling up and she leaped from the bed, dashed downstairs to crash out a Chopin Polonaise on the piano—loudly, with tears streaming down her cheeks.

The children followed in her wake, like two laughing little tugboats, and danced around the room as she played.

Far away, in his castle on the Rhine, James woke imagining he heard laughter and music in the last seconds of his sleep. It hung over into the waking day as he went through the routine of washing, shaving, drinking the colored hot water they called coffee, and eating the thick bread smeared with dripping that was his breakfast. It was November 10th, 1918. Ten in the morning—though he had no idea of the real time, any more than he knew the date, except that it was late autumn. Looking from the window, he saw a large staff car laboring up the incline, toward the main castle gates.

Ten minutes later the Commandant sent for him. An officer of great importance was waiting. They went into one of the cold, small offices, and there he met a tired-looking man in mufti who introduced himself as Walter Nicolai.

"You've come to tell me something," James announced before Nicolai could open his mouth. "I'm to be shot?"

Nicolai raised a hand to stop him. No. He had come to take him. They would have to move quickly. There was someone else in the car—two people actually. By eleven o'clock tomorrow the war would be over. This was not yet known by anyone—the people, he meant: neither in Germany nor England. It was finished, so it was important that Mr. Railton should be out of Germany before eleven tomorrow. Tomorrow was the Armistice, Nicolai said.

James, in his bewilderment asked, "But who has won?"

Nicolai told him, adding that he felt Mr. Railton should meet with the other two people, in private, before they went on their way. They would be driven for part of the journey. "After that, I have arranged for an aeroplane to fly you into Switzerland. Messages have been sent. You will be expected at Zurich." Nicolai almost did not meet James' eye, and was about to leave, saying he would see to the others, but James reached forward, holding his sleeve, feeling the weakness of his own body as he tried to pull the man back. He came of his own accord, standing close, looking, at last, into James' face. "Why?" James asked.

Nicolai spoke slowly: "Because you were protected. Because an arrangement was made. Now, I'll get the others."

He had no idea what to expect, or whom to expect. He did not even recognize the woman, thin—like himself, he supposed—and dressed with care in shabby, worn clothes, a small child, a little girl of about three years old, peering anxiously from behind her skirts.

They looked hard at each other, glimmers appearing, as though their eyes were mirrors flashing messages between friendly armies.

"James?" Her voice was immediately recognizable.

"Marie?" He could not believe it. "Marie! My God, Marie!" And they both knew what the Biblical words meant, for they fell on each other's necks and wept, repeating each other's names.

The child began to cry, and James, who had missed his own so desperately during the years of captivity, released Marie and bent to pick her up, trying to comfort her, holding the little body close.

For years after, the child remembered her first sight of Uncle James—a thin face, sad and red and blotched with tears. The thought was always one of anguish.

"Yours?" he mouthed over the child's shoulder to the equally tear-stained Marie Grenot.

With a look of incredible despair and sorrow, she shook her head. "Charles' bastard, by some German girl he interrogated. That's what they told me, but I've had charge of her since birth." She began to sob again. "I named her Josephine, after my mother."

Nicolai hovered in the doorway, speaking words they hardly heard, or even understood. "You are related, we know. It is good that cousins should be reunited. We try. We have looked after you both, yes? Now we must go."

They pulled themselves together and took little Josephine's hands, leaving the room like a bedraggled family of refugees.

In the courtyard, the Commandant fawned and bowed, and a soldier stood, looking miserable, by the car.

"You will not forget me . . . ?" The Commandant bent so low that James thought the man would kiss his hand.

Emotionally and physically worn out, they sat in the back of the car, not hearing Nicolai as he pointed out views and sudden glimpses of beauty, as a man will talk in order to cover some embarrassment. Then the child began to point also, and say things like, "Tree . . . Water (which she pronounced Vorter) . . . and House (Ow-se)."

After two hours they stopped at an inn, and Nicolai demanded food and drink while the landlord bowed, pleading they had nothing, then went away and returned with his wife, who found eggs and cooked an omelet.

Nicolai finally realized that they did not want him near, so he sat apart from them, with his driver, while they ate, each helping to feed Josephine by turns.

Only then did they exchange stories, and guardedly at that. Marie indicated that she had been separated from her German lover as soon as they got into Berlin. "It was a trap." She spoke low. "A lure. I've never felt so suicidal." After that she stopped talking, and did not speak of it again until they reached the comparative safety of Switzerland.

By midafternoon they had passed through Karlsruhe, and James was shaken by the feel and look of the place. There they also saw the first soldiers, grimed, muddy, cold, walking in a shambles, defeated. Later, James was to say that it was only then that he really believed it was over.

At four in the afternoon the car turned through gates in a high wire fence— they had seen the aeroplanes from the road for the last fifteen minutes, and James was amazed at their size. Neither side had flown monsters like this when he left England. Now they stood in ranks, silent and massive angular giant predatory insects—things from an alien world of the future, not the present.

"What are they?" he asked Nicolai as Josephine happily shouted, "Aiwopanes!"

These, Nicolai said, were the great Zeppelin Straaken R VIs. "Four engines. They bombed London; did considerable damage."

James marveled, and the car drove up to what he supposed was the Officers' Mess. They were given more watery coffee and introduced to four men who were to be their crew.

The Zeppelin Straaken had been painted white, with great red crosses marking the fuselage and the huge slab wings. They seemed to have removed all visible weapons.

Nicolai shook hands with them and said he hoped they understood. "In our kind of business, there have to be terms: you know—rules, terms of trade. Sometimes a life for a life; or a life for information; even a death for a death. They are hard, the terms of our trade."

By six they were in Zurich, met by a prim man from the British Foreign Office who said that his name was Smythe-Gilbert, but without any conviction. They would go on by train, and be made as comfortable as possible.

There was no time to rest, but a good meal was provided. Neither of them could eat much, though Josephine succeeded in getting a great deal on her hair.

"He doesn't like us," Marie commented when Smythe-Gilbert left them alone for a few seconds.

"I fear that we're an embarrassment." James realized that he had not been thinking clearly. The full possibility now struck him, "Maybe we're going to be an embarrassment to everyone. We could possibly be ghosts: risen from our graves."

"At least you'll be some kind of hero." Marie's eyes flooded but the dam did not burst. "Me? I suppose they can charge me. Shoot me."

"Don't be silly!" James snapped.

Smythe-Gilbert remained uneasy during the first leg of the journey, to the frontier, where he passed the three of them over to an escort—military policemen who behaved impeccably and acted more like servants than the jailers they appeared to be. One of them asked, "Any truth about this Armistice business, sir?"

James said he believed there was a lot of truth in it.

During the long overnight journey, Marie told him the remainder of her story. How they had interrogated her, used her also, she guessed, against the British clandestine services. How she had been set up as bait, and made to take part in question and answer sessions with intelligence officers. "They even made me look into a cell and identify you after your capture. Sorry, my dear, I was past caring by then." They did not sleep, though Josephine went out like a light as soon as the train started.

At dawn they reached the coast and a Royal Navy destroyer which took them, choppily, across the Channel. From Dover, another car, with men who looked like detectives, transferred them to Warminster.

At eleven o'clock, as they drove through a hardly believable England, one of the men turned around and said flatly, "That's it. It's all over. The war's finished."

His companion muttered, "God help us now."

2

Caspar waited for them at Warminster. Marie wept again when she saw he was crippled, and James marveled at his exuberance as he stumped about on his peg leg, agile, and using the makeshift metal arm to open doors for them. He laughed a great deal, and said C would be down, with one or two other people, to go through their tales of "derring-do." Marie began to weep again, asking what would happen to her?

"Happen? What d'you mean, happen?" Caspar looked aghast. "You went for King and country, Marie, old thing. I don't know many people who'd leave husband and children and sacrifice herself to the Hun as you did."

She opened her mouth to speak, but felt James' hand on her arm as Caspar continued: "Even Grandfather had us fooled with his 'The wretched girl will never darken my doorstep again' stuff. But he came clean to C when he dismantled his private agents. Told him everything—how he'd persuaded you to have a ring-a-ding with the Hun fellow in Paris, and run off with him to get information back if you could." He nodded, his face beaming. "And they locked you in, I gather. Even old James was sent to the rescue and landed in the muck trying to get you out."

In an effort to assist, James told her that because of the danger she was in, and the possible ramifications, he had even been instructed to kill her if he couldn't get her out: "Uncle Giles certainly did all he could." Again he nudged her. "Did you know you were putting on that show specially for me in Berlin?"

They had made her dress up and walk out— "Just down the road to a cab, with a young Military Intelligence officer who looked like von Hirsch. Made me do it, morning and evening for a week. They called me the cheese to catch a rat. I didn't know the rat was you, dear James."

Then Caspar became sober and slowly broke the bad news: about Mildred, and Charles; about Marie's father—James' uncle—Giles. "You'll want to see him, of course..."

"Yes," Marie said grittily. "Yes. Will he live long?"

"Seems not. I know C wants to get all the debriefing over quickly, and I'm pretty sure Denise wants to see you, Marie. We haven't told her yet. Only some of the family know...."

"Margaret Mary—?" James started.

"Knows you're safe. Thought it best not to commit ourselves that you were back in England yet. A few days, that's all it'll take. My God, it's going to be one devil of a Christmas with everyone together at Redhill, eh?"

Already they had taken little Josephine away. Nanny Coles was hustled down from London with instructions to travel with the child to Redhill, where she was already looking after Sara's baby son, with William Arthur due to join them in the holidays. As yet, the family had not ratified all this, but Sara had made up her mind that Redhill would be the great place of growing up for all the orphan Railtons, legitimate or not. From Redhill, in time, they would go off to their various schools but it would be their home, a place of refuge and a happy shelter from all the world's storms. Had not John told her it was the most wonderful place for growing up? And had not she, the strident town mouse, been put under its enchantment?

After C's arrival it became clear to James that whatever he knew or suspected, Marie was to be let off the hook. C was his usual bluff self, though courteous in his questioning. James and Marie each told their stories, were passed on to other officers, signed statements and were welcomed back.

Within the week they were free to return to their homes—James to his beloved M-M, and Marie to join Denise and the others at Redhill. Before she left Warminster, she asked James to go with her to Eccleston Square. Marie Grenot wanted to see her father for one last time.

He lay, looking very small, all the coldness and shrewd darkness of his trade now gone; his eyes fever-bright and full of fear.

Nobody knows for certain what happened. But one story, relayed to Andrew on the following evening by the nurse who waited outside the door, has gained credibility over the years.

According to this nurse, Marie asked to be left alone with her father. The nurse, concerned, for the old man had become agitated during that morning, waited outside the door, and so heard the short monologue.

Marie stood over him, looking into the eyes which had, so often in the past, regarded her with cold affection; and the feeble, slavering mouth that had lulled her into putting her emotions in jeopardy.

Here hung those lips that I have kissed I know not how oft.

Then she spoke softly:

"Goodbye, Papa. You almost damned me. I hope you burn, and when you do, think of me." Then she spat straight into his face. That part was certain, the nurse said, because she washed off the spittle after Marie left.

Giles Arthur Railton OBE died on the following afternoon, November 20th, 1918, at five minutes past six.

His son Andrew, together with the others, visited Eccleston Square that evening, and it was then, says the myth—the truth according to the Railtons and Farthings—that he made the final discovery, which was the penultimate piece of treachery in that part of the family's history.

3

Andrew and Charlotte were at Giles' bedside when he died. Caspar and Phoebe arrived a little later. Nobody seemed to know what to do once the first arrangements had been taken care of and the telephone calls made to the rest of the family.

Robertson offered the drinks tray, and at about seven o'clock Andrew suggested the others should go back to their respective homes. "There's nothing you can do. I'll wait for the funeral people. They said about half past seven."

Caspar and Phoebe were happy to be freed, but Charlotte, who could see Andrew had not taken his father's death in his stride, said she would stay and wait.

When the younger couple had gone, Andrew, with uncharacteristic sentiment, asked if she minded his going upstairs again. "Just want to be with the Old Man."

Charlotte nodded. "Better like this, Andrew. He hasn't really been alive since the seizure, you know."

Andrew nodded absently, went upstairs and opened the bedroom door quietly, as if not to waken the shrouded figure. At the bedside, Andrew lifted the sheet to take another look at the face. His father seemed to have become younger again now that death had taken over, removing the pain and fear.

Covering the face, Andrew looked around the room as if it were for the first and last time. He had heard, in his mind, his father quoting Shakespeare as he came up the stairs. The Railtons were weaned on it.

And our little life is rounded with a sleep.

Then, he could never say why, Andrew sensed something not quite right. Slowly he turned, and looked, turned again, looked again.

Everything was normal. The bed, the dressing table clear but for his father's watch. The leatherbound copy of Shakespeare's works on the bedside table.

He looked again. He had visited his father almost each day since the seizure and not noticed before. It was the book that had been there all the time, and Andrew simply took it to be his father's Shakespeare because it was always there. But this was not—this was a large, leatherbound Bible. Never had he known his father to keep a Bible by the bed—or anywhere else.

He picked it up, turning it over. It was relatively new—a year possibly— and with a wide, thick, leather marker. Perhaps old Giles Arthur really had a premonition after all, and he *had* set his house in order.

Inside the flyleaf, Giles had written carefully, *Seek and Ye Shall Find. Giles Railton 1917*, in copperplate handwriting, neat and small.

Seek and Ye Shall Find.

Andrew, who had spent his life, since adolescence, communicating with his father in simple cipher, felt the tingle of a voice from the grave.

Where be your gibes now?

He opened the Bible and saw the marker, with its gilt embossed pattern of arrows slanting toward one corner. The corner was slightly frayed, and he put down the book and looked closer. The marker was made of leather which had been folded, fitted together with minute clasps. If you inserted your thumbnails, and those of your forefingers, between the seams, the leather came away. Two long, thin pages of paper were stuck firmly to the leather, and filled with Giles' tiny writing.

It took only a glance for him to see what it was. The simplest of ciphers, the old book cipher he had so often used with his father. This time it came complete with the book.

Pencil poised, Andrew began. He had the whole thing unbuttoned in fifteen minutes. Charles, he imagined, had taken almost an hour over it. Andrew wondered how his cousin had felt—shaken—by the news. Unholy news. Even diabolical. Andrew understood well enough. He had always been able to understand his father.

At the time he said nothing to Charlotte, but, when the undertakers left, he took the book home and made a copy of the message, putting in his own punctuation, for there was no doubt of his father's intentions. He would read it to the family—the adults—at Christmas. It was only fair that the whole family should be admitted to the final whims and machinations of Giles Railton's life.

Yet Andrew had the grace, and sense, to show it first to Mary Anne, for the knowledge this last message gave them had a particular bearing on her own father. The accusations, and Charles' final silence, had undoubtedly come from obedience to Giles and this message. Like so many others, Charles had been lured and deceived by a master traitor.

"It took me a few seconds to work out some things," Andrew told Mary Anne in the privacy of the General's Study at Christmas: MARY is obviously Marie, and THE BROTHER OF JOHN can only be your own poor father. I was foxed with MARK and DAVID until I remembered that the general code name for LENIN was—and probably still is—DAVIS. If you take DAVID as DAVIS we have LENIN, which makes MARK into MARX. The rest is easy." He passed her the paper, knowing the cipher began 1 Ep John 1.1,2,3,4,5,6. Which meant The First Epistle of John, Chapter 1, verse 1—the first six words: "That which was from the beginning. . . .

The whole, long decode read: THAT WHICH WAS FROM THE BEGINNING MY BELIEF I HAVE BETRAYED THRICE WITH HEART HEAD AND BODY. ALL THINGS SHALL PASS AWAY. THE EMPEROR AND KING WILL CEASE AND THE HOST WILL RISE UP AND THE PEOPLE WILL SHARE EQUALLY ONE WITH ANOTHER. THIS I HAVE LONG COME TO BELIEVE THROUGH THE TEACHINGS OF MARK AND DAVID. I HAVE SERVED MY COUNTRY BUT BETRAYED IT FIRST WITH MY HEART FOR I NEEDED TO PROTECT THE TWO WHO APART FROM MY WIFE I LOVED ABOVE ALL OTHERS AND HAD ALREADY BETRAYED. I SPEAK OF JAMES AND MARY. BECAUSE OF ME THEY HAVE FALLEN AS SHEEP AMONG RAVENING WOLVES AND I HAVE HAD TO BETRAY TO SAVE THEM. I

HAVE SOLD SECRETS TO THE ENEMY FOR THEIR SALVATION AND USED THE BROTHER OF JOHN TO COVER MYSELF AND KEEP SAFE. HE WAS MORE FOOL THAN KNAVE AND SHOULD BE FORGIVEN EVEN THOUGH HE WAS LAID OPEN TO BETRAYAL BY HIS FOLLY FOR HE HAS A CHILD AT THE ENEMY'S MERCY. FOR LONG HAVE I BELIEVED REVOLT MUST COME THROUGHOUT THE WORLD. THERE SHALL BE A NEW KINGDOM AND IT SHALL BE HASTENED BY VICTORY AGAINST US AND A GREAT RISING WILL COME FROM THE EAST. GOD SAVE THE NEW KINGDOM OF THE PEOPLE AND MAY ALL MY SINS BE FORGIVEN. IF THE BROTHER OF JOHN READS THIS BEFORE ANY OTHER THEN I BEG HIM TO REMAIN SILENT FOR THE SAKE OF JAMES AND MARY AND HIS OWN CHILD. HE SHOULD REMAIN SILENT EVEN UNTO THE GRAVE. THERE IS BLOOD ON MY OWN HANDS THROUGH A WOMAN'S NECK AND A WHITE HANDKERCHIEF.

It said everything. And the family sat in stunned, shocked silence as Andrew read it to them, after dinner, on Christmas Night.

It told the whole story of Giles' political change in the evening of his life, and how he had embraced—for his own reasons—an ideological faith which came close to what was now known as Communism.

It told of the way in which Giles manipulated Charles' misfortunes and folly to his own advantage; and how he had managed to deal with the enemy by trading intelligence, perhaps only small things, through The Fisherman, using Charles as his perfect foil—and so keep James and Marie safe.

It told clearly who killed Hanna Haas. Giles Railton, who believed a new social order to be inevitable: and that sooner rather than later. His belief had become so strong that Giles had even turned it into action—betrayal to advance a German victory, and so bring the revolution quickly to fruition. Nobody could tell when his political vision had first struck. All of them knew that Giles had turned the vision to action.

The decode is now, according to mythology, kept in a locked steel box at Redhill Manor, together with the Bible and the marker which contains the cipher.

4

This should be the end of the story of those fledgling years spent by the Railton family in what we now know of as MI5, MI6 and Government Communications Headquarters. But there is no end to the whole story, and, certainly, if we deal with Giles' horrific betrayal, "the first of the really great modern traitors," they say in those endless seminars at Warminster, the rest should be told. Yet it cannot be fully related, for decades were to pass before the whole truth, and the last twist of Giles' actions, was made fully known.

By rights we must now our quietus make, not with a bare bodkin, but with a date—an arbitrary date. Sometime, let us say, in October of 1935. First, though, much was to happen in the seventeen years between. The world was changed. Empire tilted, though few felt the start of its slide. The Railtons, and, for that matter, the Farthings of America, flourished.

That Christmas of 1918, which should have been so full of joy, with its returned warriors and the influx of children to Redhill, was probably the most gloomy since the war had started.

Not only was the family saddened by the deaths of Charles and Giles, but also the facts which came with Andrew's reading of the "Giles Decode"—as it became known—were totally bewildering. The acts of treachery, the drawing in of weak, silly Charles, and the duplicity were hard enough to bear; but it was even more difficult to accept that this pillar of Establishment, the great secret man, had been so swayed by a political ideology alien to all of them.

The men endlessly discussed possibilities. In particular, Caspar, James and Dick Farthing tried to make sense of it.

"The conundrum," ventured James, "is why he protected Marie, myself and Charles' child by selling out to the Germans, when he was so attached to social change through disorder."

"Easy." Caspar appeared well up in the state of play, and the fighting still going on in Russia and its neighboring countries. "We were all his disciples, weren't we? Every one of us. His devious disciples. He ran us like a puppet-master, and manipulated the entire family."

"Sara apart," added Dick. "I am never sure if I was manipulated, but probably it was so. He sold out, though, Caspar. Sold to Prussians to let the revolutionaries in."

"I suppose"—Caspar had almost completed the Giles jigsaw—"that The Fisherman was a go-between—passing the messages—and a threat, if the old man got out of hand."

In the end, they all realized that, whatever the reason or rhyme, it simply had to be accepted. Within himself, James thought it was just possible that the Old Man, in the twilight of his years, suddenly felt guilty—a sense that there were too many men and women like him: people of wealth, rank and great privilege. The labyrinthine passages of power were stocked full of men with his background, who had risen by education, influence, money and the fact that their charmed lives had been set while still in their cradles. The world of diplomacy, and, almost to the same extent, politics, the military and naval services, were led by what amounted to feudal power.

"I believe he suddenly saw that way of things had to end, and he made an intellectual grab at the first straw that came to hand," James told Margaret Mary.

Her response was typical of her own view at that time: "Oh, to blazes with bloody Giles," she grumbled. "Why did he have to pick on poor old Charles? *I* liked Charles, idiot that he was. Oh, poor Charles. . . ."

"Poor Charles, my foot!" James' eyes, for a second, took on the same ruthless look which had once rested often in Giles' own eyes.

"Come to Mama," chirped Margaret Mary brightly, for the transitional period of adjusting to his being there was over. Now, no hesitation or embarrassment stood between them as they went about their own particular nightly—and often daily—rituals.

Caspar spoke, confidentially, about it to C, who remained as wise as ever, putting nothing on paper. C was the only person, outside family, who had first-hand knowledge of the business. "Road to Damascus." C never smiled when Giles' name was mentioned. "Straight road-to-Damascus stuff. Think about it, Caspar, and you can pinpoint the very moment, and, in the future, mistrust those who have undergone a sudden conversion. Personally, I'd have had the watchers out on St. Paul for a long time if I'd been in charge of the Christian Secret Service when he came blundering into Damascus yelling that he'd gone blind, and Christ was the Messiah. I'd have set the dogs on him, whipped him down to Warminster and had him squeezed—sharpish." He dropped into silence, pondering before he sadly admitted, "Just as I should have done with Giles Railton when he began to sell off his own private informers and little covens of spies he had stashed away over the years."

"And it was my grandfather who backed the sly Ramillies," Caspar added darkly.

To which C grunted, "And the last we know of your little brother, Caspar my boy, is that he was picked up in Petrograd and carted away. Probably shot that day. So many of our people in Russia have gone, or are going." He thought again for almost a minute. "You know, I had one devil of a row with Giles Railton. He was dead against any British military or naval intervention in Russia against the Bolsheviks. DNI went through the same business with him. Now we know why."

There was a final act in the whole Railton drama of those times. But this was not to be revealed completely for several decades. Yet Giles did point the way. James and Caspar both maintained they had an inkling as soon as they heard Giles' testimony. The secret historians say Giles Railton was but the first of many to exchange class and privilege for the hidden hair shirt of treachery. Yet he managed that without giving up anything—except those he loved. The first hint of that last knife twist, which Giles had built into his treason, came about 1935.

Epilogue

1935

In the wake of strikes and a world recession, there were many young un-
dergraduates living in the rarified atmosphere of the great Oxbridge universities
who became affected—some would say infected—by what they saw as the class
struggle of Socialism. They had come, late, to Giles Railton's own cause. And
one such was another Railton—Donald, eldest son of James, who in 1935 was
in his final year at Cambridge.

"Talks a lot of half-digested, emotional tommyrot!" James said angrily to
Caspar. Both had grown wise in the ways of the secret world—and high in
rank. "Workers of the world, unite. March under the banner of freedom!" He
gave a sarcastic snort. "Let them go. Go to the cradle of the Revolution and
see if they like the purge of freedom."

"A phase." Caspar chuckled. "He'd have got on well with your uncle, Grandfather Giles. Member of the Young Socialists, is he?"

"Don't think it's quite gone that far."

It had not gone that far, but neither James nor Caspar was to know that
young Donald was not a member of the Labour Party because of strict instructions. "You can serve the Party better," a friend told him, "if you do not
publicly display your politics. Keep clear of Labour meetings; don't get mixed
up with demonstrations; and for God's sake don't join the movement!"

It was in October 1935 that this same friend invited Donald to his rooms,
in Trinity, to "meet a comrade who will instruct and help us. He has British
origins, but has lived in the USSR for some time." The friend's name does not
matter. It is now as familiar as any well-known brand of cleanser.

Donald went to the rooms, in Trinity, on a damp, bitter, late October night
when the wind cut into the university city, straight, as some often said, off
the steppes.

The comrade from Russia spoke for almost two hours, to an audience of six.
He offered help and instruction in fighting "with stealth for the Cause and the
Party," and invited questions. He was tall, in his forties, but with prematurely
gray hair.

Donald went, with one of the other young men, to see him off on the late
train to London. There was something terribly familiar about the comrade from
Russia, but Donald could not put his finger on it—something in his voice,
mannerisms, walk, features.

On the train itself, their visitor sat back and closed his eyes. He was tired.
Tomorrow he would speak with others in London, then it was time to return

to Moscow. Progress reports to write; names to be passed on; a meeting with the Cheka hierarchy—they were in the midst of merging the NKVD, OGPU and UGB.

He smiled to himself. So that was James' son. Like his father. Very like his father. So much so that he would have to show extreme caution. Ramillies Railton—now known under a dozen aliases—wondered to himself about the circular progress of history. Who would have thought he'd have met his kinsman, unrecognized, in these circumstances? Grandfather would not have been surprised, naturally. . . .

Many, many years later—and that is a different tale—when the truth of that night, its aftermath, and dramatis personae became certain knowledge, Caspar stood, looking out onto a damp and drizzling Whitehall. "Bloody Giles," he said, softly. Then, the inevitable Shakespearean tag: *"And is old Double dead?"*